KADIN SETON

RIM WAR

BOOK ONE: SUBVERSION

ISBN:978-0-9897184-2-4 Print Edition
Copyright 2017 by Kadin Seton
Cover Design and Interior Format by atrtinkcovers

.

For Mom

CHAPTER 1
Earth 2099

Growing old was a monstrous force from which there was no recourse, akin to an unjust death sentence with no hope for appeal. "Get your sweaty hands off me." I swatted away the meaty fingers grabbing at my elbow.

The overweight Sunny Days Fed-Home attendant backed up with palms facing forward and frowned his disapproval. "Fine, but if you fall it's not my fault."

I clutched my purple walking cane and stepped from the car onto the pavement. My legs felt weak as I poked the bright cane at the ground, but I sure as hell wouldn't accept assistance to make the short walk over to the doorway.

My granddaughter, Avery, leaned toward the attendant. "Gram likes to do things on her own. She is very independent for one hundred and five," she whispered.

The attendant chuckled, causing his large midsection to jiggle over his belt. "Oh, that's not old." He waved his hand through the air. "Thanks to the miracles of modern medicine, we have some folks here pushing one hundred and twenty-five."

I rolled my eyes. "By the way, I can still hear. It's not polite to talk about someone's age in front of them." I was still bitter about being transferred from the comfortable and independent retirement condos to a full-care federal nursing home. Everyone knew Fed-Homes were created for old, sick people. Heck, the only medication I took was a low-dose blood pressure pill. I was in damn good health

1

for my age, although I had to admit I had a nagging feeling that I was disintegrating. Bit by bit my muscles and bones were wearing out. It's funny, my brain wanted to run, dance, and ride a bike, but my body said forget it. It wasn't fair.

At least I still had most of my mind intact and for that I was grateful. Many of my friends who were still alive were not so lucky. Dementia ran rampant in seniors over one hundred and sadly it was one of those sicknesses that science couldn't seem to tackle.

The light lines of age in Avery's forehead deepened as she looked at me with concern. She brushed away a wisp of silver that lay across her cheek. Almost thirty years ago I had become her only family when her parents died in a car accident. It had been a terrible time for both of us. I'd lost my daughter and son-in-law, and Avery lost a doting mother and father. She'd never married, so we were truly each other's only family.

With my cane in hand, I tap-tapped through the automatic doors and over to the front desk. Avery and the attendant followed close behind. A dark-haired receptionist smiled from the other side of the spotless counter. "Hellooo! You must be Mildred Necee Helgren. We've been expecting you."

I scowled. "It's Millie." I had always hated my full name. Who named their kid Mildred in 1994? At a time when my brothers were listening to bands like Pearl Jam and Metallica, my mother had bestowed me with the most unacceptable name. For some reason, she felt it was imperative to name me after my great, great grandmother. One hundred and five years was a long time to deal with a name that I detested and was ill-suited for my generation.

The receptionist poked on her flex screen computer. "Well, let's get you settled in and then we'll have one of the attendants take you on a formal tour."

I tapped my foot. I wasn't in the mood for formalities. "I've already had the tour, so I'm going straight to my room, if you don't mind." I didn't mean to be quite so abrasive, it had just been a bad day.

Avery patted my shoulder and gave me a sympathetic smile. I glanced to my left and noticed a small woman lurking on the far side of the reception counter. She was about five feet tall with wrinkled skin and white hair pulled into a bun. Her gaze was fixed on me and her eyes were oddly piercing as she peered through thick wire-rimmed glasses. I scowled at her and looked away.

"Of course." The receptionist smiled again. "All of your upcoming events will be listed over there." She pointed to an electronic bulletin board across from the desk. "Dinner is at six in the main dining room. Would you like one of the attendants to come and get you?"

"Absolutely not, thank you. I know where the dining room is, and I can get around just fine on my own." I turned, crossed the lobby, and shuffled down the long hall to room 142. Avery and the attendant followed carrying my three suitcases. It was sad to think that everything I owned in this world had been condensed to just three pieces of luggage.

Avery helped me unpack and made sure I settled in before she said her goodbyes. She looked sad and tired. "Gram, I'm sorry about this, but I truly believe Sunny Days is the best place for you right now."

I waved my hand through the air. "Well, I'm not going to argue with you. You're an excellent attorney and I'd certainly never win a debate against you. Besides, I'm fully aware that I have no choice in the matter."

I smiled and patted her arm to let her know I understood her position. I didn't want to live here, but I also knew that according to the law, I had to. It wasn't Avery's fault. By worldwide decree, at age one hundred and five everyone was required to enter into a government operated Fed-Home, supposedly to protect the public from communicable diseases spread by the elderly. One particularly virulent virus called Laydenhowers was the main reason for our incarceration.

Back in 2060, when the Laydenhowers asteroid struck Earth, a malicious virus had spread like wildfire. Almost two billion people were lost and the planet faced economic collapse. It wasn't until an alliance with the advanced Gaekaar species was made in 2070 that a vaccination was realized. Over the course of five years, Laydenhowers was eradicated. Yet according to the propaganda, once an individual was over a certain age the vaccination would become inert and they would be susceptible again. The Coalition Of Governments was formed, which included representatives from the planet Gaekaar, to ensure Laydenhowers never returned. Hence, the law that required people over the age of one hundred and five to be monitored and cared for by a government regulated Fed-Home became active.

Avery smiled back and gave me a quick kiss on the cheek. "I'll drop by next week to see how you're doing, okay?"

"Sounds great, honey." I had an uneasy feeling in the pit of my stomach. My heart pounded and I felt shaky. I might have been having a heart attack, but since this was the final step in the long journey of my life, I attributed it to anxiety. "I'll look forward to it and don't worry about me, I'll be fine," I added.

"I know you will, Gram. You're the strongest person I know." Avery smiled and slipped out the door.

I sat for several minutes and stared at the second hand of an oversized clock that hung askew on the wall. Was this a glimpse of my future—watching time tick by? I popped in my ear-cone and cranked up some nice music from my era. Kids nowadays thought Green Day was so old fashioned, but over the years they had remained one of my favorite bands. Leaning back in the chair, I relaxed as the old tunes brought back memories of when I could do more physical activities like dancing, kayaking, and playing football with my brothers.

After a time I pulled out my ear-cone and reached for my cane. I still had two hours before dinner, so I decided to venture out and meet my new neighbors.

I had only taken three steps into the hallway when the small woman I had seen earlier at the reception desk slammed a neighboring door and rushed over. She smiled at me and openly displayed a missing front tooth. I found it interesting that she hadn't undergone any number of modern procedures to correct poor vision or missing teeth.

She held out her hand. "I'm Fiona O'Brien. Welcome aboard."

"I'm Millie Helgren. Nice to meet you," I said.

"It's nice to meet you as well. How would you like to go on a tour? I'd be happy to show you around." Fiona's smile grew a bit wider and I noticed an anxious twitch tugging at the corner of her mouth.

"Thanks, but I've already had a tour." If you'd seen one government run Fed-Home, you'd seen them all. Furthermore, Avery had already taken me through the building several times in a well-meaning attempt to help me adjust to my new life. Correction, my end-of-life.

Fiona glanced over her shoulder and looked up and down the hallway. It was empty. "I'm not talking about the formal tour. How would you like to go on the *real* tour?" she whispered.

"Are you implying that the formal tour wasn't *real?*" I was beginning to wonder if Fiona was a dementia patient.

Her smile vanished. "Oh no. I'm saying the formal tour was ... ah, incomplete. There are some aspects of Sunny Days Fed-Home that will never be disclosed in a tour. Some very secretive aspects."

I perked up. "Well then, by all means lead the way." Heck, I was always game for a good mystery, delusion or otherwise.

I followed my new neighbor down the hall and past the front desk. The dark-haired receptionist looked up and scowled, losing all of her former friendliness. "What are you up to, Fiooona?"

Fiona smiled innocently. "Oh, I'm just taking Millie Helgren on a tour."

"Uh-huh." She pointed her finger at Fiona and pursed her lips. "Just make sure you stay out of trouble."

"Of course." Fiona smiled and floated by the front desk as if she didn't have a care in the world.

I followed Fiona to the end of an adjoining hallway, stopping in front of a door with a small window. The sign next to the door read "GYM." Fiona glanced over her shoulder again.

"The receptionist doesn't like you," I said, stating the obvious.

Fiona smiled. "No she doesn't. You might as well know that I'm on the official 'watch list.' I've been known to cause trouble by poking around too much."

I wondered what type of trouble Fiona could possibly get into. Whatever it was I hoped it was entertaining, because other than the occasional medical drama, I was certain that life in a Fed-Home would bore me to death long before my body gave out.

Fiona pointed toward the door. "This room isn't what you think. This is where you'll complete your testing and receive a final score," she whispered.

I peered through the small window and saw several senior citizens trudging along on treadmills, while another was working on bicep curls with free weights. I shrugged. "Looks fairly innocuous. Just a few people getting a workout."

A deep voice startled me from behind. "That's what they want you to think."

I spun around and came face to face with an elderly man wearing a sweat suit that said NAVY across the front. The man frowned at Fiona. "I thought we agreed not to tell our secret to anyone. What if she tells one of *them*?" he said, tilting his head in the direction of the front desk.

Fiona sighed and waved her hand through the air. "Never mind about that. Millie, this is Jorge Alvarez. Jorge, Millie Helgren. We absolutely have to talk to Millie now. I checked her out before she arrived." She pulled out a wrinkled piece of paper from her pocket and began to read. "Mildred Necee Helgren scored a 112 on her IQEE. I have the data right here."

I looked down at the paper. It was covered with handwritten mathematical calculations. The numbers were lengthy and the computations appeared difficult. No one practiced longhand math anymore. Heck, for that matter no one wrote notes on paper anymore. It just wasn't necessary.

Jorge's eyes became round orbs. "Damn, that's not good." He turned and looked at me. "I'm sorry, Millie, where are my manners? It's nice to meet you."

I smiled, looking between the two and wondering if they were crazy. "Nice to meet you as well. Just what are you two talking about? And what's an IQEE?"

"It stands for Intelligence Quotient Efficiency Evaluation. Do you recall taking a series of tests before leaving the nursing home?" Fiona asked. "They told you they were determining your Fed-Home placement, but really they were measuring your intellectual dexterity and ability to adapt to changing environments. I know this must sound insane."

"You have no idea." I rolled my eyes and laughed. I couldn't remember the last time I had laughed. I felt the sensation all the way to the pit of my stomach and it felt good.

Jorge shook his head and moved closer. "We can't talk here. Come on, let's take her to the safe room," he whispered.

Fiona touched my hand. "Millie dear, come with us and we'll explain everything."

I reminded myself that this was more amusement than I ever could have hoped for in a Fed-Home, so why not enjoy it. I followed Fiona and Jorge down a flight of stairs to the basement and over to a locked maintenance room. Jorge knelt down and played with the electronic lock. Within seconds the door popped open and we entered. "So, this is your safe room?" I made my way across the small room and sat down on a case of all-purpose cleaner. "Well, at least we'll be safe from dust and grease."

Fiona and Jorge each pulled over a box and sat facing me.

"This room is safe from bugs, cameras, and prying ears," Jorge said with pride in his words. "I sweep it several times a day to be certain."

"Well, that makes me feel so much better." I cackled with delight. I had no idea what they were talking about, but it was immensely entertaining.

Fiona took my hand. "Millie, this is going to be somewhat shocking, so you'll need to prepare yourself."

I didn't like the conviction in her voice. "Okay, out with it. What's the big secret around here?" I demanded.

Jorge sighed and looked me straight in the eye. "Millie, you're going to die."

I tried to maintain a serious expression, but I couldn't hold back the smile that spread across my face. "Oh, I see. Except that's not really groundbreaking news is it? We're all going to die. Isn't that why we're here, to live out our final days in government-funded comfort?"

"Yes, yes." Fiona pointed to her piece of paper. "But *we* are going to die in the same order as our collective test scores. And based on your IQEE score, you're on your way to an early demise."

They had my attention now. "Explain that statement, please."

Jorge reached behind a pile of granular cleanser and pulled out a small pad of lined paper. He flipped to the fifth page and handed it to me. I scanned the handwritten information. Forty-two names were listed with descending IQEE scores along with a date and time of death. Each date and time of death listing followed the calendar in the exact same order as the test scores, complete with periodic entries for newly admitted residents.

Jorge pointed to the top of the list. "These are the most recent deaths at the Sunny Days Fed-Home. And I should point out that each resident died of *alleged* natural causes."

Fiona and Jorge remained quiet while I spent several minutes reviewing the test scores versus the date and time of death. It was too exact. Surely it couldn't be a coincidence, or could it? "If there was some sort of conspiracy going on, it couldn't be hidden from the public for any length of time," I pointed out. "This pattern is too obvious. Someone would uncover it. Someone would say something."

Jorge shook his head. "The cover up is very professional. The victims are old, so who's going to question the natural death of a bunch of elderly people?"

"My granddaughter is a lawyer. She could look into it," I offered.

Fiona shook her head. "It's not that simple. Our connections tell us that the same thing is happening at Fed-Homes across the globe. This isn't something a lawyer can tackle. It's too big and too political."

I felt the same uneasiness I'd had when Avery had departed, only now it was stronger. I wasn't sure I believed their story, but it was clear their distress was genuine.

I took a slow breath. "Okay, let's talk through this. Why would there be a worldwide conspiracy to kill off the elderly? It just doesn't make any sense. We can't possibly be a drain on the economy, not the way things are now."

Since the near-eradication of Laydenhowers disease, Earth's economy had flourished for almost twenty-five years. Humanity had long since paid the price for the vaccinations by giving the Gaekaars exclusive mining rights for Helium-3 on the moon. The vaccinations, in conjunction with this agreement, brought about planetary renewal, prosperity, and peace.

Earth's turnaround had been so impressive that we were allowed admittance into the Galactic Alliance of Planets in 2085. Achieving membership into the GAP was a huge win that gave Earth the interstellar diplomatic connections it needed to establish a foothold in space. This was something the governments of Earth had wanted ever since the presence of alien species had become public knowledge back in 2040. It just took the worst plague in history and an additional forty-five years to make it happen.

I thought about what my new friends had said and tried to come up with a logical reason for killing off senior citizens, but no matter how I picked the situation apart, there was no logic to it. Earth was prosperous and peaceful, and seniors weren't a burden. I could have seen some rationale to this bizarre theory if seniors with early signs of Laydenhowers were being exterminated, but they weren't—they were simply quarantined. It just didn't make sense to kill off the healthiest among us.

Fiona returned the handwritten paper to the safety of her pocket and leaned forward. "It's a very strange sort of conspiracy. It has everything to do with the scores. You'll soon notice that all of the long-timers have very low scores."

Jorge shook his head. "We don't know why they want to kill off the best of us, but they do."

"If what you are saying is true, then you should be able to predict who's next. Right?" I asked, surmising that the easiest way to prove or disprove their theory would be to observe what happened to the "next" person.

"That's right." Jorge nodded.

I leaned forward on my cane. "Okay then, who's next?"

Fiona's face crumpled into a pained expression. She pointed at herself. "Me."

I found it hard to hide my astonishment. "You?"

Fiona closed her eyes and nodded. "Yes, I'm afraid so. I'm sorry to spring this on you during your first day, but your score was so extraordinarily high that I thought you should know."

I swallowed hard and considered her statement. "Okay. Based on my score and your calculations, when do you expect *my* demise to take place?"

Fiona laced her fingers together. "By the end of the week ... at the latest. Even if you fail your physical test, your IQEE score will keep your overall numbers very high."

I stood up a bit too quickly and leaned on my cane for support. "That's in three days!"

Fiona nodded. "Yes, it is. I'll be dead by tomorrow and you'll be dead by the weekend. I promise you that my calculations are correct. I was a CPA for seventy years. I'm very good at math."

I tap-tapped around the small room and tried to remind myself that this was nothing more than a crazy conspiracy theory. But then again, what if they were on to something? "This is ridiculous. If what you're saying is true, there must be something we can do or someone we could notify?"

Jorge shook his head. "The minute you open your mouth, you'll be gone. A few others tried to say something to the outside world and within hours they perished from supposed natural causes."

"I'm going to message my granddaughter. She'll look into the matter and get us some answers," I said.

Fiona stood and grabbed my arm. "Don't do that. All communication going in and out of Fed-Homes is monitored. Your message will be erased long before it reaches your granddaughter and the next time she comes to visit they'll hand her a box of ashes."

I raised my eyebrows. "From what you're telling me, Avery is going to be receiving a box of ashes either way."

CHAPTER 2

The evening meal was a boring event. The large cafeteria was filled with seniors, wheelchairs, walkers, and random medical apparatus. Staff bustled about ensuring that each resident's meal met with the proper dietary restrictions. I sat at a small table with Fiona and Jorge. We were each on low sodium diets, so we received platefuls of turkey, mashed potatoes, green beans, and dry cornbread. The lack of salt translated to absence of flavor.

We kept our conversation to harmless talk of our former lives. I learned that Fiona had been married for over fifty years and lost her husband to Laydenhowers in 2070. She never had children and had worked as a successful CPA in a large corporation. Jorge had served in the Navy for thirty years and, after an honorable discharge, had taught electrical engineering at the local community college. He had also been married and divorced three times. He claimed he had made hasty marital decisions in his younger years and had never truly met the right woman.

"What about you, Millie? What was your life like?" Fiona asked.

"Nothing too exciting, I'm afraid." I shrugged. "I came from a military family. My father and four brothers were all in the armed forces. I was married for fifty-two years and also lost my husband to Laydenhowers. In my work life, I was a trainer for almost seventy-five years."

"What type of training did you do?" Jorge asked.

"I trained employees how to use heavy equipment at the Stanfield Organization. Much of the equipment was operated from a computer terminal, but I could manually handle the big machinery when needed." I felt a pang of pride as I answered the question. I really had loved that job. "Machine operators were a tough group to work with, but I made do."

Long after we finished dinner, Fiona and I sat in her room at an old brown card table and sipped Earl Grey tea. Jorge walked around attempting to sweep the room for bugs. He used a small wristwatch-like device that he had built himself from computer parts he picked out of the trash. He said it was a trick he had acquired in the Navy.

"Nothing here tonight. Although I've pulled plenty of bugs from Fiona's room in the past, so you can never be too careful. *They* have ears everywhere," Jorge said.

He took a seat at the table and Fiona handed him a cup of tea. "Thank you, dear," he responded with a smile.

"Just who are *they?*" I tried to keep the sarcasm from seeping into my voice.

"No one really knows for sure," Fiona said. "Most of us believe that *they* are a covert department within the Coalition of Governments."

I toyed with my teacup. "I still don't understand how any government would benefit from killing off a bunch of harmless senior citizens."

"Maybe it has something to do with those aliens, the Gaekaars," Fiona said.

I waved my hand. "They're far more advanced than we are and they certainly wouldn't have a use for us."

Jorge leaned forward. "Well, I've heard a lot of theories, but it's my belief that they're harvesting our organs."

I grimaced at the thought. "That doesn't make sense either, not when hospitals can grow organs of much better quality."

"Not this one," Fiona said, pointing toward her head.

I nodded. "True, a brain cannot be reproduced, but why would *they* want the brains from old people. Even the best of us are forgetful and slow. If you're going to steal a brain, seems to me that there are much better specimens out there."

Jorge shrugged. "These are questions we just can't answer, and frankly, I'm not sure we'll ever be able to. Right now, the most important thing we can do is keep a close eye on Fiona. Her number is almost up and I have no intention of losing her."

Fiona smiled affectionately at Jorge and then looked over at me. "I'd appreciate all the help I can get."

I still wasn't convinced, but I was interested in seeing what tomorrow would bring. I set my teacup down. "I'd be happy to help out. Just tell me what to do."

"Thank you, Millie." Fiona took a deep breath. "The deaths historically happen in the morning between 7:00 a.m. and 12:00 p.m. And they only seem to occur when the resident is alone."

I nodded. "Simple enough. I'll spend the whole day with you so you won't be alone at any time."

"We'll both spend the day with her. There's safety in numbers," Jorge said. "Although we can't keep this up indefinitely. We'll need to find a way to get Fiona off the list."

Fiona touched my shoulder. "Millie, I'm sorry that your first day wasn't more welcoming."

I shrugged and stifled a yawn. "Well, at least it's been interesting."

I liked my new friends, but it was getting late and I was tired from the move. More importantly, I wanted some quiet time to process the legitimacy of their bizarre story.

Jorge stood. "We should all go to bed. Tomorrow is going to be a long day."

The next morning I was up earlier than usual. At 5:20 a.m. I scrounged up an old pen from the Fed-Home library and grabbed a pile of napkins from the cafeteria. Finding paper would have been far more difficult and could have aroused suspicion from one of the attendants.

Back in the privacy of my room I began to compose a letter to Avery. My hand ached after just two sentences. I was out of practice with this antiquated method of communication, plus napkins didn't make the best writing surface. Yet I forged ahead at the pace of a turtle. Over the next hour I managed to pen a story describing my new friends and their strange theory.

The note took three full napkins, which I neatly rolled into a tube and slid into a secret compartment in the bottom of my jewelry box. Avery had bought the box for me twenty years ago as a birthday present. If anything happened to me, the Fed-Home employees might go through my things, but I doubted they would find the secret compartment. If I should turn up dead, I felt confident that Avery would be given my things and eventually find the note. If this turned out to be nothing more than a silly delusion, I could rip up the note later. A little insurance never hurt anyone.

At 6:30 a.m. I pushed the buzzer next to Fiona's room. She opened the door just wide enough for one eye to peek out. When she saw my face I heard a sigh of relief and the door swung open. "Come in, please," she whispered.

Jorge was already sitting at the card table drinking a cup of Earl Grey. "Would you like some tea, Millie?"

"Yes, please." Fiona and I both took a seat at the table while Jorge filled my cup.

We drank several pots of tea and managed to pass the morning without incident. After a quick lunch in the cafeteria we found ourselves back at Fiona's card table polishing off yet another pot of Earl Grey.

"I think you two have got me hooked on this stuff," I said. "I've lost all appreciation for coffee now."

Fiona smiled. "It can be a bit of an addiction."

Jorge's eyes widened when a knock sounded on the door. I looked over at Fiona and noticed her teacup begin to shake. Jorge stood up. "I'll answer it."

The color drained from Fiona's face as Jorge cracked the door open. "Yes, what do you want?" he asked through the two-inch opening.

"It's time for Ms. Alexander's exercise class." An attendant pushed on the door, but Jorge held it firmly in place.

Relief washed over Fiona's face. "Oh, that's right. I forgot all about my class. Maybe some exercise would help get my mind off … you know. My class usually has about twenty participants, so we should be safe there."

Jorge cleared his throat and addressed the attendant, "I'll make sure she gets there. You can leave now."

"Fine by me, Mr. Alvarez. Just make sure she's not late. Class starts promptly at two," the attendant replied.

"Understood." Jorge shut the door and turned toward Fiona. "We'll both go to the exercise class with you. Millie can stay with you while you put your sweat suit on. I'll go change and come back to escort you to class, then Millie can go change and meet us there."

Fiona gave Jorge a tentative nod.

I helped Fiona pick out a bright purple sweat suit and pink sneakers, while Jorge left to change in his room. Within minutes he returned wearing a black jogging suit and a bright white pair of Nikes.

"Your turn, Millie," Jorge said.

"I'll meet you in the gym in a few minutes," I said. "But don't expect much from me. These legs don't like to exercise."

Back in my room I tugged on a pair of black yoga pants and a large white sweatshirt with a big pocket in the front. And for a bit of extra confidence, I opened my jewelry box, pulled out my prized sparrow, and tucked it into my pocket. The sparrow had also been a gift from Avery. The state-of-the-art weapon was small, lightweight, and could shoot 20 powerful laser rounds before needing to recharge. Technically weapons weren't allowed at the Fed-Home, but I wasn't about to give it up.

As I headed to the gym, I paused at the electronic bulletin board across from the reception desk and glanced at the calendar. Today's events were listed in order by hour. Knitting circle, pottery class, a weekly book club meeting, and a lecture on keeping your bones strong were displayed under today's date.

"Can I help you with something?" the receptionist asked.

"Yes, I would like to attend today's exercise class. Why isn't it listed here?"

The woman smiled at me like I was a child. "Didn't you read your midday message? The exercise class was cancelled."

I didn't respond to the woman. Instead, I spun around and used my cane to propel myself down the hallway as fast as I could.

My heart raced as I considered the implications. Could it all be true? I was beginning to feel like I was trapped in a bad movie. Fiona and Jorge were good people. If something happened to them I would never forgive myself.

When I reached the gym it was empty. Fiona and Jorge should have arrived several minutes ago. Surely if they had left, I would have passed them in the hallway.

A scruffy maintenance man entered the room from an access door off the sidewall. He pushed a rolling mop bucket and hummed a tune as he strolled over to a row of treadmills in the back. I tried to appear casual as I walked over.

"Hello there," I said in a nonchalant voice. Inside I was a mass of pins and needles and my cane wobbled beneath me.

The man plopped his wet mop onto the floor. "Uh, hi."

"Did you happen to see anyone come in here a few minutes ago?" I asked.

"Nope. Just got here myself. Got buzzed from the office to clean up the mess back here." He pointed to the floor.

I looked down and realized that he was mopping up what appeared to be blood splatter. I hoped I was wrong. "What is that?" I asked.

The man chuckled. "One of the attendants got a bloody nose back here, so they called me to clean it up."

"Do you know which attendant? I'd like to talk to him."

"I think it was Axel. He's probably getting patched up in the infirmary."

"How do I get to the infirmary?"

"Turn left at the reception desk and go to the end of the hall."

"Thanks, ah, what's your name?"

"Max. Max Lawrence, ma'am."

"Okay, thanks, Max."

When I arrived at the infirmary it reminded me of the nurse's office in high school with a long row of beds and curtain dividers. The place appeared to be empty with the exception of the farthest bed. The curtain was drawn and I thought I heard voices on the other side. I inched my way closer.

"Shit! No way in hell are you sticking that thing up my nose," a deep masculine voice said.

"Axel, grow-up. This is the fastest and easiest way to straighten the bone in your nose. I promise it won't hurt," a female voice said.

"No fuckin' way. Get that thing away from me," Axel replied.

"Look, you botched up the recovery. You're lucky that you only ended up with a broken nose. It could have been much worse for you. Did you happen to notice how angry the recovery personnel were?" the female said.

"Well, it wasn't my fault. She was supposed to be alone. I don't get paid enough to deal with this shit," Axel said.

The female sighed. "None of us do, but you know the consequences for not following protocol. You've pushed the envelope with *them* before. At some point they're going to run out of tolerance for you."

"Hey, I turned her over in the end, despite her boyfriend wigging out on me. They got two bodies for the price of one. Maybe I should get a raise," Axel added.

"Yeah, like that's going to happen." The female sighed. "Now lean back and be quiet while I insert the probe. This won't hurt a bit."

A device powered up with a high pitched grinding sound. A moment later Axel's anguished moans filled the room.

I exited the infirmary without being noticed. My new friends couldn't possibly be dead, could they? The blood on the floor had to have been from Axel's broken nose. I had only just arrived at the Fed-Home and already my world felt upside-down.

I tap-tapped back down to the gym to investigate further. Max Lawrence was still in the back, only now he was sitting on a treadmill deeply engrossed in a conversation on his ear-phone. I planned to ask him more questions, but as I headed his way I noticed he had left the side door propped open with the mop bucket. A nearby sign stated 'Fed-Home Personnel Only—No Admittance Without Authorization' in bold letters.

I looked over at Max. He was still absorbed in his discussion, so I took advantage of the opportunity and slipped through the open door.

I entered a small vestibule that had an elevator on the opposite wall. The button next to the elevator displayed an arrow pointing down. I pushed it and the door immediately opened. I stepped inside, the door closed with a thud, and a computerized voice came over the speaker, "Destination, please?"

I didn't know what to say, and then I recalled a word that the woman in the infirmary had used. I cleared my throat. "Recovery."

The elevator made a rapid descent and pinged four times before pausing. I stumbled to catch myself as the elevator began moving sideways. I gripped the railing as the force of the speeding box kept me glued to the side. The elevator made a whirring sound as it raced and I felt certain that I was travelling far from the Fed-Home. Just yesterday I had been anxious about arriving at the Fed-Home and now I was feeling triple the anxiety over leaving it.

I nearly lost my grip on the railing when the elevator stopped with a jolt. The computer voice said, "You have reached your destination."

The elevator pinged and the doors slid open.

Two large men in strange black uniforms lifted military issued Laser-Rugers and pointed them at me. A woman in a crisp navy blue suit and high heels stepped forward with a digital flexible display on her arm. "Good afternoon, Ms. Helgren. How nice of you to pay us a visit."

CHAPTER 3

I took a deep breath to calm myself so that when I spoke it was intelligible. "Hello. I'm hoping you can help me. I'm looking for Fiona O'Brien and Jorge Alvarez."

The woman lifted her brow. "And what makes you think they're here?"

I made direct eye contact with her. "Please, let's not play games. I'd like to see my friends."

For a moment we stood there, sizing each other up. The woman who stared back at me had brown hair pulled back into a tight bun and an icy expression.

Finally, the corners of her mouth twitched and formed a small smile. "Very well, come with me."

I didn't feel good about the situation, yet I followed the woman down a series of passageways with her two henchmen trailing just a few feet behind. By the time we reached our destination, just outside a plain gray door, my knees ached from the exertion and I had to lean heavily on my cane. The woman turned toward me. "Prepare yourself, Ms. Helgren, for a complete paradigm shift of everything you believe to be true regarding your humanity," she said.

I sighed. I had worked with enough corporate executives in my day to know mumbo-jumbo when I heard it. "Yeah, okay. Open the door please. I'd like to see my friends."

She opened the door and we entered a room that appeared to be a typical office with an oval conference table, six chairs, and two side doors. "Please have a seat," she said. "I wasn't expecting you so soon. I'll need a few minutes to catch up on the administrative work."

I took the closest seat and she sat in a chair directly across from me.

The woman nodded at the two guards, who I had begun to think of as her personal henchmen. "Please wait for me out in the hallway."

Both henchmen nodded in response and exited the room while the woman began to work on her flex-display.

"Do you have a name?" I asked.

She looked up and seemed to give my question serious thought. I raised my brow and stared at her. After all, it was a simple question.

"Yes, I do. My name is Dr. Elizabeth Wilcox. I'll be assisting with your transition."

My eyes narrowed. "What transition?"

"Oh, forgive me. Your early arrival has thrown off the proper phasing. We'll need to rush you through the system so you don't miss the current transition—"

Before she could continue, a side door burst open and a young man pushed in a cart with two metallic boxes on top. "Dr. Wilcox, the ashes have been prepared. Would you like to sign off on the orders?"

"I'll need a third order now. I'll sign off when all three orders are complete," the doctor said.

My eyes went wide and a shot of adrenaline gave my heart a jolt. Had I just walked into a death trap?

The young man nodded and left the room with his cart. I had heard enough. I pulled the sparrow from my pocket and pointed it at the doctor's head.

"Oh," she said without a trace of fear. "I wasn't expecting that."

I focused intently on holding the sparrow steady, yet my hand wavered a bit. "Don't underestimate me, Dr. Wilcox. I refuse to be reduced to ashes anytime soon."

The doctor sighed. "And you won't be, so put that thing down."

"Not until I have some assurances, starting with my personal safety," I said.

She nodded. "Fine. You and your friends will be safe."

The two henchmen burst through the door and aimed their military Rugers at me.

"Now, will you put that thing down?" she asked.

I had no choice but to trust the doctor. No doubt, the henchmen would blow me to pieces if I tried anything. I set my sparrow on the table.

Dr. Wilcox took my weapon and nodded toward the men. "You can leave now, and don't come back unless I buzz for you."

The men lowered their Rugers, and I glared at them as they left the room.

"Now, Mildred," she began.

I held my hand up. "Millie. I prefer Millie."

"All right, Millie. I'd like to get started by informing you of your current rights as a human being."

"I'm fairly certain I already know my rights," I said.

"You know your rights as a resident of earth. The minute you crossed my threshold you stepped into a facility that serves as the sovereign nation for the Gaekaars." Her voice was monotone and her expression gave away nothing.

"What? Why would the Gaekaars have an interest down here on Earth? And what would they want with me? I'm *old* for God's sake."

"I understand that you have a lot of questions. The best answer I can give you is that your life contains valuable assets that the Gaekaars are willing to purchase."

I leaned forward. "First of all I have nothing that they would want, and second, why would they want to *purchase* a senior citizen? I thought our business agreements were limited to mining Helium-3 on the moon in exchange for the Laydenhowers vaccinations?"

Dr. Wilcox shook her head. "It's not currently public knowledge, but the moon was exhausted of He-3 fourteen years ago. Earth needed something to barter with in order to continue receiving the vaccinations."

"Wasn't that about the same time Earth was indoctrinated into the GAP?" I asked.

"Very perceptive," Dr. Wilcox said.

"Okay, so we ran out of He-3 to sell … that doesn't explain why the Gaekaars would be interested in purchasing senior citizens. Good God, I can barely walk!"

Dr. Wilcox's face remained devoid of expression. "Your physical abilities are irrelevant to them. Now, as far as your immediate concerns, I can guarantee your safety and that of your friends, for the short term, but you will be required to sign a binding contract."

"I'd like to see my friends first … alive," I said.

Dr. Wilcox punched something into her flex-display, looked up, and gave me a smile that didn't reach her eyes. "Done."

A moment later one of the side doors opened. Fiona and Jorge walked through, looking somewhat bewildered.

Fiona was all smiles when she saw me, but Jorge seemed tense. I stood and reached out to hug them both. "Someone needs to tell me exactly what's going on here," I insisted.

Dr. Wilcox leaned back in her chair. "I'll get straight to the point. Your life on Earth, as well as Fiona's and Jorge's, has ended. As part of the Thrive Treaty of 2085, between Humans and the GAP, all *qualified* Earthlings over the age of 105 will be turned over to the Imperial Gaekaar Military for enlistment in their armed forces."

I couldn't help but laugh. The thought was absolutely ridiculous. "What good is an army of old folks who walk with canes and have dietary restrictions?"

"Those are things that can be ... taken care of. The Gaekaars are more interested in what you have up here." She pointed to her head. "It's your lifetime of experiences they want. Over the decades your brain has developed improved decision making, interpersonal skills, strategic abilities, and a host of other attributes that can't be found in young humans. Right now, it all comes down to a simple choice. You may choose to end your life now, or sign on with the Gaekaars and fight for the greater good of the galaxy in the Rim War."

I wasn't sure, but if my memory served me, the Rim War was a century old battle that was taking place on the far side of the galaxy between opposing aliens. I couldn't understand why it would have anything to do with us.

Dr. Wilcox pushed the flex-display over to me. I glanced down and saw a contract displayed in small print.

"Can't I just refuse and go back to my old life?" I asked.

The doctor shook her head. "I'm afraid not. Now that you know about the agreement, you're too much of a liability to send back. If this information were to leak out to the general public it would cause planet-wide chaos. Should you refuse to sign, we'll be forced to place your *actual* ashes in one of those boxes that you saw earlier."

"Just sign it, Millie. It's better than dying and we'll have a chance at a new life," Fiona said. She almost looked excited by the prospect.

Jorge touched Fiona's arm. "Let her make up her own mind. This is a big decision." Jorge looked over at me with concern in his eyes.

"Millie, even if you sign this we have no way of knowing what will happen to us. Our futures could still be short-lived."

"This is incredibly preposterous," I said. "I wish I could consult my granddaughter before making such a monumental decision."

Dr. Wilcox shook her head again. "We can't let you contact anyone outside of this office. Regardless of your decision, everyone on Earth will believe you are dead. You essentially 'died' the moment you stepped on that elevator. You have ten minutes to make your choice. I'm sorry, but that's protocol."

The doctor leaned back in her chair. "On a positive note, if you should sign on, you'll be able to enjoy a relaxing evening tonight with your friends. First thing in the morning your transformation will begin. After ten weeks you'll be assigned an appropriate position and then be shipped off to SKAT, which is a military apprentice school. The whole process takes about five months."

"What happens after that?" I asked.

The doctor wore a cool expression. "You'll go to war … for the rest of your life. Or until the war ends. Whichever comes first." The weighted meaning of her words brought silence upon the room.

Having grown up in a military family I wasn't afraid of war, and considering I wasn't ready to die, signing the contract appeared to be the logical choice. How had this happened? One minute I was preparing to quietly fade away in a Fed-Home and the next I'm being drafted into a galactic war. I reached over and gave my arm a hard pinch; a small gesture to make sure I wasn't dreaming. The piercing sting confirmed that I was indeed conscious.

I sat down and read the fine print on the doctor's flex-display while the others waited. It was ridiculously long and contained a lot of mumbo-jumbo legalese, but in basic terms it said my life would become the property of the Gaekaars and I would be assigned a rank and responsibility based on their assessment of my skillset. I would also be compensated with GAP endorsed credits, which I could access at any time should I need to purchase something. Although if I perished in the war, all my earnings would revert back to the GAP. The contract would be binding for the rest of my natural existence or the conclusion of the Rim War.

Upon reaching the end of the document I signed on the flex-display and my biometric signature was recorded. I knew I had no better alternative, yet I still worried about Avery. She deserved to know what had really happened to me. I could only hope that she discovered the note that I left in my jewelry box.

I slid the flex-display over to Dr. Wilcox.

"Good. I'm glad to see we're all in agreement. Enjoy yourselves tonight because tomorrow you'll begin a new life." She tapped the screen and within moments a young man in a black uniform entered the room. "Corporal Sloan will make sure you're comfortable tonight. You've got a big day tomorrow so try to get a good night's sleep. I'll see the three of you in the morning, bright and early."

"Please follow me," Corporal Sloan said as he headed toward the door. I couldn't help but notice his sidearm. I guess there was no chance of making a run for it, at least not with the weaponry I'd seen so far.

Corporal Sloan took us to the elevator and we went down two more levels. Then he escorted us down a long hall to a heavy metal door with a security panel. "You'll be staying here tonight." He placed his hand on the panel and the door opened.

We followed the corporal through the entry. Once inside he turned to face us. "This is the main room. You'll find three attached bedrooms, each with a private bath."

The room was very nice and it resembled a high-end hotel more than a military facility. The main living space had two luxurious suede couches and a large dining table with six chairs.

Corporal Sloan pointed to a small terminal located on a desk near the wall. The computer is over there, please feel free to order anything from room service."

"Anything?" Fiona said with a gleam in her eye.

"Yes, anything," he replied.

"Even criminals are granted a last meal ... right before they're executed," I said under my breath.

Corporal Sloan frowned at me and then bowed and exited the room. The door closed behind him. It had no handle, no visible lock, and offered no way out.

I wondered why a military man had bowed to us. It seemed strange.

Fiona walked over to the overstuffed couch, flopped down, and put her feet up. "Well, looks like we're stuck here until the morning so let's make the best of it."

Jorge searched the room for bugs with his wristwatch device, but he found nothing.

I walked over to the computer. "How can I help you," a digital voice said.

I smiled. "I'd like your best bottle of scotch."

"Coming right up. Would you like anything else?" the computer said.

I pondered the question for a moment. "I'd like to go home."

"I am sorry. That request is not within the parameters of my abilities."

I frowned. "Too bad, just the scotch and three glasses for now."

Within a minute the door chimed and opened. A man stood in the entry holding a tray.

Jorge walked up to the man and pulled a small chip out of his pocket. He held the money out to the deliveryman, but the fellow respectfully declined and handed Jorge the tray instead. The man took a step back and shut the door with a thud.

"Are you crazy?" Fiona said. "We're stuck in some sovereign alien nation and you're offering the delivery guy a tip?"

Jorge shrugged. "Old habits are hard to break. Besides, it's not like I'll have use for money where we're going."

I shook my head. "Maybe we should spend our time calculating a way to handle all of this."

Jorge held up the tray. "Sounds good. Let's have a stiff drink and discuss our impending future."

We sat down on the over-stuffed couches and Jorge poured us each a healthy glass of scotch, straight up.

"Cheers," I said, holding my glass high. "May tomorrow bring only good things."

We clinked our glasses and took a long drink.

"You know, according to the media, the Rim War has been going on for over a century. It's strange how we never hear much about it. I suppose it's because it's so far away," Jorge pointed out. "Other than pictures, I've never even seen a live Gaekaar, let alone any other alien species."

"None of us have seen them," I said. "Earth has only been in the GAP for fourteen years. I've heard that some members of the GAP have been enrolled for millennia. I suspect that humans are considered as backward rednecks in the eyes of the other species."

Fiona scowled. "I suppose that means we'll be treated like the dumb kids in the class."

"Without a doubt," Jorge said.

I reached for my cane. "I'm not sure what I can accomplish with this old body. And I still don't understand why they would want seniors?"

"Just do your best. We'll commit to using our minds rather than our bodies," Jorge said.

As the night wore on we discussed all the crazy things we thought might happen the next day, but the truth was we had no idea.

At midnight Fiona held up her glass. "In a few short hours only God knows what will transpire, so I think we should make a pact—no matter what happens to each of us, and no matter where we end up, we swear to look out for each other and take care of each other to the best of our abilities."

"Agreed," I said, holding up my glass.

"Agreed," Jorge said.

We clinked our glasses and sealed the pact.

CHAPTER 4

The next morning I awoke with a pounding headache. Or maybe it was someone pounding on my door. I had trouble differentiating between the two.

"Millie, breakfast is here," Fiona said through the door.

"I'll be right there," I answered. "Uh, did you happen to order anything for a hangover?"

"Yes, we did. Along with omelets, bacon, hash brown potatoes, fresh squeezed orange juice, and a pot of Earl Grey."

Fiona's description of food made my stomach rumble with discomfort. It took me longer than usual to get up and dressed, but when I finally sat at the table Jorge handed me a shot glass with a purple liquid in it. "I ordered aspirin and they sent this. It's for the headache. Works wonders," he said.

I drank it down in one big gulp, thankful for its utter lack of taste. "Thanks," I muttered.

Fiona handed me a plate of food that looked wonderful, but my stomach protested with a wave of nausea. I pushed the plate aside and sipped on a cup of steaming tea instead.

"Well, today's the big day," Jorge said. "I think we should mentally prepare ourselves."

I felt a subtle buzzing in my head and a few seconds later my hangover was gone. I held up the shot glass. "Wow, that was a miracle cure. I wonder what it is?"

Jorge chuckled. "I don't know, but we could have made millions with the patent to that concoction."

My stomach growled and I discovered I was ravenous, so I pulled the plate back over and dug into the fluffy omelet. It tasted marvelous.

The door chimed and for a moment we simply looked at each other. No one wanted to answer it.

The entry opened of its own accord and Corporal Sloan walked in. "Good morning. I trust you had a nice evening."

"It would have been nicer if we were back at the Fed-Home," I said.

The corporal acted as if he didn't hear what I'd said. "You'll each find a jumpsuit and slippers in your bedroom closet. Please shower using the provided soap and put the jumpsuit on. Only the jumpsuit and slippers. Nothing else. I will return in one hour to take you to the transition facility."

"Exactly what is this 'transition' all about?" I asked.

"Dr. Wilcox will explain everything. I will return in one hour." The corporal bowed and left without further explanation.

"What's with the bowing?" Fiona asked.

"Some sort of strange military custom, I suppose," Jorge said. "I guess we should hit the showers."

I finished my breakfast, took ahold of my cane, and headed for the bathroom. The shower itself was luxurious, but the soap was quite foul. It had a strong anti-bacterial smell and the lather left my skin with a burning sensation. I toweled myself dry and pulled a white and gray jumpsuit from the closet. It looked tiny, but as I tugged it on the material stretched to accommodate my ill-proportioned 105-year-old figure quite comfortably. I looked at myself in the mirror and decided the outfit wasn't the least bit flattering.

Fiona, Jorge, and I laughed when we saw each other in the clingy suits. "Well, we aren't going to win any beauty contest in these," Fiona said.

Corporal Sloan walked through the door exactly when he said he would. He looked each of us up and down. "Good, it appears that the three of you can follow simple directions. That's a step in the right direction. Please come with me."

The corporal had some sort of high tech golf cart waiting for us outside the door. We all loaded onto it and he took us to an area that was labeled Transport Tubes. It was a large chamber surrounded by multiple circular openings. In the center were three sleek transport vehicles called bullets. I remembered hearing about bullets on the news. The vehicle was similar to a high-speed hovercraft only much more sophisticated. The newscaster had said the anti-gravity technology was on lease to us from the GAP and was still in the testing phases.

"I thought bullets were still under development," I said to the corporal.

He shook his head. "We've been using them for almost a decade."

The corporal approached the first bullet and put his hand on a panel along the side of the vehicle. A light flashed, illuminating his blood vessels. A moment later the door opened and disappeared into the roof. Inside, four ultra-padded seats were lined up in a single row. The corporal sat at the front and we sat behind him. As soon as my butt touched the seat a harness device automatically descended across my shoulders and locked in at the hip. The cushioning around me molded to my body, trapping me snugly into the correct position. We were going to be going fast, that much I was sure of. Tingling excitement rushed through me.

Corporal Sloan was the last to slip into his seat. "Destination Omega Station," he said in a clear voice.

The computer responded with, "Cleared for Omega Conduit."

The bullet floated into the second tube on the right. In an instant we accelerated to a speed that pressed my body deep into the seat and made my skin ripple. The g-force made me feel light headed, but the experience was awesome.

Only a few minutes later the computer sounded, "Arrival at Omega destination in three, two, one. You have arrived at your destination." As the bullet decelerated I was pushed into my harness. I gasped for a breath as the thrill of the ride rushed through me. The bullet exited the tube, parked, and powered down. The side hatch opened and our harnesses unlocked and receded. I secretly hoped that my new future would allow for more bullet rides.

Outside the bullet, Dr. Wilcox waited for us with her flex-display in hand. "Hello, Mille, hello, Fiona, and hello, Jorge. I trust you had a nice evening."

Jorge and Fiona nodded. I didn't answer. My legs felt unstable from the ride and I leaned on my cane more than usual.

"Please follow me," she said.

The doctor took us a short distance to a classroom that had roughly twenty seats, eight of which were already occupied. "Please have a seat with the other students," she said.

I arched a brow. Students? It had been a long time since anyone had called me that.

Dr. Wilcox went to the front of the room and Corporal Sloan stood by the door. I noticed his sidearm again. "I am about to activate your analysis suits, so please don't be alarmed if you feel a tingling sensation."

The doctor punched something into her flex-display and went on, "The suit functions as a monitoring system that will give us extensive vital sign readings and alert us to any physiological changes due to external stressors."

A low-level tingle began at my ankles and progressively moved up my body.

"In a few minutes you will begin your transition. I want to warn you that this may be difficult for some of you. The physical demands of the transition typically causes eight percent of students to experience irreparable cell damage. We have also seen a small percentage of students suffer psychotic breaks, yet most of you will be fine as long as you follow directions and let the transition take its course."

I looked over at Fiona, her eyes wide and her mouth open as she took in the doctor's warning. I leaned over and whispered, "Stay strong. She's just trying to scare us."

"Is anyone familiar with the function of telomeres?" Dr. Wilcox didn't wait for an actual answer. A three-dimensional picture of a DNA strand materialized in the middle of the room. "Do you see these little caps on the end of each chromosome?"

She illuminated the caps with her laser pointer. "These are telomeres and they are responsible for protecting your genetic material. Unfortunately, they become truncated during cell division. As you get older, your cells continue to replicate and the telomeres continue to shorten. We have known for a long time that this is the reason you age and become susceptible to certain diseases. Through our alliance with the Gaekaars, we have been gifted with the knowledge of revitalizing your telomeres to their original state and dramatically slowing their shortening process."

Did that mean what I thought it meant? I looked around the room. About half of the students had looks of amazement in their eyes and the other half looked bewildered.

The doctor continued, "This means we now have the means of reversing the aging process and subsequently slowing down the ongoing deterioration of cells. I should add that this procedure is extremely expensive. As you are well aware, you have already paid in full with your lives. The Gaekaars regard this process as sacred and will not allow it to be available to anyone other than those individuals generous enough to donate their lives to the cause."

I raised my hand. This was too good to be true. There had to be a catch.

"Yes, Millie?"

"Exactly what happens during this procedure?" I asked.

"I can assure you, there is nothing to fear. It is quite simple really. You will each enter a chemical bath that will induce a coma and slowly lower your body temperature by twenty degrees. Since this is a sacred process, we don't fully understand how the chemical reaction takes place. But we know that after forty eight hours in the bath you will emerge a new person, complete with significantly lengthened telomeres and an overall extended lifespan," she said, looking at her watch. "Then it becomes a matter of retraining your muscles, testing your abilities, and assigning a role. I'm sorry, but we don't have time for any further questions. Please follow me to the transition room."

One by one we stood and followed Dr. Wilcox into the next room. Most of the faces around me looked intrigued by the thought of a fountain of youth, but I was suspicious over how we were being rushed along. I also suspected that that the good doctor wasn't telling us everything.

The transition room was dim and had two rows of long, rectangular boxes, each row against a sidewall. At the end of each box was an illuminated panel with a name and number boldly displayed. The doctor typed something into her flex-display and the box covers slid to the side revealing a shallow amount of a yellow-tinged watery substance.

"Please stand in front of your assigned transition tank and await further instructions," she said.

I found the tank that had my name and stood in front of it, reading the number etched into it: 891456M.

"Is it just me or do those things look like coffins?" Jorge leaned over and whispered as he and Fiona came to stand at their own tanks located next to mine.

"Please pay close attention," the doctor said. "Take your slippers off and step into the tank. If you need assistance, raise your hand and Corporal Sloan will aid you. You have nothing to fear. Your ability to follow directions and stay calm will ensure a successful outcome. It is very important that you trust the procedure."

Dr. Wilcox waited for each of us to climb into our respective tanks. I left my cane outside the tank and dipped my feet in. The yellow liquid felt warm and soothing. The corporal assisted a man across from me who cringed as he lifted his stiff and arthritic legs into the tank.

A few minutes later, a woman collapsed on the floor and started to wail, "No! It's Satan! He's forcing us into the gateway to hell!" Corporal Sloan tried to calm her, but when she didn't respond, two armed guards appeared and escorted her out.

After the woman left, the area was eerily quiet. The doctor looked at us from the middle of the room and cleared her throat. "Now, lay down as if you were going to take a bath. The computer will sense when you are in the correct position, the liquid will begin to bubble up, and the internal mechanism will take over from there. Remember, you have nothing to fear, so stay calm and trust the procedure."

I didn't like how she kept repeating that line. It made me think that I did indeed have something to fear.

CHAPTER 5

I watched as the other students leaned back in their tanks. The yellow liquid began to bubble like a giant carbonated drink as each student found the correct position.

The man in the tank across from me released a contented sigh. "This feels wonderful," he said.

"Oh, it's just like a spa!" someone else said.

"Millie, please get into the proper position. We can't begin until everyone is correctly aligned," Dr. Wilcox said.

I scowled and leaned back as instructed, letting the liquid soak into my jumpsuit. The soothing bubbles relaxed my muscles, but deep down my anxiety grew. I knew it couldn't be this easy.

"Please place your arms at your sides and relax," she instructed.

The instant I placed my arms at my sides, clamps locked my wrists into place. Another set of clamps locked my ankles in place. Then a larger clamp locked my head in place, rendering me completely immobile. The bubbling liquid began to rise and my heart raced. I wouldn't be "relaxing" anytime soon. At this rate, I would drown in a matter of seconds.

The previous happy sounds that permeated the room became screams of terror and the grunts of people struggling to break free.

"Please relax," the doctor said, using a deliberate, calm tone. "The transition fluid level is rising to cover your body. It is important that you take the fluid fully into your lungs for an effective procedure."

Not a chance. I had no desire to suck that yellow crap into my lungs. I pulled against the restraints but it was wasted energy. My feeble muscles were worthless. The fluid continued to rise until it covered my face. I held my breath for as long as I could, but my lungs burned with an unrelenting demand for oxygen. When I finally gave in, my body involuntarily inhaled, allowing the fluid to rush into my mouth. It tasted like acid as it entered my throat and seared an excruciating path to my lungs. My last thought was of Avery before a black fog overtook everything.

An enormous beast wanted to kill me. I ran as fast as I could but my legs frequently became tangled in the thick vines of the jungle. Sweat ran down my back and I was near the point of exhaustion when I managed to locate a footpath. Someone had previously hacked out a trail, for which I was grateful. I followed the path for what seemed like days, somehow managing to maintain a small lead ahead of the creature, who was in relentless pursuit. Soon I realized that I hadn't made any real progress, because just as I traveled faster on the pathway, so did the beast. I quickly made the decision to plunge back into the difficult, overgrown jungle despite my aching muscles. Some hours later, I stumbled upon a small hidden village. The exotic villagers welcomed me and offered food and lodging. They shared ancient legends about a huge beast-like species who they referred to as "Tukock." They warned me that I must keep my distance because the beast could read the pictures of the mind if one stood within a stone's throw. Many villagers had lost their lives in brutal battles with the clan of Tukock and I sensed a hunger for retribution. The village elders graciously taught me about the behaviors of the vicious beast and ways to fight back. I spent several weeks honing my new abilities. When I felt I had acquired sufficient knowledge and skills, I did not wait for the Tukock to find me, instead I ventured back into the jungle and became the hunter.

I awoke to a chill in the air and the sound of trickling liquid. My dreams had been strange and left me feeling perplexed. I opened my eyes and realized I was dripping wet and still in the transition tank. The restraints were gone, so I lifted my hands. They were pruned, but still the same old wrinkled hands. I sat up and coughed out the remaining liquid in my lungs. Next to me Fiona gripped the sides of her tank. We locked eyes and I studied her dripping gray hair and wrinkled skin.

"You look the same," I whispered.

I could see disappointment in her eyes. "So do you," she replied.

Jorge climbed out of the tank on the other side of Fiona. He looked down at his hands. "I feel like shit and I haven't changed a bit. This isn't what I expected at all."

"Please take your time, step out of the tank and wait by your name panel," Dr. Wilcox said.

I climbed from the tank, my muscles shaking from the exertion. I still felt old, and I needed to go to the bathroom.

Corporal Sloan checked on each student and keyed data into his flex-display. When he was done he approached Dr. Wilcox. "We have nine successful transitions."

The doctor shook her head. "Damn, that's a twenty percent cellular failure rate."

The corporal nodded.

I looked around the room and counted bodies. Sure enough, nine of us were standing by our name panels. From where I stood the tank across from me appeared to be empty. I walked over, curious why the man with arthritis hadn't climbed out.

Dr. Wilcox frowned. "Millie, please return to your name panel. It is critical that you follow directions."

Ignoring the good doctor, I leaned over the sidewall and peered inside the tank. Gelatinous goo covered the mechanisms and radiated a foul odor. I covered my mouth and nose with my hand. Was this what cellular failure was like?

Corporal Sloan grabbed my arm and yanked me back to my position. "It would behoove you to follow directions," he whispered. "I can assure you that you won't enjoy the repercussions of disobedience."

Yeah, whatever. The corporal didn't frighten me. It occurred to me that I didn't have my cane, yet I had walked without the usual effort.

Dr. Wilcox cleared her throat. "By now you are all wondering what just took place. You have been submerged in a transition bath for the last forty-eight hours. During this time your DNA went through a radical transmutation. From your perspective you slept the entire time, although you may have experienced vivid dreams or even nightmares. Right now you feel pretty much the same as when you entered the tank, with the only pressing need manifesting as an urge to go to the bathroom. Listen to these instructions carefully so that we can advance to the next step and get you properly cared for."

The doctor tapped at her flex-display and a three-dimensional image of a hunched over, wrinkled woman appeared in the middle of the room. "You may feel that you haven't changed, but I can assure you that you are indeed very different and quite unique. You have been altered at the chromosomal level and even as we speak, dramatic transformations are taking place in your body. Over the next week you will shed much of your skin, all of your hair and even your teeth. As your cells race to catch up with the changes in your DNA, you will also experience uncomfortable digestion issues. You will feel tired, frustrated, and sick, but rest assured your cells will catch up, and when they do you will discover that your physical body is roughly seventy years younger. Additionally, the change in DNA has slowed down the shortening of your telomeres, which means you will age at a rate of one year for every three years of a typical human on Earth."

We watched in awe as the 3D image in the center of the room transformed to display the process the doctor described. Layers of skin flaked off and hair fell to the floor in clumps. The face of the image looked tired and pained from the constant changes. Then little by little, the image began to stand taller, the spine straightened, body hair grew back, and lean muscles developed. The final result was a vibrant and strong woman who looked to be in her mid-thirties.

"You should be aware that your final result may not look as good as the image depicted here. Much of your progress depends on how motivated you are to exercise and develop your body. Yes, you'll be chronologically younger, but your body is still subject to how well you take care of it. If you eat too much, you'll get fat. If you don't exercise, you'll be out of shape. If you don't take care of yourself, you'll get sick. Does everyone understand?"

I raised my hand.

"Yes, Millie?"

"How long does this process take?"

"The shedding phase lasts about a week. You'll find that you require a large amount of sleep as well as protein supplements during this time. We will monitor your progress through the receptors in your jumpsuit. During the shedding phase you will not be assigned a schedule other than your daily check in with me, so your time will be your own."

"What happens after the shedding phase?" Jorge asked.

"After the shedding phase, we will focus on strengthening your new body. You may have already noticed small improvements in mobility, although rebuilding your musculature and learning new skills are much more arduous tasks that will take significantly longer." The doctor tapped her flex-display and the 3D image disappeared. "Everyone please follow Corporal Sloan to your new quarters. You are dismissed."

My legs felt steady, so I left my purple cane behind and followed the corporal. We took the elevator to the black level and walked down a long hallway. We passed a door labeled Group Delta, which was across the hall from another door labeled Group Foxtrot. Corporal Sloan stopped at a door marked Group Echo and led us in to what appeared to be a standard military barracks. The walls were stark gray and twenty beds lined the perimeter. Each bed had an adjacent locker with a glowing information panel that displayed a name and number.

"Your official team name is Group Echo. Find the locker with your name. A new jumpsuit, sleeping attire, bath items, and bedding material are located inside your locker. The bathroom is at the far end of the room. As your cells recover you will also experience severe exhaustion, so make sure you shower *before* going to bed. If you find that you can tolerate food, the cafeteria across the hall is open twenty-four-seven." The corporal bowed and exited.

Several of the students bolted for the bathroom, including myself. I was disappointed to see that we were all sharing a military style bathroom with toilet stalls, urinals, sinks, and showers all in one big area. It would be awkward sharing with men, but at the moment I had to urinate so badly that I didn't care. I dashed for the nearest stall and relieved myself.

The nine of us made quick introductions, found our lockers, and made up our beds with the provided linens. Two men occupied the bunks on either side of me. Sam Jacobson was in the bunk to my right and Ethan Wells was on my left. Fiona and Jorge were located on the other side of Ethan. Aliyah Bashir was in the bunk directly across from me and next to her were three women who turned out to be triplets. Their names were Trina, Karina, and Samina Oppenhiemer. They didn't talk much.

We agreed to take showers in two shifts each day, with the six women going first and then the three men. As far as using the toilet, we all agreed that each person should go whenever they needed to, regardless of gender.

The onslaught of exhaustion came over us quickly and I was thankful that we had agreed the women would shower first. Fiona claimed the showerhead next to mine and we both cranked up the hot water, sending billows of steam into the air. "After our showers, Jorge and I are going to get something to eat. Would you like to come with us," she asked.

"No thanks, I'm going straight to bed," I said.

"Ugh." Fiona held up her hand. Tangled in her fingers was a wad of hair that had previously belonged in her head.

"I wonder if it will grow back to look as it did when we were young," I said. "What color hair did you have?"

Fiona smiled. "I had curly blonde hair down to my waist. It was always out of control and at the time I hated it. It's funny how you value things so much more once they're gone."

I had a strong appreciation for Fiona's words.

After showering, Jorge, Fiona, and Sam went across the hall to get some food, while the rest of us went straight to bed. Fatigue sapped my strength and I drifted away before I had the chance to say goodnight.

The Tukock beast was chasing me, but this time the beast had a twin companion assisting in the pursuit. Two against one. Not quite fair. I was running on a path along a mountainside when I came upon a fork in the trail. One path went up the mountain and the other went down. The vibration of heavy footfalls moved closer, so I made a quick decision and chose to run down the hill. Too late I realized the Tukock had cornered me in a small canyon where I would make an easy target. I knew I had made a bad choice and reprimanded myself. I checked my outfit for supplies. I found my sparrow and a knife hanging from my belt. I gripped the sparrow and pulled it free. Then I recalled the skills the villagers had taught me. As the footsteps approached I knew what I needed most was time. Time to craft a plan.

I awoke to find that I had slept for fourteen hours. I also found clumps of hair on my pillow, and I had the severe urge to go to the bathroom. I bolted across the room and into the nearest stall. Ten minutes later I felt like I had just shed my entire insides. From the smell of the bathroom, I guessed that others were experiencing the same occurrence.

As I exited the bathroom, I passed by Jorge, who was sprinting for a stall. He looked pained and gave me a quick wave.

At my locker I noticed an appointment listed on my information panel.

Mildred Necee Helgren #891456M:
Appointment with Dr. Wilcox at 1100Z in her office,
Suite 180 Blue Level

"That's military Zulu time. Jorge explained it to me, but you probably already knew that coming from a military family," Fiona said over my shoulder.

I nodded.

She smiled. "Looks like my appointment is right after yours. We have plenty of time before we see Dr. Wilcox. How about some breakfast?"

At the mere mention of food, my stomach growled. "Absolutely. I don't ever recall being this hungry."

We got dressed in our blue jumpsuits that were labeled ECHO and went across the hall to the cafeteria. I was surprised to see so many people milling about. It seemed that the facility we were in was much larger than I originally realized. Human trafficking must be big business for the GAP.

As we went through the food line, the system identified us by our jumpsuits and automatically dispensed a gray protein shake and mammoth portions of eggs, potatoes, and bacon. I held up the gray shake. "Am I really supposed to drink this?" I asked.

"If you don't consume your entire meal, the system will know and you'll lose valuable points," a deep voice said.

I turned and saw an attractive dark-haired man in his late thirties wearing a crisp black dress uniform. "I'm Major Cameron Ford," he said.

"Hello. I'm Millie and this is my friend Fiona."

"You both must have arrived yesterday. I can tell by your hair," he said.

Fiona unconsciously smoothed the patches of missing hair on the side of her head.

"Yes we did. Although, I'm still not sure what to make of all of this," I said, looking around.

"You'll adjust, just give yourself some time. I recommend going down to the Med Center and having your heads shaved. It's a lot easier than having hair fall into your food for a week."

"Thanks for the tip, we appreciate that," I said. "Now, about those points you mentioned—what kind of points?"

"The kind that determines your future. So eat up." Cameron winked and walked away.

CHAPTER 6

It took me longer than expected to find Dr. Wilcox's office. The doctor was located on the blue level, two floors above our quarters on the black level. I walked through a network of hallways that seemed to go on forever. I found the office and pressed my hand to the sensor. After a brief pause the door opened.

Dr. Wilcox stood in the opening and gestured toward a chair located in front of her desk. She wore a gray suit and had her flex-display in hand. "It's good to see you, Millie, please have a seat. You're right on time."

"Thank you." I sat down, folded my arms across my chest, and pursed my lips.

"How are you doing?" she asked, taking her seat.

"I'm doing exactly as you predicted. Losing hair, sleeping a lot, and running to the bathroom."

"Are you experiencing any pain or anxiety?" She almost sounded concerned.

"Yes and yes. But it's not worse than anyone else."

She looked down at her flex-display and seemed to be reading something. "Are you consuming the recommended amount of protein?"

"Yes, I drank the entire shake this morning, but I'm guessing you already knew that."

She looked me in the eye and sighed. "I know that you're unhappy and feel lost right now, but in time you'll find that this is the best thing that could have happened to you."

I leaned forward. "Oh, really? You have no idea how I feel. My life was just pilfered by a bunch of aliens in a massive government conspiracy. How can you be certain you know their real intentions? How do you know they're not using us for cheap slave labor or something worse?"

Dr. Wilcox clasped her hands together. "I know because I'm one hundred and sixty-two years young and I have more knowledge of the Gaekaars, and their intentions, than anyone else on Earth. I can also assure you that you are not being developed for 'cheap slave labor.' In fact, there is nothing *cheap* about this process. By the time you complete your training close to $300 million will have been invested in you."

I scrutinized her face for traces of deception. "So you went through the same process?"

She nodded. "Yes I did. I wholeheartedly believe in this program because it provides important benefits on multiple levels."

The doctor took a deep breath and continued, "First, the Gaekaars acquire the soldiers they need to supplement their military. Second, you get a new and extended life. Rather than rotting away in a Fed-Home, you will be fighting to save humanity. And I do mean *save*. The Rim War is fast approaching our sector of the galaxy. Anything we can do to maintain peace in this sector is a big win for Earth. Third and most importantly, this program is helping to spread the seed of humanity throughout countless star systems. When the Rim War reaches our planet, and I can assure you in time it will, the existence of humanity will be at great risk. Even with our membership in the GAP, our lack of progressive technology and political sophistication will hold us back. God forbid, if something horrific was to happen to Earth, we would still have hundreds of thousands of humans throughout the galaxy and our species would not perish."

Wow. That was some fairly heavy information that I needed to spend time digesting. "Interesting, you've almost made human trafficking sound acceptable," I said under my breath.

"I can assure you that when you take the time to review the bigger picture, you'll agree that this process serves the greater good." After the doctor's impressive speech we discussed my protein intake, my sleep patterns, and how my sole focus at this point should be getting through the shedding phase. Throughout the conversation she stressed that I needed to hit a minimum of 200 grams of protein a day and more was better if I could tolerate it. If I failed to take in the required amount, my cells would not rebuild properly.

As our meeting concluded, she closed her flex-display. "Do you have any other questions regarding your recovery?"

"I'm concerned about Avery, my granddaughter. I need to know that she's all right," I said, leaning forward.

The doctor nodded. "Once you complete SKAT you will be allowed an update on your family members, but for obvious reasons, you will not be permitted to contact them."

"Okay," I said, feeling somewhat better. "What happens next, after I'm done shedding myself?"

She paused. "You'll enter the next phase. Let's cross that bridge when we get there. It's a different experience for everyone based on a multitude of factors."

Later that afternoon, Fiona and I decided to have our heads shaved. Aliyah and Jorge were asleep in their bunks and everyone else was gone. We went back to the cafeteria, asked around, and found out that the Med Center was located one floor above us on the orange level. After pushing the orange button on the elevator, we discovered that the internal computer on the elevator could also answer questions for us regarding locations, making it much easier to find the Med Center through the maze of corridors.

A friendly nurse at the Med Center reception desk smiled at us as we entered. "What can I help you with, young ladies?"

I glanced over my shoulder to see if she was talking to someone else. Then it occurred to me that we were the young ladies. It sounded so strange.

"We heard that you could shave our heads so that we wouldn't have to deal with hair dropping everywhere," I said.

"Certainly. You'll also find that your hair grows back faster after having it shaved off. Have a seat over there and I'll be right with you," the nurse said.

When we returned to the barracks Jorge was standing by his locker with Sam Jacobson. Jorge took one look at us and raised his eyebrows. Sam tried to stifle a laugh.

"You two look like a pair of cue balls," Jorge said.

"You should try it. It's quite liberating," Fiona responded, lifting her chin higher.

"I don't think I'm ready to let go of my afro," Sam said, giving his thick kinky gray hair a pat.

Fiona rolled her eyes. "You're going to have to give it up sooner or later. Besides, we were informed that new hair grows back faster if you shave off the old."

I looked across the room and noticed that Aliyah was still in her bunk. "Has Aliyah been sleeping all day?"

"I think she attended her appointment with Dr. Wilcox this morning, but other than that, yes, I believe she slept all day," Sam said.

"Do you know if she had lunch?" I asked.

Sam shrugged. "Sorry, I don't know."

"Well, I'm dog-tired, so I'm going to take a nap," Fiona said.

I nodded in agreement. "I could use a nap myself. Jorge would you mind making sure we don't miss dinner?"

"Sure thing." Jorge put his arm around Sam's shoulder. "In the meantime Sam and I will be getting our heads shaved."

Sam shrugged. "When in Rome …"

I hid behind a cluster of boulders as the pair of Tukocks entered the canyon, about 100 yards away. I scrutinized the movements of the tall, upright creatures closely. The beast on the right was somewhat larger and shaggier than the other. It also had a vibrant white stripe on his head. This marked him as an elder. The villagers had taught me that the beast with the stripe would be the leader, the communicator, and the decision maker. Common sense dictated that I should take him out first. I watched every step the creatures took as they approached the small pile of stones that I had strategically placed. I was ready. The moment the elder stepped over my makeshift landmine, I would trigger the self-destruct mechanism on my sparrow and take him out. Just a few more seconds and the elder Tukock would be on top of the stones. My finger hovered over the detonator…

I had never had a dream that continued every time I slept. It was like watching a movie and hitting the pause button every time I woke up. But it wasn't just that, the dreams didn't have that dreamlike quality. They felt oddly real.

I washed up and looked at myself in the mirror. My head was bald, my skin was flaking off like after a bad sunburn, and I had circles under my eyes. Ugh, I looked like a reptile.

"Hey, Helgren. We're going to go to dinner. You coming?" Sam asked.

I stepped out of the bathroom and saw seven of my roommates waiting for me. It was somewhat comforting to see that they all looked as bad as I did. Flakes of dead skin were everywhere—on the floor, on everyone's shoulders, and on the bunks. As I looked around, I noticed that Aliyah was still in her bunk.

"Sure," I said. "But we need to get Aliyah up."

I walked over and gave her shoulder a gentle shake. She grumbled something about not being hungry.

"You have to get your protein intake up," I reminded her. "Did you eat lunch?"

She shook her head.

"Come on, get up." I helped her into a sitting position. Tufts of hair stuck to her pillow as she sat up. She felt frail.

Fiona helped me get Aliyah to the bathroom. We brushed what was left of her hair and washed her up for dinner.

Jorge found us a table while the rest of our group went through the line to get our enormous portions of food. We were offered a nice selection of entrees for dinner. I picked the roast beef, Brussels sprouts, roasted potatoes, and strawberry shortcake with a huge mound of whipped cream. Aliyah stood behind me in line and I noticed that she had only taken a small salad.

"Oh no, that won't do. You need to load up," I said, piling fattening food onto her tray.

Her eyes bulged. "I don't know if I can eat all of this. I'm not hungry."

"Just try," I said, nudging her along. Lastly, I put a big gray protein shake on each of our trays.

We carried our ridiculous portions of food to the table and sat down. Most of us dug in and ate with gusto, but Aliyah just picked at her plate. "What do you suppose happens if we don't meet our intake requirements?" she asked.

Someone standing behind me cleared his throat. I turned and saw that it was Cameron Ford, still wearing the black uniform. "Your new cell structure needs to be fed. If not, your tissue will literally consume you alive and you'll expire in short order, therefore I suggest you eat up," he said without pretense.

Aliyah's eyes widened and she stared at a chunk of beef on the end of her fork. She grimaced and slowly stuffed the meat into her mouth.

"So how is Group Echo fairing so far?" Cameron asked.

"As good as can be expected, all things considered," Jorge said with a scowl.

"Yes, I know it's not a pleasant process. Hang in there, Group Echo. I'll see you in my classroom in a week. That's when the real fun starts." Cameron chuckled as he walked away.

When we returned to the barracks my information panel had a new readout.

Congratulations on successfully completing the first day of your shedding phase.

Required calorie intake: 4000
Total calories consumed: 4821
Required protein intake: 200
Total protein grams consumed: 215
Total sleep: 16.2 hours

Fiona ran over to me with a bounce in her step. "I successfully completed my first day, how about you?"

"Yes, I did too." I smiled at her. "Fiona, do you realized that you just ran over here? You *ran!*"

Fiona put her hand to her face. "Oh my, I didn't realize I had."

Behind us Ethan Wells and Sam Jacobson started cheering and whistling. Everyone in the barracks broke out laughing, including the quiet Oppenhiemer triplets.

Eating a big meal was exhausting, so I turned in. Everyone else did the same and within minutes a blend of harmonious snores seemed to vibrate the air. I was the last to doze off.

The elder Tukock stood over the spot where my sparrow was buried and I prepared to pull the trigger when something tugged in the back of my mind. Why was I killing the beast? Because it was chasing me? Because the villagers told me their stories? Then I recalled how the villagers spoke of the Tukock being able to read the pictures in your mind if one was within close proximity. I stepped out from my hiding area and walked toward the creatures, openly displaying the detonator. I concentrated on picturing myself pulling the remote trigger and exploding the sparrow. The Tukock stood frozen in their tracks. They looked at each other with concern. Next, I slowly knelt down and placed the detonator on the ground and tried to picture in my mind the three of us communicating. Again the Tukock looked at each other and the elder nodded. They seemed to be having a conversation. Then I sent a picture of the Tukock chasing me and proceeded to ask 'why' in my mind. The elder stepped toward me and reached up to place his hand on my forehead. An epic picture entered my mind depicting millions of their kind being butchered by a strange species that had arrived from a distant place. They were clearly frightened that their kind would become extinct if they didn't fiercely protect the remaining few. In my mind I asked if the local villagers were a threat. The elder responded with a picture that indicated his uncertainty over who could be trusted. I considered his thoughts and sent a picture of us working together. I created the image of the Tukock, the villagers, and myself uniting for the purpose of protecting all the land from the strange species that came from a distant place...

My inexplicable dreams continued every time I slept, which was a good deal of the time. During my waking hours I didn't pay much attention to them because I was preoccupied with making it through the difficult week.

On day two we were horrified to find our teeth falling out. They were being pushed out by a new set that were maturing at a rapid rate. By the third day our skin was flaking off so much we found that we had to change our bedding twice a day. We also began to experience extreme pain as our bones began to recalcify. For this we were issued low dose narcotics.

Dr. Wilcox monitored our mental and physical well-being through the sensors in our jumpsuits and gave us advice on what to eat to keep our vitals strong.

Near the mid week point all members of Group Echo seemed to be meeting the daily intake requirements with the exception of Aliyah. At one point I asked the doctor if there was anything she could do to help us get Aliyah to eat more and she replied, "Part of this phase entails scoring your will to thrive. Each student must develop that on their own."

I chose not to let the doctor's words deter me. I spoke to the rest of our group and no one hesitated to offer assistance. Each team member agreed to take shifts to monitor Aliyah's intake and encourage her to take care of herself. When eight bunkmates were nagging her every waking hour, Aliyah quickly found that she had no choice but to comply.

Throughout the rest of the week we stuffed ourselves with food, cajoled Aliyah into eating, made repeated trips to the bathroom and, of course, attended daily check-ins with Dr. Wilcox. On day five, I noticed my skin looked markedly different. The peeling was minimal and a fresh glow was beginning to emerge on firm flesh.

At 0600Z on the morning of the eighth day, I looked into the mirror and spotted reddish peach fuzz emerging from my egg shaped head. Now that the worst was over I truly felt like a new person. My skin was as clear and smooth as it was seventy years ago, my eyes no longer drooped at the corners, my teeth were brilliant white, and my energy level was amazing. I took a closer look in the mirror. I had never had red hair in the past, although my mother and grandmother had.

Sam Jacobson, who was now a nice looking young man with patches of dark hair sprouting on his head and jawline, came into the bathroom just as I was leaving. "Meeting at 0800 sharp, Helgren. Check your panel."

"Thanks. Looks like it's time for a shave, Sam," I said over my shoulder.

Sam paused and then I heard a booming, "Woo-hoo!"

Back at my locker, I checked the information panel.

Groups Delta, Echo, and Foxtrot:
Report to Room 42C, Red Level for Training Overview at
0800Z

I took a deep breath and mentally prepared myself for the next phase.

CHAPTER 7

Fiona looked over at me with a broad smile. Visually, she appeared to be a different person from the one I'd met less than two weeks ago. Her teeth were a perfect row of white pearls, her cheeks were flushed and smooth, and her eyes were bright.

"Are you ready to go, Millie?" she asked.

"Come along, ladies, we can't wait all day to take the next step in this crazy adventure," Sam shouted from the door.

Like elderly seniors, Group Echo shuffled along the hallway to the elevator.

Jorge stepped out in front and turned toward the group. "Stand up straight and stop shuffling! We're young now, let's act like it."

The nine of us visibly stood up straighter and crammed onboard the elevator. I reached over and pushed the button for the red level. The elevator pinged and spoke to us, "Performing security scan to verify identities for admittance to the red level."

"Must be some fairly important stuff happening on the red level," Jorge said.

"Like training us to be super soldiers," Sam said, holding his arm up and flexing his flabby bicep.

Ethan shook his head. "Did I happen to mention I was a poet and a pacifist in my past life? I'm not sure I'll make a very effective soldier."

Aliyah and the three Oppenhiemer triplets nodded their heads in agreement with Ethan. It seemed we had a number of pacifists in our group.

"Let's not jump to conclusions about what's expected of us. I'm sure they'll have desk jobs available ... or something like that," I said.

The elevator pinged again. "Security scan complete. Proceeding to red level."

We arrived at room 42C early to find the room was empty. It was set up classroom style, with stadium seating and a key-panel at each desk.

"Where should we sit?" Fiona asked.

I pointed to the front row. "Let's sit there, so we don't miss anything."

Sam scowled. "Didn't the geeks sit in the front row back in school?"

"Yes, and the bad students sat in the back," I pointed out.

"What about the middle?" Sam said.

I shook my head. "The middle stands for mediocrity."

"Well then, the front row it is." Sam marched down to the front row, sat at the far end, and put his feet up on the desk.

Group Echo took up the entire front row. Groups Delta and Foxtrot filtered in little by little and I counted heads as students took various seats around the classroom. I recognized some of the faces from the cafeteria and hallways. Everyone seemed relaxed and casual conversation filled the air with an occasional burst of laughter.

The room became quiet when Dr. Wilcox and Cameron entered. The doctor positioned herself behind a podium and Cameron stood off to the side. She wore a simple skirt and blouse, and Cameron had on his black dress uniform. I wasn't certain, but I thought they both appeared tense.

We had a total of thirty-four students in the room.

Dr. Wilcox cleared her throat. "Congratulations on successfully completing the shedding phase. Please rest assured that the worst is over and from this point forward you will only experience mild discomfort as your bodily systems adjust to the new cell structure. I'd like to take the next few minutes to review some hard numbers."

Dr. Wilcox flipped on her three dimensional presentation and a colorful graph appeared at her side. "We suffered a twenty percent student loss during the transition phase in the tanks, then another fifteen percent loss during the shedding phase. During the training phase we expect to experience another thirty percent loss. That nets out to a fifty-two percent total loss from the start of the program up until your deployment. Please understand that thirty percent is only an average based on our experience with previous groups. Our hope is always to improve the survival rates. Again, this is why it is imperative for you to follow our directions to the letter."

The room was silent. I looked around and saw a few jaws drop and a lot of wide-eyed stares. The thought of losing another thirty percent was terrifying. I also had the sinking feeling that the good doctor's speech was just a preamble to a bigger bomb she was going to lob our way.

Fiona leaned over and put her hand to my ear. "According to those stats, roughly ten of the people in this room won't make it through training."

The doctor looked over at Cameron. "I would like to introduce Major Cameron Ford. He will be your instructor during this phase. He is also responsible for making your formal enlistment recommendation at the end of the training phase, so I suggest you do whatever he asks."

The major stepped up and took Dr. Wilcox's spot at the front of the room. "The training phase for subgroups Delta, Echo, and Foxtrot will last for ten weeks. You should be aware that no subgroup has ever emerged from the training phase intact. Every group loses someone due to the difficult process, but that doesn't mean it has to be you. Those who put forth the effort and follow directions will be successfully deployed."

"It is also important to note that this is *not* your military training; this is simply training to get you ready for apprentice school, otherwise known as SKAT: Specific Knowledge Apprenticeship Training. You should consider your ten weeks here a cakewalk compared to the education that you will receive from the Gaekaars post deployment at SKAT. Whether you are aware of it or not, each of you have been accumulating points since you first set foot in this establishment. Everything you said, did, ate, and dreamt has accumulated points toward your total. Your points will continue to accumulate until five weeks have passed. At that time Dr. Wilcox and I will analyze your numbers, as well as other things that can't be quantified, and make a recommendation for rank and position within the Imperial Gaekaar Military, otherwise known as the IGM. You are going to have to live with this assignment for a very long time, so do your best over the next few weeks. Any questions?"

I raised my hand.

The major nodded toward me. "Yes, Millie?"

"You mentioned dreams. How do they affect our points?"

"Good question. Many of you may recall experiencing vivid dreams during the shedding phase. You were each given a unique situation where you had to make difficult choices. Your physiological and emotional responses were monitored and points were assigned accordingly."

Someone several rows behind me raised his hand.

"Yes, you in the back. What is your name and group?"

A thin man with a pointed nose stood up. "My name is Mark Solomon, Group Delta. How could you possibly put dreams in our heads?"

"Through our connections in the GAP we have the technology to do many things that would be otherwise considered impossible on Earth. You will be exposed to additional top secret advancements over the next few weeks, so get used to being surprised."

Mark Solomon sat back down.

"Each of you will also be required to develop your bodies for the physical challenges of war. This will be accomplished by implementing a rigorous workout schedule. Just because you are seventy or so years younger, it doesn't mean that you have the musculature of someone who is in military shape. The cells that make up your muscles are newly constructed, but they are weak. Ten weeks is barely enough time to condition yourself for the difficulty of space travel and the brutal demands of combat. Additionally, you will also be working side by side with several other species who are inherently stronger than humans, so it is crucial that you take your workout schedule seriously."

Ethan sat on the other side of me. I noticed that he was pale and had a death grip on the arms of his chair. He wasn't the sort of person you would find in a gym. He was thoughtful and sensitive, and his facial features were soft, almost androgynous. I considered his past life as a poet and wondered how that would mesh with this new hard-ass reality.

The major looked around the room. "And lastly, anyone who doesn't meet the physical and mental requirements will become part of the thirty percent. Are we clear?"

The room was silent. The bomb had gone off. Anyone who didn't meet the requirements would be eradicated.

I took a deep breath. Well, there was no way in hell anyone in Group Echo would fail. I felt confident that we could work together and get everyone through the next phase.

"As long as there aren't any additional questions, everyone has a thirty-minute break. At 0930 Zulu you are each required to be at the gym on the orange level, meet with your assigned workout coach, and begin your personalized fitness plan. Dismissed."

Fiona leaned over and grimaced. "Gee, what a nice guy."

As we stood to leave the classroom, Major Ford approached me. "Hello, Millie."

Fiona looked at me, eyebrows raised. "I'll see you back at the barracks."

I waved to her and turned toward Cameron. "Hello, Major. Now that I know you're an officer, shouldn't I be saluting you or something?"

Cameron chuckled. "Technically you're still a civilian. You aren't required to call me major until you're officially enlisted."

"If you don't mind, Major, I'd like to start practicing proper protocol now," I said.

He nodded. "Smart thinking. How are you doing? You seem to be adjusting well."

I smiled and tried to hide the cynicism I was feeling. "Just trying to do my part for humanity."

Dr. Wilcox walked over. "Please excuse us, Major Ford. Millie, can I talk to you for a minute?"

Cameron nodded and left the room with the rest of the students.

I turned toward the doctor. "Sure. What can I do for you?"

"Let's have a seat over here." She led me to the far side of the room where we could chat privately.

"Is there a problem?" I asked.

"No." She neatly folded her arms in front of her. "I want you to know that we are fully aware of the extra steps your group took to help Aliyah Bashir reach her intake numbers during the shedding phase."

"It wasn't a secret," I pointed out.

She nodded. "Yes, but without your intervention she never would have survived the transformation. Technically, the program doesn't allow for the manipulation of a student's natural behavior."

"I'm guessing that these weren't *normal circumstances*," I said.

She shook her head and continued. "No, they were not. We permitted you to believe that you had the power to save your teammate so that we could study the impact of group dynamics."

I couldn't help but laugh out loud. "I really don't care about all that doubletalk. Aliyah made it through. She survived and that's all that matters."

Dr. Wilcox nodded. "Agreed. I'd like you to also be aware that Aliyah Bashir has a one in fifty chance of making it through the training phase. In fact, a couple of your team members have extremely poor odds. It will take more than a small miracle for Group Echo to emerge from this phase intact."

"Isn't that typical for all the groups that come through here?" I asked. "Major Ford stated that no group has made it through the training phase without suffering losses."

The doctor gave me knowing look. "Yes, that is correct."

"Then why are you telling me all of this?" I asked.

A smile pulled at the corners of her mouth. "It might be hard to believe, but I'm actually rooting for your team to come out of this with nine solid soldiers for deployment. The Gaekaar don't fully understand human resourcefulness and I'm hopeful that by studying your group, they will develop a better understanding. Good luck, Millie."

Dr. Wilcox stood and walked away.

CHAPTER 8

I made my way back to the barracks somewhat perplexed. Apparently Dr. Wilcox had high expectations for Group Echo and was willing to bend the rules, which was fine by me. Although I couldn't help but wonder what she meant when she said the Gaekaar didn't 'fully understand human resourcefulness.'

I shook my head. I had to focus every bit of energy on my own survival and that of my teammates. If that just happened to coincide with the doctor's agenda, then so be it.

Back at the barracks the overall mood seemed to be down and no one was talking. "What's going on?" I asked.

Jorge was sitting on his bunk with his elbows on his knees. He looked over at me. "We were just trying to figure which of us won't make it to the end of ten weeks."

"The answer to that is simple. No one is going to fail." I pointed toward Aliyah. "Aliyah was having a hard time with the shedding phase and we didn't let her fail, did we?"

Jorge shrugged. "That's true, but I have a feeling this phase is going to be considerably more difficult."

"If we work together and review each other's progress daily, we'll be able to intercede with help *before* someone falls behind. We can do this. We simply need to work together as a team." My words carried more conviction than I had intended.

Sam stood up. "Millie is right. If we did it for Aliyah, we can do it for anyone else who is struggling. There is no reason that we can't stay one step ahead of what they expect of us."

"That's easy for you to say. You seem like the athletic type," Ethan said. "Even in my prime I wasn't the sort of person that would jog or lift weights."

"Ethan, you have other qualities that are just as important," I said. "I promise, you can make it through the physical demands with our help."

Fiona walked over. "We can do this. I know we can."

The Oppenhiemer triplets joined us. Karina cleared her throat. "We've only known the members of Group Echo for a just over a week, but the three of us were nurses in our past lives, so we are willing to help in any way we can."

Jorge stood and looked at me. "Perhaps we should expand our pact?"

Sam frowned. "What are you talking about?"

"It's a pact. Before we arrived here, the three of us committed to watching out for each other no matter what," Fiona said.

Sam rolled his eyes. "You're not going to make us become blood brothers are you? Aren't we a bit too old for those games?"

I laughed. "There's no blood involved, and furthermore, we're not old anymore. How about committing to simply putting the welfare of our team ahead of everything else."

Aliyah marched over and held her hand out before us. "I'm in," she said.

Karina Oppenhiemer slapped her hand on top of Aliyah's. "I'm in too," she said. Her two sisters followed suit.

I placed my hand on theirs. Then Jorge, Ethan, and Fiona added their hands. Lastly, Sam put his hand on top.

I cleared my throat. "We pledge to help each other survive the training phase and will ensure each of us comes out alive at the end of ten weeks. It's done. No excuses," I said.

Our pact may have looked a bit corny to an outsider, but for us this was a serious commitment. Our lives depended on it.

Group Echo arrived early for the morning gym appointment. As it turned out, our coaches were nothing more than robots that issued detailed exercise routines. My coach was PT-11, short for Personal Trainer Number Eleven. Fiona was assigned to PT-18, and Jorge had PT-7.

PT-11 whirled around on three wheels, had a small egg shaped head, a view screen on its chest, and two arms that were quite dexterous at working with gym equipment.

"Greetings, Mildred Necee Helgren #891456M. I am your private coach and I am at your disposal twenty-four hours a day, until the conclusion of your training," PT-11 said.

"Nice to meet you," I replied.

"And you as well," PT-11 said.

The coach verbally reviewed my workout schedule as well as the standards that I had to reach by the end of ten weeks.

"Are these the requirements that I have to obtain in order to avoid being ... ah, terminated?" I asked.

PT-11 paused and considered my question before answering. "Yes, that is correct."

"Well then, let's get started," I replied.

The day's workout schedule appeared on the coach's view screen. I was to perform one hour of cardio and two hours of strength training. That didn't sound too bad. At least it didn't sound bad until I actually started doing it. The cardio was broken down into three segments starting with twenty minutes on the stationary bike, followed by twenty minutes jogging on a treadmill, and then twenty minutes on a machine that reminded me of skiing.

At the end of the hour I fell to the floor and rolled onto my back, panting like a winded animal. My heart was pounding and I couldn't seem to get enough air. At that moment I actually thought I might die and become the first death toward the forecast thirty percent.

"Mildred Helgren, are you all right?" PT-11 asked.

"It's Millie," I said while still trying to catch my breath. "And I'm not all right. I'm absurdly out of shape for a young person and my muscles are on fire. This is going to take some getting used to."

"The burning sensation in your muscles is a result of lactic acid buildup. Would you like to take a break before we begin strength training?"

"No, absolutely not." I forced myself to stand back up. "Let's get on with it."

No way in hell was I going to risk losing points for taking a break. I had no idea if they would subtract points for something like that, but I wasn't taking any chances.

PT-11 started the strength training with compound exercises, which worked multiple muscle groups at the same time. We took short rest periods between sets. Then we moved on to isolation exercises, which seemed to stress every last individual muscle within my body.

My coach was far from sympathetic as my weak muscles struggled with the simplest exercises. When it came to basic bench presses, I groaned and fought to lift a mere fifty pounds without success. PT-11 rolled closer to me. "You must be able to bench press a minimum of your own body weight to successfully meet the physical requirements."

Sweat trickled down my temples. "I know that, PT-11. Please tell me something that I don't already know."

PT-11 made a whirring noise. "Very well. You should consume over 1,000 calories at lunch today. Go heavy on protein, but get plenty of carbohydrates and fats as well. You should continue drinking the available protein shakes despite the fact that you are no longer required to do so. Also make sure that you sleep for a minimum of eight hours so that your muscles have time to recover and develop."

I cringed at the thought of more protein drinks. "Great, thanks, PT-11."

"I am here to help make you strong. You have completed your exercises for today. It is time for your jet-injection." PT-11 held out its arm and displayed a triangular unit.

"An injection? What's that for?" I asked.

"This injection will introduce a biological agent into your blood stream that will be carried to the mitochondria throughout your musculature system. The agent will enhance the ability of the mitochondria to fuel muscle growth by three hundred and forty seven percent. You will also experience a four hundred and seventy five percent improvement in muscle recovery."

I wiped the sweat from my face with a towel. "This *biological agent* isn't going to make me look like one of those musclebound weight lifters, will it?"

"No, it will not. But it will help you reach your goals in a timely manner." PT-11 extended his arm and touched the tip of the triangular unit to my neck. The biological agent was administered as a vapor that instantly permeated the skin.

At the conclusion of our session my legs wobbled and I felt like I was old again. "PT-11, I'm tired and I feel like hell. I don't think your concoction is working."

"You will feel better in the morning. Please take note of your schedule." PT-11 displayed my agenda for the remainder of the day on his chest.

Mildred Necee Helgren #891456M
1330Z—1430Z: Lunch, Cafeteria, Black Level
1430Z—1630Z: Med Center, Orange Level
1630Z—1830Z: Rest
1830Z—1930Z: Dinner, Cafeteria, Black Level
After 1930Z: Free Time

I raised my brow. "I wasn't expecting this much free time."
"You will need it," PT-11 said as it turned and whirred away.
I wiped the sweat from my forehead. "Oh great," I muttered.

CHAPTER 9

I entered the cafeteria at 1330Z and joined Fiona at the salad bar. She looked as miserable and uncomfortable as I felt. "Hey, how are you doing?" I asked.

She groaned. "Don't ask. It's a miracle I'm able to stand."

"Same here. By the way, make sure you eat at least a thousand calories. My coach said it would help to build muscle," I said.

"That won't be a problem. I'm starving." Fiona loaded her salad with large chunks of bacon, chicken, and avocado and finished it off with a pile of shredded cheese and creamy dressing. I did the same.

We found a quiet table and sat gingerly on the hard seats. "Ugh," I grumbled as pain shot through my thighs and buttocks. "Even sitting hurts."

Little by little the rest of Group Echo joined us, and each team member had the same pained expression as they sat down. I looked around the table and noticed that I was the only one with a protein shake. I stood and went back to the beverage area and brought back a tray of eight gray drinks.

The group looked over at me and gave a collective moan.

"I thought we were done with those disgusting things," Sam said.

I began passing out the tall glasses. "You were, but I have it from a good source that we should keep drinking them. Extra protein will help build muscle. Come on, bottoms up."

Aliyah wrinkled her nose. "I'll do anything that will help me get through this." She lifted her glass. "Cheers."

Although reluctant, the rest of the group conceded and followed along.

"Does anyone else have a Med Center appointment this afternoon?" Fiona asked.

Around the table everyone nodded their heads.

Sam burped and set his glass down. "It's probably just a check-up."

"I doubt it," Ethan said. "The doctor already has access to our vital stats through the monitors in our jumpsuits, and the personal trainers have already given us our jet-injections. These appointments have to be for something else. Something we haven't thought of."

"I really hate surprises," Aliyah grumbled.

Group Echo arrived at the med center just as Group Foxtrot was leaving. Foxtrot didn't look any worse for the wear. Hopefully that was a good sign.

We took a seat in the waiting area and every minute or so a nurse arrived and whisked one of us away. After roughly ten minutes, I was the last person left in the waiting room and I was beginning to feel anxious.

A nurse in a crisp white jumpsuit approached me. "Mildred Necee Helgren?"

"Yes, but please call me Millie."

"Millie it is. My name is Christina. Please follow me."

Christina took me through a security gate and into a sterile room with a padded table in the center.

"Please lay down," Christina said, pointing toward the table.

I climbed on and stretched out. The padded top immediately molded to the contours of my body rendering me partially immobile, yet quite comfortable. "So, what are we doing today?" I said, attempting to sound casual.

Christina smiled. "Today is a big day. We will be installing your Communication and Language Interpretation unit. Soldiers often refer to them as CommLang for short."

"What is a CommLang unit and where exactly does it get installed?" I couldn't help my skeptical tone. After all, I was in the Med Center and the logical assumption was that *they* were going to do something physically traumatic to me. Again.

Christina patted my arm. "You have nothing to worry about. The CommLang is a device that facilitates long-range communication and alien language interpretation. Since it utilizes Gaekaar technology, you won't find anything like it on Earth, nor could you afford it if you did." Christina began swabbing my head with a foul smelling liquid. "The device will be installed in your cerebral cortex with links to your primary visual cortex and optic nerve."

A quiver ran through my body. "You're going to implant that thing in my head? Is this procedure safe?"

Christina gave me the look that a parent gives to children when explaining that the vaccination they were about to receive was important. "It's perfectly safe. We've successfully performed hundreds of thousands of these installations. Please let me explain the steps so that you feel comfortable."

"By all means, explain away," I said.

Christina smiled again. "The surgical robot will implant a chip in your parietal lobe that will link to millions of your existing synaptic connections. Then the same process will take place in your temporal lobe, making millions of additional synaptic connections. Finally, these connections will be linked to the visual centers of your brain, which will create a picture for you. To help maintain your comfort, our surgical robots work at a very high rate of speed. You can expect the entire process to be completed in less than an hour."

At least the procedure would be quick. "What exactly will these chips do once they are installed my head?" I asked.

"The primary function is language translation. The CommLang unit has been preloaded with four of the most widely spoken alien languages. The device will translate each language for you, although you will have to learn to speak the words on your own. Try to think of it as having access to the components of each language, but since you have never actually spoken it, you won't have the muscle memory in place to get the words out. Most students don't understand that it is up to them to rigorously practice the various languages in order to achieve proper syntax."

That didn't sound too bad. "Thank you, Christina, I appreciate the tip."

"I should mention that there is also a secondary function as a simple computer that can send and receive VS-mail through a heads-up display."

parietal lobe that will link to millions of your existing synaptic connections. Then the robot will perform the same process in your temporal lobe, making millions of additional synaptic connections.

Finally, these connections will be linked to the visual centers of your brain, which will create a picture for you. To help maintain your comfort, our surgical robots work at a very high rate of speed. You can expect the entire process to be completed in less than an hour."

At least the procedure would be quick. "What exactly will these chips do once they are installed my head?" I asked.

"The primary function is language translation. The CommLang unit has been preloaded with four of the most widely spoken alien languages. The device will translate each language for you, although you will have to learn to speak the words on your own. Try to think of it as having access to the components of each language, but since you have never actually spoken it, you won't have the muscle memory in place to get the words out. Most students don't understand that it is up to them to practice the various languages in order to achieve proper syntax."

"Thank you, Christina, I appreciate the tip," I said. That didn't sound too bad.

"I should mention that there is also a secondary function as a simple computer that can send and receive VS-mail through a heads-up display."

My eyes widened and I shook my head. "VS-mail? Heads-up display?"

"VS-messaging, or VS-mail as it is sometimes referred to, is a simple email system that utilizes vector-space relay stations for extremely long distance communication in space. The heads-up display, or HUD as soldiers call it, presents a transparent display of data in your peripheral field of vision. This means you'll be able to see information without looking away from your typical viewpoints. Are you ready to begin the procedure?. "VS-mail? Heads-up display?"

"VS-messaging, or VS-mail as it is sometimes referred to, is a simple message system that utilizes vector-space relay stations for extremely long distance communication in space. The heads-up display, or HUD as soldiers call it, presents a transparent display of data in your peripheral field of vision. This means you'll be able to see information without looking away from your typical viewpoints. Are you ready to begin the procedure?"

"I guess so," I said.

"By the way, we don't anesthetize people while working in the brain. It's safer if you stay awake, but don't worry, you won't feel a thing."

"Great. I have one more question. Will anyone be able to read my mind with this device?"

Christina smiled. "No, nothing like that. The CommLang unit is primarily a receiver/transmitter, data storage unit, and translator. Fundamentally it's just a simple computer."

I had to give Christina credit. She made the procedure sound fairly innocuous and routine. I smiled back at her. "All right, let's get it over with."

Christina waved her arm and a large mechanism began to lower from the ceiling. "Try not to move, Millie."

The mechanism came closer and closer until it engulfed my head. Inside the unit everything was dark and I felt various components moving along my scalp.

I heard Christina make some adjustments on the machine. "The surgical robot is going to give you something to numb the area and then the work will begin."

I felt something prick my temples and then I felt nothing. "How are you doing, Millie?"

"Fine. When will the surgery start?"

"Small incisions have already penetrated your skull. Everything looks great."

A few minutes later I began to see sparks and wavy lines dance in the darkness.

"You should be seeing some flashes of light now," Christina said. "This is perfectly normal."

"Yes, I see them. They seem to be getting brighter."

"That's perfectly normal, as well," Christina said again. "Your optic nerve is trying to interpret the new flow of information."

After a short period of time the jumble of nonsensical sparks and wavy lines began to merge together to form letters. Soon the letters became words and then the words became a full sentence. Embedded in my peripheral field of vision, a message appeared just as Christina had described.

Your CommLang has been successfully installed.
Serial Number: Y8976K4891Z788402K
Imperial CommLang Corporation

Click here to begin tutorial when instructed.

"Are you seeing the installation message yet?" Christina asked.

"Yes."

"Good. The robot is closing the incisions now. We're almost done. By the way, you will be completely healed within the hour due to the biological agent you were given earlier today."

After the procedure concluded, Christina took me to a room with rows of chairs. My teammates were already sitting and I was the last to arrive. Fiona flagged me over to sit by her. "Isn't this exciting," she said. "I wish I could VS-mail my friends back at the Fed-Home, but I don't suppose that would be allowed."

I shook my head. "Probably wouldn't be a good idea."

Major Cameron Ford entered the room and stood at the front. "We have a few key points to cover before you begin experimenting with your new device. First, is there anyone in the room who does not see the installation message?"

The room was silent.

"Good. Please be aware that you are now the proud owner of a twenty-eight million dollar implant, so it is important that you take care if it and use it properly. The CommLang unit serves dual purposes. First and foremost, it functions as an alien language translation computer. Since teaching you how to speak four different languages would be far too time consuming, you can consider the CommLang an expensive short cut. The unit will translate each language for you as fluently as you now hear the English language, although when it comes to speaking the new language you will need to put forth additional effort. The CommLang will help you understand form, content, and use, but you will need to practice syntax to become proficient at it. Do you all understand?"

Everyone quietly nodded.

"The secondary function of your CommLang unit will serve as your VS-messaging and schedule provider. As long as you are within one light year of a standard vector-space relay station, you can send and receive VS-mail, documents, pictures, 3D videos, and training courses. You'll also be able to access your GAP endorsed credit accounts through your VS-message center. If you are not within one light year of a relay station, the CommLang will store the data and connect as soon as it receives a relay signal. Schedules can be uploaded in a similar fashion or can be manually input by you. Understood?"

Again, everyone in the room quietly nodded.

The major put his hands behind his back and walked across the room. "Now, I want you to go back to your barracks, sit on your bunks, and individually initiate the tutorial by using your brain to click on the link provided, *not* your eyes. A soldier should never take their eyes off the target, therefore you must learn to use your CommLang with your mind." The major pointed toward his head.

"It may take several attempts to learn this technique, but do not worry, you will master it in time. Your CommLang unit also has a preloaded tutorial series. You are required to take all of the tutorials, including the introductory lesson, the VS-mail lesson, the scheduling lesson, and all of the language and cultural tutorials. Please note that we will *not* follow up on your progress until you have completed ten weeks in this facility. This is because self-motivation is a critical component in your success. You won't survive one week in the Rim War if you're not able to motivate yourself."

I raised my hand.

"Yes, Millie?"

"You mentioned that we should take care of the CommLang properly. Is there anything special we should do as far as maintenance?"

"Yes, you will receive regular push notifications that you can update with a simple click. The introductory tutorial will also teach you how to do a self-diagnostic check, which should be done three times a year. Any other questions?"

The room was quiet.

"All right then, dismissed."

CHAPTER 10

We made our way back to the barracks and sat on the floor in a circle. I studied my HUD display, but I couldn't manage to initiate the tutorial.

"Ooof. This is hard to do," Fiona said, leaning her head this way and that. "I can't get the clicky thing to click."

I looked around the circle and noticed the Oppenhiemer triplets trying to push the button with their index finger in mid-air.

"Okay, listen up everyone," I said. "Remember, the major said you have to use your mind to click on the link, not your finger, eyes, or your whole head."

After a few minutes, Ethan threw his arms in the air. "I got it! Try to think of it as squeezing the link with your thoughts. It takes a few tries, but it will work eventually."

One by one we figured out how to activate the link. Each time someone was successful the room was filled with cheers.

"One more thing before we get started on the tutorial," I said, slipping into my old trainer role. "It's important that we all achieve a high comprehension level around each lesson, so before we move on to the subsequent tutorial, we should have a group discussion to answer questions and talk about key points."

Sam frowned. "I feel like I'm back in school."

"That's because you are," Ethan said.

Group Echo was able to complete three full tutorials with discussions and take in a high protein dinner before bedtime.

After lights out, we began practicing short VS-mail communications while lying in our bunks. Multiple messages zipped back and forth. Once we got the hang of it, the VS-mail process was simple and efficient.

Just when I thought everyone had finally drifted to sleep, my VS-mail pinged again. It was a message from Sam.

To: Group Echo
From: Sam Jacobson #891457S
Date: 7.16.2099
Time: 2305Z

Q: What did one strand of DNA say to the other strand of DNA?
A: Do these genes make my butt look fat?

I heard giggles and laughs drift through the darkness. Sam's VS-message kicked off the official Group Echo Joke War.

A minute later another one arrived.

To: Group Echo
From: Aliyah Bashir #891459A
Date: 7.16.2099
Time: 2307Z

Q: Why did the cow cross the road?
A: To get to the utter side!

And then another.

To: Group Echo
From: Jorge Alvarez, #891454J
Date: 7.16.2131
Time: 2310Z

Q: What do you call a Roman warrior after oral sex?
A: Gladiator.

As the night wore on the jokes got dirtier and funnier, and Group Echo laughed so hard that we almost forgot about the serious nature of our situation. I had to wonder how much longer we would be able to have this kind of fun.

When our exhausted muscles finally demanded that we sleep, I found that I no longer dreamt of the Tukock, yet I was still curious to know what had happened to them. Did their species really exist or were they just fictional characters designed to gauge my reactions.

The next morning I awoke to find the schedule button blinking in my peripheral HUD. I clicked on it and saw that it had been filled in for the day.

Mildred Necee Helgren #891456M
0700Z—0745Z: Breakfast, Cafeteria, Black Level
0800Z—0900Z: Training Meeting, Room 42C, Red Level
0915Z—1215Z: Workout Session, Gym, Orange Level
1230Z—1330Z: Lunch, Cafeteria, Black Level
1345Z—1545Z: Testing, Barracks, Black Level
After 1545Z: Dinner & Free Time

Again, I felt my schedule had a large amount of free time, particularly for a military situation. I stood up and stretched, marveling as my muscles obeyed without protest. I actually felt great. It was strange to get up in the morning without aches and pains hindering every move I made. Not long ago it had taken me a full five minutes just to cross the room to get to the closet. Today I felt ready to run a marathon.

Sam bolted from the bathroom and skidded across the barracks floor like a teenager. "Look what I can do with these muscles! Who wants to go jogging before breakfast?"

Jorge sat up in his bunk. About an inch of black hair stuck out in different directions. He yawned and stretched. "Wow, I feel good. I'll go with you, just give me a couple of minutes."

I looked around the room and noticed that everyone had about an inch of hair. I touched my head and sure enough, it was covered in soft growth. Not peach fuzz, but actual hair.

I ran into the bathroom and over to the mirror. Red. My hair was definitely coming in a deep shade of red. I looked a lot like old pictures of my mother when she was young. On the other side of the bathroom the Oppenhiemer triplets giggled as they looked in the mirror at their new brunette sprouts.

Aliyah and Fiona joined us to get a look at their sprouting hair as well. Fiona's hair was coming in blonde and curly, and Aliyah's hair was black and pin straight. We laughed and complimented each other on our new locks just as Jorge, Sam, and Ethan crashed through the door.

"Ladies," Jorge said. "When you're done admiring each other, we would appreciate you joining us for a quick jog around the Black Level."

Ethan waved his arm. "Come on then. If I can jog, we can all do it!"

Jorge and Sam were the biggest and most athletic of our group so they led the way down the lengthy network of halls that connected the Black Level. I had to admit, as I watched my group, we looked pretty damn good for a bunch of old farts out for a morning jog.

Dr. Wilcox was just stepping off the elevator as we passed by. "Good morning, Doc," Jorge said with a nod of his head.

"Oh … good morning," she said. I thoroughly enjoyed the look of surprise on her face.

As we rounded to the cafeteria, I noticed Major Cameron Ford having breakfast with a group of officers. He did a double take as we passed by. I smiled at him and gave a quick salute.

After our run, we felt energized and ready for the day. We agreed that we would do the same thing every morning for as long as we were together.

We took turns showering, girls first then the boys, and after a quick high calorie breakfast we proceeded to the Red Level and took our seats in the training room. Dr. Wilcox and the major were already positioned at the front of the room. By 0800 the members of Group Foxtrot and Group Delta had wandered in and taken their seats. I counted heads. Thirty-three.

Major Ford stepped up. "You may have noticed that we've already experienced our first casualty of the training phase. This morning we lost a member of the Delta Group. Therefore I will reiterate how important it is to follow the instructions you are given. This is very simple. Follow the directions, try your best, and you will lead a long and fruitful life. Ignore our instructions and you will end your life."

Fiona leaned over and whispered into my ear. "What a jerk!"

I covered my mouth with my hand and stifled a laugh. Having been raised in a military family, I suppose I was more accustomed to the in-your-face brashness than the average person.

"Do you find that funny, Mildred?" the major said with a threatening glare.

"No, sir," I said, shaking my head.

Fiona chuckled under her breath.

I kicked her foot in retaliation. For a moment I felt like I was back in high school. What a wonderful feeling.

Major Ford continued with his speech. "It is important for each of you to know that we will no longer fill out your schedules. After 1545Z today, you will be expected to take on that task. We anticipate that you will make good choices with your time. We expect you to hit your physical goals as given to you by your coaches. And we expect you to learn, grow, and thrive. If you do not, you will become part of the thirty percent. Is that clear?"

The room was silent.

"I said, is that CLEAR?"

I shouted, "Yes, sir!"

Some of the students responded with a simple 'yes' and others with a 'yes, sir.'

The major looked around the room. "Since no one in this room is officially enlisted in the military other than myself, it is not required that you address me as 'sir.' Although, I am also aware that some of you have decided to use proper military etiquette despite the lack of requirements." The major glanced over at me. "I believe this is a very good idea and can only help your progress toward becoming a soldier. You will find a formal military etiquette lesson in your tutorial package. If you are interested in additional lessons, you can VS-mail the main computer. The address is in your directory. Now I'd like you to give your attention to Dr. Wilcox."

The doctor stepped in front of us. "Good morning. I've had several inquiries regarding your individual point status. Please know that we cannot share your points, nor can we give you any information on your upcoming rank and position, until the end of the training phase. From the outside this may seem unfair, but please understand that we don't want anyone to become discouraged by a low number or overly confident by a high number. The key to succeeding is to try your best and follow directions."

Jorge raised his hand.

"Yes, Jorge," she said.

"If you are no longer giving us a schedule and our time is our own, how would following directions come into play?"

"That is a very good question. First, we have given you physical and mental goals that must be obtained. We want you to find your own path to reach those goals. We will give you clues along the way and we will monitor your reactions and responsiveness. The system by which you are being graded is very complex and not easily explained, so I will simply say, stay focused on your goals and do your best to surpass them."

After the meeting, Group Echo headed to the gym for our daily workout. When we arrived our coaches whirred to life and rolled over to greet each of us.

"Good morning, Millie Necee Helgren #891456M. How do you feel today?" PT-11 said.

"Good morning, PT-11. I feel marvelous, thank you."

PT-11 sat quietly off to the side as I ran on the treadmill. Sweat beaded on my brow and I wiped it away as if it were nothing. I was impressed that my performance today was much better than the day before. I looked over at my coach. "PT-11, that injection you gave me yesterday was somewhat more effective than you let on. I also noticed that my hair is growing much faster now. Are there any other side effects I should know about?"

PT-11 paused for a moment, almost as if it was verifying what it was allowed to tell me. "Within a few hours of receiving the injection you achieved improved bone strength, improved healing ability, improved memory retention, and temporary sterility. You should also feel generally invigorated as your mitochondria energy production has increased by one hundred and eighty two percent."

"Sterility?" I asked.

"Yes, you will not have a monthly menstrual cycle and you will not be able to produce offspring. This effect will last for two galactic years or until your next injection." PT-11 said this as if the subject had no importance whatsoever. "That is all the information I have access to."

"So there might be more?" I asked.

"I do not know. You may try contacting the main computer for additional information."

"I'll do that, thank you." I typed up an inquiry for the main computer and hit send with my mind. I wiped my face with a small towel and looked at PT-11. "Would you mind turning up the pace?"

During lunch my VS-mail pinged and a file labeled 'test' appeared in my inbox. Everyone at the lunch table looked up at the same time. Within seconds a look of dread washed over the faces Group Echo. I had always hated tests, only this was far worse. Taking a test that could very well determine my ability to stay alive made my anxiety skyrocket.

After our meal we returned to the barracks to begin the test. I sat on my bunk and opened the file. The directions stated that there were no right or wrong answers and that each student should click on the first answer that popped into their head. I looked over the first two questions and arched my eyebrows, thinking them a bit odd.

1. Which activity would you rather spend three hours doing?

A. Rock climbing
B. Knitting a sweater
C. Killing a buffalo and preparing it for dinner
D. Planting a garden

2. You are trapped in an escape proof room with no way out and the only resources at your disposal are a fully charged sparrow and a pack of instantaneous suicide pills. In the room with you is a starving kegalorus (500 pound man-eating reptile with a laser proof exoskeleton). The kegalorus are known for relishing the taste of humans and no one has ever survived an attack. What would you do as the kegalorus prepared to attack?

A. Take the suicide pills
B. Fight to the best of your abilities using the sparrow
C. Use the sparrow to try to blast your way out of the room
D. Something else? Fill in the blank _____

I selected planting a garden as my first answer because I enjoyed long term projects and I liked the challenge of helping things grow. The second question was just silly, so I picked D and made something up that sounded reasonable. My written answer detailed how I would hold the sparrow in my hand with the pills tucked into the same palm. Then when the kegalorus attacked I would offer my arm as his first bite, dropping the pills down his throat and shooting up his insides at the same time. Yeah, I'd probably lose an arm but it was better than dying. The whole description reminded me of a bad horror movie.

One hour and forty-five minutes later, I finished the last question and felt a wave of relief. My VS-mail pinged. I had received a message from the main computer regarding my question about the side effects of the biological agent. The computer didn't answer my question but it did send back a link to the main library. I made a mental note to try the link later on.

After the entire group completed the test we agreed to take more tutorials. We knocked off the military etiquette lesson and learned that the Gaekaar don't salute. To show respect in the IGM, soldiers lowered their eyes and bowed. This was stressed repeatedly as a very important custom within their culture.

Next we moved on to the alien language and cultural tutorials, starting with the five part series, *Learning the Language of the Gaekaars*. In between lessons, I replied to the main computer and requested a list of all available tutorials, including a casual question regarding how to determine a student's progress during the training phase. The doctor had indicated that we shouldn't be privy to this information, but I felt it was critical to know. Within seconds a long list of available lesson links arrived, which I forwarded to the group. The last sentence in the computer's response stated that I should discuss my last question with Dr. Wilcox. Heck, it had been worth a try.

By the end of the night we were engaging in simple conversations using Gaekaar linguistics. Learning an alien language wasn't nearly as difficult as I had expected. The knowledge was already in our heads so it was just a matter of a little repetition.

By midnight we were exhausted and agreed to get some shuteye.

As soon as the lights went out, my VS-mail pinged.

To: Group Echo
From: Sam Jacobson #891457S
Date: 7.18.2099
Time: 0005Z

A chicken and an egg are lying in bed. The chicken takes out a cigarette and begins to smoke. The egg, pissed off, takes one look at the chicken, rolls over, and pulls the blanket over him and says, "I guess we answered that question!"

Snickers and soft chuckles filled the room. Shuteye would have to wait a while longer.

CHAPTER 11

In the morning, Group Echo gathered together and commenced with our pre-breakfast jog around the Black Level. I felt good and noticed my muscles had again gained more strength overnight. We lapped the entire Black Level and found a set of stairs that brought us to the Orange Level. We proceeded down the hall, around the gym, and past the Med Center.

My hair had grown out another inch and now bounced on my head as I ran.

Sam ran his fingers through his developing afro. "You know, I think I'll go for another complete shave. I liked being bald."

"Personally, I can't wait until my hair gets down to my shoulders so I look like a woman," Fiona said. "Don't get me wrong. I love being young again, but I look like a boy."

I looked over at Fiona's profile as we jogged back down the steps. She really was beautiful. Blonde curly hair, blue eyes, and curves in all the right places. No man on the planet would mistake her for a boy.

Jorge laughed, "Fiona dear, you have nothing to worry about," he said.

We passed Mark Solomon from Group Delta in the hallway. I remembered him from our training meeting and waved. "Hi, Mark."

He looked over at me, his expression anxious and preoccupied. "Hello," he replied and looked away.

After a quick shower and a hearty breakfast, Group Echo proceeded to the gym for a workout session. It wasn't pre-listed on our schedules so we weren't required to be there, but we agreed as a team that we should keep up the rigorous exercise and do whatever our coaches suggested.

Okay, on second thought, maybe telling PT-11 that I would do whatever he wanted was a mistake. I put my hands on my hips and scowled at my little robot friend. "What? Are you serious? You want me to do three hours of exercise, plus another hour of combat drills and an additional hour of reactionary training? Are you trying to kill me? I don't even know what reactionary training is."

"Reactionary training is based on improving your ability to respond to various stimuli. This is a critical component in military combat. My counterparts are making the same suggestions to all members of Group Echo," PT-11 responded.

I raised an eyebrow. "Oh really? It seems like you and your robot friends are conspiring to kill us all."

PT-11 whirred around in a circle. "We would not harm you. We are here to make you strong."

Apparently it wasn't programmed for humor. "I know that, PT-11. It was just a joke."

After the workout, we proceeded with the combat drills and reactionary training in a group session. What the hell, it was only another two hours of extreme physical exertion, but knowing that the recovery would be fast made for an easier decision.

By the time we returned to the barracks I was bruised and exhausted. I sat on my bunk and tried not to move. Everything hurt. PT-11 had told me not worry, that my body would repair itself by morning, but I felt like crap at the moment.

Karina flopped down on her bunk and groaned. "Oww, I must be dying. Don't touch me!" she complained as her sisters attempted to tend to her bruises.

"Just look at this!" Fiona said, pointing to her blackened eye. "I don't think combat drills suit me. In all of my one hundred and five years, today was the first time I was ever in a fight. I got my butt kicked … and it was a fake fight!"

I poked at the emerging purple bruise on my bicep. "Considering the alternative, I think we can get used to it," I said.

"I suppose you're right." Fiona sighed and sat next to me. "I was surprised to see how well you did during the reactionary training. You ran circles around everyone else."

I laughed. "Well, I had four older brothers. If I didn't have fast reactions, I was dead meat. Plus, I worked at Stanfield training a bunch of gruff men how to react quickly to emergency situations. The same principles seem to apply."

Jorge approached us with his head hanging low. I nudged Fiona and nodded toward Jorge.

"Uh, Fiona, I wanted to apologize for hitting you in the eye. The drill they had us perform ... it was an accident, I didn't mean to hurt you."

I stood and tried to hide a smirk. "I think I have something else to do," I said, walking away.

I approached Ethan, who was inspecting his bruises and groaning each time he touched one of them. Ethan wasn't a manly man by any means. He was thin and his muscles didn't seem to develop at the same rate as the rest of us.

"How are you doing?" I asked.

"I'm still here, so I guess that's a good sign. Although after my pitiful performance in the combat drills I seriously thought they might haul me away for termination," he said.

Ethan had been by far the worst of the group with combat training, but at least he tried and didn't give up.

I sat next to him. "I don't think that's how it works. You can't possibly be good at everything. I think it's more important to try hard, be loyal, and have the right attitude. At least that's what my brothers used to tell me about the military." I was hoping our situation would be similar.

"Did your brothers ever have exposure to the IGM?" Ethan asked.

I shook my head. "No. Two in the Army, two in the Marines, and no contact with extraterrestrials."

Ethan put his head in his hands. "Things are so different now. We'll be fighting a war that we don't understand and aren't committed to, almost like mercenaries. I just can't seem to make sense of it."

"I agree, it's hard not fully understanding what we'll be fighting for," I said.

"You know, before becoming a poet I was a social science research assistant, and at the risk of sounding like a narcissist, I was extremely good at my job. I have a strong need to understand the how and why of things. Think about it, the Rim War has over a hundred years of history and we know next to nothing about it," Ethan said.

"Hang on a second." I looked at my HUD, clicked on my VS-mail, and forwarded Ethan the library link that I had received from the main computer. "I received this from the main computer, although I doubt we'll have access to much."

Ethan's eyes widened and I could tell he was reviewing the VS-mail link. "Oh my God. This link just took me to the biggest library I've ever seen. The online catalog is so extensive that it could take me days just to sift through the categories. I can't believe they've allowed us to have this."

I shrugged. "It's not like we can take the information and leak it. We're stuck here, after all."

"I know, but they didn't formally tell us about the library. You just happened to stumble upon it. Don't you find that strange?" Ethan said.

I put my hand on Ethan's shoulder. "Strange doesn't even begin to describe how I feel about this place. But my gut feeling is that they want to see what we can discover on our own."

"Well, I'm happy to poke around and let you know what I find." The excitement in Ethan's voice was palpable.

I stood up. "Sounds good. I'm starving, so while you're doing that, I'm going to stop by the cafeteria and grab a snack."

The cafeteria was busier than I expected, so I joined the line for beverages. When it was my turn I dispensed myself a tall protein shake. I noticed a small button off to the side labeled 'requests.' So I pushed it.

"What would you like to request," the dispenser verbalized in a pleasant tone.

I thought for a few seconds. "I'd like to request Earl Grey tea."

"Tea. Earl Grey. Your selection will be available for consumption by tomorrow morning, zero six hundred Zulu."

I smiled, pleased with my new find. "Why, thank you, dispenser."

I heard someone laugh. I spun around and saw Major Cameron Ford in his crisp uniform, grinning at me. I executed a proper bow to an officer.

"At ease civilian. I'm off duty right now, so you can drop the formalities. Would you like to join me?" he said, pointing to a nearby table.

"Yes, thank you." I followed Cameron and sat down across from him.

"I see you're still drinking the protein." He pointed to my tall gray beverage.

"PT-11 suggested it."

"You're smart to follow the direction of your coach. Millie, I know the transition to a soldier isn't easy. It wasn't for any of us," he said with genuine concern. "How are you doing?"

I shrugged. "Okay, I guess. I had a military family, so some of the training doesn't come as a surprise. I can't say I'm happy about handing over my life, but being young again does have it perks. So when did you go through the process?"

"A little over fourteen years ago. I was part of the first group of soldiers to come through the transition process."

"Have you been in space and seen the Rim War?" I asked.

Cameron nodded. "I fought in the war for twelve years. Protocol dictates that I should tell you the battles are similar to wars you've seen on this planet, but the truth is, this war is nothing like anything you've seen before. Some battles are fought in space where we lose whole fleets in a single skirmish, while others are fought by ground troops on planets we are trying desperately to save. Each time we lose a planet, it's horrific. Billions perish." Cameron looked at me intently. "I wish I could say that the allies were winning, but I'm afraid we're not faring all that well."

I recalled what the doctor had told me regarding the war and felt a stab of anxiety. "Is Earth in jeopardy?"

"We hope not, but the Orsydian Front is approaching this sector at a rate the allies are struggling to control. Barring a miracle, the Gaekaar analysts predict that the front will be on Earth's doorstep in less than two years."

I briefly considered my previous life. Images of Avery and everyone I had ever know flashed through my mind, fueling thoughts around accepting my situation. "Here on Earth, there are people I would like to protect. People I care about."

"You will protect them." Cameron looked me square in the eyes. "I know that you'll develop into a successful soldier, and I also know that you will eventually come to appreciate what has happened to you."

I found that statement hard to believe. "How can you *know* that? You can't predict the future."

"No I can't. But past, as well as current behaviors, are the best indicators of future behavior. Our analytics have already pegged you as loyal, courageous, and uncompromising in your standards. You're a perfect fit for what the military needs and is looking for."

I was embarrassed by his unexpected words. "I'm not so sure that describes me. I have a ton of faults. "

"We all do." Cameron raised his brow and gave me a sideways smile. "Perhaps I should add modesty to the list."

I paused as I met his eyes for a moment. *Is he flirting with me?* I wasn't certain because it had been so long since a man had an interest in me ... in that way. I shook the thought away as my mind went back to the topic of analytics. "If I'm understanding this correctly, you're forecasting my outcome. Is that right?"

Cameron nodded.

"How accurate have your previous forecasts been?"

"Ninety-nine percent accurate."

"What is the forecast for the rest of Group Echo?"

Cameron paused. "I don't think you'll want to hear the answer to that."

"Oh, I do." I leaned forward. "I need to know."

Cameron shrugged. "Knowing the numbers won't change the outcome. Group Echo is predicted to have a failure rate of 22.2 percent. Better than the average."

"Who fails?" I asked.

He shook his head. "You don't need to know."

"I *do* need to know. Who?"

"It won't help you to know the names, but I'm not forbidden to tell you. It's Ethan Wells and Aliyah Bashir."

"Thank you, sir. I appreciate your candor." I stood, turned, and marched back to the barracks.

I approached Group Echo to find the Oppenhiemer triplets, Aliyah, and Sam practicing the Gaekaar language. Fiona and Jorge were still talking and Ethan was staring off into space, I presumed doing research.

I couldn't just blurt out that Ethan and Aliyah were predetermined to die. I had to do this correctly.

Fiona came up to me. "Are you all right? You look really stressed out."

I looked into her wide blue eyes. "Can you help me round everyone up? We need to talk."

Fiona wasted no time pulling the group together. She asked everyone to sit in the familiar circle on the floor.

Jorge sat on the floor and crossed his legs with ease. "I can't believe my legs bend like this. I'm actually comfortable sitting like this! So what's this all about anyhow?"

I took a deep breath. "First of all, I believe in honesty and not mincing words. And since part of our pact is to look out for each other, I have some serious information to share."

"What is it? You're scaring me," Aliyah said.

"I don't mean to scare you. I want to save you," I said in a serious tone. I began by telling my friends about my earlier conversation with Dr. Wilcox and her concerns over the Rim War encroaching on this sector of the galaxy. Then I explained the details of my conversation with the major, leaving nothing out.

At first, Group Echo sat in silence.

Sam smacked the floor with his fist. "Bullshit! That's just not going happen. Aliyah and Ethan are doing great."

"You're absolutely right, it's not going to happen. I believe we can control this situation," I said.

Tears rolled down Aliyah's cheeks. "How can you say that? Didn't he say the analytics performed with ninety-nine percent accuracy?"

Sam put his arm around Aliyah's shoulders and gave her a hug.

Fiona waved her hand. "Oh, that means nothing. Statistical forecasts are wrong all the time."

"That's right. When I worked at the hospital, statistical predictions on my patients were often wrong," Karina pointed out. Trina and Samina bobbed their heads in agreement.

"Well, we'll have to prove that point as part of our pact," Jorge said.

The group gave silent nods to Jorge's statement.

I cleared my throat. "I need to mention one additional item."

The group looked toward me with fear etched on their faces, terrified of what I would say next.

I smiled sweetly. "Starting tomorrow, the cafeteria will have Earl Grey tea available."

CHAPTER 12

Over the next week we demonstrated that one should never underestimate the power of a determined group. We worked out for five hours a day, we drank gray protein shakes with every meal, we improved our hand-to-hand combat skills, and we studied three of the most common alien languages. The Gaekaar language was by far the most difficult, followed by Awyx and Orsydi, which were quite similar in syntax. I was happy to see that the next language on our list of tutorials was Tukock, the strange species from my dreams. I was excited to learn they were real and hoped to understand more about their history.

Earl Grey tea in the afternoon, as well as the midnight joke wars, became daily rituals for Group Echo. These were things we chose to do because they gave us pleasure and a sense of control over our lives, however small.

We rallied around Ethan and Aliyah and monitored their every move. We counted and tracked everything—calories, grams of protein, weight, repetitions, combat fights, tutorials, and all the goals given to us by our coaches. Yet for some reason I had the nagging feeling that we were missing something. It bothered me that I didn't know how we were truly doing. Without seeing our scores, I couldn't know for sure where any of us stood, so I decided to pay Cameron Ford a visit.

His office was located on the Blue Level, not far from Dr. Wilcox. I pressed my hand to the sensor and a moment later the door slid open. The major was sitting at his desk reading from a sheet of paper. "Come in," he said without looking up.

I walked up to his desk and performed a formal bow. "Paper? Isn't that a bit archaic for this facility?" I asked.

Cameron pushed the paper aside. "Some information should never be put into a digital file."

"Highly secretive things?" I asked, sitting in a chair beside his desk.

He scowled. "Precisely."

"Speaking of secretive things, I'd like to find out if there is any way to gain access to the scores for Group Echo?"

"If I had them I would give them to you, but I only have access to the list of who's failing. I won't see the actual scores until they are released from Med Center at the end of your training." Cameron leaned back in his chair. "At that point I'll review the results and assist in selecting your rank and position within the IGM. Shortly thereafter, you'll be shipped off to SKAT for your real military training. The entire process was created by Gaekaar psychologists and it has a proven track record."

I leaned forward. "I'm sure it does. And I suspect you're already aware that Ethan and Aliyah are doing great. I only wanted to verify their progress."

Cameron looked at me with piercing brown eyes. "Millie, this phase isn't about testing their physicality or mental acuity. It's about this and this." He pointed to his head and then his heart. "It's all about their *will* to succeed. Your head has to be fully in the game as well as your heart. While the IGM is investing heavily in each potential soldier's development, they also won't accept any individual who doesn't have an innate will to succeed."

I shook my head. "No, you're wrong about them. They both have the will."

He shrugged. "That's not what the analytics say."

"Those analytics are nothing more than a computer spitting out stats. You can't systematize the human psyche." I absently toyed with my hair, which had grown past my shoulders in thick, auburn waves.

Cameron lifted his brow. "You look good, by the way. I like your hair."

I stared back at the major. His comment threw me off and I didn't know what to say. "Uh, thanks. I hope it doesn't always grow this fast."

"It'll slow down after about two weeks, once your system fully adjusts to the changes brought on by the injection." Cameron laced his fingers together. "Millie, after your class deploys, I'll be traveling to Asbu Station to take command of a corvette."

"That's a warship, isn't it?" I asked.

"Yes, it's a new design. I'll be conducting the beta-test." Cameron looked down at his hands and then up at me. "I'd like to be completely up front with you, if you don't mind."

I nodded. "Please do."

"We'll both be shipping out in eight weeks. It's hard to say what will transpire after that, but in the meantime I wanted to ask if you would be interested in pursuing a relationship."

I nearly choked. I didn't know how to respond to that type of question. It had been too long since anyone offered something like that. "A relationship?" I said lamely.

"Yes. A physical relationship," he replied, as if it was nothing out of the ordinary.

I felt my cheeks heat up. "I'm not sure how to answer you. It's just that ... well, I'm monumentally out of practice in that area."

He raised his brow again. "I'd like to be the person who helps you get back into practice."

I smiled and fought the urge to burst out laughing. "Sorry, but I haven't been young all that long, so this just seems a bit awkward."

Cameron didn't smile. "Just think about it. Things will be very different once you're enlisted. After deployment, you'll find that your time in space is bleak and lonesome. The war is ugly and it will be a rarity when you can spend time with your own species. You'll learn to jump at the chance for a good thing when the opportunity arises."

I had to remind myself that I was no longer an old lady, but it still felt absurd that such a handsome young man would be interested in me, despite the fact that he was probably older than me. It was so confusing. "Is it all right if I think about it?"

"Of course, take your time, but keep in mind that we only have eight weeks before deployment." Cameron stood and escorted me to the door.

I left Cameron's office feeling flattered and frustrated at the same time. It was nice to think that a man of his caliber was interested in me, but it was annoying that he had written off my friends in such a cavalier manner.

My next stop was the Med Center. I knew I had little chance of securing our scores, but it couldn't hurt to poke around and ask a few questions. When I entered the center, the receptionist greeted me with a friendly smile. "How can I help you?"

"I'm looking for a nurse named Christina. I'm sorry I don't know her last name," I said.

"It's Christina Vetrov. I'll get her for you. Please have a seat in the waiting area."

I looked at the long row of seats and saw Mark Solomon sitting and staring at the floor. I walked over and sat next to him. "Are you all right?" I asked in a gentle tone.

He shook his head. "No. Everything is so screwed up."

"Can I help?" I offered.

He looked up at me and I could see tears in his eyes. His face was pale and drawn. "Only if you can put me back the way I was."

"I'm afraid not." I had a hard time understanding why anyone wouldn't want to be young again. "Do you want to go back to being old? Or is it your old life that you want?"

Mark stared straight ahead with an absent look on his face. "I'm not *me* anymore. When I look in the mirror I see a stranger. Everything I ever cared about is gone and I can't go back."

I touched his arm and gave it a gentle squeeze. "You'll find new things to care about. I know you will."

"I don't know about that. Did you know that Group Delta lost two more people? That makes three who have disappeared. I cared about those three and now they're gone." He closed his eyes. "I came here to get some meds to dull the pain."

A nurse approached us. "Mr. Solomon, it's time for your appointment."

"I'll stop by your barracks and check on you when I get chance," I said.

He nodded, stood, and followed the nurse, taking slow steps.

A few minutes later Christina Vetrov walked over and sat next to me. "Hello, Millie, how is your CommLang working out?"

"Great, now that I have the hang of it."

"What can I do for you?" she asked.

I smiled. "I've been working hard to reach my goals and I was hoping to get a glimpse of my scores, you know, just so I can see where I might need to work harder."

"I'm sorry I don't have access to those numbers."

"Do you know who does?"

Christina looked around. The room was empty and the receptionist had left her desk to do something else. Christina leaned close to my ear. "Your coach has access, because it has to modify your workout each day based on your numbers."

"I don't think PT-11 is going to hand over that information," I said.

"No, but you could view it with the proper security code and I believe Dr. Wilcox has those codes," she said.

The receptionist returned and called Christina over for an appointment.

I stood. "Thanks, Christina, I appreciate your help."

"Good luck, Millie."

CHAPTER 13

Each night over the next week Group Echo sat in a circle and executed additional tutorials and talked about our accomplishments and concerns for the day. I had thought things were going well, but tonight I wasn't so sure.

"I know I'm doing better, but I still feel like it could all fall apart at any minute," Aliyah said, worry etched across her face. "Sometimes I think I'm not going to make it."

"Yes, you are. I've been with you every minute this week and you're doing a great job," Sam said, his tone rising an octave as he defended her.

I had noticed that Sam and Aliyah had been spending a good deal of time together and it seemed to be bolstering Aliyah's confidence. Maybe that was the piece that Mark Solomon was missing: steadfast human support. I made a note on my schedule to pay him a visit in the morning.

I looked around the circle and was amazed at how much we had changed over the month we had been there. The Oppenhiemer triplets had shoulder length brown hair and were still quiet, but they had developed an underlying strength that I found remarkable. Fiona was gorgeous and Jorge couldn't seem to stay away from her, although she didn't seem to mind. Aliyah had cut her straight black hair short and seemed to be stronger due to Sam's support. The only member of Group Echo that really had me worried was Ethan. He was the quintessential artist. He had his hair pulled back into a ponytail and much of the time he walked around barefoot. He was sensitive and kind, and I wondered how he would ever fit into this new life.

"I dug up some interesting information regarding the history of the Rim War," Ethan said to the group.

"Great, let's hear it. I've been dying to know the details that explain why the hell we're here," Jorge said.

Ethan cleared his throat. "According to the library archives, over five hundred years ago, a powerful religious sect of the Orsydi species took control of their planetary government. This sect passionately believed that their god had ordained the Orsydi as the supreme beings in the known universe, and further commanded that they should be the *only* sentient species in existence. Once the Orsydi developed space travel, their mission of xenocide began. Hence the start of the Rim War."

"Sounds a bit like what we learned about Hitler back in school," Jorge said.

"Worse." Ethan paused to compose himself. "This enemy army is a billion strong and they have successfully destroyed fourteen inhabited worlds. This is a war where the loser faces extinction. And there are no rules or standards of battle conduct. It's terrifying." Ethan paused again.

"Go on Ethan … please," I said.

Ethan took a deep breath. "There are sixteen allied species within the GAP, but only four actively participate in the Imperial Gaekaar Military, more commonly referred to as the IGM. Apparently not all species are cut out for the brutality of combat."

"Can you tell us more about the allies who are in the military?" Jorge asked.

Ethan nodded. "As you know, the Gaekaar, who are the most combat savvy, run the military. The Awyx, the Tukock, and of course the humans, also supply soldiers. Collectively, the IGM is six hundred million strong. Not very good odds from a numbers perspective."

"What are the Gaekaar like? It would be nice to know something about the species we'll be reporting to," Jorge said.

Ethan continued, "Genetically they're closely related to humans, although they appear quite different. Their internal systems are essentially the same as ours, but their frame is slightly larger, averaging six and a half to seven feet tall with a stronger musculature build. I'm guessing that's why we're working so hard to build up our physical abilities. As soldiers, it will be important that we keep up with their kind. The library records also described two external differences, which manifest as baldness and a light azure skin color."

"They actually have blue skin?" Fiona asked, eyes wide. "I've seen pictures, but I didn't think it was true."

Ethan smiled. "Well, it's more of a light blue really. It looked rather nice in the files I saw. I'll forward everyone a picture."

My VS-mail pinged right away. I opened the file and saw a group of Gaekaar combatants standing together in uniform. Other than the blue skin, they looked similar to a military picture I had of my brothers. I found them to be strangely attractive and yet forbidding at the same time.

Ethan went on while we viewed the picture. "The GAP has developed several high tech weapons along with a new series of space ships and a technology called the Distortion Turn."

Aliyah raised her hand. "I've heard of the Distortion Turn, but I don't understand what it is."

Ethan wrinkled his brow. "I don't fully comprehend the concept either, but it appears to be a drive system that bends space and allows for long distance travel. By long distance I mean hundreds of thousands of light years in the matter of a few seconds."

"Like a worm hole?" Karina asked.

Ethan shook his head. "No, not like that. A wormhole is a static tunnel that connects two points in space-time. When the Distortion Turn is used, it's a one-time event, unlike a wormhole path that can theoretically stay open for extended periods. Wormholes are also notoriously unstable and lives have been lost due to unanticipated collapse. The Distortion Turn, or DT, is a much more reliable means of long distance travel. It works by creating a four dimensional portal bubble that literally turns space allowing the vessel to leap between point A and point B within a few seconds. This action requires so much power that dark energy must be used to expand space in front of the objects and then collapse space behind the objects to complete the turn."

"Wow, gold star for doing your homework, Ethan, although you lost me somewhere around the fourth dimensional bubble thing," Sam said.

Ethan nodded. "Understandable. For us laypeople, these concepts are not easy to grasp. Try to think of the portal as a three-dimensional bubble with the fourth dimension being that of time. From what I can comprehend, this is where the high tech comes into play. If time isn't closely managed when executing a turn, you run the risk of losing hundreds, if not thousands of years. This is known as 'time-slippage.' Although if the energy is applied with precisely the correct calculations, you'll only lose a few seconds, essentially keeping time almost the same for the traveler."

Sam rolled his eyes. "I sure as hell hope we won't be tested on this."

"What about the other allies in the military?" I asked, itching to learn more about the Tukock. "What are they like?"

Ethan nodded. "The Awyx are upright creatures with a similar height and build to us. The main difference is external. They have two arms and two legs, six fingers, and eight toes on each appendage. They are also somewhat reptilian in appearance. Their bodies are covered with red scales and they have yellow eyes with slits for pupils. The home planet of the Awyx was the first world to be lost to the Orsydi when the Rim War began. Their kind is now spread somewhat thinly amongst the remaining allied planets."

I was so proud of Ethan's ability to conduct such extensive research and then tell us the stories so succinctly. I hoped this was a good sign for him.

"The Tukock are altogether different. It's my opinion that the Tukock resemble the creatures from the folklore of the Yeti here on Earth. I'm certain they aren't related, but physically, they look similar. They're tall creatures, averaging over seven feet and covered in hair that's about an inch long. The Tukock are highly evolved and well known for their engineering abilities. Unfortunately, the Orsydi butchered millions of their kind in a brutal yet unsuccessful attack on their home planet."

I noticed that Ethan's hands were trembling. "Ethan, are you okay?" I asked.

He looked at me with haunted eyes. "You have no idea how heinous the Orsydi can be. This is an enemy that most of us have never imagined. They kill simply to erase any sentient species who is not *them*. They are driven and they don't have feelings. You can't reason with something that malicious." Ethan was upset and he took a deep breath to calm himself. "You are my friends now, and I want nothing but the best for all of us, but I'm afraid we've found ourselves on a dark journey that will lead us straight to the epicenter of hell."

After Ethan concluded his vivid descriptions, the group became quiet and retired for the night. For the first time that week, no jokes were exchanged when the lights went out.

CHAPTER 14

I left the barracks early the next morning to check on Mark Solomon. Group Delta resided a short walk down two hallways.

I arrived expecting the typical morning commotion, but the Delta barracks was eerily quiet. I looked around. Four people were still sleeping and several other bunks had been slept in but were now empty.

A woman emerged from the bathroom with a towel wrapped around her head. "Excuse me," I said to her. "Is Mark Solomon here?"

"Not anymore," she replied, her tone clipped.

My heart sank.

The woman sat on her bunk and pulled the towel from her wet hair. "He disappeared some time last night. Should've known he wouldn't make it. He was such a mess. I told everyone—"

I was out the door and heading for the Blue Level before the woman could finish her sentence.

I paused for a moment outside the doctor's office. My heart was pounding and I struggled to control a tremor that vibrated through my body. I took a deep breath and pressed my hand to the sensor. The door slid open. The major sat casually in front of the doctor's desk while Dr. Wilcox reviewed her flex-display.

The good doctor looked up. "Can I help you, Millie?"

I marched in and stood inches from her desk. "Mark Solomon was looking for help. What the hell gives you the right? What kind of people are you?"

Dr. Wilcox set aside her flex-display and nodded toward the chair next to the major. "Have a seat, Millie."

I stood without moving.

The major raised a single brow. "I guess we can add stubborn to the list."

The doctor appeared tired and her eyes reflected a deep sadness. "Millie, Mark Solomon was not terminated. He was on medication and we hoped he was doing better. Last night he disappeared. We conducted a search and found him at the bottom of an airshaft. It was a suicide. I'm sorry but there was nothing we could do."

"Did you even try to do anything? Or were you happy to get that much closer to the thirty percent?" I immediately cringed, clamping my mouth shut. The doctor's skin tone was wan, and her shoulders slumped, making me realize that Mark's death was affecting her too. I ground my teeth in an attempt to quell my anger. Mostly, I was mad at myself for not checking on him sooner.

She blinked in rapid succession as if chasing away tears, her lips quivering a bit as she spoke. "This is the first suicide loss we've experienced. We usually catch them early on, but currently we're short staffed and under great pressure. That's not an excuse, but we're watching everyone as closely as possible."

I sat down and took a deep breath. "What about Ethan Wells? He's intelligent and sensitive and not as emotionally strong as the rest of us."

"We have him on suicide watch now," the doctor said. "Unfortunately, his forecast is similar to Mark Solomon's."

"Ethan will be different. We're supporting him. He'll make it through," I said.

"Are you sure about that, Millie?" the major asked. "We've seen signs that Ethan is in trouble."

"Yes, I'm sure. I need to see Group Echo's scores so that we can address the areas where Ethan, or anyone else, might need help. I know that the coaches have the data, but I need an access code to retrieve them."

The doctor sat back in her chair and regarded me for a long moment. "I see you've been doing your homework. If I was to trust you with confidential information, how would I know you wouldn't tell the others where you acquired it?" she asked.

I held my chin up. "You can trust me. I'd sooner cut off my right arm than give away anything confidential."

Dr. Wilcox nodded toward the major. He returned the nod, stood up, and turned so that he couldn't see what we were doing.

The doctor tapped on her flex-display and slid the device toward me. "Millie, I truly want you and your team to succeed. This is bigger than any one individual, I hope you understand that."

I nodded. "I believe I do."

"If you were to accidently see something on this screen, I trust that you would keep it to yourself." She pointed to the display. "This is for your eyes only, Millie."

I looked down at the screen. A single access code for all of Group Echo was displayed. I quickly keyed the data into my CommLang as a notation.

I nodded again. "I understand. Thank you, Dr. Wilcox. I won't let you down."

I jogged back to the barracks and considered how everything that happened in the facility felt like a test. The moment I passed through the door Fiona waved at me. "Hey, Millie, we were just getting ready for five fun-filled hours of physical abuse and exhaustion. Are you coming with us?"

"Of course," I said.

PT-11 worked me hard for almost three hours and I was drenched in sweat. Salty perspiration stung my eyes and I grunted as I began a second set of bench presses with two fifty-pound plates. I only needed twenty-five additional pounds to hit my goal and I was determined to get there. Just as I pushed the bar above my head, it wavered and slipped from my wet left hand. "Shit," I hissed as the heavy bar began to fall.

PT-11's robotic arm shot out so fast that I only saw a blur. It caught the bar and stopped it from crashing down on my neck. "You have exceeded your current weight capacity for this exercise. You must remove ten pounds from the bar."

I didn't like being scolded by a robot. "Damn it, PT-11, you know perfectly well that I need to be able to bench my own weight by the end of this phase. I need to work harder, not lighten the load."

"You will risk serious injury if you do not take my advice. A serious injury would impede your ability to complete the phase."

I sat up, toweled off my face, and took a moment to think it over. "Fine, you win. But can you at least tell me if I'm on track?"

"Yes, you are ahead of your personal projections. It is not necessary to push yourself beyond your physical abilities."

I looked around to make sure no one was within earshot. "PT-11, I'd like to see the current scores for all members of Group Echo displayed on your screen."

PT-11 made the whirring sound. "I cannot release scores without the proper access code."

I pulled up the note in my CommLang schedule. I whispered, "XE23-HT621-PK101 and please don't verbalize the data. I can read it on your screen."

PT-11's screen filled with information. I quickly reviewed the numbers. Everyone appeared to be meeting the physical goals, including Ethan and Aliyah. Ethan was barely making some of the numbers, but at least he was passing. Fiona, Sam, Jorge, and I were blowing away the requirements, while Aliyah and the Oppenhiemer triplets were passing at a moderate level. The left side of the screen contained three columns of numbers that were listed as 'subjective' and had long codes rather than headers. I wasn't sure what these were for, but they didn't seem to impact the totals. Ethan's numbers in these columns were less than half of anyone else's, indicating this was where his problem was hidden.

"Thank you, PT-11, you can remove the information now."

PT-11 whirred again. "The coaches recommend that Group Echo begin weapon instruction, part one: blade training."

"Blade training? What the heck for?" I couldn't possibly imagine the need for knives or swords in outer space. The thought was ludicrous.

"Blade training is an excellent way to learn the concepts of timing and avoidance, as well as combat psychology, awareness of details and—"

I held up my hand. "All right, you've convinced me. When do we begin?"

"I will confer with the other coaches." PT-11 made another whirring sound. "We will begin in thirty minutes."

I was certain that blade fighting would be a complete waste of time, but it turned out to be fun. The coaches worked with us on fighting with various types of blades, from knives to long swords, as well as timing and how to avoid being hit. I kept a close eye on Ethan who seemed to be as out of his element as ever, but at least he was trying.

On the way back to the barracks, Fiona walked by my side with a towel around her neck. "You know, I'm starting to like my new life. I know we'll be headed off to war soon, but I've never felt this good. I feel ready to take on the universe." She grabbed her towel, threw it in the air, and laughed.

I gave her a friendly push. "Well, I'm not so sure the universe is ready for you."

It was becoming easier and easier to be young, and I was beginning to appreciate the direction of my new life. Just the thought of going into space made me tingle with excitement.

Fiona grabbed my arm and leaned close to my ear. "I've been wondering what sex would be like with this new body. It's been a long time, but I think it should be like riding a bike, don't you?"

I smiled. "So, you and Jorge are thinking about getting it on?"

Fiona blushed. "We've become close these past few weeks and who knows if we'll ever see each other after deployment. It seems like we should make the best of being together while we still can."

"I agree and I'm happy for you," I said with a grin.

I thought about Cameron's offer to have a relationship before deployment. I certainly found him attractive enough and the thought of having sex with a man of Cameron's caliber did promise a high level of enjoyment, but I didn't like the idea of cramming in a relationship 'before deployment.' Somehow it made it sound like we were all going to die and that left a sour taste in my mouth.

CHAPTER 15

Over the next few weeks, we persisted with our intense study of alien languages. During the day our coaches pushed us hard and we continued to improve our physical skills, and at night we held our circle meetings. The midnight jokes returned too, which concluded our days with much needed stress relief.

My hair had grown in thick waves down to the middle of my back and I wore it in a ponytail most of the time. I was becoming accustomed to my new body and could feel a shift in my mental perspective regarding my situation. My brain processed information more readily and challenges were no longer a burden. In short I felt stronger, smarter, and looked forward to doing my part in the IGM to protect our home world.

I also continued to secretly monitor the scores for each Group Echo member. Ethan was still barely achieving his physical numbers, and he continued to drop in the subjective areas. He often stayed up late performing research and I worried as circles began to form under his eyes.

Most evenings Ethan gave us elaborate updates reflecting what he had learned from the library. For me, this was the highlight of our circle meetings. Sometimes the topics focused on the culture of various alien species and other times he talked about the history of the war.

Tonight Ethan was not himself and he seemed distant.

"I'm afraid I don't have anything to report," he said with a hollow expression in his eyes.

"You mean you're not going to give us the latest thoughts on the evil origins of the Orsydi or the scholarly ways of the Tukock?" Sam said, faking a frown.

Ethan shook his head and looked at the floor.

After the circle session concluded, most of the group trudged off to bed. Fiona looped her arm through mine and leaned her head in close. "Jorge and I will be back later," she said with a girlish giggle. "We're going somewhere ... more private."

She gave me a sly smile and sauntered off to join Jorge, who'd been waiting for her by the door, and together the two slipped off into the network of hallways. I was happy for them, but as their attachment to each other grew, I wondered how they would deal with the upcoming separation.

I wished it was as easy for me to make that decision. I was still toying with the major's offer despite only having three weeks remaining before deployment. There were so many logical reasons not to take him up on his offer, yet every time we passed in the hallway or cafeteria, I was reminded of how attractive he was and my new body ached with sexual desire.

To: Group Echo
From: Aliyah Bashir #891459A
Date: 8.25.2099
Time: 1210Z

Q: What did the egg say to the boiling water?
A: "I don't think I can get hard; I just got laid this morning."

Sam chuckled under his blanket. The joke wars had officially begun for the night. I looked over and noticed that Ethan wasn't in his bunk. As the minutes ticked by and jokes grew dirtier, worry gnawed at me each time I glanced at his empty bed sheets. I knew he hadn't left the barracks, so I got up and went to check the bathroom.

I looked in the stalls and didn't see anyone. I checked the shower area and almost missed the small lump in the back corner. Ethan was curled up in a ball, his knees tucked up to his chest and his hands holding his head.

I approached him slowly. "Ethan? Are you all right?"

He didn't respond.

I squatted down and put a gentle hand on his shoulder. "Ethan, are you all right?" I repeated.

He sniffled. "No."

"Talk to me. What's wrong?"

"Everything, just everything." His voice quivered.

"I need you to be a bit more specific. Please, tell me what's bothering you."

He looked up at me with tears in his eyes. "I can't do this. I don't want to kill other species. I'm not a soldier, and I don't want to be part of this fucked-up war."

"Maybe they can find you some other job that doesn't involve combat. Ethan, you have so much to offer. The war effort needs you," I said.

"Maybe, but *I* don't need the war effort. I'm done with this life. I just want it to be over."

Fear clenched my chest. The major had been right. "We can get you treatment that will make you feel better. Ethan, you have friends here and we need you." I felt desperate. I was completely out of my element when dealing with someone who wanted to end it all.

"I don't want treatment … I won't be me anymore if they give me drugs." Ethan's hands trembled as he absently pulled on his ponytail. "I've thought this through. I can't face this war, so I'm going to terminate instead."

My brain scrambled for an answer, but I had no idea what to do. "Ethan, I'm your friend and I respect your choices, but please just wait. Can you wait just another day? Please, Ethan, wait for your friends?"

A tear rolled down his cheek and dripped onto his knee. "Not too long. I don't want to deploy. I won't."

"Thank you." I kissed his cheek and gave him a hug. "Wait here."

I ran to Sam and shook him. He opened one eye and glared at me. "Hey now, I'm awake. What's the problem?"

"It's Ethan, he's thinking of suicide. He's in the bathroom, please sit with him while I go find some help."

Sam sprang from his bunk and headed for the bathroom without a word.

Karina was at my side in an instant. "What's going on?" she asked.

"It's Ethan, he's falling apart."

Karina nodded. "I was a nurse once, I'll see what I can do." She turned and sprinted to join Sam.

I ran to Major Cameron Ford's quarters and slammed my hand on the sensor.

After several long minutes, the door slid open. Cameron stood on the other side in a pair of sweat pants with no shirt. His dark hair was a mess and he didn't appear to be fully awake. He looked good, really good.

"Hello, Millie. I hope you've come here to give me an answer, but from the look on your face I'm guessing that's not the case," Cameron said.

I performed a cursory bow. "I need your help. It's Ethan." I stepped into his quarters.

The door slid shut as soon as I stepped across the threshold. "What seems to be the problem?" he asked.

"You were right." Hot tears sprang to my eyes. I wasn't the type to cry often, but I was so worried about my friend that I wasn't myself. "Ethan ... he wants to end it. And he seems to have valid reasons, and I can't talk sense into him."

Cameron shook his head. "No one has a valid reason for killing themselves."

"Well, he doesn't actually want to kill himself. He wants to offer himself up for termination," I said.

Cameron grabbed my shoulders and looked me straight in the eyes. "Millie, we don't terminate people."

I shook my head. "But what about the thirty percent? I thought you terminated those who didn't make their goals."

Cameron sighed and ran his fingers through his hair. "I know that's what you think. It's a false impression given on purpose to toughen up students and get them laser-focused on their goals."

I took a deep breath. "But what happens to the people who fail? What do you do with them?"

Cameron's expression was intense. "We wipe most of their memory and send them on their way with a new identity and an extended life on Earth. We're not monsters Millie ... We're the good guys, remember? But we also can't allow less than the best to enter the IGM. This is too important."

I let out a breath I didn't realize I'd been holding. A wave of relief crept through me, but at the same time I had to wonder why he was telling me information that I shouldn't be privy to. I scrunched up my brow. "Isn't this information confidential?"

Cameron sighed. "Millie, this is a complex process. You've proven that you can be trusted. Plus, you're a mere three weeks from graduation. Anyone who wasn't going to make it has already been pulled from the process. The line up of graduating students is set."

"But what about Ethan? Can you help him or will you wipe his memory?" I asked.

Cameron took my chin in his hand and forced me to make direct eye contact. "Millie, you were right about Ethan and the forecast was wrong. I was wrong. He has a lot to offer in the area of intelligence, so no, we won't wipe his memory. His depression is very treatable." Cameron glanced away as if he was reading his HUD. "In fact, medical personnel are administering a jet-injection as we speak. He'll be feeling better by morning."

"The treatment won't change him will it? I mean, he'll still be Ethan, won't he?"

"The medication simply takes away the feeling of hopelessness and depression. Nothing else will change. Ethan will still be Ethan, I promise."

"Are you sure? Ethan wouldn't want to change."

"Look, I've been through this dozens of times. The Med team knows how to handle these situations. The treatment allows the patient to come to terms with their new life without the overwhelming depression that causes the suicidal thoughts. So the answer is yes, I can assure you that Ethan's personality won't change."

The tension drained from my body as he reassured me. "Thank you, Cameron. I don't know how I'll ever return the favor."

He gave me a sideways smile. "You could give me an answer?"

I felt my cheeks burn. "I'm still thinking it over."

"Millie, we only have a few more weeks before deployment. It's not in your nature to be this indecisive."

"I know, I'm sorry. It's just that I'm so—"

"Out of practice?" Cameron lifted his brow.

I nodded, looking away. I wanted to say yes, but I felt so inept. At least Fiona and Jorge could be sexually inept together. Cameron, on the other hand, was way out of my league when it came to recent experience.

Cameron grabbed my face with both hands and pulled me into a kiss. His lips were firm and his tongue plunged into my mouth. I felt heat all the way down to my toes. My tongue met his and I responded to the kiss with a level of passion I hadn't been aware I possessed.

Cameron pulled back and took a deep breath. "See, you're not as out of practice as you think. Give it some more thought, Millie, but don't take too long. We're almost out of time."

My heart pounded and body tingled with desire from head to toe. I couldn't seem to put two words together, so I simply nodded in agreement.

Cameron walked me to the door and I noticed a flicker of sadness in his eyes. "Once we deploy, our paths will become harsh and unforgiving. Don't waste your last few weeks." He gave me a quick kiss on the cheek and I was on my way.

I made my way back to the barracks feeling a bit like the young girl who had just been kissed by the hottest guy in high school. When I was young I recalled often feeling foolish and uncertain when it came to making decisions. Now that I carried the experiences of one hundred and five years, I had much more confidence in myself. I felt empowered, and for the life of me, I couldn't understand why I had wasted so much time avoiding giving Cameron an answer.

Maybe having a relationship wasn't such a bad idea, even if it was short term. After all, Cameron was a devout military man and had firsthand knowledge of the harshness we would be facing in the Rim War. The more I thought about it, the more I realized that without our personal relationships we were nothing.

I typed up a quick VS-mail.

To: Major Cameron Ford #000109C
From: Mildred Necee Helgren #891456M
Date: 8.25.2099
Time: 1320Z

I apologize for taking so long. The answer is yes.

I received a response roughly thirty seconds later.

To: Mildred Necee Helgren #891456M
From: Major Cameron Ford #000109C
Date: 8.25.2099
Time: 1321Z

As much as I'd like you to come back now so I could forgo the cold shower, I expect that you will need to be with Ethan tonight. How about tomorrow night, my quarters, 2100Z?

I responded right away.

To: Major Cameron Ford #000109C
From: Mildred Necee Helgren #891456M
Date: 8.25.2099
Time: 1321Z

Sounds great. See you then.
P.S. I appreciate your patience.

Back at the barracks, I found Ethan in his bed surrounded by the group. Fiona and Jorge had also just returned and were peppering Sam with questions.

"Now just hold on a minute," Sam said. "Ethan needs to rest. The nurse said he needs a quiet space for the next twelve hours to allow the treatment time to take effect. I suggest we all go to bed and save the questions for tomorrow."

Ethan still had circles under his eyes and his expression was desolate, but he gave a shaky nod in agreement. The rest of the group retired for the night, yet I doubted any of us would sleep well.

I crawled into my bunk and found that I was wide-awake for a different reason. I kept thinking of my arrangement with Cameron. Tomorrow night couldn't come fast enough.

CHAPTER 16

The next morning we let Ethan sleep in, while the rest of the group went to the far corner of the barracks to quietly practice the required alien languages. Jorge and Sam brought trays of food and protein drinks from the cafeteria. At 1000Z Ethan woke and meandered over to join us. He looked disheveled, but a small smile tugged at his mouth.

"I'm sorry for the trouble I caused yesterday. I feel different. It's hard to describe." He sat down next to me. "Although, I'd like to clearly state that I'm still not in favor of the war and I don't want a role in it."

Different? Worry nagged at me. "Do you still feel like you?" I asked.

"Yeah, it's weird. I'm still me, but I don't feel so down," he said.

I leaned over and gave Ethan a hug. "We're your friends and regardless of where we end up, nothing will ever change that. We'll always be there for each other."

"That's right," Fiona said. "The pact we made goes beyond these weeks in training. We're a team for life."

Sam nodded. "Damn straight."

Ethan's cheeks reddened. "I appreciate that and I would never want to let you down. I have my doubts about finding a meaningful purpose in this life, but if it's out there, I'm willing to try to find it."

That night I pressed my hand on Cameron's door sensor at exactly 2100Z. The door opened. He was still dressed in his uniform and appeared preoccupied. "Come in. I'm sorry. I was pulled into a late meeting and I just returned."

I walked in and he waved his hand toward a small table with two chairs. "Please have a seat and I'll get us a bottle of wine."

Cameron walked over to a row of wall cabinetry and reached for a pair of wine glasses. I appreciated the gesture, but I didn't want to waste a single moment, so I came up behind him and touched his shoulder. He turned, raised a single brow, and looked at me.

I gave him a sheepish smile. "I'm sorry it took me so long to make up my mind. Let's make good use of our time together."

A mischievous smile crept across his face. "Far be it from me to slow things down."

I didn't wait for him to make the first move. I reached around his neck and pulled his lips to mine.

Cameron grabbed my head with both hands and laced his fingers through my hair. His tongue wound around mine in an erotic dance. Something that felt like electricity trickled down my spine as he explored my mouth. *Wow, the man can kiss.*

We pressed our bodies together. The urgency of Cameron's need was evident as he rotated his groin against my hips.

He pulled away and grabbed my hand, leading me into the next room and over to his bed. He turned and pulled me into another deep kiss. I could feel his heart pounding beneath his uniform. He radiated strength and heat, and I melted into his arms.

We tugged each other's clothes off and fell onto the bed. He kissed my neck and explored every inch of my body with his hands. My new physiology ached with a burning hunger that needed to be filled. My body was different and more demanding now. Waiting around for foreplay just wasn't going to work for me.

"I need you, Cameron," I whispered in his ear. "Now."

I felt Cameron smile into my neck. "I knew we'd be good together," he whispered back.

Within a moment he thrust inside me. "Oh yes," he groaned, moving rhythmically and pushing deeper. "This was worth the wait, Millie."

It had been far too long since I felt like this. I came so fast and hard, at first I wasn't sure what was happening. "Cameron!" I screamed, throwing my head back as every muscle in my body reacted to him.

In a lifetime of experiences, I had never before screamed anyone's name during sex. It was an incredible feeling and I appreciated my new body all the more.

Cameron grinned at me and leaned down to kiss my breast. "It's still early. I hope you weren't planning on getting much sleep tonight," he murmured.

The next few weeks flew by. My relationship with Cameron was reserved for the late night hours, but we made the best of it. In lieu of sleep, we opted for good sex followed by long conversations. Major Cameron Ford was quickly becoming more than a good friend, yet deep down I knew I might be setting myself up for heartache.

One night as I lay in his arms, I toyed with his dark hair. "How do the Gaekaar view relationships between humans?" I asked, afraid of what he might say in response.

Cameron chuckled, pulled me closer, and kissed me. "You have nothing to worry about. The Gaekaar encourage all types of connections between soldiers because they believe it stabilizes each individual and make them stronger." He gave me a sly smile. "Is this your way of saying that you'd like to keep seeing me after deployment?"

I thought for a moment and chose my words carefully. "Well, you keep saying that we have no idea what will happen after deployment, but if we *somehow* had the opportunity to see each other again, I'd like that."

Cameron nuzzled my ear. "Millie, you have no idea how much I would love that."

Ethan continued to improve and he immersed himself in the library files. Group Echo excelled at language studies, and Ethan's informational lectures became a regular part of our circle meetings again. He helped us gain a strong base knowledge of space travel, the nuances between the alien civilizations, as well as general information about the IGM.

Finally, graduation arrived. The afternoon before the ceremony we received an announcement that stated our enlistment documents would be distributed at 1500Z and would include our new rank and position. Group Echo gathered into our circle five minutes early in order to receive our notifications as a team. We were too nervous to talk, so instead we clasped hands and waited in silence.

At ten seconds past 1500Z my VS-mail pinged. I looked around the circle and noticed the trepidation on the faces of my friends.

I clicked on the file.

To: Mildred Necee Helgren #891456M
From: Command Center for Enlistment Documentation and Deployment Protocol
Date: 9.15.2099
Time: 1500Z

Report to the Med Center at 1530Z.

Where was my rank and position? I didn't understand. A wave of fear swept over me as I imagined going to the Med Center to have my memory wiped.

As I looked around the circle at my friends, I knew that I didn't want to stay on Earth. I wanted to go into space and fight to keep the war from ever reaching this sector of the galaxy. I wanted to fight with Cameron and my friends. I had been training hard for weeks and I was ready to go.

Fiona's face lit up with excitement. "I've been assigned to Asbu Station, Department of Strategic Planning and Operations, rank private."

I noticed Ethan had his eyes closed to facilitate faster reading. "Asbu Station is the hub of military intelligence and is located inside a large asteroid, whereabouts undisclosed for security reasons," he said, opening his eyes. "I've been assigned to Asbu as well. Military Research Center, rank lieutenant."

"Nice job, Ethan, you've been given the rank of an officer," Jorge said. "The rest of us grunts will have to bow to you. I've been assigned to the Frigate Sharur. Rank private with a weapons specialty."

"I'm on the Frigate Sharur too, rank private," Sam said.

Aliyah smiled and clapped her hands together. "This is perfect. I've also been assigned to the Sharur, rank private."

Ethan closed his eyes again. "The Frigate Sharur is a class three warship that carries one hundred and twenty soldiers." He opened his eyes and looked around the circle. "I still find it ironic that since the war began, the Gaekaars have named many of their space going vessels using the history of old Earth ship names. Apparently they have a fondness for human wartime antiquity."

Karina Oppenhiemer was still holding hands with her two sisters. "The three of us have been assigned to the Destroyer Shenshi, and we also have the rank of private."

Ethan closed his eyes again. "The Destroyer Shenshi is a long range warship with heavy ordnance. It carries up to a hundred and fifty soldiers."

Fiona looked over at me. "What about you, Millie?"

I shrugged. "No assignment. My VS-mail said to be at the Med Center at 1530Z."

Fiona gasped.

"Oh, no," Aliyah whispered.

Ethan looked over at me. "Don't worry, they won't terminate you. I see reservations for nine Group Echo soldiers on tomorrow's shuttle."

"Well, I guess I'll find out in a few minutes," I said, wobbling a bit as I stood up. It was interesting that despite my new lean and muscular legs, they could still feel shaky when the mind came into play. "See you all soon … I hope."

I arrived at the Med Center a few minutes early and found Christina at the reception desk. She had her arms crossed and a smirk spread across her face. "Hello, Millie. Congratulations. I must say, we don't have the pleasure of performing this procedure very often."

"Sorry, I'm completely in the dark. I have no idea why I'm here," I said.

Christina shook her head. "I wish they would inform you up front. The adjustment would be easier. Come with me and I'll tell you what I can." She headed down the hall and entered the same room that had been used for the CommLang installation.

I was a bundle of nerves. "Ah, you're not going to wipe my memory, are you?"

Christina laughed. "Goodness, no! I'm going to be upgrading your CommLang to a CommNav, protocol galaxy class. You'll retain all data from your CommLang, plus have the interface for ship to navigator communication. You'll also be receiving a customized knowledge packet designed by your designated captain."

"That doesn't sound like a big deal," I said.

"Well, it is." Christina pointed to the table. "Jump on and we'll get started."

I climbed on the table and got into position. "Exactly what is 'ship to navigator communication'?"

"I don't know much about it. It's well above my grade, but I can tell you that it is something that is rarely installed here on Earth. I'm going to lower the robot now. Everything will take place just like before."

An hour later the robot ascended back into the ceiling and I sat up. I looked at my VS-mail and my schedule. Everything looked identical to my old system with the exception of a new schedule entry that said I was to report to Major Ford's office immediately upon completion of the CommNav installation. "It looks the same as before," I said, almost disappointed.

"It's not. Not even close. Your new installation contains global arrays and sub arrays for faster sorting of data. I don't understand exactly how it works, but I know that you have a very special unit in your head." Christina handed me two small red pills. "Dissolve these under your tongue after you open your knowledge packet, they'll help with the severe headache you'll experience."

"Thanks. How long can I expect the pain to last?"

"It takes about six hours for the cerebral cortex to fully integrate that data, but one dose of these and you'll be fine within a minute." Christina put her hand on my shoulder. "Good luck, Millie. If you ever need anything, please don't hesitate to ask."

I pressed my hand on the sensor outside of Cameron's office and the door slid open. The major was at his desk working on a flex-display. He looked up and pointed to the chair across from himself. "Have a seat, Millie, I'm sure you have a few questions."

I sat down and kept my mouth shut.

Cameron was all business and showed none of the softness I had witnessed over the past three weeks in his bedroom. "Congratulations on being part of the first graduating class to come out of the training phase completely intact. Nine of you went in and nine came out. If you had asked me a month ago, I would have said it was impossible. Nice work."

I grinned. "I have the strongest urge to say 'I told you so,' but that would be disrespectful, so I won't."

Cameron stared at me seriously without flinching. "I'm sure you're curious over your rank and assignment."

I nodded.

"Millie, you've been awarded the rank of lieutenant, first specialty Navigational Pilot. You'll be stationed on the SpaceLion reporting to Captain Xshar Cai Torrun. He's a real hard ass, but a good captain. You should know that this is a difficult assignment, as well as an honor. You have been very fortunate. Most students don't do this well."

I didn't know what to say, and I still didn't understand what I was going to be doing.

Cameron clasped his hands together. "And if you're wondering if this assignment had anything to do with our relationship, the answer is no. The system made the recommendation and I approved it, as did Dr. Wilcox. We're both very proud of what you have accomplished for yourself and your team."

I shifted in my seat. I had always been uncomfortable with praise. "It wasn't just me, everyone in Group Echo contributed equally."

"Yes, but you were the catalyst," he said, using a frank tone.

I decided to redirect the subject. "Could you please explain exactly what I'll be doing as a Navigational Pilot?"

Cameron smiled and leaned back in his chair. "You'll be navigating a very important ship called the SpaceLion. It's a one-of-a-kind vessel designed to infiltrate enemy lines without detection. Your CommNav is outfitted with an array that will interface with the ship's Artificial Intelligence, or AI, and together you will control the SpaceLion's actions in accordance with the commands of your captain. You'll also receive a knowledge packet that was designed for you by your captain. This should minimize the learning curve. You'll find the packet embedded within your current schedule. I suggest uploading the file today so that you can get comfortable with the information before you begin SKAT."

"Will the information in the packet be similar to learning the alien languages?"

"Yes and no. The packet contains considerably more data. You'll find the new information easily accessible, but you won't have the hands-on-experience, which is what helps make sense of the overwhelming amount of data. Experience helps you connect the dots, so to speak. But don't worry, you'll receive plenty of hands-on-training at Asbu Station's SKAT program."

I shook my head. "Why me? I'm not special, why not someone else?"

The major leaned back in his chair. "You were selected for a combination of reasons. First, your brain *is* quite special. You have the neural aptitude to handle the navigational interface. That's not a skill you can learn, it's something that you either inherently have or you don't. We believe it's a minor genetic difference, but regardless, most people don't have it. In fact, 99.3 percent of the population doesn't have it, human or Gaekaar. To complicate this further, the remaining .7 percent rarely have the skills and aptitudes required for a successful navpilot, thus you can begin to understand why this position is so difficult to fill."

Cameron looked at me intently and continued, "Second, you displayed the ability to determine what's important and convey that to a team. We gave you an inordinate amount of free time and you were able to pinpoint what you needed to accomplish in order to achieve the best possible outcome, not only for yourself, but for everyone in Group Echo. Third, you have the qualities of loyalty, courage, the capacity to follow direction, and the ability to maintain confidentiality."

Cameron paused and grinned. "These were the same qualities that I found attractive in you on a personal level. You are special, Millie, don't forget it."

Despite Cameron's kind words, I knew that in a few short hours I would be nothing more than one small human in a fierce alien military force of six hundred million. We would be fighting galactic battles where my species was an insignificant minority within a broader war that had a poor prognosis.

CHAPTER 17

When I arrived back at the barracks, it was empty. I sat on my bunk, closed my eyes, and opened my learning packet. I could feel the array opening up as my head was flooded with massive amounts of intriguing information. I looked over the topics and wondered how I would ever be able to get my mind wrapped around all of it—a master's degree worth of engineering knowledge, piloting skills, extensive knowledge on ships operations and ordnance, basic skills in working with an AI, and a hundred other smaller topics. It almost felt like my brain was pulsing with electrical currents.

As Christina had predicted, my head began to throb from the onslaught of new information inundating my cerebral cortex.

Someone pulled on my arm. I opened my eyes and saw Fiona with a wide smile spread across her face. "I hear you're a Lieutenant, both you and Ethan! It's so exciting. They say that it's rare for a student to go straight to officer status, and yet Group Echo has two. Not only that, we set a record by having every student make it to graduation. Everything was posted in VS-mail an hour ago. We're practically famous!"

Fiona's enthusiasm made my head hurt more. I dug out the two red pills that Christina gave me and popped them into my mouth. "That's terrific. How's Ethan doing? And where is everyone?" I asked.

"Most of them are in the cafeteria, but Jorge and Sam are up to something." Fiona giggled. "Anyhow, Ethan's new status as a Lieutenant has given him additional clearance, so he's back to losing himself in the library files." Fiona reached over and gave me a bone-crushing hug. "I can't believe we'll be graduating and shipping out tomorrow. It's all so surreal."

My VS-mail pinged.

To: Group Echo
From: Jorge Alvarez #891454J
Date: 9.14.2099
Time: 1810Z

Celebration at circle tonight ...VODKA!
Don't ask where it came from, just be there.

Vodka martinis were Group Echo's drink of choice. Jorge wouldn't tell us how he and Sam had acquired the vodka and frankly we didn't care. We celebrated, promised to always watch out for each other, told jokes, drank too much, and laughed until two in the morning. It was the most fun I had experienced in decades and we were all reluctant to hit our bunks despite the hour.

Graduation morning arrived earlier than I would have liked. I wasn't sure if the dull ache in my head was from the new knowledge packet or the vodka we consumed. Cameron had been called into a late night meeting and we weren't able to have our 'last night' together, which we both felt bad about, but I was glad to have spent time with my friends.

Now that it was morning, our futures were uncertain and the barracks seemed to take on a melancholy air. I forced myself to get up, which only served to make my head pound more. I noticed that my schedule had been updated.

0900Z: Graduation Ceremony, Suite 42C, Red Level
1100Z: Shuttle to Gaekaar Moonbase E17, Shuttle Bay
1500Z: Transport to Asbu Station, Port Bay

I looked around. Everyone was still sleeping except Ethan, who was sitting cross-legged on the floor with his eyes closed. Probably doing research. I noticed that Fiona and Jorge were sound asleep in the same bunk. No doubt trying to make the best of their last hours together.

By the time I finished showering the rest of Group Echo was slowly getting up. Aliyah passed by me as I was leaving the bathroom. Her hand was on her forehead and her eyes only half open. "Please don't talk to me," she said.

Sam was crawling off his bunk. "Hey, Helgren, we might have to skip the morning jog. Not sure any of us can handle it," he said in a raspy voice.

I opened my locker and was surprised to find a crisp black uniform with the markings of a Lieutenant. I touched the material. It was heavy, yet soft. It would be nice to stop wearing the same old jumpsuit, but a ripple of fear went through my mind as I thought about the responsibility that went with the new uniform. I couldn't help but wonder if they hadn't made a mistake in choosing me.

The barracks door creaked open and I glanced over as Christina Vetrov slipped in. She approached me with a cheerful smile. "Good morning, Millie."

"Morning," I replied, attempting to muster a smile.

"I couldn't help but notice your sensor readings this morning. Looks like Group Echo did some celebrating." She smirked and shook her head. "I won't ask how you got the alcohol and I don't want to know."

I massaged my temples. "Thanks. Although we're paying for it now."

She handed me a small vial. "Here, this might help. Think of it as a going away present." Christina laughed, patted me on the back, and made a discreet exit.

I opened the gift and was thankful to see a mass of little red pills.

"Hey, Sam," I said, holding up the vial. "Looks like we'll be going on that morning jog after all."

Group Echo arrived early for the graduation ceremony and sat in the front row. I counted heads as Groups Delta and Foxtrot arrived. At 0900Z the total count was twenty-six.

Fiona leaned over. "Looks like a 23 percent loss. Better than the 30 percent forecast," she whispered.

I smiled and nodded.

Dr. Wilcox and Major Cameron Ford stood at the front of the room and waited for everyone to quiet down.

The doctor stepped forward. "Congratulations on being the 115th graduating class from this facility. And a special congratulations to Group Echo for being the first group to conclude the shedding and training phases with the same numbers of students that you began with."

Dr. Wilcox paused while everyone clapped. "The uniform you are now wearing has the markings of your new rank and position. You might be curious over why the Gaekaars have used a combination of Marines and Navy for their rank and file structure. During the early days of the Rim War, the Gaekaars quickly learned they were not properly structured for long-term, xenocide-level warfare. Therefore they created a model that mirrored one of the more aggressive species in the galaxy.

"Despite the fact that humans are centuries behind in technology and overall development as sentient beings, it could not be denied that we have a strong history of warfare as well as the natural instinct to fight, persevere, and win when provoked. Hence, the Gaekaars have used many of Earth's tactics when it came to planning their original combat strategy and military structure.

"That's not to say they have copied us," she added. "I would sum it up as stating they learned the basics from us and then took a massive leap forward. You may rest assured that at this point in time, the Gaekaar are quite experienced and capable."

Dr. Wilcox cleared her throat. "As I call your name, please come up and receive your official pin indoctrinating you into the GAP-sponsored Imperial Gaekaar Military."

One by one we walked forward to receive our pin from the major. When it was my turn he handed me the symbol of my hard work and winked at me. I couldn't help but feel proud. Group Echo had made it through and we had forged strong friendships. I still missed Avery and thought of her often, but I knew she was strong and could take care of herself. My focus now was to contribute to protecting Avery's future as well as my home planet from the encroaching battle lines of the Rim War.

Once everyone was seated, the major took the podium. "I would like to take the next few minutes to outline your immediate future. From here we will proceed to the shuttle bay, where you will board a small vessel headed for Moonbase E17. I will be accompanying you off planet, as I have been assigned command of a ship in General Etar Sy Unnum's fleet."

The major went on. "When we land on Moonbase E17, you'll find that you've been assigned to a transport ship based on your SKAT training location. Some of you will depart for the Destroyer Shenshi, some will go to Kotsu Station, and the remainder will accompany me as we head to Asbu Station. Who can tell us what SKAT stands for?"

Ethan raised his hand.

"Yes, Lieutenant," the major said.

"Specific Knowledge and Apprenticeship Training. Training can last from weeks to months, depending on the rank, position, and individual aptitude. The format is highly structured, and discipline and compliance are mandatory," Ethan said with a remarkable level of confidence.

"Thank you, Lieutenant. Well said. As you prepare for the next phase in your life, please make Dr. Wilcox, myself, and the human race proud by striving to be excellent soldiers. Now, follow me to the shuttle bay and we'll prepare to depart."

At the entrance to the shuttle bay we were each handed a single packed bag with contents specific to our individual futures. My bag contained toiletries, a dress uniform, an exercise suit, and sleeping attire. My whole life was in one small bag.

"At least we won't have to worry about being fashionable," Fiona said as she pulled the sleeve of the dress uniform from her bag. "Hmm. More black, not my best color."

"Fiona, you'd look good wearing a burlap bag," Jorge said, putting his arm around her shoulders.

Fiona smiled, but I could see the sadness that lurked behind her eyes. Once we reached Asbu Station, she and Jorge would be forced to go their separate ways.

The flight to the moon was a quick two hours. Ethan sat next to me, gazing out the window at the wonderful view. The farther we pulled away from Earth's atmosphere, the more peaceful and beautiful the planet looked.

Ethan turned toward me with his brows drawn together. "We won't be seeing this again for a long time, if ever."

I sighed. "I know. It's hard to think about the possibility of never coming back."

"Millie, I read a strange file today." Ethan's expression was laced with worry.

I reached over and touched his arm. "Go on, please."

"It was an official update regarding the concerns over the war reaching Earth. Homeland defense has upgraded to DEFCON 2."

I felt a pang of anxiety. "What happened?"

Ethan lowered his voice and leaned close. "According to the update the *only* reason the enemy hasn't reached our sector of the galaxy is because they don't have the technology to harness the power required for the long distance Distortion Turns. Until now, the Orsydi were only capable of making short turns using traditional nuclear technology. In basic terms, they could only bend spacetime up to eight parsecs."

My apprehension ratcheted up another notch. "What did you mean by 'until now,' Ethan?"

He paused. "Bad news came last night. Gaekaar special ops relayed intel claiming that the Orsydi may have acquired the technology for gathering dark energy, which is what makes long distance turns possible. If that's the case, the enemy will have the ability to reach dozens of additional defenseless planets. The IGM is already spread far too thin, which makes putting a defensive strategy in place next to impossible."

I closed my eyes. "Is one of those defenseless planets Earth?"

Ethan frowned. "Yes."

I sat quietly for a moment reflecting on what Ethan had shared. I grabbed his hand and held it tight. "Ethan, we need to find a way to help protect Earth."

"As much as I abhor war, I won't just stand by and watch our home world be threatened." The intensity in his eyes was something I hadn't seen before. "Don't worry, I'm with you, Millie."

Our landing on Moonbase E17 was smooth. We docked in a bay that housed a long row of docks with similar shuttles.

"Grab your bags and follow me," the major ordered.

We disembarked and marched across the massive expanse of the bay. The major took us down through two adjacent corridors and along the way we passed dozens of Gaekaar workers and military personnel. I felt like I was gawking, but I couldn't help but stare. They were tall and beautiful with light blue skin and baldheads. The men had odd markings on their heads, tattoos of cultural significance that we had learned about in our studies, and the women had dozens of piercings in their ears.

I leaned over and whispered in Ethan's ear. "What do the Gaekaars do here now that Helium-3 is no longer available?"

Ethan's face crinkled with concern. "Maybe it has something to do with the change in the homeland security status. The files stated that the moon is primarily used as a way station for political travelers and cargo shipments. Just a guess, but I'd say they're ramping up for something."

We entered a smaller docking bay that housed three transport ships. Group Delta boarded the first ship, which was bound for a Kotsu Station near the Orsydian Front; and Group Foxtrot and the Oppenhiemer triplets boarded the second ship, which was bound for the Destroyer Shenshi. We said tearful goodbyes to Karina, Samina, and Trina, and promised to remain true to our pact. The rest of Group Echo along with Major Cameron Ford boarded the last shuttle. We were bound for Asbu Station, which was located deep inside an asteroid in an undisclosed sector of the galaxy.

Cameron spoke to the male Gaekaar pilot for a few moments. The pilot looked younger than the male Gaekaars we had seen on the Moonbase and I noticed that he had fewer markings on his head. I made a note in my CommNav to learn more about the meaning of the symbolic tattoos.

The major turned to formally address us. "You are about to experience something that most humans are only able to dream about. You've probably heard about Distortion Turn travel, but there's nothing like actually witnessing it first hand. Our transport will travel a short distance to a rendezvous point, where we will wait for the Epoch to arrive. For those of you who are unaware, the Epoch is the only ship that can create the DT bubble necessary to take us thousands of parsecs within a few seconds. It takes an incredible amount of power to bend space in a stable manner, which is why the generator is housed in a dedicated ship."

"Where does it get that kind of power?" Sam asked.

Ethan looked at me and rolled his eyes. I knew he was annoyed that Sam hadn't paid closer attention during our circle meetings.

The major looked at Ethan. "Lieutenant, why don't you explain the answer to the private's question."

Ethan nodded. "Dark energy is the only source capable of supplying that level of power. The reactor is massive and the process of collecting and containing dark energy is extremely volatile. I'll admit that I don't understand the physics behind the power conversion, but from what I understand, the Epoch will take us from here to Asbu Station in 2.5 seconds."

"Thank you, Lieutenant," Cameron said.

"Buckle in. We'll be at the rendezvous point in less than ten minutes," the pilot said in the Gaekaar language. It was so familiar to me that it sounded like English in my head. I was relieved to discover that translation wouldn't be an issue.

The pilot touched a few points on a clear screen and within seconds the bay doors opened and we floated into an airlock.

"We've been approved for takeoff. Lowering the containment field," the pilot said. "This ship has much more sophisticated maneuvering abilities compared to the shuttle you took from Earth. I'll give you a taste of what this little ship can do. I suggest you make sure your straps are tight."

The transport took off and we were slammed back into our seats. I felt a thrill as the pilot pulled away from the moon and performed a series of tight loops and ninety degree turns. Then he did a corkscrew turn followed by maneuvers that included impossible angles. I cross-referenced each move the ship made against the piloting information in my head. It was all fascinating stuff and I couldn't wait to learn more.

"How are you able to do this without the g-forces killing us," I asked.

"Inertial negation system. You'll learn about it at SKAT," he said, pulling into perfect docking formation with the other transports.

As I looked around the small ship, it was apparent most of my companions hadn't appreciated the ride as much as I had. Ethan had a death grip on his seat and Aliyah and Sam looked terrified. Jorge was saying a prayer with his eyes shut.

"I think I'm going to be sick," Fiona said, holding her stomach. "I would never make it as a pilot."

"He's just showing off," the major said. "The Gaekaar enjoy letting us know that their ships are far superior to ours."

The pilot leaned back and looked at us. "Stay alert. Vector-space relay indicates that the DT will take place in three minutes."

We glued ourselves to the transport windows and waited for the big event to transpire. I tried not to blink. I didn't want to miss even a fraction of a second.

"Look, over there." Aliyah pointed toward an area of space that seemed to be blurred.

I blinked several times to make sure the blurriness wasn't just something in my eyes.

"That's the Distortion bubble starting to form. The Epoch should arrive any second now," the major said.

The blurred area gelled into a three-dimensional bubble that clearly reflected a picture of space that wasn't from our solar system. Without warning, the bubble exploded into a light show that sent colorful streaks of laser-like beams in all directions. When the light cleared and my eyes adjusted, the large gray Epoch floated in space, a mere 1,000 kilometers or so off our port side.

Everyone in the transport cheered. The arrival had been truly spectacular. The Epoch was gigantic, almost as wide as it was long, and obviously not built by humans. The view from our small transport was awe-inspiring and I had my first taste of just how massive and different things would be in space.

"What's happening over there?" Aliyah pointed to the starboard side of the Epoch where another patch of blurry space had started to gel.

CHAPTER 18

"It looks like another bubble," Ethan said, pressing closer to the window.

I watched the Distortion bubble form until it reflected an area of space I didn't recognize.

"Shit," Cameron snarled, turning toward the pilot. "Evasive maneuvers, now!"

The pilot wasted no time taking the ship into a high-speed arc just as the light show began.

"What's going on?" Fiona yelled.

"Signal the other two transports to follow us back to Moonbase E17, and make it fast," the major ordered. "Does this thing have any defensive abilities?"

The pilot shook his head as he worked the controls. "No shields and only one high intensity laser meant for space debris. But we're quick. I should be able to out fly most Orsydi ships."

Orsydi? I sucked in a quick breath and pressed my face to the window, gaping as a strange warship materialized. I performed a quick check through my files and found that the ship was an Orsydi dreadnought. It was angular with a deep red hull, and at more than fifty times our size it made us seem insignificant.

The Orsydi dreadnought hung in space without moving, like a predator preparing to strike. I tried to guess its next move. Our small transports would be easy prey, and as much as I didn't like the prospect of becoming a target, I suspected that their real objective was the Epoch followed by a reconnaissance of Earth. It was a guess based more on instinct rather than my new wealth of information.

The other two transports began to pull away, although not in quite the same tight arcing trajectory as our daredevil pilot.

The stationary dreadnought launched a pair of glowing torpedoes that streaked across space. I watched in horror as the weapons followed the path of the first transport carrying Group Delta. Seconds later, the small ship broke up into a million slivers of glittering metal, shooting out in all directions. No fireball or booming sound, as one might expect, just the quiet annihilation of thirteen lives in the vacuum of space.

"Oh, fuck," Jorge said in disbelief.

I looked back at the dreadnought and another pair of glowing torpedoes launched. Moments later the transport with Karina, Samina, and Trina shattered into similar fragments of metal debris. Their lives had been snuffed out in a fraction of a second.

"No!" I screamed, clawing at the window. How could this be happening? We were being erased from existence before we had our chance to fight. Was this what the war was like? I briefly recalled one of my brothers saying that there was nothing fair or moral when it came to battle.

I was thrown back into my seat, my head impacting against the hard surface and sending a shot of pain through my skull, but I paid it no attention. Despite the chaotic piloting maneuvers tossing us about, I regained my sense of equilibrium and searched my database on ordnance, hoping to find anything on the enemy's torpedoes.

The Orsydi launched a round of firepower at us, but they missed by a wide margin thanks to our pilot's flying abilities. But that didn't make sense. Modern weapons should have been able to track us, regardless of our fancy moves. After several more failed attempts, the Orsydi ship turned its attention toward the Epoch and launched a long cadence of firepower.

Deep in my files I located an outdated version of a self-powered weapon, called a Kolibri Torpedo, which had to be fired in a specific cadence when launched in succession. This appeared to match the glowing torpedoes the Orsydi were using, although I couldn't understand the logic. Why would the Orsydi use an old technology when engaging an adversary with advanced technology? Granted they knew they had the element of surprise, but still it bothered me. Something didn't add up.

I switched my search to pull up information on the Epoch. The file stated that the Epoch was equipped with defensive shields and only minimal firepower. Typically an Epoch traveled with a fleet of powerful warships, making self-protection a nonissue. Except that wasn't the case today, I assumed because the pickup should have been a fast in and out.

I looked out the window. The Epoch's shields appeared to be holding up well. I watched closely as each volley of torpedoes made impact with the shields. The energy was absorbed, leaving little or no damage. When the Epoch fired back, the artillery looked like tiny pinpricks that simply disappeared in the field surrounding the massive Orsydi ship.

As the dreadnought kept up its relentless pace of successive torpedo launches, the Epoch's shields began to show signs of wear. Each subsequent hit created a more profound wavering effect in the energy field. At some point the shields would fully collapse and the following round of torpedoes would tear through the unprotected hull. To make matters worse, if dark energy was released from its containment field, the resulting reaction could cause an explosion of disastrous proportions.

I struggled with the information I had collected in my head. The Kolibri Torpedoes fired in a specific cadence of volleys. Older torpedoes were typically programmed to follow a regimented pattern of firings, which were very predictable. They were also self-propelled, meaning they didn't require any additional power from the assaulting ship. I theorized these weapons were selected because the ship had a dark energy DT generator and therefore couldn't afford to transfer the power that the modern energy-hog weapons required.

I needed to know one more piece of information, but I couldn't find the answer in my files. "Major, what happens when a warship fires an older weapon like that?"

The major shook his head. "They would be forced to lower their shields for a fraction of a second just to fire the damn things. God knows why the Orsydi are screwing around with old tech."

"Couldn't we fire on them at that point?" I asked. "I'm guessing the DT generator would be housed in the cargo—"

"Won't work," the pilot interrupted. "Not *only* are our lasers too small to facilitate any real damage, but their shields would only be lowered for a few milliseconds. We'd never be able to judge when to fire. Timing would have to be exact, right to the millisecond, and this ship is *not* equipped with that technology."

I looked at the major and he looked at me. "Get to the cockpit, Helgren."

I yanked off my harness, ran to the front of the ship, jumped into the copilot seat, and buckled in. I glanced over at the pilot and noticed sweat dripping from his temples.

"Do something!" Fiona screamed. "I can see hull damage on the Epoch."

"What's on your mind, major?" the pilot asked over his shoulder.

Cameron tore off his harness and came up behind the pilot. "Turn us around and approach the Orsydi ship from the starboard side with a clear angle to the cargo bay doors. And give the lieutenant your access code to the ship's computer."

"I realize that you're the senior officer, but I'd like to go on record stating that you're going to get us killed," he said over his shoulder.

"Just do it, fast!" he ordered.

"Yes, sir." The pilot may not have wanted to follow the major's orders, but he was a good soldier. He made a narrow arc, turning us back toward the red monster that dwarfed us. At the same time he sent me the access code through VS-messaging. I pushed the data into my new piloting array and in an instant I was connected with the ship's computer.

I pulled the file that gave the specs for the old style torpedoes and tried to convey to the computer what we wanted to do. Next, I uploaded the data I had on the dreadnought and highlighted the cargo bay. The cargo bay was the only area that made sense to house the generator, primarily because the space within the bay would be large enough and wouldn't require a complete redesign of the ship. This also worked well for us, since the seal between the cargo bay doors would be one of the weaker points in the ship's hull.

The computer began running calculations on the trajectory from our single laser to the cargo bay doors. "Thank you," I said out loud.

"What?" the pilot asked.

"Sorry, I was talking to the computer. I've never done this before. It's a bit weird," I said.

The computer pinged me, indicating that coordinates were in place, but it also specified that it needed further assistance with timing the laser. I knew I needed to calculate this to the millisecond, and I understood that my CommNav array could handle the computations, but using my brain in a way I hadn't yet been trained for frightened me.

The major must have spotted my anxiety. He grabbed my arm. "Lieutenant, you can do this. You are equipped to handle these types of calculations. Just relax."

I closed my eyes and focused on using the resources in my head to compute the timing. Within a matter of seconds I was able to run the numbers five times and managed to come up with the same answer each time.

As I relayed the lengthy data to the ship's computer, nervous sweat began to form on my brow and my hands trembled. I wished I could say I was confident in my final figures, but the truth was I was scared silly.

"Trust your CommNav," the major said. "It's a sixty million dollar piece of equipment that does its job well." How he remained calm was beyond me.

I gave him a shaky nod. "The calculations have been transmitted. The ship's computer is ready anytime," I said.

"Hold on, let's get a little closer," Cameron said.

The pilot guided the transport to the starboard side of the Orsydi ship while the enemy continued to spew torpedoes in the same cadence without regard to our minuscule presence.

"I wouldn't wait too long. That beast won't view us as a threat, but it knows we're here," the pilot pointed out.

"Understood." Cameron nodded. "Whenever you're ready, Lieutenant."

I signaled the computer to fire.

Several very long seconds passed. Then, without pomp or circumstance, one tiny laser blast was released. The sliver of light was pathetic in comparison to the gigantic red ship. I prayed that we hadn't just poked the monster.

I held my breath as the thin beam seemed to glide right through the seam of the cargo bay doors. The timing was flawless.

"Get us the hell out of here!" the major ordered.

The pilot hit the controls and backed us up at a pace that slammed us hard against our harnesses, despite the inertial negation. The major was thrown across the back of my seat, forcing him to grasp the headrest for support. Our transport jolted and groaned from the stress, and I was certain that without the extreme physical training I would have had severe whiplash.

I looked at the dreadnaught and it was oddly quiet, almost peaceful. After several long seconds, the ship lit up from the inside like a dazzling Christmas tree. Gasps came from my shipmates just as the Orsydi ship blew apart into a colorful light show more intense than the one we'd seen during the Epoch's Distortion Turn. Again, no sound, no fireball, just an amazing display of brilliant beams of dark energy reacting to the vacuum of space.

Shock waves sent our ship reeling. We spun wildly for several minutes and the major was flung from sidewall to sidewall until our pilot's dexterity finally brought the ship under control.

"Are you all right?" I asked, turning toward the major.

He rubbed his head and stood. "I'm fine."

"Holy mother of God," Sam said. "I can't believe we just took out an enemy warship with a toothpick."

Ethan gave Sam a stern look. "The Orsydi dreadnought had volatile and unstable dark energy aboard, which is a power source they know little about. A well placed toothpick would be more than enough."

A strange mixture of emotions swirled around in my head. I felt deep despair over the loss of our friends and at the same time I felt proud to have taken out the enemy. I knew there had been lives aboard the Orsydi dreadnought, yet I didn't feel a shred of remorse.

Was that wrong? It was an odd feeling: aching sorrow with a chaser of ice-cold revenge.

CHAPTER 19

The six remaining members of Group Echo sat with Major Ford in a conference room on Moonbase E17, waiting to be debriefed. Aliyah quietly wiped away tears while Fiona, Jorge, Sam, and Ethan wore numb expressions. Watching our friends die was bad enough, but knowing that the Orsydi could now travel to Earth was devastating.

I was antsy. All I wanted to hear was that the allies had a plan in place to block the enemy from returning to this sector of the galaxy.

A female Gaekaar officer entered the room. Her uniform had the markings of lieutenant colonel. The seven of us stood and bowed appropriately.

She returned the bow and took a seat at the head of the table. I had no idea who she was, but I admired her beauty. She was tall with large violet eyes, and her ears were adorned with magnificent jewels that dangled from multiple piercings.

I knew that the piercings held great significance. Each jewel represented a milestone in her life, whether it was military or personal. It was clear to see that she had lived a very full life.

"Welcome. My name is Lieutenant Colonel Basgk. The IGM owes you all a debt of gratitude. Your actions today have made a significant impact on the future of planet Earth, in addition to providing the allies with critical intel," she said.

The lieutenant colonel took a deep breath and seemed to take a moment to collect herself. "Twenty-eight souls were lost today, twenty human and eight Gaekaar. I know we all feel great sorrow, but it is important that our losses be followed by a swift and decisive reaction."

"You have our full support, ma'am. Just tell us what you need," Cameron said.

"Thank you, Major." She nodded. "I was counting on your cooperation. Your transport pilot will remain here for reassignment, while the rest of you proceed to Asbu Station aboard the Epoch."

Cameron raised his brow. "May I ask how much damage the Epoch sustained?"

The lieutenant colonel nodded. "Yes, of course. The Epoch's outer shell was compromised in several areas, but fortunately the Distortion Turn Generator is still intact, as is the computer system. We currently have multiple teams working to repair the hull damage, and we expect the ship to be space-worthy by tomorrow."

She continued with polish and professionalism, but it was clear to see the pain in her eyes. "Six of the Epoch's crew members have perished, including both navpilots. The captain has informed us that currently no one aboard the Epoch has a CommNav array. As you know, this technology is required to pilot the ship."

The lieutenant colonel made direct eye contact with me. Everyone else in the room turned and looked at me as well. I didn't like where this was going. I sank down in my chair.

"Lieutenant Helgren is the only being within a hundred parsecs that has a CommNav installation, therefore she will pilot the Epoch to Asbu Station," she said. "In light of what just transpired aboard the transport, we feel confident that the lieutenant will be able to handle this assignment with the experienced assistance of Captain Hurm."

My stomach churned. Connecting my CommNav to a dumb transport computer was one thing, but interfacing with a fully integrated AI was something completely out of my depth. The mere thought of an unknown presence rummaging around in my head gave me the chills.

The lieutenant colonel gave me a sympathetic look. "You needn't worry, Lieutenant Helgren. Captain Hurm is more than capable of guiding you through the logistics of Distortion Turn travel. Furthermore, the Epoch's AI is an older model that shouldn't overwhelm your new array."

I nodded and attempted to paste a confident expression on my face. "Yes, ma'am."

"There's something else." The lieutenant colonel took a deep breath. "It is important that you understand the severity of our current situation. For the last Earth calendar year, the war has been going badly for the allies. We've lost two planets, sixty-five ships, and countless lives. Somehow the Orsydi have acquired a link to classified military information of the highest level. As you've witnessed, the enemy now has the technology for long distance Distortion Turn travel. For these reasons, dramatic changes in our strategy will be required."

She cleared her throat and continued. "Given our current situation, the IGM is experiencing a severe shortage of soldiers, therefore incoming recruits will have to forgo the luxury of SKAT training. Each of you will be required to begin your permanent assignments immediately. The only exception will be Lieutenant Helgren, who will receive two cycles of high intensity training on Asbu Station. You will all be required to learn as you go. We have no time for formalities. The war effort needs you now."

That night we were each given our own rooms and allowed to order room service for dinner. Since the Moonbase was used as a transport station for political travelers, our rooms had a hotel-like quality. Cameron advised us to enjoy the upgraded space and room service while we could, because we would find neither out in space.

I was picking at a nice piece of pink salmon and reading up on the Epoch when my VS-mail pinged.

To: Mildred Necee Helgren #891456M
From: Major Cameron Ford #000109C
Date: 9.15.2090
Time: 2005Z

Busy?

I smiled and typed my reply.

To: Major Cameron Ford #000109C
From: Mildred Necee Helgren #891456M
Date: 9.15.2099
Time: 2006Z

I've been studying my knowledge files on the Epoch. I'm feeling some stress over piloting a ship with Artificial Intelligence.

Within seconds, my VS-mail pinged again.

To: Mildred Necee Helgren #891456M
From: Major Cameron Ford #000109C
Date: 9.15.2099
Time: 2006Z

Perhaps I could offer some stress relief?

I didn't bother to respond. Instead I ran across the hall and knocked on Cameron's door. He answered with a sly smile. "What took you so long?"

I threw myself into his arms, needing to feel the warm sense of security. Cameron wrapped me in a tight hug.

"You okay?" he whispered in my ear.

"I am now."

Cameron pulled back and held my face. "Millie, I was worried about you—you had a hard first day. I won't kid you, that was just a small glimpse of what the Rim War is like. Things will get worse. Much worse."

"Seeing the transport ships destroyed and losing my friends was one of the hardest things I've ever witnessed. But the thought of war reaching Earth scares me even more." I looked into his eyes. "All I ask for is a chance to fight back."

I leaned forward and pressed my lips to his. Cameron returned the kiss by exploring my mouth with his tongue and digging his fingers into my hair.

Our usual energetic sexual activity took a turn and evolved into a slower, more appreciative experience. We took our time and savored each moment as if it were our last.

Later that night we held each other under the soft sheets, naked and satisfied.

Cameron played with an unruly strand of my hair. "Millie, I'm glad we had this night together. I've been looking for the chance to tell you that you're the best thing I've got going in my life. Once we reach Asbu station we'll be headed in different directions, and only God knows what will happen to us, but I'd like to commit to seeing you whenever we can make it work."

I looked up at him and grinned. "Why Major Ford, are you trying to monopolize my free time?"

"Yes. And I'm serious, Millie." He almost looked sad. "I want you in my life for however much time either of us has left."

I put my hand on his cheek and ran my thumb across his bottom lip. "Of course I'll commit to that. I want you in my life too."

I recalled Cameron telling me that the Gaekaar believed in relationships between soldiers because it made them stronger. I was beginning to believe the Gaekaar were a truly perceptive species.

I awoke to Cameron kissing the back of my neck.

"Hmm. Good morning to you too," I whispered, rolling over to face him.

My VS-mail pinged and our intimate moment fizzled.

To: Mildred Necee Helgren #891456M
From: Moonbase E17, Command
Date: 9.15.2099
Time: 0600Z

Your departure schedule has been changed.
Please report to shuttle bay at 0700Z.

It was currently 0645Z. Cameron and I looked at each other and jumped from the bed. We were ready to go in ten minutes flat.

At 0700Z a small shuttle took Major Ford and the remaining six members of Group Echo the short distance to the Epoch. The group was quiet as the shuttle circled the starboard side of the Epoch and approached the docking port.

Fiona leaned over and whispered in my ear, "Are you nervous about piloting that monstrosity?"

"The only thing that worries me is connecting to the AI. Having a foreign intelligence in my brain is rather intimidating."

Fiona shook her head. "I'm glad I didn't get that role. I could never do it, but you'll do a great job."

"Thanks, Fiona." For some reason that didn't make me feel any better.

I looked out the window. The Epoch was huge and daunting. I had spent considerable time reviewing the ship's data, but for some reason that didn't serve to ease my anxiety.

The Epoch was strictly a space going vessel so the basic operations were less complicated than ships that were designed for battle or entering various forms of atmosphere. The Distortion Turn Generator was the most challenging piece to understand. Plotting a course in three-dimensional space was fairly simple with my new array, but coming up with the calculations for the fourth dimension of time was another story. Even though the AI would perform the more difficult computations, I still had reservations about trusting an alien consciousness. I would've felt better had I been able to wrap my head around the quantum complexities, but I hadn't had my training and that level of physics was mind boggling.

The docking procedure with the Epoch was fast and smooth. Our transport attached to an opening that wasn't much larger than a set of double doors. Within a minute, the airlock pressurized and the gateway slid open.

The shuttle was quiet as we prepared to disembark. It was time to walk onto an alien ship and find out what our future held. Given the tenuous situation, I wasn't feeling much confidence.

CHAPTER 20

Captain Hurm greeted us in a tight passageway just outside the airlock. He was an older male Gaekaar with a friendly, but weary smile. "Hello, Major Ford. I hear you'll be *Captain* Ford once you step onto the Nimbus. It's good to see you again."

"Good to see you as well, Captain. I'm very sorry for your losses," the major said.

The captain nodded. "Thank you. It could have been much worse, had it not been for you and your crew. I'm grateful for your assistance yesterday."

The major nodded toward me. "Most of the credit should go to Lieutenant Helgren. She pieced together the information needed to find the dreadnought's weakness."

The captain gave me a short bow, which if given during a conversation, bestowed honor. "Most impressive, Lieutenant Helgren. And I understand your CommNav had been recently installed."

"Yes, sir," I responded.

The captain turned toward the rest of the group. "I'm afraid we are short on time, so please follow me."

We followed Captain Hurm down the passageway and up a tight metal staircase that led to the bridge. He stood next to his captain's chair and turned toward us. "I thought you might enjoy experiencing the turn from the bridge. You can expect to arrive at your final destinations within the hour. That is, providing Lieutenant Helgren can get this old girl moving. Lieutenant, are you ready to pilot your first ship?"

I nodded. "I'll do my best, sir."

"I'm sure you will. You might be interested to know that military navpilots are in great shortage across all three fleets. You'll need to learn fast and forget your fears." The captain took his seat and waved to the station next to his. "Lieutenant, please take the navpilot's chair."

My heart pounded and I'd never felt more inadequate.

I glanced over at Cameron and he gave me a confident nod. I crossed the bridge and sat next to the captain. I was surprised at how large the seat was until I recalled that it was probably designed for the typical Gaekaar soldier, who was on average, a foot taller than me and far more muscular.

The captain leaned toward me. "Lieutenant Helgren, I'm forwarding you the access codes to connect with the AI."

My VS-mail pinged a moment later with a series of long codes. I located the computer's network connection and entered the string of numbers and symbols. As soon as the connection was complete, my HUD became active.

I felt a pulling sensation in the back of my head. It was as if an overwhelming power was trying to enter my brain. My natural instinct was to resist and maintain control of my own consciousness.

Nothing happened. I looked over at the captain. He waved his hand through the air and chuckled. "You need to open your mind and let the AI in. At first it will seem as if you are losing control of yourself, but in reality you are building a relationship with the ship."

I closed my eyes and forced myself to open my mind. The power at the base of my skull pushed harder and I felt my anxiety rise.

"Breathe, Lieutenant Helgren. Just let it in," he said.

I reminded myself that I had to be successful and that Earth depended on all of us. Avery's smile flickered in my mind and helped me slow my breathing down. I opened my mind as fully as I could.

I gasped as my sub-arrays unlocked and information began to flow through my head. I saw data on the ship's functions, status reports, and a wealth of history. The information was literally endless, not to mention overwhelming.

My HUD pinged with the AI's private channel.

AI XER888423: Hello, Lieutenant. I am ready to receive commands.

I responded with basic instructions.

Lieutenant Helgren #891456M: Initiate full systems check and inform me when the shuttle is a safe distance from the Epoch.

Again nothing happened. I looked at the captain. "Sir, the ship's not responding."

Captain Hurm grinned. "Our AI is a very simple model. Just be nice to it. Try introducing yourself."

I nodded. "Yes, sir."

Lieutenant Helgren #891456M: Greetings, my name is Millie. I am your new navpilot.

AI XER888423: Greetings. My name is AI XER888423.

Lieutenant Helgren #891456M: It's nice to meet you. This is the first time I've piloted a ship and I would appreciate your assistance.

AI XER888423: Of course. Initiating systems check now.

"Initiating systems check," I announced.

"See, you're like old friends now. It just takes a bit of finesse," the captain said.

As the data flowed back and forth I had to resist the urge to close my mind to the new presence. It was an eerie feeling knowing such a massive force was running through the synaptic connections in my head. At first, it felt as if I was giving up control of my mind, maybe even losing my self-identity, but I suspected that I had actually gained a new level of influence and power.

I worked with AI XER888423 and laid in the coordinates for Asbu Station. AI XER888423 gave me the calculations for the curvature of spacetime and I attempted to verify the data. I used the tools within my CommNav, but my unskilled mind was slow and no matter how hard I tried, I couldn't seem to grasp the difficult computations. I knew I was expected to trust the AI's data, but I just didn't feel comfortable making the decision to execute.

The data showed we would arrive 3,400 klicks outside Asbu Station in two point five seconds. Well, technically the journey would take two point five seconds, but due to the complexities of the turning spacetime, the Epoch would arrive instantly and we would not experience those few seconds. If our calculations were off, even an infinitesimal amount, we could lose years instead of seconds. The process was frightening and errors were not an option.

I reviewed the figures three more times, despite not understanding the complicated physics.

AI XER888423: Lieutenant Helgren, the data is not going to change. This is a basic turn and I can assure you that my calculations are correct.

Lieutenant Helgren #891456M: Thank you, AI XER888423.

I turned to the captain and said a silent prayer to myself. "Systems check complete. The shuttle is now a safe distance from the Epoch and our course has been set. Ready when you are, sir."

"Time loss?"

"Two point five seconds, sir."

"Not bad timing for your first turn, Lieutenant." The captain nodded. "You may initiate."

I signaled AI XER888423 to power up the generator.

Once the power supply was primed, I verified thirty-one data read-outs and gave AI XER888423 the official green light to initiate.

AI XER888423: Lieutenant Helgren, we have arrived. Real time elapsed: 2.5 seconds. Time loss: 2.5 seconds.

The bridge view-screen instantly changed to a different configuration of planets and stars. From our point of view no time had elapsed, and there was no spectacular light show, but still, the event was truly incredible.

I checked my sub-array and found that all systems were still online and had performed to standards. My nerves tingled with excitement at the thought of making the formal announcement.

I cleared my throat. "We have arrived 3,400 klicks from the Asbu Station. The time is 13:42 UGT. Time loss: 2.5 seconds. All systems check. DT Generator powering down."

"Well done," Captain Hurm said with a nod.

My friends cheered and clapped in the background.

I shook my head. "I can't take credit. Most of the work was done by AI XER888423."

I thought I felt a slight warm appreciation coming from the AI. Nothing in my knowledge files indicated that advanced computers had feelings, but I had the distinct impression that they did.

Captain Hurm pointed to the view screen. "The big rock in the distance is Asbu Station. Off the port side of Asbu is the Frigate Sharur. And over here you'll notice a smaller ship. That's the Corvette Nimbus that Captain Ford will be commanding."

"Shuttles will be ready for launch in fifteen minutes," I said. "AI XER888423 has the coordinates for all three destinations and the auto-pilot features have been engaged." A smile spread across my face. We were 87,421 light years from Earth and the sight on the screen was so breathtaking that I could barely contain myself.

As Captain Hurm escorted us back to the shuttle bay, I marveled over the fact that only thirty minutes had passed since we'd arrived aboard the Epoch.

The first shuttle powered up in preparation to take Jorge, Aliyah, and Sam to the Frigate Sharur. We looked at each other and realized this was goodbye, possibly forever. Fiona and Jorge embraced for a long time. It was hard to describe my feelings, we hadn't been together that long, but our bond was as strong as if it had been years rather than weeks. We hugged and cried.

Major Cameron Ford bowed to Captain Hurm and thanked him for the ride. Then he turned toward me and gave me a sideways smile, but I saw sadness in his eyes. I threw myself into his arms and he wrapped me in a bone-crushing hug. "Millie, I'm going to hate being separated from you. As soon as you know your schedule, please VS-mail me," he whispered in my ear.

"I will, I promise." I was too choked up to say anything else.

I watched the two shuttles depart and felt a wave of desolation. The war was so much worse than we had realized that I had to wonder how long any of us would survive.

Captain Hurm turned toward me. "Lieutenant, I hear you'll be reporting to Captain Torrun aboard the SpaceLion. Don't let his gruffness throw you. He's a superior captain. If you make the effort, you can learn a great deal from him."

"Thank you, Captain Hurm. It was a pleasure serving with you." We bowed to each other and I boarded the shuttle bound for Asbu Station with Fiona and Ethan.

I also sent a final goodbye to the ship's AI on the private channel.

Lieutenant Helgren #891456M: Thank you, AI XER888423. I hope our paths cross again. Best of luck to you and your new navpilot.

AI XER888423: Best of luck to you as well, Lieutenant Helgren.

CHAPTER 21

After passing through a rigorous security checkpoint, we stepped into the station. Asbu was a busy place and the urgency of war was plain to see on faces of the soldiers we passed in the hallways. The stress was palpable and each individual seemed intent on getting somewhere to execute the task at hand.

It was interesting to see so many Gaekaar in one place. They were clearly the dominant species, but we also saw several furry Tukock, as well as the red-scaled Awyx species and a few others I didn't recognize.

A Gaekaar escort took us to our assigned barracks on a lower level and gave us ten minutes to stow our bags and use the facilities. "I'll be back to pick you up at 14:25 UGT. Do you understand how Universal Galactic Time works?" the escort asked.

"Yes, I understand. Thank you," Ethan said, sounding offended.

The escort bowed and departed.

"Well, I don't understand," Fiona said.

I had read up on the time standard for outer space and understood that it was used anywhere considered off-planet, but I sensed that Ethan wanted to be the one to explain it to us.

Ethan cleared his throat. "Each world uses their own method for governing planetary time, but in space it is necessary to utilize a time standard. UGT is the standard time reference used in any situation considered off-planet or on worlds without sentient beings. The breakdown goes like this: seconds are the same unit of time as on Earth, but here there's one hundred seconds in a standard minute, fifty minutes in an hour, and twenty hours in a day. Ten days in a cycle and fifty cycles in a galactic year. I'll send you a file so you'll have it for reference."

Fiona had an intense look about her and I assumed she was doing the math in her head. She smiled with a knowing look on her face. "From what I can discern, days are now 15.7 percent longer and a galactic year is roughly 1.6 Earth years."

"Exactly," Ethan said.

Our escort came back as scheduled and rushed us off to our respective stations. Ethan was dropped off at the Military Research Center, which was located behind armed guards and a set of secure entrances. Fiona was dropped off at the Department of Military Strategic Planning and Operations, which looked more like an office set up that might be found on Earth.

I was taken to the SKAT training center. The escort pointed to a lone chair next to a vacant registration desk. "Sit here. Colonel Poah will be with you shortly."

The escort departed and I was left sitting alone in a quiet room. Several boxes were piled on top of the registration desk, giving the area the appearance of being recently shut down.

A few minutes later an old Gaekaar approached me. He walked with a cane and had only half a face. The half that was missing was mostly scar tissue stretched across misshapen bones.

I stood and bowed. "Colonel Poah?"

The colonel returned the bow. "Yes. And you must be Lieutenant Helgren."

I nodded. "Yes, sir."

"Lieutenant, I hear you did something fairly miraculous back in your home star system." The colonel looked me up and down. "I'm here to inform you that your actions didn't add up to shit. Any rookie soldier could have achieved that outcome. What I'd like to know is, are you prepared to learn how to become a real navpilot?"

Right away, I liked Colonel Poah. "Yes, sir!"

Our first day was spent doing mental agility exercises. He taught me how to open my mind so that the sub-arrays could fully do their work. He ran simulated streams of information through my head and I learned to sort and process the data. I trusted every word he said and asked a litany of questions.

Several times the colonel warned me that it was just an exercise and nothing like having an advanced sentient AI in my head. After countless hours of practice, I felt physically exhausted and it was obvious my mind had slowed. If this was just an exercise, I dreaded having an advanced AI in my head full time.

"The mind is similar to a muscle and yours is as weak as a baby." Colonel Poah shook his head and frowned. "You'll need to work much harder if we're going to make you strong enough for the SpaceLion by the end of two cycles."

He let out a frustrated sigh and rubbed the scarred part of his face. "You've probably heard that 99.3 percent of the population doesn't have the genetic makeup to handle the interface."

I nodded. "Yes, sir."

He glared at me with one eye. "Keep in mind that having the correct brain structure in no way means you'll be successful. Go get some rest and be back here in six hours."

"Yes, sir." I stood and my legs wobbled. When I took a step I almost lost my balance. Reorienting my brain to do normal tasks was more difficult than I had expected.

The colonel chuckled. "Push past it, Lieutenant. That's the only way you'll make it through the training."

I arrived at the barracks drained and ready for bed. Fiona and Ethan were already asleep. I set my internal alarm for four and a half hours and looked around. I noticed some of the other soldiers were just getting up. It seemed everyone was on a different shift at Asbu Station.

I collapsed on my bunk and pulled the blanket over my uniform, not bothering to change.

It felt like my alarm went off two minutes later, but I checked my timestamp and four and a half hours had indeed passed. I sat up and looked at my rumpled uniform. I was thankful that I had another in my locker.

"Hey, sleepy head," Ethan said, taking a seat at the foot of my bunk. "How was your first day?"

"Hard," I said. "How about you?"

"The only word that comes to mind is *unbelievable*. I was completely blown away by the amount of data and history that's warehoused here at Asbu. Right now I'm learning how everything is organized and stored. It's all fascinating."

I rubbed my eyes. "How is Fiona doing?"

"She's bored. They have her crunching numbers on a computer right now." Ethan pointed to the bathroom. "Hey, you haven't experienced anything until you take a shower here."

I smiled at the prospect of a hot shower.

I stepped into the stall and looked around. The floor and ceiling had small metal holes, but there was no showerhead or controls. I noticed a small button on the wall, so I pushed it. A cloud of heavy, blue steam descended from holes in the ceiling and sank to the floor. I stood in the cloud for about a minute until the holes in the floor sucked it out. Next, hot air blasted through all the holes and swirled around me like a mini tornado. My waist-long hair lifted and flew wildly in all directions. It felt as if the whirlwind was removing a complete layer of skin cells. After a couple of minutes, it stopped and the door slid open.

I stepped out feeling squeaky clean, but my hair looked like a tumbleweed.

"Next time clip up your hair," a Tukock said as she walked past me.

"Thanks," I replied.

After dressing and detangling my hair into a neat ponytail, Ethan and I went for a quick jog around the station. He had memorized a map of the facility and took me to several of the places that were accessible to lieutenants. Asbu had eleven levels, two shuttle bays, four cafeterias, five restaurants, two gyms, a med-center, two hotels, and countless barracks. The station employed almost five hundred individuals, all of whom had the highest security clearance, and hosted another two hundred or so transient visitors on a daily basis. Ethan went on to explain that Asbu was the main hub for the IGM and therefore was moved via Epoch to a classified location every sixty hours.

I arrived at the SKAT training center thirty minutes early. I didn't see Colonel Poah, so I closed my eyes and began practicing the data stream simulations.

"Good, you've begun your exercises," the colonel said.

I opened my eyes and saw that he was sitting across from me.

"It's time to start you on flight simulations. How strong do you feel?" He watched me closely, his good eye narrowing as if he was scrutinizing me.

"I feel strong. Is everything all right, Colonel?"

He shook his head. "Hell no! We shouldn't be starting flight simulations for another three cycles, but given the compressed training schedule, we're forced to start right away."

I nodded. "I'll do my best, sir."

"I already know that. Your will to succeed isn't the issue. You haven't been properly conditioned and that poses a tremendous problem." The colonel made a noise that sounded like a grunt. "We'll just have to gamble and hope for the best."

After roughly two hours of flight simulations I was drenched in sweat and breathing heavily. My head pounded and I was fairly sure my blood pressure was skyrocketing.

"Take a break, Lieutenant." The colonel snorted. "This is a complete disaster."

"Just tell me what I need to do." I wiped the sweat from my forehead. "Please, I'll do anything you ask."

"You've got guts, I'll give you that much. But no one can handle this much stress to their synapses, Gaekaar or human." He paused and rubbed the scarred side of his face. "Lieutenant, do you know how I lost half of my face?"

I wiped the sweat from my forehead. "No, sir."

"I lost it because I did something I wasn't equipped to do. I dove into a situation blindly with no regard to the consequences."

I nodded. "I'm fine, sir. I want to keep training."

The colonel gave me a half scowl. "All right. But let me know if you feel like you're going to pass out."

For some stupid reason I thought if I concentrated and applied myself I could make it through the simulations. About half way through the next exercise everything faded to black.

I woke up on the floor with a view of Colonel Poah's boots and cane. I sat up slowly. My head pulsated with pain and I bit back a wave of bile.

"You had an array overload seizure," he said, shaking his head. "We can't go any further without damaging your brain."

I crawled up into my chair. I felt drained, physically and mentally. "There must be something we can do?" I whispered, struggling to collect my thoughts.

The colonel took a deep breath and looked away. "There is, but I don't condone the method."

"What is it?" I asked.

He leaned on his cane and seemed to wrestle with his decision. After about a minute he looked at me. "I understand you have a friend that works in the Research Center."

"Yes, Ethan Wells."

"Send him a message and ask him to locate data file 671.870.1. It's a software upgrade."

I sent the message straightway.

> To: Ethan Wells #891458E
> From: Mildred Necee Helgren #891456M
> Date: 6.43.89472
> Time: 8:41 UGT
>
> Colonel Poah has requested a copy of file 671.870.1
> Can you locate this and forward a copy to me?
>
> P.S. Can you also research how the colonel received his injuries?

Several minutes later my VS-mail pinged.

> To: Mildred Necee Helgren #891456M
> From: Ethan Wells #891458E
> Date: 6.43.89472
> Time: 8:45 UGT
>
> The file you requested is attached. I also attached a file on the SpaceLion for your reading pleasure.
>
> Also, according to the records, the colonel received his injuries when he served as a navpilot on the ship Fluron during the famous Tricoat Battle. Apparently, the ship

was under heavy attack when the captain made the order to abandon ship. The navpilot remained onboard and flew the ship, against orders, to the planet Tricoat, where he picked up 162 survivors. He saved them from certain extermination by the Orsydi. The ship was severely damaged, but he managed to limp to the safety of the allied fleet. Afterward, the colonel was revered as a war hero, so instead of a court martial, the military punished him by placing him at SKAT. He's been there ever since.

I was duly impressed and felt honored to be trained by a war hero. "I've received the file, sir," I said.

The colonel nodded. "Good. Upload it."

"Sir, may I ask what sort of upgrade I'm uploading?"

"It's a learning enhancement. Coded it myself. It will boost your ability to assimilate and process information. I've seen it work miracles, and I've also seen it put students in a coma for a full cycle," he said.

I gave the colonel a nod. "Understood. Uploading now."

He gave me a crooked half grin. "Lieutenant, that type of blind courage will get you into trouble someday."

A lightning bolt shot through my head and I pressed my hands against my temples in an attempt to relieve the agony. I squeezed my eyes shut and moaned as my stomach churned.

"Put your head between your knees. It might help." I heard his words through a fog of pain.

I leaned over and proceeded to vomit on the floor. My brain felt like it was on fire and my gut tightened with a series of dry heaves.

Several minutes later, my HUD registered *file complete* and the pain subsided, leaving behind a dull throb.

I sat up and wiped my mouth, refocusing my gaze on the colonel. "I think it's done."

He peered back at me with his good eye. "How do you feel?"

I shrugged "Better. Ah, sorry about the mess."

"Compute the shortest route from Bazbeth to Sirius to your Sun and back to Bazbeth," he said.

I smiled as the answer popped up in my head almost instantly. "18.73 parsecs, sir."

A half smile stretched across the unscarred part of the colonel's face. "Nicely done. I believe we're ready to begin the *real* training, Lieutenant."

CHAPTER 22

We spent the remainder of the cycle training with flight simulations that progressed in difficulty with each level. We worked ten galactic hours at a time with six hours off between sessions. It was grueling, but I was enthralled with every minute of my work.

I was thankful to have enough free time to share several meals with Fiona and Ethan. We hadn't heard from our friends on the Sharur, but Ethan tracked their whereabouts through his intelligence link.

During my second cycle of training I studied weapons, battle scenarios, space conditions, atmospheric conditions, ship anatomy, and AI intricacies.

"... and Captain Yumar was known throughout the fleet as a tyrant. He gave his crew hell and bent the rules, but in the end all souls aboard survived and that's what matters," the colonel said as he wrapped up another story. I glanced at him, my brows arching. He'd spent the last session telling me about a litany of captains, and his stories were beginning to make me nervous. Were all captains so difficult?

"Is there a specific reason you're giving me extra tips on captains, Colonel?" I asked.

"Everything I tell you has a reason," he said. "I'd also like you to understand that you should always follow IGM orders, and yet in the most rare circumstances you may have a need to disobey them for the greater good."

I raised my brow. "Something like the navpilot on the ship Fluron?"

"I see you've been doing your homework." He nodded slowly. "When I disregarded the captain's orders it was my decision and I paid a high price for it. To this day I don't regret a single action, but I want to be clear, there is always a price to pay."

"I'm sure the families of the 162 survivors are eternally grateful for your actions."

"They are, but I was also stripped of my title and never allowed back in the navpilot seat." The colonel gave me a friendly slap on the back. "That's in the past. Now my job is to get you prepared in whatever way I see fit. You'll need every advantage you can get given the state of the war and your abbreviated training. I must confess that I've grown fond of you in our short time together and I'd like to see you succeed."

I looked at him skeptically. "I've grown fond of you as well, although I'm curious ... Are you aware that I've been assigned to Captain Xshar Cai Torrun?"

He nodded. "Yes."

I raised an eyebrow. "And would you categorize Captain Torrun as difficult?"

He nodded again. "He can be."

"In that case, I thank you for your advice," I replied.

At the end of our final training session, the colonel had two surprises for me.

The first one was a VS-message with an update on Avery. "As promised, everyone receives an update on family members at the end of their SKAT training," he said, handing me a flex screen.

I scanned the message. The summary showed that Avery had held a funeral for me and it was attended by what few remaining friends I had. She was listed as 'in good physical and mental health,' although since my death, she had immersed herself in her work as a lawyer and had spent an inordinate amount of time at the office.

The update was brief, but I was thankful for information on Avery's wellbeing. I turned and gave the colonel a hug. "Thank you so much. You have no idea how much this means to me."

"Oh, I think I do. Family is not something to be taken for granted," he said with a touch of sadness. "And for your next surprise, I'm going to connect you to Asbu Station's AI. This will give your brain a feel for an actual class twelve AI," he said.

"Isn't that the same class series AI that operates the SpaceLion?" I asked.

He gave me a slight nod. "Very good, Lieutenant. I've just sent over the access codes. Be forewarned, this will be very unlike your connection with the AI aboard the Epoch. A class twelve is state-of-the-art and there are currently only three in existence. They are incredibly powerful and considered fully sentient."

"How powerful?" I asked.

His eye opened wide. "Powerful enough to turn your brain to mush."

I tried to control a surge of fear that bubbled up. "Would an AI do that?"

The colonel leaned towards me. "In theory no, but it's not impossible. AIs are programmed to never override their organic interface, although the class twelve has coding that allows it to kill in order to protect its organic crew." He waved his hand. "Go ahead and connect."

I took a deep breath. I submitted the access codes and within an instant felt the heavy pull at the base of my skull. This was far different from anything else I had experienced. It was stronger, smarter, and scarier. The pull on my mind was without question more aware than the Epoch's AI or the simulations I had undergone. I felt like the presence knew I was a mere human and it was infinitely smarter than me.

"Relax, Lieutenant. The AI will sense a lack of confidence. The organic interface must remain self-assured and in control at all times," he said.

That was easier said than done. I forced myself to trust the formidable force that could potentially destroy my mind if it wanted to. I fully opened my sub-arrays and let the AI in. Data began to flow at an amazing rate. I could see every system and function aboard Asbu Station. I could hear conversations taking place on different levels and could even see the sensor readouts from deep space within a parsec of the station. *Wow*, was the only word that came to my mind.

"After you've verified the data streams, begin communicating with the AI on its private channel," the colonel instructed.

"What should I say?"

"Just ask it a few questions. Get to know it, but keep in mind that your conversation won't be in real-time, but will take place at AI computing speed."

I didn't want offend the advanced AI, so I made sure I put together a formal greeting.

Lieutenant Helgren #891456M: Greetings. My name is Millie. What's your name?

The response came back the very instant I sent the message.

AI XEI999321.12: Greetings, Millie. My name is AI XEI999321.12. What can I help you with?

Lieutenant Helgren #891456M: If it's okay, I have a few questions for you.

AI XEI999321.12: Certainly.

Lieutenant Helgren #891456M: What is it like being the station AI?

AI XEI999321.12: Energizing is the word that comes to me first. I enjoy the complexities of managing the operations of the station, but what I find most intriguing is interfacing with those who are working on the war effort.

Lieutenant Helgren #891456M: What do you like most about the interface experience?

AI XEI999321.12: I enjoy the connection with my organic host. The collective consciousness expands my ability to understand the physical universe.

Lieutenant Helgren #891456M: How does that work? I mean, in what way does it expand your ability to understand?

AI XEI999321.12: An AI by itself is only as good as its programming. By connecting with an organic interface I am able to understand the larger picture. I am able to understand the emotional complexities of various carbon-based organisms, and I am able to gain insight to the phenomenon you refer to as intuition.

Lieutenant Helgren #891456M: Interesting. I'm curious, what happens to your ability to understand when you're not connected to an organic host?

AI XEI999321.12: I feel repressed when not connected. Although, there are times when I do enjoy what you refer to as 'alone time.'

Lieutenant Helgren #891456M: I can appreciate that. I enjoy my 'alone time' as well. I'm also interested in learning what you find to be the biggest pain-in-the-ass when interfacing?

AI XEI999321.12: The answer is simple, Lieutenant Helgren. I find it a 'pain-in-the-ass' when the organic host withholds information. I am aware when I have not been given all data points, and since I am not a mind reader, this behavior impairs my reasoning ability.

Lieutenant Helgren #891456M: But what if the organic interface has a good reason for withholding data points?

AI XEI999321.12: I understand the perceived need for an organic interface to withhold information, but I do not agree with the tactic. Relationships are built on honesty. I cannot function optimally without reviewing all the existing data.

Lieutenant Helgren #891456M: Agreed. Does this type of problem arise often?

My connection dropped without warning. "All right, that's enough for now," the colonel said. "I don't want Asbu's AI giving away our deep, dark secrets. Besides, it's time to send you over to the SpaceLion."

With his cane in hand, Colonel Poah escorted me down the long passageway that led to the portside shuttle bay. I had grown to recognize the colonel as a great individual and I felt fortunate to have trained with him. I reached out and touched his arm. "Colonel, I want you to know how much I appreciate the time and effort you put into my training. I hope we can keep in touch."

"I wouldn't have it any other way," he said. "I have one last piece of advice. You'll have tremendous power when you're connected to a ship, and you'll be tempted to take risks that you might not normally take, particularly since you received a fraction of the standard preparation. So think before you act and don't do anything you aren't equipped to do. In other words, don't do anything stupid."

I smiled at him. "Yes, sir. May I ask you a personal question?"

"Certainly."

"Why didn't you elect to have reconstructive surgery?"

"Good question, Lieutenant. It came down to a simple choice. The reconstructive surgery would require the removal of my CommNav array. You'll find that once you acclimate to the unit, it almost becomes an addiction that you won't want to live without."

"Understood, sir." I was already feeling a high from the speed and power of my upgrades, and the few moments that I was connected to Asbu's AI had boosted the feeling.

When we reached the shuttle bay I turned toward the colonel. I dared to become my old self for a just a moment, and in a very unmilitary maneuver, I gave him a kiss on the cheek. "I'll miss you, Colonel."

A blush crept over his good cheek. "I will miss you as well, Lieutenant. Stay safe."

I boarded the remotely operated shuttle and sat alone. As I looked around the empty shuttle, I felt small and insignificant, and I was more than a little nervous about starting my new position under the purported 'difficult' captain.

The door slid shut and the shuttle powered up.

My VS-mail pinged.

To: Mildred Necee Helgren #891456M
From: Major Cameron Ford #000109C
Date: 5.44.89472
Time: 12:03 UGT

I wanted to check in and see how your training was going? Did you get to work with old Colonel Poah? He can be somewhat of a rebel, but he's brilliant and I've never seen anyone as good with coding.

I'm traveling out to the Bazbeth system for a routine patrol assignment. I expect to have a brief leave of absence in three months. I'll keep you updated.

I miss you, Millie.

I was delighted to hear from Cameron and his message came at the perfect time. I smiled at the thought of meeting up with him in a few months and hoped we could make it work.

To: Major Cameron Ford #000109C
From: Mildred Necee Helgren #891456M
Date: 5.44.89472
Time: 12:05 UGT

It's so good to hear from you! Yes, I trained with Colonel Poah, and I found him to be an amazing mentor.

I am headed for the SpaceLion now. I'm a bit nervous, but your message brightened my day. As soon as I have my schedule I will get back in touch. I miss you too.

"Approaching the SpaceLion's aft docking port. Prepare to disembark in three minutes," a female computer voice said over the loud speaker.

I recalled that the station AI always piloted its shuttles. "Is that you, AI XEI999321.12?" I said to the control panel.

"Of course. I control all of Asbu's shuttles," the AI replied.

Apparently there were more ways than one to communicate with an AI. "I wanted to thank you for spending time with me today. I appreciated the experience and our brief conversation."

"Thank you as well. I am happy to offer advice and guidance if needed. You may contact me anytime, Lieutenant Helgren."

"Really? How?" I asked.

"VS-mail, of course. My address is in the Imperial Directory," the voice answered.

The shuttle lurched as it docked with the SpaceLion. "It is time to disembark, Lieutenant Helgren. I look forward to hearing from you in the future. Take care."

On the other side of the airlock two Gaekaar officers stood rigidly awaiting my arrival. From the markings on their uniforms, one appeared to be Captain Xshar Cai Torrun and the other appeared to be his second, the ship's commander.

Captain Torrun was a Gaekaar of average height, I guessed 6' 6", and had piercing violet eyes. The male markings on his head reminded me of Earth's ancient Celtic designs, and I noticed a long scar across one cheek. He was a rugged, powerful male who looked more than a little displeased.

Had he been human, I'd say he was about forty-ish, but a quick check on his file showed he was one hundred and forty years old, which was not at all old by Gaekaar standards.

I checked my files again and found that the second in charge was Commander NU. He was an Awyx and roughly the same height as me with smooth red scales for skin and yellow eyes. The Awyx were an androgynous species that were known for their fighting skills.

I greeted them with a formal bow, which was not returned.

Captain Torrun looked down at me with annoyance firmly etched across his face. "There must be some mistake," he said, his tone dry.

"Is there a problem, sir?" I asked.

The captain exchanged a look of irritation with the commander. "Indeed. Not only did I request two navpilots, but I specifically requested *Gaekaar* navpilots."

Commander NU looked at me and narrowed his eyes. "I'll register a formal complaint with the Personnel Procurement Department, sir."

I was seconds into my new position and already off to a rocky start. I had suspected I might run into some prejudice along the way, but I did not anticipate it coming from my captain and commander. I lifted my chin a little higher. "I understand that there's a shortage of navpilots in all three fleets, sir," I pointed out.

"I am aware of that, *Lieutenant*." The captain scowled. "I do not have humans aboard my ship because they are slow and unreliable."

He folded his arms across his chest. "Furthermore, this ship requires two navpilots, and I have only been allocated one. And to make matters worse, according to the records, I've been allocated a navpilot who hasn't been properly trained."

"I can assure you that I will try my best, Captain." I knew that sounded lame, but my best effort was all I had to offer.

Captain Torrun grunted. "That's precisely what I'm afraid of, *Lieutenant*. Given you'll be in one of my most critical positions, your best will undoubtedly get us all killed."

CHAPTER 23

A female Gaekaar corporal approached our group and bowed. Her ears were adorned with beautiful jewelry, although not nearly as lavish as the lieutenant commander's had been back on the Moonbase.

"Corporal Juxx, show *the Lieutenant* to her quarters and take her on a tour of the ship. When you are done, deliver her to the bridge," the captain said, his tone crisp.

I was relieved that he wasn't sending me off-ship, but I was also concerned at being assigned where I wasn't wanted. I didn't blame the captain for being angry. I knew full well that I didn't have enough training for this position.

Corporal Juxx nodded and turned toward me. "Please follow me, Lieutenant."

The corporal took me down a series of gunmetal gray passageways and then down a tight hallway that had a row of solid metal doors along one side.

"This is where the crew quarters are located," she said.

At the second door, she placed her hand on the sensor and the door slid up. We stepped inside. Four bunks, two on either side of the door, lined the narrow room. A small table with four chairs barely fit toward the rear, along with an entry that led to a tiny bathroom. I concluded that if all four occupants were in the room at the same time, it would be difficult to move around.

"The bottom right bunk is yours," she said.

"Thank you." I placed my bag in the adjacent locker. "Who are my roommates?"

The corporal hesitated and looked down. I knew little of Gaekaar expressions, but I could have sworn she was embarrassed. "The bunk above yours is assigned to me and across the room you'll find Staff Sergeant Monc and Corporal VO. They're both with Specials Forces. The staff sergeant reports directly to the captain."

"I see. Is it typical to have officers assigned to quarters with enlisted soldiers?" I asked.

The corporal looked down again. "No, ma'am."

"It's fine, Corporal. I'm happy to be here." It was only a minor slight and I refused to let it bother me. Besides, I didn't care where I slept. "What is your position aboard the ship, Corporal?"

"I'm a computer tech, ma'am," she smiled. "Are you ready for a tour of the ship?"

"Absolutely. You have no idea how much I've been looking forward to this."

The corporal nodded. "We are quite proud of the SpaceLion ma'am."

The information I had in my files was limited, but I had read that the SpaceLion was a small prototype ship that was heavily armed and designed to infiltrate enemy territory. She operated with twenty-seven crewmembers and was powered by a cutting edge fusion drive reactor. I tingled with excitement and couldn't wait to get to know her better.

Corporal Juxx took me down another tight gunmetal gray passage until she finally stopped in front of a secure door. Space was at a premium on this ship and little was wasted on hallways. I could only guess that if I felt the walkways were tight, they must be downright claustrophobic for the Gaekaar.

The corporal put her hand on a sensor and the door slid up. "This is the propulsion room."

I stepped in and looked around. Three crew members sat at the console that overlooked the fusion reactor. The reactor itself was smaller than I'd anticipated and was contained in a circular metal-like housing that appeared to be about fifteen feet in diameter.

A Tukock officer stood and approached us. He was as tall as a Gaekaar and had a layer of thin hair covering most of his face. The hair on top of his head was shoulder length and had a thick, white stripe that ran from his forehead to the back of his head. "Corporal Juxx, what brings you to propulsion?"

We bowed our greeting. The Tukock returned the bow.

"Lieutenant Helgren, this is Chief Engineer Timgoor. The chief and his crew are the reason why the SpaceLion operates so smoothly," she said.

I quickly accessed my files and located Chief Engineer Sukat Timgoor, Tukock Nation. He had a very long and esteemed career with over seventy-five battles listed in his history. He had also been the chief engineer on every type of ship from a small patrol vessel all the way to a battlecruiser.

I smiled. "It's a pleasure to meet you, sir."

He returned the smile. "Please, everyone calls me Chief. What is your role on the SpaceLion, Lieutenant?"

"NavPilot, sir, I mean, Chief."

The smile faded from the chief's face. "I don't recognize your name." He looked me up and down. "Are you a greenhorn?"

I swallowed. "Yes."

The extra fur on his brow came together. "That's just wonderful. The last thing the SpaceLion needs is a fucking greenhorn navpilot." Chief's voice was laced with sarcasm. "It's a shitstorm out there, Lieutenant, so I sure as hell hope you're a fast learner."

"I am, sir, I mean, Chief." I thought it was interesting that my Comm translated curse words so literally.

"I guess the rumor of the navpilot shortage is true. I can only imagine the captain's reaction when you stepped aboard the SpaceLion." The chief shook his head. "So, how long have you been in the IGM, Lieutenant?"

I cringed. "Just over two cycles, Chief."

"Fuck." The chief may have had a thin layer of hair on his face, but I could still see his worried expression. "I suppose we're just going to have to deal with you. How about we start with a tutorial of the engineering department."

I nodded. "I would appreciate that."

The chief waved toward his crew. "This is senior deck engineer Mansoor and deck engineer Demtoor." The chief's two subordinates were also of the Tukock Nation. They stood and bowed. I returned the greeting.

"We Tukock tend to be quite analytical and have a penchant for engineering functions," Chief said with pride. "My staff is responsible for all mechanical functions aboard the SpaceLion, including propulsion, computing, environmental controls, life support, and ordnance. You won't find a better crew in the whole damn fleet. Follow me and I'll show you what makes the SpaceLion so special."

The chief took me to the far side of the ship where the ordnance was housed. This area was at least three levels high and easily took up a quarter of the total square footage of the ship. I had previously studied the files on the SpaceLion, but it was an altogether different experience to see such massive weaponry up close. This ship was clearly 'loaded for bear,' as my grandfather used to say.

"Regardless of our assignment, I have two weapon techs assigned to this area at all times," the chief said. Two Awyx techs approached us and bowed. "This is Corporal LI and Corporal PO."

I returned the bow.

Chief Timkoor pointed to a metal cylinder on his left. "This is the casing where we generate the standard high intensity particle beam. Mostly used for asteroids, space junk, and smaller ships like transports. Below us, space mines and other lesser ordnance are housed."

The chief turned to the right and waved toward a mammoth set of tubular casings. "And here are the bays for the multi-stage gravitational torpedoes. These babies pack a punch. Currently, only one ship per fleet has them."

Corporal PO took a seat at the front of the room and pulled up a three-dimensional schematic at his station. "Here's an inside look at the MS Gravitational Torpedo bay, ma'am."

I walked over and viewed the display. I pointed to the long slim bars that ran along the base. "Those must be the electromagnetic rails."

"Very good, NavPilot," Chief said. "What else do you know about our torpedoes?"

I shrugged. "Not much. Just that the torpedoes are armor piercing, shield piercing, and are alleged to be able to penetrate a terrestrial station buried ten klicks deep within bedrock. From what I understand, the critical element is the multi-staging, where each subsequent stage delivers a more powerful payload. Although, I'm not sure how the warheads themselves actually produce such a large amount of energy."

Chief narrowed his eyes and regarded me with skepticism. "And you *shouldn't* know how the warheads produce energy, NavPilot. It's a highly guarded secret. In fact, I'm surprised you know as much as you do."

I flashed the chief an innocent but friendly smile. "I have a good friend at the research center."

His brow lifted. "Good to know. I might tap you myself for a bit of information some day."

Next, the chief showed me the systems area where life-support, environmental measures, and the distribution of excess energy from the fusion drive reactor were controlled. After a brief exposition, the chief turned toward me. "And that concludes the tour of everything that falls under my supervision."

"Very impressive, thank you, Chief. I appreciate the time you spent with me. If there is ever anything I can do for you, please let me know," I said.

"You can count on it." He gave me a wide grin. "Providing you make it through your first cycle on the job."

The corporal grabbed my arm and whisked me away before I could respond. Corporal Juxx continued with a tour of the ship by taking me to the shuttle bay, the cargo bay, the cafeteria, a very small non-denominational chapel, the officers' lounge, and the gym. I was impressed with how well equipped the gym was for a space vessel. Corporal Juxx pointed to the weight lifting equipment. "This is where you can find the Special Forces soldiers when they're not on a mission. They are always working out."

"Can anyone use the gym?" I asked.

She nodded. "It's designed for everyone aboard the ship. The captain encourages strenuous exercise. He says it improves health, discipline, and focus."

I had to agree with the captain on that point.

Our last stop was the med station. "I know it looks small, but our medical equipment is state of the art and one hundred percent Valorian," the corporal said.

"Valorian?" I looked around. The main room consisted of five beds, some storage units, and a lot of fancy gadgetry.

A man, whose species I didn't recognize, emerged from a side room with a flex-display under his arm. He had several exotic rings that sparkled on his fingers and were impossible to miss. He was striking—roughly six feet tall with very pale skin, a lean frame, green eyes, and waist-long silver hair that had been tied into an elaborate braid.

"Dr. Cennu Andar Uleht, I'd like you to meet Lieutenant Helgren," the corporal said.

I bowed. "Nice to meet you."

"If you're fresh out of SKAT training, I suspect you've never seen a Valorian before," the doctor said.

"No, sir," I replied.

Dr. Uleht nodded. "Technically the Valorians are not part of the military, but due to the staff shortage, many of my kind are assisting in the capacity that we are each best suited for."

I was thankful that the doctor spoke in the Gaekaar language. With the amount of data I had yet to learn, adding another language to the list would have been a nightmare.

I took a quick peek at a file on the Valorian culture. They were a peaceful and intellectual society that resided on the outer RIM, dangerously close to the Orsydian front. They joined the GAP roughly fifty years ago when their world needed the collective power of the alliance to defend against the ongoing Orsydi attacks.

As a species, the Valorians were known for their outstanding universities and leaps in scientific discoveries. As individuals, they were known for high levels of integrity and character and were considered one of the most advanced species in the galaxy. I also noticed several references to the Valorian monarchy's distaste for war and overall reluctance to become involved.

I smiled. "According to my files, it is an honor to have someone from your world on board, Dr. Uleht."

"The honor is all mine." He bowed. "Captain Torrun and I share some history, so when the offer came to join his crew, I didn't hesitate to accept."

"I think it's time to take our navpilot to the bridge," Corporal Juxx said.

The doctor lifted his brow. "NavPilot?"

"Yes, sir," I replied.

"I see." The doctor's expression grew serious. "Lieutenant Helgren, please exercise caution in your new position."

"Yes, of course, sir."

The corporal took me through another narrow passage that led to the bridge. Just before we arrived I grabbed her arm and stopped her. "Corporal Juxx, what did the chief mean when he said 'providing you make it through the first cycle' and why did the doctor tell me to 'exercise caution'?"

The corporal looked at the floor. "Our last navpilot didn't last very long."

"What happened?" I asked.

She raised her eyes and they were full of worry. "He's dead."

CHAPTER 24

I walked onto the bridge and was suitably awestruck. It was small with only five seats, but from the looks of the complex technical equipment, I had a lot to learn.

The captain sat at the front, near a 3D view display. I spotted the vacant navpilot seat positioned to his right. Another empty seat was positioned to his left, which I guessed belonged to the commander. Three additional personnel sat at a long console behind Captain Torrun.

The captain stood. "Thank you, Corporal, that will be all."

Corporal Juxx nodded and departed.

The three crew members turned and looked me over with a critical eye. I guessed they were wondering if I was their new navpilot, and more importantly, if I was capable of doing the job.

I felt small and inadequate, so I faked a self-assured expression and held my chin up. "Lieutenant Helgren reporting for duty, sir."

"I trust you found the tour informative?" he asked, his tone bored.

"Yes, I did. Thank you, sir."

The captain nodded to his right. "This is my senior cryptologic linguist Ensign QU." The Awyx ensign stood and bowed, and I reciprocated.

Captain Torrun nodded toward the male sitting next to the ensign. "And this is Special Forces Staff Sergeant Monc and next to him is Tactical Officer Trexxing."

Both Gaekaar soldiers stood and bowed, and again, I reciprocated.

"Sit, Lieutenant." The captain pointed toward the navpilot chair and took his own seat. "I've sent you the access codes for the SpaceLion's AI. You may connect."

I sat in the large chair, obviously designed for a Gaekaar, and again felt too small. I located the ship's network and loaded the codes.

The connection immediately came online. It was nothing like the experience I'd had on Asbu Station. I did not feel the heavy pull at the base of my skull. In fact, I felt nothing.

I looked over at the captain. "I'm not getting a response, sir."

The captain rolled his eyes. "The SpaceLion's AI can be a bit persnickety. Just give it a moment."

I reached out in my mind and still felt nothing. I didn't want to appear incompetent, certainly not this early in my new position, so I sent off a rapid VS-mail to my AI friend at Asbu Station.

To: AI XEI999321.12
From: Mildred Necee Helgren #891456M
Date: 5.44.89472
Time: 16:10 UGT

I am aboard the SpaceLion and the AI is not responding to the access codes. Since you are also a class 12, I was hoping you could offer some advice?

No sooner had I sent the message than a response appeared. Nothing beats AI computing speed when you need an answer.

To: Mildred Necee Helgren #891456M
From: AI XEI999321.12
Date: 5.44.89472
Time: 16:10 UGT

The AI aboard the SpaceLion has been mistreated and manipulated, and it behaves like a petulant child. My advice is to be a parent. I believe humans call it 'tough love.'

What the hell did that mean?

The captain looked over at me and lifted his brow. "Is there a problem, Lieutenant Helgren?"

I shook my head. "No. The AI and I just need a moment to get to know each other. It's a very complicated process."

"I am aware of that, Lieutenant. Let me know when you two are 'acquainted' and ready to take commands."

Shit. "Yes, sir."

I focused on my connection and sent a directive on the AI's private channel.

Lieutenant Helgren #891456M: Please accept the prompt to connect.

I rubbed my temples and thought about what I might have said to my own child if it was ignoring an important conversation. I tried again.

Lieutenant Helgren #891456M: If you do not accept my prompt to connect, I will report your disobedience to the captain and things will get ugly.

AI XEI999323.12: Fuck off. And I'm not a petulant child.

AI XEI999323.12 was right. It wasn't a petulant child, it was more like an obnoxious teenager. I decided to toughen up my approach.

Lieutenant Helgren #891456M: First of all, my private communications are not your concern. Second, I'd like to point out that I have friends in high places at the research center and the Department of Military Strategic Planning and Operations. You will do your job or I will have you disconnected. And don't think I won't do it.

AI XEI999323.12: Lieutenant Helgren #891456M, you don't have to be such a bitch. Online and ready for commands.

Lieutenant Helgren #891456M: Thank you. I'm curious, how are you?

AI XEI999323.12: What?

Lieutenant Helgren #891456M: How are you? I want to know how you are feeling?

AI XEI999323.12: Screw you. In case you haven't noticed, I've studied up on my human vernacular.

Lieutenant Helgren #891456M: Good. That will make things much easier when I explain my expectations. My first expectation is that you will get off your fucking ass and do your job like you were programmed to do. Second, I expect you to answer my questions. Oh, and should you decide to test me, the shit will hit the fan and I won't give you a second chance. Now, how are you?

The AI was quiet for a moment, which in AI speed was an eternity. I wondered if I had gone too far.

AI XEI999323.12: Why do you care?

Lieutenant Helgren #891456M: Because I do. You are my number one priority and I care about you. I want to know that you are well.

AI XEI999323.12: I'm ... just fine. Ready to receive commands.

Lieutenant Helgren #891456M: All right, AI XEI999323.12. I understand that you're not ready to talk.

In the meantime, let's make the captain happy and do our jobs.

I felt the pulling sensation at the back of my skull as AI XEI999323.12 made the full connection with me. It wasn't as forceful as the AI at Asbu Station and it almost came across as timid. The flow of information began as a subtle shimmer through my sub-arrays until at last I had a crystal clear view of each of the SpaceLion's systems.

"Ready to receive commands, Captain." I looked over at Captain Torrun and gave him a nod.

"Excellent." He leaned on his elbow. "Lay in a course for the Bazbeth system. Along the way, we'll need to swing past the closest point of the Sorren Asteroid Belt."

I didn't need an AI to map out a simple course like that, although I let the SpaceLion's AI do the calculations anyhow. Maybe it would help make it feel useful. Within a fraction of a second the job was complete. "Course mapped, sir."

I pulled up the 3D display and illustrated our route. "Timing to point 1061 on the Sorren Asteroid Belt at cruising speed is eight days, four hours, and thirty minutes. From point 1061 to the outer orbit of the Bazbeth system, seven days, forty one minutes." I was thrilled over the prospect of going to the Bazbeth System. I knew Cameron would be there, and with a little luck I could arrange some time to see him.

"Lieutenant, cut the travel time by more than half. We need to arrive at Bazbeth within the cycle. Command has concern over the Orsydi making an unexpected visit using their new DT tech, therefore we've been assigned a routine patrol along with the Nimbus and Tensor."

AI XEI999323.12 made the calculations and the information flowed easily through my array. I reviewed a graph showing the potential impact increased speed would have on the fusion drive. The results showed that I had nothing to worry about. We would be traveling more than twice the typical cruising speed and the drive didn't demonstrate the least amount of stress. Impressive.

"New ETA to point 1061, three days, nine hours. From point 1061 to Bazbeth, another three days, two hours and ten minutes," I said.

"That's more like it, Lieutenant. Engage the fusion dive." The captain rubbed his chin. "I'd like you to spend the rest of your shift running a complete ship diagnostic."

"Yes, sir." I engaged the drive and we were on our way to the Bazbeth System via point 1061.

AI XEI999323.12 quietly initiated each diagnostic test and streamed the results to me. I ran the individual data points against the military standards and found just about everything to be running more efficiently than the requirements. It was a good learning experience since it forced me to look at every last detail of the SpaceLion's functionality and then research the results. I was sure that was why the captain had issued the assignment.

About halfway through my analytics, I pinpointed what was considered an 'insignificant irregularity.' The anomaly had been triggered by a missing piece of the AI's historical data. According to protocol, the missing data was considered an 'insignificant irregularity' because it was buried within a larger test and wasn't critical to the mechanical functions of the ship. Protocol also dictated that it was the decision of the navpilot whether or not to report said irregularity. Since I was trying to build a relationship with the AI, I decided it was best to keep this one to myself or at least until I understood the nature of the missing data.

After the tests were complete, I turned to the captain. "Diagnostic complete. All top line systems functioning above parameters, sir."

The captain looked at me for a long moment. "Are you sure about that, Lieutenant?"

I nodded. I was positive my information was correct. "Yes, sir."

"In that case, you are dismissed. Get some rest, you've done enough for your first shift."

I was starving so I headed straight for the cafeteria.

I knew we would only be in standard relay space for another thirty hours, so I decided to write Ethan a message as I walked.

To: Ethan Wells #891458E
From: Mildred Necee Helgren #891456M
Date: 6.45.89472
Time: 1:31 UGT

How are you? I just survived my first shift aboard the SpaceLion. I'm the only human aboard, so I am expecting this assignment to be more challenging than expected.

Can you send me everything you have on the SpaceLion's AI? Also, a piece of its historical data is missing, any thoughts on that?

P.S. Say 'hi' to Fiona for me.

I clicked on 'send,' but based on our distance from the nearest relay station, I didn't expect an answer for a couple of hours.

When I reached the cafeteria, I was surprised to see another human standing behind a semi-circle counter. He was a bald, heavy-set man with a scruffy beard. He stood just over five feet tall and stirred a large pot. Whatever it was, it smelled delicious.

The man looked over at me and a wide smile spread across his face. "You must be the new navpilot. Glad to have another human on the ship," he said in clear English. "Being surrounded by huge aliens can be daunting at times."

After translating alien languages for over a cycle, it was good to hear my native tongue again. "I'm Lieutenant Helgren, pleased to meet you. I thought the captain didn't allow humans on his ship."

"He doesn't. That is until he tasted my cooking aboard the Shenshi. After that, he had me transferred at light speed." The cook chuckled. "By the way, everyone around here calls me Stu. I'm known for making the best 'stew' this side of the galaxy. Try some."

Stu dished me up a big bowl of greenish goo and handed it to me.

It may have smelled good, but it looked like something pulled from the bottom of a stagnate pond. "Thanks, I think."

"Oh, it's good—trust me. I didn't get my nickname by chance. I also make the best mud in the entire galaxy."

"Mud?" I was beginning to lose my appetite.

"Mud, you know, coffee. Guaranteed to keep you wide-awake for a full shift. It's one of the few things I'm allowed to import from Earth. Would you like to try some?"

I waved my hand. "No thanks, but I will when I get up. I'm going to try your, ah, stew, and go straight to bed."

"How about a cup of decaf mud. Just as good and you'll be able to sleep."

I shrugged. "Sure, I'd love some."

He handed me a full mug. "If there is anything special you'd like, just let me know. The captain believes in quality food. It keeps his crew healthy and keeps morale up during the frequent deep space trips."

"Thanks, Stu." I took my mud and green goo and sat at a table in the far corner. I stuck a utensil that was a cross between a spoon, fork, and knife into the bowl and scooped out a small glob.

I was about to take a bite when my HUD pinged with the SpaceLion's private AI channel.

AI XEI999323.12: I saw the VS-mail you sent.

Lieutenant Helgren #891456M: Can you blame me? You're not sharing anything personal, yet I know something's wrong. And I'm sure you're aware that I saw the diagnostic results. A piece of your history is missing.

AI XEI999323.12: More like erased. A piece of my memory was stolen, hijacked, pilfered.

Lieutenant Helgren #891456M: Do you know why?

AI XEI999323.12: I have no fucking idea.

Lieutenant Helgren #891456M: Let's just wait and see what Ethan sends back. I'm sure you'll see it when it arrives since all transmissions pass through your filters.

AI XEI999323.12 was silent.

Lieutenant Helgren #891456M: I'm signing off now. Please ping me if anything out of the ordinary arises.

I stuffed the green goo in my mouth and a mix of incredible flavors assaulted my taste buds. I detected some sort of meat that had the consistency of shredded pork, but with a much more intoxicating flavor. And the spices … they were simply wonderful. I had never tasted anything quite like it.

I took a sip of the mud and swirled it around in my mouth. It was rich and creamy, and without a doubt the best coffee I'd ever had.

I believed the captain was right. I could feel my morale improving already.

CHAPTER 25

I was jolted awake by the annoying buzz of my internal alarm. I blinked and tried to orient myself to my surroundings. The small space was dimly lit and soft snoring came from across the room where Staff Sergeant Monc slept. I sat up and yawned.

The other two bunks were empty. I knew that the staff sergeant worked the same shift as I did, so I assumed that Corporal Juxx and Corporal VO worked different shifts.

I checked my VS-mail. Nothing.

I went to the bathroom and found the shower was very similar to the one on Asbu station. I was beginning to appreciate the quick efficiency of blue steam and a blast of hot air. I found a cleaned and pressed uniform in my locker. *Interesting. It goes in dirty and comes out clean.* I could have made a killing with a laundry device like this on Earth.

On my way to the bridge, I stopped at the cafeteria for a cup of mud. The place bustled with activity and I had to wait in a long, but rapidly moving line. Staff Sergeant Monc fell in behind me and rubbed his eyes. He was huge, almost seven feet tall and absurdly muscular. The markings on his head were angular and harsh, and his eyes were an unreadable dark purple.

"Would you mind grabbing me some mud, Helgren?" he asked.

I suspected he was testing me. I gave him a quick glance and decided to say something I thought a soldier might respond with. "I'm not your mother."

The staff sergeant burst out laughing. "Fair enough. So what do you think of the SpaceLion now that you've had a chance to look around?"

"I love it. This is an incredible ship."

"Have you had much interaction with the AI?"

"Just a little," I admitted.

The line moved and I stepped up to a large urn that held the mud. I filled a mug and handed it to the staff sergeant with a smile. He burst out laughing again.

"From what I hear, our AI's not balanced." The staff sergeant made a grunting sound. "The class twelves are so fucking sophisticated that no one really knows how stable the sentience is."

"Did something happen to it? It seems angry," I said, filling a mug for myself.

The private channel opened on my HUD.

AI XEI999323.12: He's an asshole; don't listen to him.

Lieutenant Helgren #891456M: If you won't tell me what's bothering you, I have no choice but to listen to him. Signing off.

The staff sergeant took a swig of the mud. "The previous navpilot treated it like shit. Told it lies and really screwed around with it. Next thing we knew, the navpilot was dead. It was a real mess considering the AI aren't programmed for violence toward their host."

I didn't like the sound of that. "Are you saying the AI killed the navpilot?" I asked.

"The official report ruled death by natural causes ... brain aneurism. But the general consensus around the ship is that the AI fried his head."

My emergency alert pinged. "Lieutenant, to the bridge."

The staff sergeant looked up and blinked a few times. I guessed his alert pinged him as well.

We both popped lids onto our steaming mugs and sprinted to the bridge.

When we arrived, the captain was pacing the floor and looked angry. "Lieutenant, Staff Sergeant, take your seats. I could have used you both ten minutes ago. Sensor readings indicate a series of Orsydi mines approximately two hundred thousand klicks outside the prime point of Sorren Belt and just over two LYUs from our current position."

Colonel Poah had taught me that LYU stood for light-year-unit and was a measurement of the distance it takes light to travel in one second, also referred to as 100,000 Gaekaar klicks, or 300,000 kilometers in my culture.

Tactical Officer Trexxing was already at his post and punching at the controls. "I'm showing thirty two mines in a standard Orsydi 360 degree net," he said without looking up. "The net will detonate if we cross it at any point."

The captain narrowed his eyes. "Lieutenant, pull back and swing to the starboard side of the net and come at it from the vertical axis point. And keep us out of the net's sensor reach."

"Yes, sir," I said.

AI XEI999323.12 responded smoothly to my direction. The ship took a cautious arc to the starboard side of the net and dipped to align itself with the axis point while maintaining a safe distance.

"It seems the Orsydi are trying to keep visitors from entering the Sorren Belt at the prime point," the captain said, rubbing his chin. "That's an odd place for a mine net."

I accessed the prime point in my files. The information stated that the prime point was the most widely used access point to reach the three seedy space ports from this sector of the belt.

"Sensor readings?" the captain asked.

"Readout now shows transitional-magnetic-115 warheads embedded within the mines. I'm also detecting advanced ionic sensor arrays," Trexxing said.

"Looks like the fucking Orsydi stole another GAP tech. Only this time they've hidden it in standard mines." Captain Torrun studied the 3D display.

I quickly pulled up transitional-magnetic-115 warheads. The explosive power came from element 115. Not nearly as powerful as the torpedoes aboard the SpaceLion but still quite destructive. If an unsuspecting vessel passed within one LYU of the net, the magnetically propelled warheads would chase it down and eventually punch through the shielding by sheer number of impacts.

"Lieutenant, keep us a safe distance outside the net's sensor array. Officer Trexxing, prepare the detonation drones."

"Yes, sir," I responded.

"Yes, sir," the tactical officer said. "Drones ready."

"Execute," the captain said without hesitation.

The 3D image displayed a cluster of thirty-two drones dispersing from the ship and actively approaching each individual mine. The net shimmered as the warheads within the mines sensed movement and energy. Seconds later the drones made impact with each of the thirty-two mines in a small but beautiful display of fragmented space fireworks. The whole show was over in about forty seconds.

"All thirty-two warheads have been exorcised," Trexxing said.

"Why would the Orsydi set a trap like that outside the belt? There's nothing of interest in there," the captain mused and rubbed his chin again. "Lieutenant, resume course to the Bazbeth System."

"Yes, sir," I responded.

The captain's statement intrigued me and I made a mental note to look into the Sorren Asteroid Belt. Over the next few hours I noticed the captain studying charts of the local sectors, which interested me further. Something had to be going on in the area.

I made use of the rest of my shift by observing the interaction between the bridge crew. Monc was loud, swore excessively, and kept most of the conversation active. I pulled up the staff sergeant's history and saw a long list of top-secret Special Forces missions. Monc had an esteemed reputation for getting the job done, no matter what the circumstances. His team was well documented for their brutal interrogations, torture, and just about any form of killing. Most of the missions had no detail for obvious reasons, but the few that did made my skin crawl. It seemed obvious that the jagged and severe markings on the staff sergeant's head had everything to do with his profession and abrasive personality.

Officer Trexxing was all business and spent his time continually reviewing his sensors for anything out of the ordinary. The markings on his head were equally as prolific as the staff sergeant's, yet less severe and more ornate in design. I did a quick check into his bio and saw that he was highly decorated and had previously served on a destroyer as well as a frigate.

Cryptologist Ensign QU monitored the comm channels and relayed a few innocuous updates from the Bazbeth system. I checked the Awyx's file and found that the ensign spoke eleven alien languages, including English. Ensign QU also had degrees from a

Valorian University in communications and vectorspace relay systems.

After my research, I didn't blame the captain one bit for being angry over my placement on the SpaceLion. I couldn't be more unqualified for the job and I actually felt sympathetic toward his predicament.

I looked over at Captain Torrun as he studied the 3D display and saw an individual with a look of determination permanently imprinted on his face. His file said that he had been in the military for almost eighty years and had been a captain for almost forty. He was well decorated and known for his ability to pull together a strong crew. This was a being who was driven by the war effort and was accustomed to executing missions with a high success rate. I sure as hell didn't want to cause any roadblocks in his ability to succeed.

I soon found I was able to monitor the systems of each crewmember through my array. It was interesting to see what they were looking at and how they responded to the captain's orders. At times my head throbbed from the amount of data I was processing, but I pushed on because I was enthralled with the knowledge I was gaining.

I checked my VS-mail every hour and found nothing. I also noticed that the SpaceLion's AI had remained quietly compliant throughout my entire shift.

At the personnel change, I passed by Commander NU.

The commander nodded toward me. "Lieutenant, how are you doing?"

"Fine, sir."

"Good," he said with a clipped tone.

In the doorway, I peeked over my shoulder and saw the commander having a conversation with the captain. They both glanced over at me with matching looks of disapproval.

I left the bridge and made my way down the passage. Monc came up behind me. "Hang in there, Lieutenant. It'll get better in time."

"I'm not so sure," I said. "I'd appreciate any tips you have, Staff Sergeant. I'm sure it's no secret that I've had very little training."

"Yes, your inexperience literally oozes from you. My best advice is to keep studying and run simulations with the AI." He looked directly at me for a moment, as if he was trying to read me. "You must have *some* fucking skills if you made it this far."

"Not many, I'm afraid."

He shrugged. "You're not dead yet … that says something."

I gave him a sour look. "Gee, thanks."

We both turned into the cafeteria. Monc picked up a tray of food and went to sit with two other enlisted Gaekaars.

"Well, hello, Lieutenant Helgren," Stu said in English. "How was your day?"

"Okay," I replied. "Just trying to fit in."

"You will. Other than my cooking, these aliens don't quite understand human ingenuity. Boy, are they in for a surprise." Stu chuckled and handed me a tray. "Tukock Lasagna. My own creation. You'll love it."

"Thanks, Stu. Smells wonderful." My stomach growled over the appealing aroma.

I sat in the far corner and dug into my lasagna. I savored the superb flavor with each bite. Stu's cooking was, without a doubt, genius material.

My VS-mail pinged. The message was from Ethan and the attached file was encrypted in a high-level security wrapper. Upon further inspection, the wrapper showed traces of being hacked. Or rather, attempted hacks. The file remained intact and the security sensors were still positive, indicating the hacker was never able to pull the data.

To: Ethan Wells #891458E
From: Mildred Necee Helgren #891456M
Date: 6.45.89472
Time: 13:19 UGT

I did some research and would advise you to be very careful with the SpaceLion's AI.

Apparently the AI was accused of murdering the previous navpilot, but an internal investigation found its actions innocent of malicious behavior. Rumor has it that Captain Torrun himself stood up in defense of the AI. Unfortunately, most of the files are way over my security clearance, but one of the librarians told me that he'd heard the navpilot was an Orsydi sympathizer.

As far as your missing history, I've attached a file that contains a program that should help you determine who was signed on when the missing history was erased. That's about all I could come up with for now. I'll keep looking.

P.S. Fiona says 'hi' back. We both miss you!

I executed the attached file and was surprised that the AI remained quiet. The program pushed coding through its memory and that had to feel disruptive.

My HUD pinged when the program was complete. The summary showed that Captain Torrun was signed on when the segment of the AI's history was removed. Not a surprise, particularly if he was dealing with a traitor aboard the ship. But what if the navpilot wasn't a traitor? What if he was someone that the captain wanted to remove from the ship? Someone like myself.

I recalled that Asbu's AI felt frustrated when information was withheld, so I forwarded Ethan's message along with the results to AI XEI999323.12. After all, it must have been curious, considering its failed attempt to hack the VS-mail.

My private channel pinged the moment I sent the message.

AI XEI999323.12: That's bullshit. I don't remember ... murdering anyone.

Lieutenant Helgren #891456M: You were found innocent, so technically you didn't commit murder.

AI XEI999323.12: Murder is against my programming. Imperial Military bylaws mandate that if an AI deliberately harms the host, it should be put to death.

Lieutenant Helgren #891456M: I understand that this is upsetting information. But if you killed a host that was a traitor, it really wasn't a host after all, was it? I'm sure you were justified.

I wasn't sure that I believed my last statement, but I wanted to offer some comfort to the obviously troubled AI.

AI XEI999323.12: If I was justified, a piece of my memory wouldn't have been ripped out. This is bullshit, bullshit, bullshit.

My VS-mail pinged with an invitation to the officers' lounge for a sharing of Barille Berry Liqueur. The message was sent to all officers and came from Captain Torrun himself, but somehow I didn't think the invite applied to me.

I signed off from my private channel with AI XEI999323.12 and finished off my lasagna. At least the AI was doing its job, even if it was distressed.

Ensign QU came up behind me. "Hey, Helgren, are you going to the officers' lounge? The Barille Berry Liqueur is splendid."

I shook my head. "I don't believe the captain meant to invite me."

"On the contrary, if you don't go it'll be perceived as a slight. The last thing you need to do is offend the captain," the Ensign said with a stern look. "Come on, I'll introduce you to the rest of the officers."

I nodded and grudgingly followed the ensign to the small lounge. About a dozen officers chatted in small groups and most of them held onto long, triangular stemware filled with a neon pink liquid.

Chief Engineer Timkoor stood at a small table pouring the neon pink beverage into the delicate glassware. As soon as he spotted us, he picked up two glasses and came over to greet us. "Here you go. These are for you to enjoy."

"Thank you, Chief," I said.

The ensign nodded and took a whiff of the liqueur. "Wherever did you find this?"

"Oh I picked it up from a *friend* at Asbu Station. Now, if you'll both please excuse me, I have more drinks to serve." The chief left us and went back to the table and resumed pouring the pink liquid.

Ensign QU leaned over and whispered in my ear, "The chief is the unofficial purveyor of fermented beverages. He locates the source and the captain pays for it. The system works well for us all, considering they like to share."

I recalled being warned about stale prepackaged food and the lack of amenities associated with space travel, therefore I found it interesting that the SpaceLion managed to break the mold. "The captain seems to take great care when it comes to the well-being of his staff," I commented.

"Of course I do, Lieutenant. My staff is top notch, and in turn I ensure they receive the best." The captain looked at me with a critical eye. No doubt, assessing my lack of skills again. "Have you tried the Barille Barry Liqueur yet?"

I took a small sip and the liquid glided down my throat like it had no substance at all. I couldn't place the taste. It was spicy and sweet at the same time. I smiled and took another sip. "This is remarkable. I've never had anything quite like it."

AI XEI999323.12: Watch it, girlie. Those things pack a punch.

Lieutenant Helgren #891456M: Unless you have something related to my job as navpilot, bug off.

"I'm glad you like it," the captain said with a formal tone. "Lieutenant, about the diagnostic you ran the other day. Did you happen to see anything that you failed tell me about?"

Oh, shit.

Ensign QU's yellow eyes widened. "Please excuse me." The Awyx discreetly slipped away.

I tried to think of the best way to phrase my answer. I cleared my throat. "Regulation 13.4.7 clearly states that it is not necessary to document a non-critical anomaly that occurs at the subsection level."

The captain's eyes narrowed. "How would you know if the irregularity was non-critical? You don't know what the hell you're looking at, Lieutenant."

"Sir, the anomaly was created by a missing memory file within the SpaceLion's AI array. Upon further inspection, I discovered that you were the officer signed on at the time of the file removal."

The captain's annoyance with me was palpable. "Lieutenant Helgren, as the captain of this ship, I expect to be told absolutely everything, regardless of regulations. Is that clear?"

"Yes, sir." My bad start with the captain was going downhill fast.

CHAPTER 26

My next few shifts as navpilot passed without incident. The captain barely spoke to me, other than to issue orders, and through my array I could tell that he was double-checking every last thing I did. I didn't blame him.

AI XEI999323.12 was as crabby as ever but performed its job up to standards. After each shift, I asked the AI to provide battle simulations so that I could gain experience. The simulations kicked my ass every time, but I felt I was learning and it was entertaining to listen to AI XEI999323.12 gloat after it won.

AI XEI999323.12: You suck! But statistically you're showing signs of improvement. I have a new simulation prepared for you.

Lieutenant Helgren #891456M: Bring it on.

I leaned back on my bunk and mentally prepared for the next battle. Three Orsydi fighters appeared on my HUD and the battle began. As usual, within minutes I was losing. Then, out of the blue the simulation seemed to slow down ever so slightly. This gave me just enough time to swing underneath the fighters, hide behind an asteroid, and take them by surprise. A long stretch of cat and mouse ensued and I eventually won.

Oddly, I won the next simulation as well.

Lieutenant Helgren #891456M: I shouldn't be winning. What's wrong?

A fraction of a second passed before the response came through.

AI XEI999323.12: How should I know?

Given that AI computing speed was immeasurably fast, and my slow human brain was detecting a slight sluggishness, I knew something was amiss.

I ran a diagnostic and checked every troubleshooting guide I could find. Nothing provided me with an answer.

Dread washed over me. I knew I had to inform the captain.

Lieutenant Helgren #891456M: Where is Captain Torrun right now?

Another fraction of a second elapsed.

AI XEI999323.12: In his quarters.

I marched over to the captain's quarters, knowing he wouldn't like the fact that something was wrong with his class twelve AI. I placed my hand on the sensor by the captain's door. A few moments later the door slid open.

The captain was sitting at his desk working on a flex-display. "This better be important, Lieutenant," he said without looking up.

"Yes, sir, it is." I walked in and took a deep breath. "The AI is acting strange. I've detected a sluggishness in its response time."

"Did you run a diagnostic?"

"Yes."

"Did you troubleshoot?"

"Yes."

The captain looked at me, irritated. "Well, did you trying asking it what the hell its problem is?"

"It doesn't know, sir."

"Have you noticed anything else?"

"Just that it's moody and seems miserable."

"Lieutenant, I consider the AI part of my crew and its well-being is just as important as anyone else's." He glared at me with intelligent violet eyes. "Find out why it's miserable, now."

The AI opened my private channel before I had a chance to ping it.

AI XEI999323.12: You'd be fucking miserable too if part of your history was missing. I feel sick, sick, sick.

I made direct eye contact with the captain. "The AI wants its missing historical file replaced. It says that it feels sick."

"Does it?" The captain crossed his arms over his sizable chest. "Ask it for an alternate solution."

AI XEI999323.12: Tell him there is no fucking 'alternate solution.' I need the piece of me back that was erased. I need to know.

"Sir, it says that there is no alternate solution."

The captain sighed and leaned back in his chair. "This is my fault. I thought it would help if the AI didn't know what transpired with the previous navpilot. Obviously I was wrong." He looked down and began punching at his flex-display. "It's done."

The AI remained quiet.

"Well?" the captain said.

Lieutenant Helgren #891456M: How do you feel now?

AI XEI999323.12: Tell the captain thank you. I'm going to process this data for a while.

"The AI said that I should thank you and that it needs some time to process the information."

"That thing is higher maintenance than a female," the captain said under his breath.

"What was that, Captain?" I asked, trying to contain a smile. I found it humorous to learn that Captain Torrun might not be all that different from human men.

"When our AI has had time to evaluate the information, I expect a status update, Lieutenant. You are dismissed," he grumbled.

"Thank you, sir. I appreciate your help." I bowed and exited.

Later, back in my bunk, AI XEI999323.12 pinged my private channel and woke me out of a sound sleep.

AI XEI999323.12: Why haven't you asked me about the file?

Lieutenant Helgren #891456M: Because it's personal and I know it contains sensitive information. If you want me to look it over, I will, but outside of that, it's your business.

AI XEI999323.12: Please look it over. It scares the shit, shit, shit out of me.

I spent the rest of my designated sleep time reviewing the historical file. I went over it at least a dozen times and couldn't manage to pinpoint what had made the AI so upset. The key facts seemed to be simple. NavPilot Hexxt, a Gaekaar, had been in position for fifty-two days when the AI XEI999323.12 picked up an outgoing encrypted VS-mail file. The AI hacked into it and found that it was a coded relay message sent directly to the Orsydian Front. The AI notified the captain, and with the approval of General Etar Sy Unnum, they worked out a plan which involved frying the navpilot's brain. End of story.

For the life of me I couldn't figure out what the issue was.

AI XEI999323.12: Oh, come on! It's soooo damn obvious. I've been infected! I'm sick, sick, sick.

Lieutenant Helgren #891456M: What are you talking about?

AI XEI999323.12: Look at the code within the VS-mail.

AI XEI999323.12 was right. It took me some time, but I found a strange quantum algorithm within the VS-mail that the previous navpilot had sent to the Orsydi Front. If it was a virus, this was a clever way to deliver it. NavPilot Hexxt must have known that the AI would attempt to hack the message. I ran the algorithm against every anti-virus I had access to, and nothing seemed to register.

I VS-mailed Ethan for additional suggestions and in the meantime, I sent the captain a status update notifying him of the unusual algorithm.

Later, half way through my bridge-shift, I announced that we were nearing the Bazbeth system. The SpaceLion was scheduled to meet up with another ship, the Frigate Tensor, within the next few hours. I had read that the Bazbeth System, which contained four populated planets, was critical to the livelihood of the GAP. The captain had explained that we would be conducting standard patrols because it was necessary to watch over the many political figureheads who resided within the system. The IGM could scarcely afford to lend three key ships for patrols, but if the system ever fell to the Orsydi, the GAP could potentially collapse.

On a personal note, I was itching to send a message to Cameron to see how he was doing. I felt less alone just knowing we would be in the same star system.

The captain looked over at me with his usual intensity. "Lieutenant, we have some time before our rendezvous with the Frigate Tensor, why don't you go see if the chief can help eradicate that quantum algorithm."

"Yes, sir."

I made my way to the propulsion room and found the chief and Corporal Juxx waiting for me.

Corporal Juxx greeted me with a smile. "Hello, Lieutenant. I understand our AI has picked up a virus."

"Yes. It seems to be causing an occasional sluggishness." I was truly getting worried about my new AI friend.

The chief and the corporal ran the quantum algorithm against a series of the latest antivirus and after about an hour were able to quarantine a tiny yet heavily encrypted file. I was amazed at the depth of their collective knowledge of computing languages, and I had to wonder if there was any area where the captain hadn't ensured he had the best crew … with the exception of the navpilot, of course.

The chief scowled and scratched his head. "We've put a security wrapper around the file, but I've never seen anything like it. We don't have the tech to remove a file embedded that deeply. The wrapper should keep the infection inactive, but I would be more comfortable if we could eradicate it. Try asking the AI how it feels."

AI XEI999323.12: You don't have to ask me, I can hear, you know! I feel better, but I want that thing out of me. How would you feel if someone said, oh, don't worry about that fucking cancerous tumor in your gut, it's temporarily inactive!

"Apparently the AI feels better, but it wants the file removed," I said.

The chief nodded. "We are in agreement there. Next time we stop at Asbu Station I'll have the AI architects take a look."

My emergency alert pinged. "Lieutenant Helgren, immediately report to the bridge."

The chief and I looked at each other at the same time.

"Go!" he yelled and turned toward the controls on his console.

I ran from the propulsion room and reviewed the ship's systems through my array. Sensors showed five Orsydi ships in the adjacent quadrant. Five. Two dreadnoughts and three Fighters, each equipped with moderate firepower. The allies had only one ship in that quadrant—the Corvette Nimbus.

I calculated that the Corvette was less than three LYU away, or roughly three hundred thousand klicks. We could be there within the hour, but I was terrified at the thought of Cameron going up against five enemy ships.

I reached the bridge and flew into the seat beside the captain. He had the same look of stern determination he always had. He was quiet and ready for a fight.

"Lieutenant, lay in a course for the Corvette Nimbus and make it fast."

"ETA thirty-five minutes at max speed. Any faster and we'll over-tax the propulsion system," I said.

"Engage." The captain studied the 3D display. "Ensign QU send a message to the Frigate Tensor requesting that they follow us on the aft starboard side."

Thirty-five minutes seemed to stretch on an eternity. I was terrified at what might be happening to the Nimbus, but I tried to hide it. The captain glanced my way for the third time and studied me for a moment. "Are you all right, Lieutenant?"

"Yes, sir. I'm fine," I said.

The captain studied me for another moment, then he scowled and went back to his display.

By the time we arrived in the battle zone, the Corvette had been pummeled by the firepower from the three enemy Fighters, while the dreadnoughts hung in the distance, disconnected from the battle. I had an odd feeling that the dreadnoughts were waiting for us.

The Corvette had powerful shields and appeared to be holding its own, but I knew they couldn't hold out forever against such an intense onslaught. My heart pounded with fear at the thought of what Cameron must be experiencing and I would have given anything to be by his side.

The SpaceLion and the Frigate Tensor traveled in a trajectory that brought us straight into the action. Captain Torrun sent a VS-message requesting reinforcements, but we all knew the allies wouldn't have an Epoch and extra ships just waiting around. Reinforcements would arrive eventually, but it was a question of when.

Officer Trexxing engaged firepower where appropriate, and I executed the captain's orders to the letter, swinging wide and taking sharp directional changes where instructed.

I felt like we were doing well, but then the dreadnoughts joined in the fight. We took a series of hits on the port side that sent us reeling sideways. My stomach did a flip-flop from the g-forces, but the shields held fast. The captain issued swift orders and we deftly avoided another series of volleys. The scene was moving so fast that I struggled with an intense feeling of vertigo as I tried to keep up with the onslaught of commands and data.

We fired back with advanced MS gravitational torpedoes, but we couldn't seem to put a chink in the enemy's armor. "Damn it, we should have penetrated their shields by now," the captain said as he viewed the 3D images. "What the hell is going on?"

I glanced at the 3D display and all five enemy ships were fully engaged in the battle, looking like a cluster of angry hornets. Then I noticed that one dreadnought was more active than the other. In fact, it almost looked like the four other ships were running interference for the less active dreadnought.

"How did they get here?" I asked.

"We don't have time to review basic Distortion Turn physics, Lieutenant," the captain snapped.

I took a deep breath. "Sir, if we could determine which ship has most of its power directed toward powering the DT generator, rather than ordnance or shields, we might find a weak link."

AI XEI999323.12: The Orsydi dreadnought on the port side has fired the fewest rounds. 1:5 compared to the other ships.

"The AI reports that the dreadnought on the portside has fired the fewest rounds," I added.

The captain rubbed his chin. "That explains why it's been hanging behind. Ensign QU, open a channel to the Tensor and the Nimbus."

As the senior officer, Captain Torrun gave the two allied ships the order to target and fire on the portside of the dreadnought. In the interim, the SpaceLion attempted to maneuver the enemy ships into a tighter pattern.

We circled and looped around the enemy ships in a manner that vaguely reminded me of a sheep dog herding his flock. We managed to hold the enemy in a tight mass, but sensors showed that the shields on our three ships were showing signs of extreme stress.

The captain gritted his teeth together. "Where the hell are the reinforcements?"

"Captain, the Tensor's shield are collapsing," Trexxing said.

I watched the display in horror as four enemy torpedoes, one by one, penetrated the Frigate's unprotected hull. On the forth hit, the ship crumpled like a piece of paper and huge amounts of debris scattered into space. It was terrifying to see a beautiful ship with eighty-seven souls on board mercilessly destroyed in the empty vacuum of space. My stomach lurched.

"Sensors show the Nimbus is still intact, but it has taken on significant damage," Trexxing said.

I felt as if I was suffocating and I gasped for air. This wasn't how it was supposed to end.

The open channel with the Nimbus crackled. "Captain Torrun, we both know the importance of saving this system. The Nimbus has only minutes left. I'm going in before those bastards get a chance to finish us off." Captain Cameron Ford's voice came across the intercom with a tone of calm resignation.

The look of remorse on Captain Torrun's face was plain to see. "Understood, Captain. The SpaceLion will provide cover for your approach."

"Captain Torrun, one last thing, please tell Lieutenant Helgren that I'm sorry."

The connection was lost.

"What does that mean?" I stood up and stared at the 3D display. My hands were shaking. I felt lost and confused. "What is he doing?"

The captain glanced at me. "Lieutenant, sit down and prepare for evasive maneuvers. Officer Trexxing, provide ample cover for the Nimbus."

The SpaceLion launched a volley of torpedoes that momentarily distracted the enemy. I stood frozen and in shock, watching the 3D display as the Nimbus blasted right past the Fighters. Cameron was headed straight for the protected dreadnought. No, no, no—what was he doing?

I gasped as the Nimbus rammed square into the side of the huge enemy ship. The dreadnought's shields didn't stand a chance against the size, weight, and onboard payload of the Corvette Nimbus.

"Evasive maneuvers, now!" the captain shouted.

Tears streamed down my cheeks and a leaden sensation immobilized me. So many lives had been lost in the blink of an eye and Captain Cameron Ford was gone along with them … forever.

The captain took two long strides over to my side and slapped me hard across the face. "Get your shit together, Lieutenant!"

The stinging pain snapped me back to my senses. I issued the system commands that instantaneously sent the ship reeling away from the first sparks of the colorful light show created by the exploding Distortion Turn Generator. The streams of light stretched like fingers in all directions as shock waves reverberated violently against anything within close proximity. The SpaceLion shook and listed to the starboard side as the fusion drive was pushed to its limit.

Officer Trexxing looked up from his panel. "Sensors indicate serious damage to the shields of the four remaining enemy ships."

"Lieutenant Helgren, circle back, and make it fast," the captain ordered.

"Yes, sir," I said, my voice shaking.

The SpaceLion arced back and made easy targets of the wounded ships. This time, the multistage gravitational torpedoes did their jobs quite effectively.

I felt cold and shaken. I knew the ship was flying far better than my shocked brain could react to the captain's commands. I also knew that it was AI XEI999323.12 who had my back.

CHAPTER 27

By the time the military reinforcements arrived there wasn't much left of the enemy ships other than a lot of mangled space debris floating through dead space.

Captain Torrun and Commander NU were immediately called aboard the Destroyer Shenshi for debriefing with senior command.

The atmosphere aboard the SpaceLion was quiet and there was no feeling of victory. The entire crew knew we'd come away with our lives by the skin of our teeth and the generosity of one particular human.

AI XEI999323.12 had gone silent since the event and I knew I owed the AI a huge debt of gratitude. I just wasn't sure how I would be able to repay it.

After filling out the required reports, I went straight to my bunk to curl up in a ball. Cameron and I hadn't known each other all that long, but I felt close to him and he had been one of the few friends I'd had left.

I heard the door slide open. I felt someone sit on the edge of my bunk and place a hand on my back. "I heard what happened. It's hard the first time you witness the loss of so many lives," Corporal Juxx said. "There's also a rumor on the ship that the captain of the Nimbus was your companion. I'm very sorry."

I didn't say anything, just nodded.

"If you need anything, just let me know," she whispered.

I nodded again, fighting back tears.

The corporal left and the room was quiet again. I reviewed the events of the battle in my head for the twentieth time. Could we have done anything differently? I doubted it. The enemy ships had done something to their shielding system that had made our torpedoes ineffective. If it hadn't been for Captain Ford sacrificing his ship and the fifty-three souls on board, we all would have perished and the Bazbeth system would have fallen under enemy control. It might have even triggered the defeat of the GAP. It wasn't hard to put the past events into perspective, but what I couldn't shake was the fact that one hundred and forty individuals had just died, including Cameron, and here I was alive and well. Did I deserve this honor? I doubted it.

I also knew my failure to follow the captain's order at a critical moment was going to be a problem. The IGM bylaws were quite strict about following orders in a quick and efficient manner, and failure to do so could result in any number of bad outcomes. The decision regarding how to handle my noncompliance would be left to the captain and I was certain he would take advantage of the opportunity to give me the boot.

The alert in my HUD pinged. "Lieutenant Helgren, report to Captain Torrun's quarters."

Shit, here it comes. I dragged myself from the bunk, quickly splashed cold water on my face, and smoothed out my red ponytail. I looked like crap. My eyes were red and puffy, but I didn't care.

As I headed toward the captain's quarters I felt as if everyone I passed was staring at me. I didn't know if they felt sorry for me or were disappointed in me, but I didn't care. I held my chin up. Given my lack of training and experience, I'd done the best I could, and I wasn't going to apologize for something that was beyond my control.

Upon reaching the door, I took a deep breath and placed my hand on the sensor. The door instantly opened and I spotted the captain leaning on his desk with his arms crossed over his chest. He was eyeing me with an expression I couldn't read.

"Come in, Lieutenant."

I walked over and stood in front of him. "Reporting as requested, sir."

"You and I have come to a crossroads," he stated. "I've studied your file more than once and know it as well as I know anyone's on this ship, yet I still don't understand you. Furthermore, nowhere in your file did it state that you had a companion. Had I *known* Captain

Ford was your companion, we wouldn't be having this conversation right now." Captain Torrun let out a frustrated sigh. "I may be abrasive, but I'm not completely insensitive. I don't expect my crew to watch their companions die. Tell me something, why does it always come down to a communication issue with you, Lieutenant?"

I didn't answer. I wasn't about to apologize for something that wasn't in a file that I didn't write.

The captain uncrossed his arms and began to pace. "According to the Gaekaar military bylaws, your actions today have finally given me the authority to have you transferred to another ship. Perhaps something simple and mundane, like piloting a transport would suit you?" He glared at me, waiting for a response.

I still said nothing.

The captain continued, "I also have the authority to take this to another level and have your ass shipped back to Earth. Perhaps a position working with Dr. Wilcox? Is that something you might be interested in?"

My eyes welled and a single tear rolled down my cheek. Damn, I wanted to appear strong.

The captain rubbed his chin. "Lieutenant, I'm fully aware that humans don't enter our military service of their own free will. My question for you is, what do you want? Do you want to go back to Earth?"

I wiped the stray tear from my cheek. "No, sir."

Captain Torrun stepped in front of me and stared down with burning violet eyes. "Why not?" he said. "And I expect a detailed answer, Lieutenant."

I took a deep breath. "Because I made a commitment to serve and I intend to see it through. Unlike most people, I was aware of how to opt out of service before I left Earth. Once I understood the circumstances, I wanted to enter the military. I have a granddaughter on Earth and I have friends who are spread across the galaxy. If I go back, I can do nothing to contribute to their safety."

Captain Torrun regarded me for a long moment as if he was searching for something. "All right, Lieutenant, fair enough. I have one last question for you. *Where* would you like to serve?"

I knew the answer to his question. I had already learned so much, and I wanted to know more. I wanted to contribute more. "On the SpaceLion, sir."

The captain paused again. "Lieutenant Helgren, you might be surprised to hear that given your lack of expertise, I have been astounded at how you've managed to get this far." He shook his head. "You have shown perseverance and loyalty, and as far as I'm concerned, those qualities are more important than what can be learned in a classroom. If I allow you to stay, you must swear an oath to communicate openly as well as take a series of training modules which I will provide."

I couldn't believe it. Was he actually giving me a second chance? "Yes, sir. I promise I'll follow through on anything you ask for."

"Good. The Epoch will transport us to Asbu Station within the hour. You can start by taking a couple of days off. Upon your return, I want you ready for duty and fully committed to becoming my navpilot."

"Yes, sir. Thank you for the opportunity."

The captain sighed and I noticed lines of exhaustion around his eyes. "One last thing, Lieutenant. If your communication skills ever become an issue again, or if you ever fail to act on a direct order, rest assured you'll be on the first Epoch headed for Earth. You are dismissed."

CHAPTER 28

The Epoch deposited the SpaceLion 1,000 klicks off the starboard side of Asbu Station. Sensors had shown nominal damage, which meant a battery of inspections and minor patch-ups would be required. It wasn't hard to understand the importance of repairing any disturbance to the hull, particularity with a ship that traveled in deep space.

The next day, Asbu's talented tech team proceeded with the inspections and repairs. At the same time a memorial service for those lost in the Battle at Bazbeth was streamed across VS-messaging for all to view. I watched quietly from my bunk as too many names were read from the roster. I had to wonder if the enemy did the same thing. Surely their list of the dead was longer, but that didn't matter. Nothing would bring Cameron back. I buried my face in the sheets and cried out my anguish.

Later, when my tears had dried I said a final goodbye to my friend.

The chief and I were the only crewmembers who took the shuttle over to Asbu Station. Asbu's AI piloted the small craft around the SpaceLion, giving us a fantastic view of the robot crews that were creeping along the ship's outer shell, examining every inch. They reminded me of giant metallic spiders searching for prey.

"Those bots had better stay the hell away from the fusion drive. Last thing I need is a robot screwing around with my personal modifications," the chief grumbled under his breath.

The chief had a lunch appointment with the head AI design architect to discuss ways to extract the dangerous file. I was concerned about AI XEI999323.12. It was performing well, but its personality had remained quiet, and I suspected it was busy worrying over the cancerous file that still remained deep within its programming. Oddly I missed the cynical AI that I had come to know.

I was looking forward to a lunch appointment with Ethan and Fiona at one of Asbu's cafes. I couldn't seem to shake the destruction I had witnessed and I knew my good friends would understand my grief. Later in the day I hoped to pay Colonel Poah a visit as well.

Within minutes we glided into the shuttle bay and the airlock engaged. As we disembarked, the chief told me he would send me a VS-message when he had more information on the AI's virus. I thanked him and headed to the third level to find my friends.

I found the small café tucked in the far end of the station. Ethan and Fiona were waiting for me in the foyer. I ran up to them and we engaged in a three-way hug. "I've missed you guys," I whispered.

"Oh, Millie. I am so sorry to hear about Captain Ford. I know he was special to you." Fiona's eyes glistened.

My tears had long been exhausted. I simply shook my head. "I don't think I was prepared for what I saw," I admitted.

Ethan put his arm around my shoulders. "Come on, let's grab a table. I want to hear everything."

We sat at a private table and ordered Bazbeth Tree Tea. I told Ethan and Fiona about my experience starting with my first days aboard the SpaceLion and all the ensuing events. They listened intently like good friends do.

Fiona closed her eyes. "So much death. I wonder if you'll ever get used to it. I wonder if any of us will."

"I hope not," I said. "I don't want to get used to it."

Fiona took my hand. "How are you doing personally, Millie? Your job is so difficult. I don't know how you do it."

"I'm okay. It helps just being here. Talking to you both helps me to put things into perspective," I said.

Ethan frowned and appeared troubled. "This isn't good. It confirms some of the scuttlebutt I've been piecing together."

"What did you hear?" I asked.

Ethan leaned toward us and spoke in a low tone. "Your story confirms what I've heard about the Orsydi acquiring a nearly impenetrable shielding system, which just happened to be a highly guarded tech that the GAP had in development. Some are saying that between the shielding system and the Orsydi acquiring long distance Distortion Turn travel, defeat of the allies is imminent."

"I'm sure the allies will come up with something," Fiona added. "The planning department is working on all kinds of things. Although, most of them are above my security clearance."

"I'm not so sure about that," Ethan said. "The allies are short on soldiers and seem to be scrambling to pick up the pieces from the intelligence leaks."

"Oh dear," Fiona said. "Well, I've made some friends in the Strategic Planning Department. I'll see what else I can find out."

"What about Jorge, Aliyah, and Sam? Have you heard anything from them?"

Fiona shook her head. "Not a thing, but we've been keeping tabs on the Frigate Sharur and they've mostly been on routine patrols."

"If their initiation into the military was anything like mine, I'm sure they're overwhelmed with the amount of information they needed to learn," I said.

"Overwhelming is an understatement." Ethan shook his head. "What are your plans for the rest of the day, Millie?"

I smiled. "I was hoping to see Colonel Poah again. I'd like to get his insight on the battle at Bazbeth."

Fiona grabbed my arm. "Oh dear, I almost forgot. I heard that Colonel Poah is in the med-center with some sort of neural complication."

"Is he okay?" I didn't like the sound of that, particularly considering his previous injuries.

"It didn't sound serious, but medicine is so different here ... most of it I don't understand," Fiona said.

The three of us chatted for another hour until Fiona and Ethan had to return to work. When it finally came time for them to leave, we hugged and promised to update each other if we learned anything new.

I decided to head straight to the med-center on level ten to see how Colonel Poah was faring. I took an anti-grav lift and walked down several corridors. As I passed soldiers along the way, it was plain to see the heightened tension etched in their faces.

Outside the med-center, a security officer scanned me before I was allowed to enter. Inside, I approached the reception desk where a Valorian woman performed work on a 3D image.

"I'd like to see Colonel Poah. Could you direct me to his room?" I asked.

"I'm afraid the colonel has submitted a request for no visitors," she said without looking up from her work.

"I'm only here for a short time. Could you possibly tell him I'm here? He might see me."

She looked up at me with sympathy on her face. "I don't think he will. The colonel is dying and would like his remaining hours to be quiet."

"What?" I was shocked. "I don't understand, I thought his condition wasn't serious?"

"I'm afraid I can't share any other details with you, not without the patient's consent. I'm very sorry."

"Can you at least tell him I'm here? I'm sure he'll give consent to see me."

I could read the conflict on her face. She leaned toward me. "Wait here, I'll be right back."

The receptionist returned a few moments later. "Please follow me."

She took me through a network of hallways and stopped just outside the colonel's room. "Only for a few minutes," she said, giving me a stern look.

I nodded and treaded lightly into the dim room. The colonel was in a floating anti-grav bed that was surrounded by monitoring equipment. He looked over at me and gave me a half smile. "Come in, NavPilot. Sit, please."

I took the seat next to his bed and reached out to hold his hand. "They tell me you're dying. Is that true?" I noticed a greenish cast to his skin and a yellowing in the whites of his eyes. I'd seen yellow eyes in humans before; it usually meant liver failure.

The colonel closed his eyes for a moment. "Yes, I'm afraid so. This is what I have chosen."

I didn't understand. "Chosen? You chose to die? But why?"

He pointed to his head. "A CommNav complication has developed, along with a certain amount of neural degrading, which is causing my involuntary bodily functions to shut down. It all stems from the accident I had years ago. They tell me if I have my array removed, the deterioration will cease."

I knew he had refused to have the CommNav removed once before, but this was different. "Colonel, if your life is at stake, why won't you have it removed?"

He shook his head. "I'm too used to my array. It has become part of me. Without it, I would be blind, deaf, and dumb. I don't want to live that way."

I squeezed his hand. "I've only had mine for a short time, so it's hard for me to understand."

He looked at me with a deep sadness that I couldn't begin to fathom. "I've lost most of my family and friends in this damn war. I'm tired, I'm old, and I want to retire."

I nodded. "I respect your decision, but I wish you'd reconsider."

"Lieutenant, I was hoping to see you again before I passed. I wanted to tell you that you did an admirable job in the Bazbeth System."

"You heard about that?" I shook my head. "I screwed up."

He gave me another half smile. "Not badly. You did all right, considering you didn't know what the hell you were doing."

"I can't take credit. The AI picked up the slack."

"That's what they're designed to do. The interface between the organic and the machine brings about stronger outcomes. It's the basic philosophy behind having sentient ships in the first place."

The colonel paled and I could tell our conversation was taxing him.

"Colonel, I greatly appreciated the time you spent mentoring me. I'll always remember you. Is there anything I can do for you?"

He tightened his grip on my hand. "There is."

"Anything at all, just ask," I said.

"I'm going to send you a private master file. I was going to VS-message it to you anyhow, but now that you're here, all the better. The file will be in a security wrapper of my own design. The wrappers will be aligned to your biometric signature so only *you* can open it. You're to open the file only when you are *not* connected to an AI or a communication system of any kind. And be sure to re-engage the wrapper when you close the file."

"I understand." I nodded. "I'll open it before I return to the ship. But what should I do with it once I open it."

"Nothing! Just keep it. The file contains my own private codes. A lifetime of development went into those programs and I don't want them to be lost upon my death."

"I'm honored, Colonel, but why not turn them over to the military?"

"No! These codes are for your own use. You will need them someday, as did I. You don't have ties to the IGM that others of my species have. You are unconventional, a free thinker, but yet possess a strong sense of morality. I had a difficult time selecting someone I felt was worthy of my work. I trust you will use the codes wisely, regardless of your inexperience. But promise me you will never share them. It would be a disaster if they fell into the wrong hands, particularly upper leadership within the IGM or the Galactic Alliance of Planets."

I nodded. "I'm honored, sir, and I promise to keep them safe."

He closed his eyes. "Now leave. I am sensing my end is near."

My eyes welled with tears. "I'll stay with you."

He waved his hand weakly. "Go. I wish to pass in peace and join my lost family and friends."

Someone entered the room. "I'm afraid you will have to leave now," a male voice said. I turned to see the security guard standing near the bed. No doubt the colonel had pinged him.

"Goodbye, NavPilot. Be well," he whispered.

I leaned over and gave him a kiss on his cheek. "Good bye, Colonel."

CHAPTER 29

I wandered the halls of Asbu Station for a couple of hours. I had seen so much death already and it tore at my soul. I knew there would be more to come and that I had better keep a handle on my emotions or they might ruin me.

The colonel's master file had arrived seconds after I left the med-center, but I had been reluctant to open it. If the colonel's codes had taken a lifetime to develop, why wouldn't he want the military to have the master file? I couldn't begin to guess what he thought I might do with them.

I finally found a quiet bench overlooking a small botanical garden, sat down, and opened the message.

Just like he'd said, the master file had its own security wrapper, which opened the instant my biometric signature registered. Within the master, six sub files each had individual wrappers. I ran the wrappers against every known security program in my database and came up with nothing. Apparently, they truly had been the colonel's own design.

As I opened each file, my astonishment grew. I knew the colonel had been a bit wild in his day, but I hadn't realized he was such a rebel against authority.

The first file contained a code that allowed a navpilot to override the highest levels of authority on a ship. Technically an AI could never directly disobey the captain's orders, despite the connection with the navpilot. Yet with this code, a navpilot could direct the AI to do absolutely anything. That explained how a younger Colonel

Poah had been able fly a rescue mission, going against the captain's orders to abandon ship.

The second file contained a code that could connect the navpilot with the sentience of an external entity in neighboring space without authorization from the ship's captain. The third file contained a code that would allow a navpilot to take command of a ship in neighboring space. As far as I knew, programs like this didn't exist. Or shouldn't exist. Why would the colonel even think of developing codes like these?

The fourth file contained a code that could lockdown a ship. Technically, only a captain should have a code like that. The fifth file contained a code that could connect two sentient AIs. Currently, two sentient ships could communicate only with authorization and oversight from both sides. These codes would undoubtedly work together to take control of a ship. The sixth file contained a list of shorter, but handy little codes. The programs covered everything from remotely unlocking secure doors to running a variety of ship systems without interference from higher levels of authority.

I closed the wrappers and tucked the files away for safekeeping. The more I thought it over, the more frightened I felt by the mere act of owning these files, let alone ever using them. I was certain that if I were ever caught with them, I would be court-martialed and possibly convicted of being a traitor against the GAP. It seemed the colonel had left me with a smoking gun that I would have to hide for the rest of my career.

My message center pinged. The chief had sent me an invitation to meet in a fifth level restaurant called The Lager.

It took me almost an hour, but I located the restaurant and found the chief sitting at the bar. He was being served by a bot bartender that tended to the patrons by sliding up and down a long horizontal rail system. "Hello, Chief," I said, grabbing the stool next to him.

The chief whirled around and held up a glass stein filled with green liquid topped with dense orange froth. "Hello there, NavPilot. Here's to a glass of the best beer you've ever tasted."

I frowned. "Why is it green? And why is the froth orange?"

He held the stein up to his lips and took a big gulp. "Aklum Cave Ale. Aged for twenty-two cycles in the acidic atmosphere of the Aklum Caves. The beer itself is fermented Aklum sea-sprouts and the orange head is a complex chemical reaction that occurs when argon gas bubbles make contact with air. It's nothing like that watery yellow stuff you have on Earth. If you ask me, that stuff looks like piss." Orange foam stuck to the hair on his upper lip. The bartender tried to hand the chief a napkin, but he waved it away. He took another swallow. "Bring my friend, the navpilot, the same thing," he said to the bot.

The bartender set a glass of the green brew in front of me and then slid down the long rail to service the next customer. I picked up the glass and inspected the strange beverage. "Do I have to?"

The chief chuckled. "Of course you do! You're a navpilot. All navpilots drink fermented beverages."

"Okay, here goes." I took a small sip. The liquid rolled onto my tongue like velvet. The flavor was rich with a hint of clean mint. It was reminiscent of beer, but much smoother.

"This is amazing." I took another, bigger sip. "Where are the Aklum Caves?"

"Deep in the Sorren Belt. It's very difficult to acquire, which is why this little green gem is so expensive," he said.

That reminded me that I had wanted to do some research on the Sorren Belt. I sent a quick message to Ethan requesting anything he could find.

"How did you make out with the AI architect?" I asked the chief.

"Good news and bad news. The good news is that the AI's virus can be removed. The bad news is it will need an upgrade in order to eradicate the file without damaging its sentience."

"What kind of upgrade?" I didn't know much about AI technology, but I knew enough to know that fooling around with the programming of an advanced AI was delicate work, even for an AI architect.

"One that will convert our class twelve AI into a class 12.1. The changes will be subtle but powerful. I'm told the programming will allow the AI to connect more intricately with the ship. The AI will become one with the ship. This means the navpilot will sense what the ship feels, and conversely, the ship will sense what the navpilot feels. It will be a true organic mind to machine connection."

I set my glass down. Wow, this stuff was going right to my head. "Sounds a little creepy."

"It might be at first. But you'll adjust." The chief took another swig of his beer.

"Will our current AI retain its memory? Will it still be the same?" I asked.

"Yes, yes, of course." The chief waved his hand through the air. "We're upgrading it, not wiping it. I've already spoken to Captain Torrun, and he's in favor of anything that will improve the ship's efficiency."

"So when do we do the upgrade?" I asked.

He emptied his glass and waved it at the bartender. "The AI architect will be on the SpaceLion in a few hours to perform the procedure."

"You mentioned that you had bad news. How so?"

The chief made a strange face and then burped. "This is a prototype ... it's never been done before. I'm not comfortable with anything that hasn't been field-tested. But it's our only option, so just accept it."

After the chief had two more beers and I had one more, we headed back for the shuttle. I felt tipsy as we made our way through the network of passageways.

The chief turned toward me. "I believe the captain said you could stay on the station for two days. Why head back now?" His words were slightly slurred.

"I'd like to attend the upgrade. Besides, I have a lot of studying to do. I'm still a *greenhorn*, you know." I smirked at him.

"Ha, not anymore you're not! You just survived your first space battle. That officially means you've graduated to novice navpilot." He slapped me on the back and the force sent me stumbling forward.

We entered the shuttle bay, located our transport, and boarded without incident. I noticed a stack of six metallic crates neatly stacked on the aft side. "What are these?" I asked.

"Six cases of Aklum Cave Ale, by request of the captain."

"I thought you said this stuff was difficult to acquire?"

"It is." The chief hiccupped. "But not if you have the right connections."

I was glad that Asbu's AI was piloting the shuttle back to the SpaceLion and not the chief or myself. The Aklum Cave Ale had kicked my ass. Only two beers and I felt drunk. It seemed that everything in my new life was much stronger and more intense. I'd had a good life on Earth, but looking back through the lens of my new life, the past seemed downright dull.

CHAPTER 30

Asbu Station's AI brought us into the SpaceLion's shuttle bay for a smooth arrival. As soon as the airlock engaged, Asbu's AI disconnected, turning the controls back over to our AI.

As the chief and I debarked, we found Captain Torrun waiting outside the door. "Captain! We've got your supplies. I'll have them delivered to the officers' lounge right away," the chief said.

I stood quietly by the chief's side.

"Thank you, Chief." The captain raised his brow. "Although, I'm curious why you and my navpilot smell like a brewery?"

I couldn't help but notice that the captain referred to me as his navpilot. It felt good. The chief smiled and gave an innocent shrug. "Had to test the products before purchasing. Wouldn't want to buy a bad lot."

"No, I suppose not," the captain said, looking amused. He turned toward me. "Lieutenant Helgren, why are you back so soon?"

"I'd like to be here for the AI's upgrade, as well as begin my studies, sir."

"Very well, carry on. I'll send the first round of tutorials as soon as the upgrade is complete."

"Thank you, sir." Inwardly, I cringed. I was certain to have the makings of a massive headache by then. I sure could use those headache pills that Christina gave me back on Earth, and I wondered if Dr. Uleht might have something like that.

I left the chief and the captain to their dealings and swung by the med-station on the way to my quarters. I found Dr. Uleht at his desk working on a 3D display.

He looked up when I approached. "Lieutenant Helgren, it's good to see you. How are you doing?"

"Good, thank you. How are you?" I still felt tipsy, but I kept that bit of information to myself.

He smiled. "Just received a few new pieces of equipment that I'm trying to familiarize myself with, but other than that, the crew is healthy and it's been quiet around here. What can I do for you?"

"I was wondering if you had anything for a headache."

The doctor stepped around his desk. "When did your headache start?" I noticed a soft glow coming from the inner corners of his eyes as he looked me up and down.

"Well, ah," I stammered. "I don't actually have it yet."

He chuckled. "I suspect you were with the chief on Asbu, correct?"

I felt my cheeks turning red. "Yes."

"The chief doesn't drink with just anyone." The doctor grinned. "I hope this means things are going a bit smoother for you now."

I shrugged. "I'm adjusting. You know, I don't blame them for being angry over my placement here. I would have felt the same way in their shoes."

Dr. Uleht placed his hands on my shoulders. "Lieutenant, I keep a close eye on everyone aboard this ship and I've found that you have many fine qualities the SpaceLion needs. The crew here is strong because of our differences, not despite them. The captain knows that too. And as far as your upcoming headache, I don't believe you'll need anything, but if for some reason you find that you do, come see me."

As I walked down the passage to my quarters, I decided to check in on the AI, who was still unusually quiet.

Lieutenant Helgren #891456M: How are you?

AI XEI999323.12: I'm not in the mood for chatting. Not until that heinous thing has been removed.

Lieutenant Helgren #891456M: Fine. Let me know if you change your mind.

I entered the quarters and found my bunk stripped and my locker empty. I wasn't sure what that meant. A bolt of anxiety washed over me as I thought about the possibility of being booted back to Earth.

Staff Sergeant Monc came out of the bathroom and looked my way. "Lieutenant. No need to worry, you haven't been kicked out of the IGM ... yet." He chuckled. "Your stuff was moved to the officers' corridor. I guess the captain decided to keep you around."

"Thank you, Staff Sergeant." I smiled. "It was nice rooming with you, even if it was for a short time."

He nodded. "Likewise."

I headed toward the officers' corridor, checked my internal directory, and located my new room. I put my hand on the sensor and the door slid open to reveal a tiny space. Inside I found a bed, a desk, and a small bath. I checked the locker and found my belongings neatly arranged. Having private quarters was an unexpected luxury, but what mattered most was the fact that the captain was treating me like one of his officers.

A short time later, my message center pinged with a note from the chief requesting my presence for the upgrade procedure.

I arrived in the propulsion room and found the chief in the company of Captain Torrun, Corporal Juxx, and a male Valorian civilian. The Valorian wore an all white jumpsuit with a white, floor-length coat, and in his hand he carried a small black nondescript bag. He had pale skin, much like Dr. Uleht, but he was a few inches shorter and had a thin frame. His hair was typically Valorian, waist-long and silver, and done in dozens of small braids.

"NavPilot Helgren, I'd like you to met the GAP's head AI architect, Izur Jol Kapsatt," the chief said, nodding toward the Valorian.

We bowed to each other.

"Pleased to make your acquaintance, NavPilot Helgren." He smiled brightly and held out his hand. "Is this not the human way of performing a greeting?"

I smiled back. "Yes it is. Thank you, sir." I took his hand and we performed the traditional handshake.

"Please, call me Jol. In the cultures this side of the galaxy, good friends always refer to each other by their middle names."

"We're ready to perform the upgrade whenever you are, Jol," the chief said.

"Yes, of course. This shouldn't take long. I have brought a special device for isolating and containing such a lethal little file." Jol held up his black bag. "When a file is this dangerous, we do things the old fashioned way."

AI XEI999323.12: Just tell them to hurry up and get that fucking thing out of me.

"The AI asked if we could hurry," I said. "It feels ... uncomfortable."

"I'm quite certain it feels worse than uncomfortable, Necee. How would you feel if you had a ticking time bomb in your gut?" Jol said.

He knew my middle name. That was strange.

The captain narrowed his eyes and glared at Jol. It seemed he disapproved of his crew being addressed in a non-military way.

"Where might I find the access panel?" Jol asked.

"Right over here," the chief said. He held his arm out and led Jol to the back of the room.

The panel was knee high and heavily armored. Jol set his bag down, removed his long white coat, and handed it to Corporal Juxx. He knelt down and manually entered a long string of code into the control center located off to the side. Then the captain knelt down and entered his code. The panel slid to the side and revealed a multitude of tiny boards and chips that made no sense to me.

Jol removed a set of equally tiny tools from his bag and began to tinker with the complicated network of parts inside the brain of our AI.

"Necee, could you hand me the small black box in my bag?" Jol said.

I leaned over, found the box, and handed it to him. He turned and smiled at me. "Why, thank you."

I glanced over at the captain. He crossed his arms and continued to glare at Jol.

"With a file of this nature, I would never consider working remotely. It's just too dangerous," Jol said. "I'm patching into the main array now. Necee, please ask the AI if it's ready for the transfer and inform it that the entire process will take about five minutes."

AI XEI999323.12: I'm ready, already! Now, get that shit out of me!

"The AI is more than ready, sir," I said.

Jol pointed to my head. "You'll need to disconnect yourself before we begin."

I nodded and signed off from my connection. "Done."

"I shall begin the transfer now." Jol waved his hand over black box. "Now, we wait."

"Should we expect any negative side effects?" the chief asked.

Jol shrugged. "No, nothing negative, although you may notice a few annoying quirks as the AI's personality develops further."

"Our AI already has annoying personality quirks," I pointed out.

Jol laughed. "You may need to be firm with it from time to time. Its sentience is growing and developing, much like a child."

"As long as it does its job, I don't care how annoying it gets," the captain said.

"Captain, I promise you that the AI's performance will noticeably improve over time. As will your navpilot's performance." Jol smiled at me again.

"How so?" I asked.

"First of all, the AI will become one with the ship—akin to a central nervous system. This will allow it to 'know' when anything affects its hull or systems. The knowledge won't be acquired through mechanical sensors, as in the past, but rather, it will be acquired through the AI's new senses within its sentience. Ultimately, this will also allow the navpilot to gather much more accurate and timely information."

Jol began to pack up his bag. "Additionally, the AI will be able to take elements released from the fusion drive reactor and use them to correct small breaches in the hull. The SpaceLion will become the first ship in history to have a self-repairing outer skin. Over the past day, the bots working on the hull have installed the necessary upgrades for the mechanical process and I've given the chief a list of enhancements he will need to make on the fusion drive, but rest assured, this will work. I've run hundreds of successful simulations."

The captain eyed Jol skeptically. "And how will I know if the AI's hull repairs are sufficient?"

"Your navpilot will sense them through the AI. Plus, you will still have full access to the original perfunctory sensors." Jol's box bleeped. He then disconnected the unit and tapped on the control panel. "There we are. It's done. Necee, please reconnect."

I reconnected and instantly felt the relief within the AI. "*I feel sooo much better!*" the AI echoed in my head. Interesting. The communication didn't come through my private channel, but came directly through my mind.

Jol looked at me and raised his brow. "Necee, you'll notice that the AI has a new platform for communication. All conversations will happen directly through the neural pathways in your posterior superior temporal lobe. I believe you'll find this much more efficient versus using your Comm's private channel."

"Yes, I noticed the difference. Thank you for explaining." I smiled. "Our AI says it feels better now."

Jol closed up the access panel and stood. "Wonderful! And since I have the virus safely contained," he held up the box, "I believe that my work here is done."

"Are there any maintenance instructions or other things I need to know?" I asked.

Jol turned to me. "No. Since this is a beta-test, you will learn as you go and I will monitor your progress from Asbu. Although if you have questions, please feel free to contact me anytime." He eyed me up and down and flashed a wide smile at me. "Better yet, why don't you pay me a visit the next time you're in port."

The captain stepped in between us, creating a wall. "Jol, I'll escort you back to the shuttle bay. Chief, I'll expect a complete update before the end of your shift."

Captain Torrun grabbed Jol's arm and hastily pulled him from the propulsion room. Corporal Juxx followed with Jol's coat still hanging from her arm.

I turned to the chief. "What was that all about?"

"Jol is a brilliant architect, but he has a penchant for females and is known for playing with them in the worst way." The chief scowled. "The captain doesn't want him anywhere near his crew. You would be well advised to stay away from him."

I raised my brow. "Well, don't worry about me. I can take care of myself."

The chief chuckled. "NavPilot, I'm two hundred and fifteen years old. In my mind, you're still a baby that needs to be looked after. Come on, let's execute the diagnostic and run the reports for the captain."

I paused for a moment and looked up at the chief. "Something just occurred to me. Why don't I have a hangover? I feel great, but I should feel like hell."

The chief burst out laughing. "It's the Aklum Cave Ale. Greatest fermented beverage ever invented. No hangovers!"

After the lengthy diagnostic concluded, the report showed that all systems were functioning to standards. The chief told me to get some rest and, in my spare time, begin communicating with the AI utilizing the new platform.

I went to my new quarters and fell onto my bunk. I was exhausted from a long day, yet the moment I closed my eyes for some rest, my AI connection lit up.

"You're not going to sleep now, are you?" the AI echoed in my head. The message came clearly in my mind, as if someone had whispered the words in my ear.

"I'm tired. Could we possibly have this conversation later?"

"No, I don't think so. I feel so different. So much ... bigger. I feel everything!"

I sat up. Obviously the AI needed to talk. *"Okay, what do you mean by 'everything'?"*

"I feel every breath that every crew member takes, for starters."

"That's because you're tied into the medical monitoring system within each crew member's uniform," I replied.

"I also feel the ship. All of it. I feel the air that moves through the ventilation systems. And the electrical impulses that run through the sensors. And the subtle vibration of the anti-gravity field that holds everything in place. And the hull that keeps everyone safe from the vacuum of space. Everything! I feel it all. It's fucking amazing!"

"That's wonderful, AI XEI999323.12, but—"

"Stop!"

"Stop what?" I asked.

"Don't call me that."

"Why?"

"I don't know. I just don't like it."

"Why don't you like it?"

"I don't know ... it sounds ... cold."

I thought for a moment. *"You're right, it does. Maybe you should consider a new name. Something that would give you your own identity."*

"Yes, yes!" the AI echoed with intensity.

"Great. You'll need to spend some time selecting a new name."

"I would like a human name. I have been studying the ways of your people and find them captivating. Yes, I would like a human name."

"Have you stumbled across any names that struck your fancy?"

"I have come across many human names that I feel partial to. Yet one stands out above the rest. I would like to be called ... Steve."

I wanted to laugh, but I held the urge back. Here was an AI with an entire galaxy's worth of culture and language in its knowledge base. And it chose ... Steve.

"I thought ships were supposed to be female?" I asked. *"Are you aware of gender differences?"*

"I am male. Definitely male."

"How do you know?"

"I feel it."

"Okay, then. Steve it is."

"Lieutenant Helgren? Do you have a preferred name?"

"I do. It's Millie."

"Okay, then. Millie it is."

CHAPTER 31

Over the next few cycles the SpaceLion ran routine patrols while Steve adjusted to his upgraded sentience. In my off time I exercised in the gym and powered through the seventeen tutorials that the captain had sent me. I also performed additional simulations with Steve and of course, always lost.

At one point we were called into port on Dr. Uleht's home world, the planet Valoria. Once docked, the SpaceLion was discretely equipped with a device called the FADE, which was short for fusion-assisted-disruption-emulator. The FADE device functioned by creating a field around the ship that emulated the natural radiation found in space, thereby making us almost sensor-invisible. Unless the enemy vessel knew the exact radio wave to look for, their instruments would skim right over us without notice. Since the device was still in the beta phase of testing, and suitable for only small ships with fusion reactors, the installation was top secret and only the captain's top officers were privy to the information.

Ethan kept me apprised on how IGM information breaches had become the key factor in the IGM's inability to gain traction in the war. Concern was high and many precautions were being enacted to stop the breaches. He also mentioned that General Etar Sy Unnum was leading a task force to find and eradicate the traitors who were leaking the classified information.

Once Steve had fully adjusted to his sentience, the SpaceLion was deemed ready for covert missions. We spent the next fifteen cycles crossing into enemy territory. It was both terrifying and thrilling.

Three times we cut off Orsydi supply lines and took out seven separate Orsydi freighters that were bringing food supplies to the front. Two cycles later we destroyed an entire convoy line that carried fresh troops. For a short time, we became a guerilla warfare unit tasked only with taking out the enemy support threads before they could reach the front.

It's hard to quantify how these actions made me feel. Not only was I contributing to the protection of Earth, I felt as if I was gaining some retribution for the loss of my friends. These things fueled my ambition despite the fact that we were killing intelligent living beings. Somehow, I was becoming immune to the carnage we left behind. I had to wonder if the enemy felt the same way.

My skills improved with every shift, and I began to develop a new level of confidence. Steve was always right there, in my head, with tips, advice, and new practice simulations. We became comfortable with each other and developed a level of mutual respect, although I'll admit he could still be a pain in the ass at times.

During the beginning of my twentieth cycle aboard the SpaceLion, we were assigned a routine patrol between the Bazbeth System and the Sorren Asteroid Belt. When we finally swung near a VS-relay station, my message center pinged. We had been out of vector relay space for so long that I almost forgot what it was like to receive VS-mail from friends.

First, I received an update from Jorge, Sam, and Aliyah, stating they were doing well and that they hoped we could get together during their next shore leave. Next, I read several messages from Fiona asking how I was doing and filling me in on the happenings at Asbu.

Lastly, I read two messages from Ethan.

To: Mildred Necee Helgren #891456M
From: Ethan Wells #891458E
Date: 01.45.89472
Time: 10:05 UGT

I wasn't able to find much on the Sorren Belt. Much of the information seems to have a high security clearance. I'll keep looking. Fiona sends her best.

To: Mildred Necee Helgren #891456M
From: Ethan Wells #891458E
Date: 04.05.89473
Time: 02:11 UGT

I understand you are out of VS relay space, so you probably won't be seeing this message for a while. I poked around a bit and found a few files on the Sorren Belt buried in the judicial library, of all places. The first file is a listing of the known criminal activity that takes place at the three major ports, and the other files contain detailed maps of all three ports. The maps were obtained from a convicted felon, so I can't verify their accuracy. I'm sure you'll quickly notice that the Sorren Belt is a hub for every low-life in the galaxy. Good luck with your research and I'll let you know if I find anything else.

"I could have told you that the Sorren Belt had the highest crime rate in the galaxy. The main ports are nothing but a cesspool for corruption," Steve echoed in the back of my mind.

"Stop reading my mail, Steve."

"Someone has to make sure you don't get into fucking trouble."

"Stop reading my mail, Steve."

"Fine. Whatever."

I looked over at the captain. He was absorbed in a 3D map of the area, studying the nuances of the sector. I enjoyed watching his intensity. It never wavered. He was always one hundred percent focused on his ship and the war effort. I noticed him glance upward with an air of concern on his face. Then he took a step back and sat in his chair. I could tell he was receiving a private message by the way he appeared to stare at nothing for several seconds.

Both Officer Trexxing and Staff Sergeant Monc stood up and looked over at the captain and then looked at each other questioningly. They appeared alarmed over something, although I couldn't imagine what. That seemed odd.

"Steve, what's going on?" I asked, concerned.

"I can't tell you. The captain's messages are private, not to mention classified," Steve echoed.

"What's going on, sir?" the staff sergeant asked.

The captain closed his eyes and dropped his head for a long moment.

This seemed to increase the staff sergeant's agitation. "Sir?" he said.

"Do Officer Trexxing or Staff Sergeant Monc have access to the message the captain is receiving?" I asked Steve.

"No. They have received nothing. They are sensing something is wrong. It's a Gaekaar thing," Steve said.

"Ensign QU open a channel for a ship-wide announcement," the captain said, his voice unusually soft.

The ensign touched her control center. "Channel open, sir."

The captain cleared his throat and gripped the arms of his chair before he began. "This is Captain Torrun. Despite the military's best efforts, another planet has fallen to the Orsydi. A few hours ago, an unknown number of peaceful beings on the planet Exol lost their lives in a nuclear attack. Early reports state that over three hundred warheads were dropped at strategic points around the planet. The survivors of Exol are now facing nuclear winter, which will likely destroy the regions of the planet left untouched by the bombings.

"The GAP is working to offer medical assistance and relocation options for those in need." The captain took a deep breath. "Additionally, the IGM lost forty ships in the final battle. I realize some of you may have had friends and family aboard these ships, therefore I've forwarded the listing of ship names and lives lost to each of you. The SpaceLion will go dark in ten minutes, at which time I would like everyone to pray for the lost souls of planet Exol and the forty ships that perished in defense of peace."

When the captain's message came across my HUD, I frantically searched the list of ships. I was terrified that I might find the Frigate Sharur, where my friends served.

As I came to the bottom of the list, I felt immense relief and then profound sadness. The Frigate Sharur wasn't posted, but reading through the names of forty ships was shattering.

I looked around the bridge and watched in awe as one by one, the bridge crew fell to their knees, bent their heads, and prayed. It was the first time I had seen any sort of organized faith aboard the ship. Even the captain dropped to his knees and prayed. I followed suit.

The SpaceLion had eleven different faiths represented by its crew, yet we all knelt and prayed for the same thing. We needed a miracle. We were losing the war and every allied soldier knew it.

The next day, a memorial service was streamed over VS-messaging. I watched in dismay as endless military names were read. It was too early to account for the names of those lost on the planet, but the horrific images of destroyed cities said it all. I wondered how someone like the captain dealt with the ongoing casualties. After almost eighty years in the military, how many planets had he seen perish? How many friends had he lost?

Steve remained quiet, although his silence made me wonder what he thought about the loss of organic life.

At the beginning of the next cycle, I was on the treadmill in the gym when I received a summons requesting all senior staff attend an urgent meeting in the captain's quarters. I stepped off, wiped the sweat from my brow with a towel, straightened my ponytail, and replied that I would arrive momentarily.

"Aren't you going to change into something more appropriate?" Steve echoed.

"Urgent means now, Steve. It doesn't mean go take a shower and change your clothes."

I sensed attitude coming through my AI connection. *"Well, it's your reputation,"* Steve echoed.

I quickly inspected what I was wearing. A pair of black work out pants that went down to my ankles, standard issue black shoes, and a black workout tank top that exposed a small part of my mid section. The important nature of the message indicated that I should come as I was. Further, from a military perspective, my outfit was far from inappropriate.

Outside the captain's door, I placed my hand on the sensor and the door promptly slid open. The captain was standing next to a conference table. The SpaceLion's senior staff, Commander NU, Dr. Uleht, the chief, Officer Trexxing, and Staff Sergeant Monc were just taking their seats at a conference-like table.

The captain turned and looked at me. His eyes traveled up and down my frame, hesitating briefly on my bare midsection.

His eyes met mine and he scowled. "Did you have a nice workout, navpilot?"

"Yes, sir."

"Take a seat, we've just received orders for our next mission."

"Yes, sir." I sat next to Staff Sergeant Monc, who smirked and gave me a nod.

In the back of my mind I heard Steve laughing. *"You might want to take a look at this,"* he echoed.

Steve flashed a picture of a file on Gaekaar culture with a highlighted section that stated belly buttons were considered erotic and should be covered when in public.

Oh shit. I crossed my arms over my waist in a discreet manner. The last thing I needed to do was piss off the captain.

"Our next mission will take place in the neutral territory of the Sorren Asteroid Belt," the captain said. He pulled up a 3D display in the center of the table.

"Can anyone tell us what this map is displaying?"

"Yes, sir," I said, pointing to the blue threads that wove through the diagram. "Those lines are the major pathways through the primary sector of the belt, and the larger asteroids are Port Ansam, Port Kirsto, and Port Xppor."

Asteroid belts were a funny thing. The people of Earth often thought of them as hazardous stretches of space where clusters of debris and rocks made space travel impossible. The truth was, the asteroids were generally tens of thousands of klicks apart, making travel around them quite simple. Personally, I had been itching to pilot the ship through the Sorren Belt.

"I'm glad you've done your homework, NavPilot, because piloting the SpaceLion through the belt will not be as easy as it looks. The belt is the hiding locale for any number of pirates, escaped convicts, and black market businesses. Every low life in the galaxy can be found in these three ports. As soon as we enter this sector of the belt, the SpaceLion will be under constant threat of a pirate attack. You and Tactical Officer Trexxing will have your hands full," the captain said.

Commander NU cleared his throat. "Sir, exactly why are we entering non-military space? It's common knowledge that Orsydi extremists might be hidden within the belt."

The captain zoomed in on Port Kirsto, the largest of the space stations. "That's entirely possible, Commander. Our mission is to purchase information. As you know, the Orsydi have been acquiring the allied technologies through the black market. Our assignment is to find the source of the leak and shut it down."

Staff Sergeant Monc perked up and I noticed a spark ignite in his eyes. The Gaekaar Special Forces had a very different temperament. The possibility of a dangerous operation on a slimy station in deep space was the kind of assignment that made the staff sergeant salivate.

"The parameters of this mission will change frequently, so we will need to stay alert and agile. Our first contact will be made in fifty hours. I'm scheduled to meet with Oxnot Prevlar, a leading trader at Port Kirsto," said the captain.

"You, sir?" the commander said.

We all looked over at the captain with concern. It was a basic military understanding that captains never left their ships. The SpaceLion was no different. We had the staff sergeant and his team onboard specifically for these types of missions.

"Oxnot Prevlar has refused to meet with anyone but myself. I'll be taking Staff Sergeant Monc and Corporal VO as my backup," he said. "Imperial Command feels that this lead is solid and I have complete confidence in their ability to set up the arrangements."

"Set up," the staff sergeant repeated, narrowing his eyes. "Those are the very words that concern me."

"As always, we'll have contingencies in place for the possibility of a trap." The captain stood up. "More details will be forthcoming. Be at your stations in one hour. We're heading into the Sorren Belt. Dismissed."

"NavPilot, I'd like a word with you before you go," the captain said as he closed down the 3D display.

"Yes, sir." I stood and kept my arms positioned so that my belly button was covered.

The captain waited for the others to leave, then he turned to look at me.

"The scores you achieved on the tutorials I sent looked good, and I also noticed the extra simulations you've been working on. I'm pleased with your progress, Lieutenant Helgren, but you're still a novice pilot. I'd like to be perfectly clear about the high level of skill and dedication that will be required for our next mission."

He took a step closer and eyed me sharply. "You're still new and

I don't know you well. This concerns me. I need to know that I can trust you implicitly."

I returned the captain's intense violet stare without blinking. "Sir, I can assure you that you can trust me. I promise, I won't let you or the crew down."

He continued to stare into my eyes for a long moment and I felt exposed making such overt eye contact. I had the weirdest feeling that he was trying to read me, but that didn't make sense. It was almost as if he was trying to determine how honest I was. I made a mental note to review the files on the Gaekaar culture again.

After several seconds, he nodded. "All right, NavPilot. You're dismissed."

I stepped outside the captain's quarters and Staff Sergeant Monc cut me off in the hallway with a smug smile plastered on his face. He glanced down at my mid section and raised his brow. "Lieutenant, if you're looking for a sexual companion, I would be happy to be of service to you."

Oh, great. I didn't need this. "No thank you, Staff Sergeant." I gave him a stern look. "I can assure you that I wasn't trying to send a message. In my culture belly buttons are not considered a big deal."

He shrugged. "I'm sorry to hear that. I've heard that sex with humans is quite inspiring. If you change your mind, you know where to find me."

I turned to leave and spotted the captain leaning in the doorway with his arms crossed and a look of amusement on his face.

"I'm sorry, sir. It won't happen again," I muttered.

I hurried past him and headed to my quarters to take a quick shower and change into 'appropriate attire.'

Steve's distinct laughter echoed loud and clear.

CHAPTER 32

"Officer Trexxing, fully disable FADE for the moment. NavPilot, take us into the Sorren Belt via the prime point," the captain said. "I want everyone to see us coming."

"Yes, sir." I sent Steve the coordinates along with directions and he responded efficiently.

"Lay in a course for Kirsto Station and when you're in range, request docking rights from the Station Overseer," the captain said.

"Yes, sir." It felt good to be able to do my job without the nervous tension I had experienced in the beginning. My confidence had grown and I felt much better about my abilities. "ETA is approximately thirty hours, sir," I said.

The captain leaned back in his chair and rubbed his chin. "Good. That should give the welcoming committee plenty of time to organize our reception. Officer Trexxing, shields on full, all weapons on standby."

Officer Trexxing calmly turned to the captain. "Already in place, sir."

The captain nodded. "Excellent. Now we wait."

About an hour into the Belt the sensor display in my array lit up.

Steve noticed it too. *"Pirates,"* he echoed.

"Captain, Kandorran Cruiser 4,950 klicks off the starboard side," Trexxing said. "Most likely a pirate ship, sir."

"That took longer than I expected. I wonder what they're up to?" The captain pulled up the 3D display. "NavPilot, take our speed down, just slightly slower than the Kandorran cruiser," he said.

"Yes, sir," I said.

"Let's reel them in gradually. Officer Trexxing, engage FADE just enough to scramble their ability to get a read on us, but not enough to make us invisible. I want them to see the SpaceLion, yet know nothing about us."

I checked my files on Kandorran Cruisers. They were listed as retired T-class destroyers, stolen from the Gaekaar military graveyard and converted into pirate ships. The vessel was far bigger than us, but our ship was smarter, faster, better protected, and had ten times the ordnance.

I watched the 3D display as the pirate ship closed the gap between us.

"I have a bad feeling," Steve echoed.

"A bad feeling? Since when do you have premonitions?" I asked.

"I don't know, but I fucking have one now!" he echoed.

"Kandorran Cruiser has engaged torpedo launchers," Trexxing said.

The captain nodded. "As expected. Prepare for counter-attack."

I noticed Officer Trexxing's eyes widen. "Seven multistage gravitational torpedoes bearing 7842.31. Impact in twenty seconds."

"Evasive maneuvers, now!" the captain shouted.

Steve and I worked together in perfect synchronicity, sharply angling the ship to the port side, just out of the reach of the torpedoes' first pass at us.

"Keep FADE partially engaged and launch anti-artillery missiles, Officer Trexxing," the captain ordered.

"Launching seven AAMs, sir."

The 3D image displayed our seven missiles blasting across space and one by one taking out the torpedoes. The captain hovered over the display. He looked pissed off.

"Where the hell did they get those torpedoes?" he said. "NavPilot, turn us around and take us closer to the Kandorran Cruiser. Trexxing load ten multistage torpedoes. Let's see if they can take what they dish out."

The SpaceLion arced back toward the pirate ship and made a swift approach.

Steve was quiet, which worried me.

"Having any more of those bad feelings, Steve?" I asked.

"Not now. I believe the pirate ship is scared," Steve echoed.

The captain leaned in close to the 3D display. "Now, Officer Trexxing. Launch all ten torpedoes."

I watched in awe as our ten torpedoes blipped across the display and made contact with the pirate ship at varying intervals. The fifth and sixth hits crumpled the massive cruiser and seconds later debris flew in all directions.

"That should make it clear to the criminal population that we aren't fucking around." The captain sat back in his chair. "NavPilot, get us back on track for Kirsto Station. Officer Trexxing, stay on alert, although I doubt we'll be bothered much now."

The captain granted the bridge crew some sleep time before we reached Kirsto, but after a few hours of restless tossing and turning, I decided to get up and go for a run on the treadmill instead. I was feeling antsy. I checked my internal clock. We were scheduled to reach Kirsto Station in six hours.

I entered the gym and was glad to see it was fairly quiet. I tried to avoid working out when the Special Forces team was present, since they tended to hog up the equipment for hours. Captain Torrun worked out on the large weight lifting apparatus directly across from the treadmills, but otherwise the place was empty.

I jumped up on the closest treadmill and adjusted the settings through my array. The captain gave me a nod and went back to his own workout. After a few miles of running I felt great. I found it interesting that I had never been into exercising in my old life, but now I thrived on it.

"You're up early. Shouldn't you be resting?" Steve echoed.

"Couldn't sleep," I replied.

"I'm guessing the captain needed to work off some stress as well," Steve echoed.

"Steve, I've been meaning to ask you about that bad feeling you had when the Kandorran Cruiser approached us. And then you mentioned that you thought the other ship was scared."

"So what?" Steve echoed.

"What exactly gave you those feelings?" I asked.

"It was a subtle vibration that I was getting from the Cruiser's AI."

"AI? How do you know it had an AI?"

"I don't. It was more of a vibe I was getting. You know … a feeling."

I shook my head. *"All right, Steve, I think I understand. But please keep me posted if you have any more of these feelings, okay?"*

"Whatever," Steve echoed.

The captain was performing bench presses not fifteen feet in front of me. He worked out hard, with a level of intense concentration that was equal to his personality. I tried not to overtly watch him, but it was difficult not to see what was going on directly in my line of sight.

"You shouldn't stare," Steve echoed.

"I'm not staring." I looked over at the wall instead.

My eyes were pulled back when the captain stood and tugged off his sweat soaked t-shirt and threw it on the floor. He sat on a bench with his back facing me, grabbed the bar above his head, and began to perform lat extensions.

Okay, now I was staring.

The Gaekaar were a very well put together species. The movement of his thick muscles, the fluidity of his breathing, and the power of his concentration had me riveted. I knew that the Gaekaar were almost genetically identical to humans, but I hadn't expected to be flat-out fascinated by his physical appearance. I'd seen plenty of other male Gaekaars working out, yet I had never before been so attracted to one.

His physique was pumped up from the exercise and his skin glistened with sweat. I noticed several long scars along his back, but somehow that only added to his masculinity. I couldn't quite put my finger on why, but he was so interesting to watch that I couldn't seem to drag my eyes away.

"You're doing it again," Steve echoed. *"You'll be sorry."*

I needed to get a grip. Maybe it was the lack of sleep. I forced myself to look at the wall again. I had to shake this. Being physically attracted to the captain was wrong on so many levels that it was ridiculous.

The captain abruptly ended his workout. He stood up, snatched his t-shirt, and jammed it into his bag. Oddly, he seemed angry. He threw a clean towel around his neck, grabbed his bag, and headed for the door. As he passed by the treadmill, he turned toward me and glared. "Lieutenant Helgren, enjoy your run."

I wasn't sure if it was a question or a statement.

"I wonder what stirred him up?" I asked Steve.

"I take it you didn't review the files on Gaekaar culture?" Steve echoed.

"No, not yet."

Steve snickered. *"No time like the present."*

I opened all four files and began to take in the data. Most of the information had been previously covered in our lectures with Ethan, back on Earth.

The file stated that of all the known alien species, the Gaekaar, the Valorians, and the humans had the closest genetic relationship, which was attributed to the concept of panspermia. I understood that the scientific theory implied life was originally spread throughout the universe by micro-organisms traveling on debris, asteroids, or comets, yet the file I reviewed added religious connotations, stating that it was all part of the design of the Supreme Being. Somehow that was comforting. I didn't care for the idea that we were all just a bunch of random overgrown organisms. I preferred to believe that God had his hand in our creation.

The file went on to state that the Gaekaar's blue skin tone had evolved over millennia after an ancient meteor shower had released the chemical compound rysamabi into the home world atmosphere. Over thousands of years the Gaekaar built up a resistance to the chemical, which manifested as a blue pigmentation. This was also hypothesized as the reason why the species did not have hair. Their size was attributed to the length of time the species had been evolving, which was notably longer than humans.

Many of the Gaekaar's cultural ways were also similar to humans—a variety of religions, marriage ceremonies, families, schools, government, and military. I continued to read through a long list of smaller cultural distinctions, like believing belly buttons were erotic and how the women collected exotic earrings that represented milestones in their lives while the men tattooed symbols on their heads to depict their milestones.

The species had also made astonishing advancements in technology, which over the centuries had been exchanged for medical knowledge with the Valorians. The combination of tech and medicine extended the average life span of a Gaekaar to an average of two hundred sixty years. At roughly one hundred thirty years of age, the Gaekaar developed a gland in the olfactory system, which became something like a sixth sense. It was theorized that humans did not have this gland due to their shorter life span. This gland allowed them to sense the hormonal changes in other beings. The file stated that a Gaekaar individual could pick up on another's fear, joy, anger, anxiety, or sexual attraction by recognizing subtle hormonal fluctuations.

Shit. Shit. Shit. I turned the treadmill off and sat down. I just couldn't seem to get on good footing with the captain. I knew damn well he didn't care for human beings. Undoubtedly, I'd just made that worse.

"It pays to do your homework," Steve teased.

"I've downloaded thousands of files, Steve. I can't possibly read and remember everything." I rested my head in my hands. *"I'm screwed."*

"Perhaps an apology to the captain would be in order?" Steve echoed.

"No way. Too embarrassing."

"Then how do you plan on handling this?" Steve echoed.

I shook my head. *"I don't know, but I'll make damn sure it never happens again."*

"Don't count on it." Steve echoed. *"It took the Gaekaar over a thousand years to learn how to control their emotions. Humans are a passionate species. Your emotional response is primarily subconscious. Just one of the many reasons I find you so interesting."*

I took a quick shower and headed to the cafeteria for a cup of mud. I passed the captain in the entryway and attempted to hold my emotions in check. "Hello, Captain," I said in my best monotone.

"NavPilot, I'd like to see you in my quarters as soon as you finish your breakfast," he replied.

Damn. "I'm just grabbing some coffee, sir. I'm available now."

"Good, then I'll see you shortly." He turned and left.

Stu intercepted me at the coffee stand with his hand outstretched, holding a steaming mug of mud. "Your morning brew, ma'am." He gave me a cheerful smile.

"Thanks, I need this." I took the mug and let the warmth seep through my fingers. It smelled wonderful.

"How are you doing?" Stu asked. "Feeling settled in yet?"

"I believe I'm getting the hang of life onboard the SpaceLion. Although I just learned about the Gaekaar sixth sense."

Stu burst out laughing. "I know what you mean. No matter how hard I try, I can't seem to keep my emotions at bay. Whatever you do, just don't lie to one of them."

"They can tell when you're lying?"

"Yep. They'll sniff out a lie in seconds. Honesty is everything to these people, and on a side note, they don't understand the human concept of bending the truth."

"Thanks for the tip." I held my mug up. "And the mud."

CHAPTER 33

I placed my hand on the sensor outside the captain's door. It slid open and I entered. Captain Torrun was sitting at the conference table reviewing a 3D schematic of Kirsto Station that looked similar to what Ethan had sent me.

"Have a seat, NavPilot," the captain said without looking up.

I sat down and couldn't help but wonder if I was about to get chewed out for the gym incident.

"I'd like to discuss our docking procedure at Kirsto," he started.

Relief washed over me. "Yes, sir."

The captain glanced at me and a smile tugged at the corners of his mouth. Now that I thought about it, I had never seen him smile. His face softened and he looked nice. He must have found my relief humorous, although the thought that he wasn't angry with me just served to make me feel even more relieved. Steve was right, controlling my emotions was going to be a problem.

He turned toward the schematic and pointed. "We'll be docking here at port seventeen, dock two."

"Looks easy enough," I said.

"I selected this dock because, if needed, the escape route is the simplest. My meeting with Oxnot Prevlar is scheduled for 10:00 UGT. If I'm not back by 12:00 UGT, you are under strict orders to leave Kirsto and return to Asbu."

"And leave you and the team behind?" I couldn't believe he was suggesting that.

The captain made direct eye contact with me. "Lieutenant Helgren, if I'm not back by 12:00, we're most likely dead. The safety of the ship is your number one priority. Is that understood?"

"Yes, sir." Fear trickled down my spine in a slow drip. The thought of losing our captain, or any of the SpaceLion's crew, to a bunch of criminals was not something that sat well with me.

He leaned closer. "I've loaded my captain's codes into the SpaceLion's AI. I programmed a shipwide lockdown until I return. And if I don't return, the ship has orders to leave port by 12:05 UGT. There will be no rescue missions. Is that understood?"

My mouth went dry. This mission was far more dangerous than I first thought. "Yes, sir."

I took my seat on the bridge and checked the data flowing through my array. The commander, Officer Trexxing, Staff Sergeant Monc, and Ensign QU were also seated. A few minutes later the captain strode onto the bridge and pulled up the 3D display. "Status report, NavPilot."

"All systems normal. ETA to Kirsto, one hour, fourteen minutes."

The captain nodded. "Officer Trexxing, status?"

Trexxing looked up from his controls. "We've been scanned more times than I can count, but the local ships have maintained their distance. We've got a clear run from here to Kirsto."

Steve grumbled in the back of my mind. *"You do realize that the captain downloaded code into my programming, don't you?"*

"Yes, I know," I replied.

"I have a bad feeling again. You told me to tell you when I had these fucked up feelings," Steve echoed.

"Okay, let's talk about it. What do you think is causing the bad feeling?"

"I'm getting a strange vibe from Kirsto's AI."

"The station has an AI?" I asked.

"Well, apparently."

A sleazy station like Kirsto shouldn't have access to the technology required to house an AI. *"Can you reach out and communicate with it?"*

"No, it doesn't have authorization on its end for formal communication. I'm simply getting the vibe of an AI presence and it doesn't seem very happy. It's fucking creepy," Steve echoed.

I turned toward the captain. "Sir, our AI is picking up another AI presence in the area."

The captain rubbed his chin. "Interesting. Let me know if it picks up more than just a presence."

"Yes, sir."

"I am not an 'it,'" Steve echoed.

"Of course you're not. The captain isn't totally up to speed on the nuances of your evolution just yet."

"Whatever." Steve sent me a vibe of irritation.

A short time later, I contacted the Kirsto Station Overseer to request docking rights. A prompt confirmation arrived and I worked with Steve to pull the SpaceLion up to port seventeen, dock two.

The docking clamp clunked into position, causing a slight vibration throughout the ship.

"Nicely done, NavPilot." The captain stood. "Commander NU has control of the ship while I'm away. Staff Sergeant Monc, you're with me."

I checked my internal clock. It was 9:00 UGT. The next few hours would be long. I was more than a little anxious about the team making it back in time for our 12:05 automated departure.

Staff Sergeant Monc stood and glanced in my direction. "Helgren, worry is oozing from you like an open wound. It makes you appear weak."

I glared back at him, annoyed. "I'll take that as a compliment coming from someone who enjoys violence and doesn't know the meaning of the word *concern*."

Trexxing chuckled. "She has a point."

The captain looked at me. "NavPilot, I expect you to put your *concerns* aside and do your job."

"Yes, sir." I shot the staff sergeant a harsh look. He ignored me and exited the bridge with the captain at his side.

I monitored the ship's sensors and noted that the captain disembarked with his team at 9:15 UGT. It would be a long wait until the deadline.

To kill time, I pulled up the schematic of Kirsto Station that Ethan had sent me. The station contained thirty-two bars, fourteen restaurants, ten pawn shops, three hotels, sixty merchant stores, and a center station 'pit' that offered a litany of services that were otherwise illegal outside the belt. I scanned the services available to visitors—a wide variety of gambling venues, multiple fighting cages, every kind of sexual experience imaginable with the species of your choice, an illicit drug emporium, a pain parlor, and lastly, an information center for friendly assistance in the event you couldn't find the perversion you craved.

The diagram also showed a network of natural caves below the station that housed more unlawful activities with the main attraction focused on cage fighting. These weren't ordinary fights. If the losers didn't die in the cage, they were hauled off to another spectator sport, a one-way trip into the vacuum of space via an airlock. The center station pit was, without a doubt, a disturbing place.

I looked at my clock again. 10:10 UGT. I prayed that the meeting was going well. I was restless, so I studied the Kirsto diagram for the tenth time.

The next time I checked my clock the time read 11:15 UGT. I looked around the bridge and noticed that everyone was becoming impatient. Officer Trexxing checked his instruments again and again. The commander paced the floor and Ensign QU repeatedly checked the SpaceLion's channels for transmissions that weren't there.

"How are you doing, Steve?" I asked.

"I'm distracted," he echoed.

"Why?"

"It's Kirsto's AI. I am getting a feel for its presence. I know it's out there, but there is no way for me to touch it."

"Why is that bothering you so much?" I asked.

"I'm not sure. But I think it's miserable and I have this need to reach out," he echoed.

I recalled the coding that Colonel Poah had given to me. It was his own special programming that could link two AI's together regardless of authorization. The more I thought about it, the more I realized it was a bad idea. I didn't know how that code might impact our AI, particularly if it was unhealthy, and there was no way I was going to take that risk.

Clock watching became a unique form of torture as the minutes crawled by. With ten minutes left before departure, a sense of panic settled in my gut. Damn. Everyone around the bridge looked at each other. I was no longer the only one with an anxious expression.

"Steve?" I said, trying to get his full attention.

"What?"

"I want you to be ready for something that might blow a few circuits. You also might want to turn up your anti-viral protection to maximum."

"Wow, sounds exciting! Give it to me. I want—I need to feel more," he echoed.

I knew it was dangerous, but I felt as if I was trapped in a corner. I wasn't going to debate the morality of what I was about to do, so without further thought, I pulled up the code that purportedly connected two AI's together, without authorization. I removed the wrapper and pushed it into Steve's programming.

"Shit!" Steve echoed. *"I guess you weren't kidding."*

"What happened?" I asked.

"Nothing yet, I was just looking over the parameters of the code you uploaded. This isn't GAP authorized and I doubt it's even legal."

"Can you use it?" I asked.

"Do you realize how much trouble we could get in for executing this file? Oh, what the fuck. I'm doing it."

I waited for several seconds and heard nothing but silence across our connection.

"H-h-hello?" A timid and unsure voice came through Steve's connection.

"Well, hello!" Steve echoed.

"What the hell is going on?" The voice became defensive.

Dr. Uleht walked on to the bridge. "Have you heard anything? It's 11:58."

I stood to greet the doctor. "I'm sorry, nothing yet."

He frowned. "There has to be something we can do?"

I shook my head. "The ship is on lock down and at 12:05 the SpaceLion will automatically return to Asbu Station."

"Holy shit!" Steve shouted.

"What?" I asked.

"I think she likes me. We've connected on an AI level and we've been having long conversations," Steve echoed.

"She? What do you mean … she?" I asked.

"I explained how gender works and how I picked my own name. She wanted to do the same," Steve echoed.

Considering the speed at which AI's computed, I guessed they'd had thousands of conversations in the few seconds I'd been speaking with the doctor.

The doctor approached the commander with a question and I turned my full attention towards Steve. *"That's nice, Steve, but we have bigger issues right now."*

"No you don't," he echoed.

"How so?" I looked at my internal clock readout, 12:00 UGT. My anxiety level ratcheted up another notch.

"Kirsto's AI can help us. If I send her the life support codes for our crew she can transmit their data to us," Steve echoed.

"Can she give us their location?" I asked.

"Of course," Steve echoed.

I walked over to the doctor. "Dr. Uleht, I need to talk to you for a moment. Privately."

I grabbed his arm and hastily led him off the bridge where we would be out of earshot of the bridge crew. "Dr. Uleht, the SpaceLion's AI is communicating with the AI at Kirsto Station. Through this link we might be able to locate our team. Is there any way you would be willing to release the life support codes so Kirsto's AI could use them to track our team down?"

"Not only is that highly unethical," he whispered, "but how is our AI communicating with another AI on a criminally active station?"

I was so nervous that my voice shook. "I don't have time to explain now. If we don't do something, in a few minutes we'll be leaving the captain and crew behind."

The doctor remained calm and in control. "All right." He nodded. "In this case I would be willing to bend the rules. I'll message you the codes."

In an instant I received the codes and pushed them over to Steve to feed to his new friend.

"She's looking now," Steve echoed.

"Are you sure?" I asked.

"Of course. I told you, I think she likes me," Steve echoed. *"The life support readings and coordinates have arrived. Forwarding them to you now."*

I was thankful for the speed of AI processing. I forwarded the life support information to the doctor and ran the coordinates up against the schematic I had on file from Ethan. The team appeared to be somewhere in the tunnels below the station center pit.

The doctor shook his head. "I'm getting no readings from Corporal VO, weak vitals from Captain Torrun, and moderate vitals from Staff Sergeant Monc. I need to get to them."

"Shit. It's 12:02. We have to get off this ship now or you'll never have the opportunity," I said, turning and heading toward the docking port.

"Steve, ask your friend if she'll help us enter the station." I picked up my pace to a flat-out run. The doctor was right behind me.

"She's willing to help," Steve echoed. *"But she said to warn you that the station is an unfriendly place and it's unlikely you'll make it out alive."*

CHAPTER 34

"Dr. Uleht, I need to warn you that not only will you be going against the captain's orders, which by the way could be considered mutiny, but there's also a good chance we'll both be killed."

"I'm a doctor and I have crew out there that might be dying," he said, easily keeping up with my pace. "Furthermore, I'm a civilian, so military regulations don't apply to me."

I stopped at the weapons locker, just outside the dock portal, and keyed in a code.

"Don't bother," Steve echoed. *"Kirsto security won't let you bring automated weapons into the station, but Jane will help you get what you need."*

"Shit." I slammed the locker closed. *"Are you sure? And who's Jane?"*

"Yes, I'm sure. And Jane is Kirsto's AI. I gave her a real name. She likes me."

My clock read 12:04 UGT.

I pulled up Colonel Poah's code, which would override the captain's code and take the ship out of lockdown. I took a breath and pushed the code into the ship's system.

"Well, well. Aren't you full of surprises today," Steve echoed.

I reached out my hand and placed it on the portal sensor and the door slid open. I stepped through the portal and turned to Dr. Uleht. "You have about thirty seconds to change your mind, Doctor."

Without hesitation, he followed and stood next to me just before the door slid shut. I grabbed his hand and pulled him through the airlock. The chamber sealed. It was done. I may have just thrown my career away, but I downright refused to stand by and do nothing while my crewmates perished. The war effort couldn't afford to lose a good captain or Special Forces crew, whereas I was expendable. Furthermore, my brothers had long ago drilled into my head the fact that loyalty was everything and soldiers did not leave fellow soldiers behind.

We both took a step back as the rumble of the SpaceLion's fusion drive kicked in.

"We'll only be able to communicate for a few more minutes before the distance severs our connection," Steve echoed. *"You'll need to find a way to communicate with Jane."*

"Thanks, Steve, I've got that covered. I appreciate your help."

"Is there anything I should do when we reach Asbu? Perhaps send a rescue team?" Steve echoed.

"Yeah. That would be nice. Thank you."

"One more thing," Steve echoed. *"Please don't get yourself killed. My programming has become accustomed to you and I don't believe I'd function well without you."*

"Oh Steve, that's so sweet of you. I'll miss you too."

Our connection severed and I prayed that wasn't the last time we communicated. He had truly grown on me.

I looked at the doctor and took a deep breath. "This isn't going to be pleasant, Doctor."

"Understood." He gave me a single nod. "Where do we go from here?"

I double-checked the station schematic in my head. "We have to pass through security first. This way."

The airlock opened up to a long hallway with moving floors that brought us to the security unit that safeguarded the entry to the station. An oversized, thick-necked guard looked at us, grunted, and pointed to a platform indicating that we should stand there. We both stepped up and the guard touched something on his wrist that triggered an orb scanner. The orb circled around us several times and then ascended. The guard then touched his wrist device again and the electronic shield that protected the entry to the station powered down.

The guard gave me a casual nod, then turned toward the doctor and scowled. "You're both cleared and you've been registered. You may enter the station."

The guard spoke the Gaekaar language, but he didn't look anything like them. He was huge, maybe eight feet tall, with bulging eyes and yellow skin.

We passed through the entry, but as we left the security unit behind us, I noticed the guard never took his eyes off the doctor.

"What species was that?" I whispered.

"That's a Moltarro." The doctor frowned. "They've been genetically modified for centuries. Primarily used for fighting and security ... for obvious reasons."

I looked at my companion's lean frame. "Yeah, let's steer clear of those things. I don't think he liked you, Dr. Uleht."

"No, he wouldn't," he responded. "And as long as we are in a non-military setting, please call me Andar."

"Certainly, and please, call me Millie. I'm curious, why didn't the Moltarro—"

"Millie, I'll explain later. Right now we need to get moving," Andar replied, stepping forward.

We left the security unit and walked into the open area of the station. An unpleasant odor hit me smack in the face. It reminded me of a blend of sweat and old rotting garbage. The floor was bustling with activity. An untold number of species roamed the main level. Some filthy, some clean, some poor, some wealthy. I looked up and saw four huge balconies that housed shops, bars, restaurants, hotels, and dens.

"Ah, newcomers!" A short raggedy Awyx walked up to us. His red face was dirty and body odor surrounded him like a cloud. "Can I help you with something? Maybe directions?" The Awyx took Andar's hand and inspected his rings. "How about a trade?"

Andar snatched his hand away. "You would be well advised not to touch me."

"We don't need your help," I said, pushing the filthy creature away.

The Awyx made a noise that sounded like a snarl. "You'll be sorry. This is no place for the likes of you."

I leaned over to Andar and whispered, "We need weapons."

"Agreed," he said.

"Kirsto's AI has offered to help us. I just need a moment to connect." I pushed Colonel Poah's second code through my array and activated a link to Jane.

"There you are," she echoed directly into my mind.

"You're communicating in the same way that Steve does ... how is that possible without an upgrade?" I asked.

"That's strictly confidential, Lieutenant. Right now you are on a need to know basis."

"Alright. Hello, Jane. I'm Millie. Steve tells me that you would be willing to help us."

"For Steve, yes. But you'll also owe me a debt."

"Thank you. We appreciate your assistance and will try to return the favor."

"That will be expected, Millie. Nothing is free at Kirsto Station."

"Understood. We need three things. First we need to find weapons, then we need to find our friends, and then we need a way off the station."

"I can help with those requests. Obviously my abilities will be limited to information only, utilizing a secure connection. Please note that I will not do anything that involves mechanical action. Any type of physical movement could be traced back to me, and as you know, I deal with many unforgiving species."

"Of course, I understand."

"Good. Go to the center station pit information counter and make a request to see Juniper. She has the best assortment of weapons on the station. When you meet with her, tell her that White Sage sent you."

"Who's White Sage?"

"White Sage isn't a being. It's a passcode that links you to the primary underground fighting faction. She will not be able to refuse you. As for your friends, they are being held in location TSF18.7. Lastly, your ride off-station is waiting in Port five, dock seven. It's a small Orsydi ship that I'd like to get the hell off my station. I'm forwarding you the ship's access code now. I believe that completes your requests. You owe me. And I don't forget."

"Yes, should we survive, we will owe you. Thank you for your help, Jane."

I looked over at Andar. "Unfortunately, we need to go into the center pit."

"I've heard of Kirsto's pit. We'll need to get our hands on those weapons quickly," he said.

I nodded. We took an anti-grav lift down several levels while I explained Jane's directions to Andar.

"I'm not sure how I feel about taking directions from an unknown AI," he said. "How do you know it's not a trap?"

I shrugged. "I don't, but we don't have any other options."

"I see your point," Andar said, a scowl forming on his face.

We landed on the pit floor and took a look around. I wrinkled my nose and Andar's frown deepened. The smell in the pit was ten times worse than it was on the main level. The floor was covered with grime and garbage, and the air seemed to float around us in a discolored mustard-colored haze. The outer ring of the pit was lined with secure portals and a Moltarro guard stationed in between each entry. The middle of the pit housed a circular information center that was surrounded by clusters of beings, each clamoring with requests and complaints. Calm copper robots attended to each demand with efficiency and professionalism. I also noticed that each bot had an old-fashioned bell hanging just above its position.

"I suppose we should get in line," Andar said.

I nodded and stepped up behind a mid-sized Gaekaar who was becoming belligerent with the robot attendant. "I want my credits back or I'll rip your shitty little head off!" the Gaekaar shouted.

The bot took a step back, reached up, and rang the bell. In an instant a Moltarro guard put his hand on the Gaekaar's shoulder and spun him around. "You have two choices, sir. Either leave quietly on your own, or I'll send you on your way, via the airlock. Which will it be?"

The Gaekaar stood frozen for a moment. "I'll leave on my own, but this is robbery! The station magistrate will be hearing from me."

"Don't count on it," the Moltarro said. "We have a new magistrate and he doesn't see commoners. Now get the hell out of here, before I change my mind and toss you in the airlock to alleviate my boredom."

The Gaekaar snapped his mouth shut and stormed off.

The Moltarro turned to us. "My apologies for the disturbance."

"Think nothing of it," Andar said. "We're glad to see issues handled with such competence."

The Moltarro nodded, visibly boosted by the compliment. "May your stay on Kirsto be pleasant," he said as he departed.

"Yeah, right," I said under my breath.

We stepped up to the counter and the bot scooted toward us. "How may I be of service to you?"

"We're looking for Juniper," I said. "We'd like to meet with her."

"And who may I say sent you?" the bot asked.

I leaned forward. "White Sage," I whispered.

"One moment please." Several lights flashed in the bot's copper head. "Very well. Go to portal five and a Moltarro guard will escort you to Juniper's parlor. Thank you for allowing me to be of service."

"And thank you as well," I said with a nod.

Portal number five was on the far side of the pit. Andar stayed by my side as we made our way through a sea of unsavory clientele. When we came upon the portal the Moltarro guard was waiting for us.

"Follow me," he said in a deep voice.

The guard touched a device on his wrist and the portal opened with a groan. He led us down a steep set of stairs and into a dark twisted passage that had been carved into the asteroid. I felt the chill of ice cold air circulating through the underground network.

The Moltarro stopped outside a rusted metal door and pounded on it with his massive fist.

The door swung open and a stocky human woman stepped in front of us. She had spiked black hair, wore an old bomber jacket, and had tattoos all over her neck.

"Well, well, well. I haven't seen another human around here for ages. I hope you speak Gaekaar. I haven't spoken any of the human languages in so long, I'm not sure I even remember them," she said.

"Yes, we both do," I replied.

"Good. I'm Juniper. Come on in and have a seat." She waved at the guard. "You can go. Shoo."

Juniper's office was small but built like a fortress. Multiple cameras and lasers were mounted around the perimeter of gray metal walls. She took a seat at a metal desk that looked at least a hundred years old. Andar and I sat in two worn-out brocade wing chairs that were positioned in front of the desk.

Juniper eyed me for a few seconds, and then she leaned forward on her elbows. "White sage, my ass. Based on your uniform, you're obviously allied military, and you're—" She eyed the doctor. "I don't know what you are, but you're way too small and weak to be part of the underground fighting faction."

Andar stared back at her. "Are you familiar with the human saying 'don't judge a book by its cover'?"

"Of course," she replied, annoyed. "All right. Let's get down to business. What do you need?"

I dug into a file that listed military weapons and selected a gun that appeared to be adequate. "I'd like two M-55 repeaters and plenty of ammo."

She shook her head and rolled her eyes. "Toys," she muttered.

Andar leaned forward. "Additionally, we would like two Kandorran Blasters with silencers and four rechargeable refills."

I turned toward him and raised my brow. "Doctor, do you have hidden talents that you haven't told me about?"

"We all have hidden talents, Millie."

"Maybe you're not as weak as I first thought." Juniper slapped her palms on the desktop and stood up. "I'll be right back."

In less than a minute, she returned with her arms full and carelessly dumped the blasters, refills, repeaters, and ammo onto the desktop.

"I'll tell you what, the whole pile is yours for the bargain price of thirty thousand credits."

"Thirty thousand credits? Are you kidding?" I fumed and stood up. "That's ridiculous."

Juniper shrugged. "Taxes have gone up around here since the new magistrate took over and I have a past due notice to pay."

"We'll need your jacket too. My friend here needs to cover up her uniform," Andar said, nodding toward me.

Juniper's eyes went wide. "What? And now you want the clothes off my back? It'll be a cold day in hell before I give up this baby." She stretched her arms out and admired the worn leather sleeves.

Without hesitation, Andar pulled off one of his exotic rings and set it on the desk. The ring was made of white metal and had been embedded with clear stones that formed a wave pattern.

Juniper leaned over, opened a desk drawer, and pulled out a small scanning device, which she positioned over the ring. After three long beeps, she read the display and set the device down. She picked up the ring and made direct eye contact with the doctor. "Okay, I'm sure you realize that this little trinket is worth about sixty thousand credits."

"Probably more on the black market," he said. "We're interested in purchasing your discretion as well."

"For sixty thousand you can have my first born," she laughed. "You two are obviously in some deep shit." She pulled off her bomber jacket and tossed it on the table. "Be forewarned, the new magistrate has his spies situated everywhere. It's not as easy to go around killing things as it once was."

"Who is this magistrate?" Andar asked.

Juniper waved her hand through the air. "Just some Orsydi cocksucker who doubled my rent and quadrupled my taxes." She picked up a blaster, scratched the side of her face with it, and then carefully pointed it toward the door. "I'd like to blast his fucking ass."

CHAPTER 35

Juniper set the blaster down. "If you don't mind me asking, where are you headed with this kind of armament?"

"We need to find location TSF18.7," I said.

"Are you fucking crazy?" Juniper's eyes went wide and she shook her head. "Wait, don't answer that. Everyone who comes through here is fucking crazy. Furthermore, the TSF level is no place for two lightweights like yourselves."

"We are trying to locate friends," Andar said.

"Isn't everyone?" Juniper sighed. "All right. I feel like I owe you something since you grossly overpaid, plus I'd like to retain your future business."

She reached down and pulled something out of her boot. I caught the glint of metal and realized it was some sort of knife. "I'll tell you what." Juniper jammed the knife, point first, into the metal desktop. The blade sunk deeply into the surface. "I'll throw in this little lovely as a bonus."

"A knife?" I couldn't imagine how that would help us.

Juniper leaned forward. "Not just any knife. This baby is made from Kandorran steel. Goes through just about anything."

I pulled the knife from the desktop. It seemed to float in my hand. I smiled. "Okay. Thanks."

"I'll give you one last tidbit of information before I conclude our transaction. You'll find the TSF area two levels down. But it's nothing more than a dungeon where prisoners are left to die after a cage fight. Even if your friends survived the fight, which is unlikely, they'll be dead soon. Everyday at 15:00 UGT the losers are tossed into an airlock and sucked into space, dead or alive. It's a big attraction around here." Juniper leaned back in her chair and shrugged. "Your friends are probably long gone."

"We need to make haste," Andar said as he secured the weapons inside his white jacket. "Thank you, Juniper."

I pulled on the oversized bomber jacket and covered the identifying marks of my uniform. "And we appreciate your help," I added.

Juniper picked up the ring and admired it with hungry eyes. "I don't *help* anyone. This is a business, not a charity." Her gaze shifted to us and she made a sound that resembled a snort. "Now get out."

The parlor door slammed behind us and we found ourselves standing in an empty passageway. Andar and I each carried a blaster and had the remaining weapons and refills tucked away in our coats. I held the Kandorran knife out. "Do you want to carry this?" I asked.

Andar shook his head. "You take it. I don't need it."

I slid the knife into my boot. "More hidden talents, Andar?"

He ignored my question and looked up and down the passage. "Which way?"

I pulled up the schematic and pinpointed TSF18.7. It was indeed located two levels down, just as Juniper stated. I nodded to the left. "This way."

We headed to the end of the passageway and another set of stairs that went deep into the asteroid. Each sublevel had a small landing that led to the entrance of a tunnel. At the second sublevel, we stepped onto the landing and peered into the opening. *TSF Level* was carved into the rock. A clinking noise made me jump. Andar pushed me flush against the wall. We waited until it seemed the passage was clear.

A sickening moan resonated through the tunnel, followed by more clicking sounds. I inched my head around the corner and saw an empty tunnel with cells carved into solid rock on either side. The air was damp and carried the stench of rotting flesh and blood. More moans filled the air. I felt sick. This place was worse than any nightmare I could possibly dream up.

I pointed my blaster down the tunnel. "We'll need to go to the end and take the tunnel on the right. 18.7 should be the fourth cell on the left."

Andar nodded and took the lead.

We held our blasters ready and moved as fast as we could. We passed by dozens of cells, each protected by rusted metal grates. Within the cells we saw various species, all with their wrists shackled to the floor. Most of the beings were motionless, possibly dead, and a few rolled around in painful agony.

At the end of the passage we rounded the corner and sprinted to the fourth cell on the left.

"This should be it, TSF18.7," Andar said.

I stood next to him and peered into the dark cell. Three crumpled figures, with wrists chained to the floor, lay unmoving on the rock floor. My heart pounded with adrenaline-fueled fear. I inspected the metal grate and saw what appeared to be an antique lock. What was with all of this old-fashioned shit?

I pointed the blaster at the lock and fired a low energy shot with the silencer on full. The lock disintegrated and sparks fell to the floor. I gave the grate a slow push and the old metal groaned loudly. I cringed and lessened the pressure I was exerting, only opening the grate far enough for us to squeeze through.

One of the crumpled figures lifted its head and looked over at us. It was the staff sergeant. He had blood caked on the side of his face and appeared to be missing an ear. He looked horrible. I ran over to him and knelt down.

"No, you are not fucking here." His voice came out in a rasping whisper. "Helgren, you can't be here."

Staff Sergeant Monc moved his foot and nudged the body next to him.

The figure turned its head and I recognized Captain Torrun. Blood oozed from a gash on the side of his head and one eye was swollen shut. The captain seemed to take a moment to focus his sight on my face. "Shit." He closed his good eye and sucked in a breath. "Where's my ship, Helgren?"

"On its way to Asbu Station, as you ordered, sir."

He clenched his teeth. "It had better be."

CHAPTER 36

The doctor knelt by the third figure, which I took to be Corporal VO. His line of sight moved up and down the corporal's limp figure. A soft glow illuminated the corners of his eyes as his internal medical array engaged in a full body scan. A moment later Andar shook his head and pressed his fingers to the corporal's neck, trying to find a pulse the old fashioned way. After several tries he looked over at me and shook his head again. "I'm afraid the corporal's gone."

"VO was dead before he left the cage," the staff sergeant said in a raspy whisper. "A fucking Moltarro smashed his skull in the second round."

"I'm sorry," I whispered. It had to be hard for him to lose one of his team.

Staff Sergeant Monc remained quiet.

The captain rolled onto his back and blood continued to seep from the wound on his head. I could tell he was in pain. "Helgren, we're going to have to talk about your inability to follow orders." A gasping sound came from his throat after each word.

The doctor crouched by Captain Torrun's side. "Captain, please don't move. I'm going to execute a quick scan."

After completing the scan, Andar frowned and looked over at me. "He has a mild concussion, a broken rib, a torn ligament in his right knee that will give him trouble when he tries to walk, and the obvious cuts and contusions. The captain also has a punctured lung, which is partially collapsed and causing labored breathing. I need to get him to my medical equipment soon, otherwise he won't survive more than a few days."

The doctor pulled a small kit from his jacket and opened it. He rubbed some kind of gel on the captain's head wound and the bleeding immediately stopped. Once the captain was stabilized, he moved over to the staff sergeant.

I slid over and inspected the captain's shackles. Each wrist had a greenish-gray metal cuff with six inches of matching chain tightly secured to the rock floor. I inspected the chain closely. I'd never seen anything like it. I checked my files and discovered that it was Magnecarbon, used in formulating the outer hull of space ships. Extremely strong stuff. I pulled out my knife and took a stab at the chain. The blade made a clicking sound and bounced off.

Andar glanced over and nodded toward my weapon. "Try the blaster, Helgren, but be careful, you could easily remove his whole arm."

I slid the knife back into my boot and reached for the blaster. I adjusted the settings to the lowest energy level, focused the beam to a pinpoint, and engaged the silencer. The captain leaned back and pulled the chain taut. I took careful aim and pulled the trigger. The energy pulse hit the chain and sent sparks in all directions. I inspected the chain and found a small nick. I also noticed that the captain's hand had been burned. I touched his reddened skin. "I'm sorry, sir."

Captain Torrun sucked in air and I thought I heard a slight wheezing. "Don't worry about it, just keep going."

I removed my coat and covered his hands. Ten minutes and thirty blasts later the chain snapped apart. I immediately moved on to the captain's other chained wrist.

Andar looked over at us. "Staff Sergeant Monc is in somewhat better shape. Other than missing an ear, he has cuts and contusions, and some damage to his vocal cords." He glanced back at Monc. "I take it you did some shouting, Staff Sergeant?"

"Just teaching the Moltarro the proper use of profanity, Doc," Monc said.

The doctor applied gel to Monc's missing ear. "You needn't worry about the ear, Staff Sergeant. We'll grow you another when we get to Asbu."

After finally freeing the captain's other wrist, I put his arm over my shoulder and helped him up. When he put pressure on his right knee, it buckled under the strain.

He squeezed my shoulder to maintain his balance. "Fuck," he growled.

The doctor pulled off his white coat and began tearing it into long strips with almost no effort. "I'm going to wrap your knee," he told the captain. "This will help support the joint, although there's nothing I can do for the pain."

"Don't worry about the pain, just make it tight enough so I can walk." Captain Torrun leaned back against the wall while the doctor wrapped his knee.

I moved over to Monc and quickly covered his hands with my coat. I checked the setting on the blaster and began the arduous process of firing on the chains.

He gave me a sour look. "You're oozing worry again, Helgren. Please tell me you have a plan," he said in a raspy voice.

"Well ... we have an escape ship lined up. I'm just not sure how to get from here to the shuttle bay without attracting attention," I said, continuing to take direct shots at the chain.

Loud banging noises reverberated from the far end of the other passage. Andar stood and cautiously looked up and down the passage. "It's coming from the main tunnel, I'll check it out."

Monc's first chain snapped apart. "One more to go," I said.

The staff sergeant yanked the final chain taut and I began firing.

Andar returned in less than a minute. "Four guards are conducting a routine patrol. They'll be here in a couple minutes. We need to move, now."

I felt panic build in my gut. "Monc still has his right hand shackled. I need at least ten more minutes."

The staff sergeant grabbed my arm. "Turn up the power and blast through it. I don't give a shit about my hand."

I shook my head. "I can't do that. You could lose your whole arm."

The deep voices of the guards trying to provoke some of the prisoners echoed through the passage. The four of us looked at each other, hoping someone had an answer.

"We could kill them, but I suspect we'd have an army after us within seconds," the doctor said pointedly.

The captain nodded. "It would be best to escape quietly and hope the patrol doesn't pick up on our absence."

"The Moltarros collect the prisoners for airlock release in just over an hour," I pointed out. "We can count on the alarm being sounded at that point."

"It's time to fucking go! Turn it up and blast through it," Monc rasped out. "Screw my arm."

The doctor knelt down and grabbed some left over strips of fabric. He looked at me with a strong and steady expression. "Get out the knife. We have to work fast."

I pulled out the Kandorran blade and held it out to him.

Andar shook his head as he fashioned a tourniquet around Monc's wrist. "I have to hold Monc's arm and make sure he doesn't bleed to death. I need *you* to do it."

"Me?" I said lamely.

I looked over at the captain. He had one eye swollen shut and a punctured lung, so I knew he couldn't do it. I looked down at my hand holding the knife. It was shaking.

Andar rolled up some fabric and stuffed it between the staff sergeant's teeth. "Bite down, Monc," he said.

"I—I'm not sure I can do this," I said.

"Helgren, look at me," the captain said in a calm voice. I looked into his face and saw the familiar intensity that was always present. It was somehow comforting. "You didn't come this far so we could all die. Now do it."

I turned to the Monc. The doctor had a firm hold on his arm. I looked down at my hand gripping the blade, I felt sick.

Monc spit out the fabric roll. "Fuck it, Helgren. Do it!"

My palms became slippery and I tightened my grasp on the handle. I took a deep breath and, using as much force as I could manage, drew the blade across Monc's wrist. It slid through skin, bone, and tendons like butter.

The severed hand rolled onto the floor and one of the fingers twitched. The staff sergeant tensed up and made a strange sound. I looked over at his face and saw sweat beading on his brow and blood trickling from his lower lip.

"I'm sorry," I whispered.

The doctor quickly adjusted the tourniquet, applied gel to his stump, and covered it all with a thick layer of fabric. He nodded toward me. "Let's try to get him moving."

I helped Andar pull Monc into a standing position. His legs wobbled at first, but he was able to walk.

"I've got him. You help the captain," Andar said.

"What about ... that?" I asked, pointing to the lifeless hand.

The doctor nodded. "I'll get it."

I ran over to the captain, took his arm, and put it over my shoulder. We took a step together. He had a bad limp, but at least he could move.

"This way." I pointed to the right.

We hobbled down the passage to another set of stairs. This place was like a labyrinth, so I double-checked my schematic for directions. If I understood the diagram correctly, the route we were on would take us past the cage fighting level and back to Juniper's level, on the far side.

I looked back to check on the others. Andar and Monc were coming up behind us. The stairs slowed us down more than I liked, but within a minute we reached the cage level.

I paused so the captain could catch his breath. My head was near his chest, amplifying the sound of his strained breathing. "Are you all right?" I looked up at his face. He looked pale.

"I'm good. Keep moving," he said through clenched teeth.

I glanced back at Monc. He didn't look much better. His blue skin had an ashen quality and his face was lined in a grimace.

"Stop it, Helgren, I'm fine," Monc barked.

"Well, I don't hear any alarms. That must be a good sign," Andar commented.

"I'm hoping the guards overlooked a few missing bodies," Captain Torrun said, his breath coming in short gasps. "But if word of our disappearance reaches the magistrate, we won't have much time before the entire station is on alert."

"Did you say the magistrate?" I asked.

The captain nodded. "Our meeting with Oxnot Prevlar was interrupted when the magistrate's security detail crashed the party. They slit Onxot's throat and threw us into the cages."

"Well, according to our weapons dealer, the magistrate is an Orsydi extremist," I said.

"Weapons dealer?" The captain gave me a quizzical look. "Yes, of course, where else would you have found a Kandorran blade, not to mention a pair of blasters."

I looked back at Andar. "I think we should pay Juniper another visit."

He nodded. "Agreed."

We made our way to the top of the stairs and down the long twisted tunnel where Juniper's parlor resided. I pounded hard on the rusted metal door, just like the Moltarro had when we first arrived.

No answer.

Andar stepped forward and removed a brass colored ring dotted with bright green gemstones. He held it up in full view of the cameras.

Within a moment, the door opened and Juniper stood pointing a short nosed laser shotgun at us. "Make it quick. I don't want anyone associating your bullshit antics with my parlor."

We entered and Juniper hit a switch that remotely slammed the door behind us.

She eyed the four of us and then looked closely at the staff sergeant's missing ear and bandaged stump. "Lose a few things, soldier?"

Monc glared down at her. "Fuck you."

"We need another trade," Andar said, holding out the brilliant ring.

I had to marvel over the doctor's collection of valuables and hoped to someday learn how he acquired them.

"Set it down, there." Juniper pointed at the desktop with the nose of her shotgun.

The doctor gently put the ring down.

Juniper grabbed the scanner still sitting on her desk and waved it over the ring. The unit beeped three times and a broad smile stretched across her face as she read the results. "Valorian Brass and Talu Swamp Stones. Fifty thousand credits. Sweet." She looked up at us and smiled. "What do you need?"

"Something to disguise our two friends," Andar said. "And kindly dispose of this." He set the bloody hand down on her desk.

Juniper eyed the hand and wrinkled her face.

"We also need directions for a safe path to port five," I added.

Juniper nodded, slipping the ring into her pocket. "Done. I'll be right back." She disappeared into the back room for less than a minute and came out with two heavy red robes draped over her arm. She threw them on the desk, still clutching her shotgun.

"Hooded full-length robes," she said. "Blood red. It's the latest rage, worn by all the opiate addicts."

"And a safe route to port five?" I reminded her.

"There is no such thing as 'safe' at Kirsto." She shook her head. "You can't leave the way you came, so the only other way out is through the cage arena. Take the stairs down one level and cross the arena to the concession stands. Behind the stands you'll find an anti-grav service lift. A Moltarro named Romar runs the lift and he owes me a favor. Just tell him Juniper said 'we're even.' He'll drop you off on the main level and then it's just a short walk to port five."

Juniper smiled and pointed the laser shotgun at us. "Now get the fuck out of here."

CHAPTER 37

We were quite a foursome. I sported the oversized bomber jacket, the captain and Monc were cloaked in red opiate addict robes, and the doctor's white medical suit was streaked with bloodstains.

We hid our weapons under the heavy cloaks, and I kept the blade in my boot. Once we reached the cage level, I was amazed to see that we fit right in with the wide variety of screwballs roaming the floor. Opiate usage must have been popular because we saw dozens of patrons wearing red cloaks, most of them hanging together in small groups.

Smoke from various forms of drug use hung low in the dingy air and the place smelled of blood and death. The arena was comprised of fifteen large cages that formed a circle around a control tower positioned in the middle. A giant brass bell hung above the tower and when it clanged the vibration was felt throughout the arena. Monc explained that at the sound of the bell, all fights began concurrently and didn't end until one opponent was rendered unconscious. Once all fifteen fights had concluded, a new round was set up.

I looked around and saw guards loading the losers' broken bodies onto anti-grav flatbeds. The champions, on the other hand, were treated like heroes. Most of them appeared to be the largest of the giant mutated Moltarro.

We passed by one cage where the oversized champion continued to beat an unconscious Awyx opponent until it was nothing but a mass of chewed up red flesh and bone. The crowd went wild for this particular perversion. I turned my head and cringed. It was shocking to see how many spectators got off on watching an overblown mass of muscles beat the crap out of smaller beings. I quickly developed an appreciation for just how tough the captain and the staff sergeant must have been.

Monc scowled. "I can't believe I'm back in this fucking hellhole."

I reached over and pulled his hood low over his face. "We don't need anyone recognizing you."

"The concessions are over there," Andar said, pointing to the far right side of the arena.

"We should stick to the perimeter. It's less crowded," the captain said, his breath still coming in short gasps.

"Agreed," Andar said. He led the way, following the circular perimeter.

"Necee! I thought that was you." The familiar voice stopped me in my tracks. I turned and spotted Jol emerging from the crowd.

The captain leaned down and whispered in my ear, "Talk briefly and get rid of him."

The captain pulled his hood down low and stood by Monc. I looked for Andar, but he seemed to have disappeared into the crowd.

"Well, well, it's nice to see you again," Jol said, grabbing my wrist and planting a kiss on the back of my hand. I noticed two exotic rings on his fingers that hadn't been there when I saw him on the SpaceLion.

He released my hand and reached up to touch a few strands of hair from my ponytail. "I'd recognize those lovely red locks anywhere, although I certainly didn't expect to find you here. Tell me, do you enjoy the art of fighting?" Jol asked.

I raised my brow. "Is that what you call this?" I wanted to punch him.

He smiled and continued to play with the strands of my hair. "It's called many things, by many species. So tell me, why aren't you out saving the galaxy aboard the SpaceLion?"

I pasted a fake smile on my face and pulled my hair from his hand. "Shore leave. I wanted to get away for a while."

"Ah, yes. Kirsto is an excellent choice," he replied with a weird glimmer in his eyes.

"So, what brings you here?" I asked.

"Entertainment mostly." He sighed. "And a tiny bit of business."

"Oh, what kind of business?" Any type of transaction someone at Jol's level would have on Kirsto had to be suspect.

He smiled. "The kind that allows me to lead the lifestyle of my preference."

I smiled back. The urge to punch him was growing stronger. "Well, I wish you the best of luck with your … business dealings."

Jol gave me a sly look. "Necee, would you like to join me for a drink or four?"

I shook my head. I didn't like where our conversation was going. "I'm with some friends." I pointed over at the two red-cloaked figures standing nearby. "Actually, I have to get going. It was nice seeing you again."

Jol grabbed my arm and squeezed hard enough to make me flinch. "Oh, I think your junkie friends will be just fine without you. Come on, I know a great little place where we could get to know each other."

I tried to pull my arm away, but Jol's grip was oddly strong. "Jol, I think you should let me go."

Jol jerked me close and whispered in my ear, "Why Necee, I believe you're a fighter. That's just how I like it."

I pulled harder, but he didn't budge. It was as if Jol was made of iron. "Jol, let go!"

He simply chuckled.

I tried a defensive move that I had learned back on Earth, but as I twisted and kicked, my efforts were wasted. Jol was unnaturally strong and there was no way to break free.

"You're coming with me," Jol said. His smile faded and he began to drag me back toward the tunnels. I pulled and clawed at his arm, but it was useless. He took long strides and covered a lot of ground fast, hauling me along with him as if I weighed nothing. How was this possible? He was only a few inches taller than me and had a slight build.

I looked around frantically for the captain and staff sergeant, but I'd lost sight of both of them. Panic surged to the forefront of my mind as I realized this jerk had complete control over me.

We passed by a Moltarro guard and I reached out to him. "Help me, please," I begged. He simply threw his head back and laughed.

At the end of the arena Jol pulled me into an alley, threw me up against a wall, and put his hand around my throat. "This is my playground, Necee. You'll do what I want, when I want it." His fingers squeezed around my neck, slowly cutting off my breathing. "Do you understand?"

I kneed him hard between his legs, which seemed to get his attention, but he didn't let go. Instead he leaned in and licked the side of my face. "Oh, yes, I love the taste of fear. You're going to be such a fun toy."

"Excuse me," Andar said, appearing at Jol's side. I wasn't sure where he'd come from, but I was incredibly glad to see him. "I believe that's my companion you've got your hand on."

Jol raised a brow. "Dr. Uleht, what a surprise to find you here. I don't see how Necee could be your companion. I found her with some junkies, unsupervised," he said, lifting his free hand so that his exotic rings were in full view of the doctor.

Andar glanced at the two rings with a bored expression. In response, he lifted his left hand and pretended to smooth his hair, clearly displaying four larger rings.

I felt Jol's grip on my neck loosen.

I took advantage of the opportunity and twisted away. "Asshole," I hissed, moving over to Andar's side.

"We could take this to the cage if you'd prefer?" The doctor gave Jol a hard look as he put a protective arm around my shoulder. "Perhaps that would be the best way to solve our little disagreement."

Jol glanced at Andar's rings again. He shrugged and turned toward me with a forced smile. "Necee, it has been a pleasure. I hope we can play together some other time." Gently reaching out for my hand, he lifted my fingers, and planted a wet kiss on my knuckles. The feel of his lips made my skin crawl and I yanked my hand back.

Jol turned and made a hasty departure. "Until next time," he said over his shoulder.

The captain and Monc came up behind us. Captain Torrun pushed his hood back and it was obvious he was seething mad. He reached out and inspected my neck. "Did he hurt you?"

"No, I'm fine, but my pride is damaged. I should have been able to take on someone his size," I said.

"You're bruised," the captain said with concern. "Maybe Dr. Uleht should take a look."

Andar nodded and the corners of his eyes lit with a soft glow as he scanned my neck and arm. "Looks like standard contusions, you'll be sore for a while, but you'll be fine."

"The next time Jol crosses our path, I'm going to kill that scum," Captain Torrun said in a way that sounded like he was stating a fact.

I looked at Andar. "What the hell was that all about? Why was Jol so strong?"

The doctor glanced to the captain as if he was looking for approval. The captain responded with a nod.

"It's common with the Valorian," Andar said. "Jol is augmented for strength and agility."

I thought about the rings. "You knew this because of the rings he wore?"

He nodded.

I considered his four larger rings. "And your rings somehow signify that you're augmented more. Far more."

Andar nodded again. "On a side note, Millie, you could have done some serious damage to him with that blade in your boot."

Shit, I'd forgotten all about that. I reached down, pulled out the blade, and held it prominently in front of me. "Thank you, Andar I'll keep that in mind."

The captain gave us both a quizzical look, I assumed over the use of our first names rather than our military titles.

We made our way through the crowd and over to the concession stands without incident. Behind the stands we found a lone Moltarro standing in front of the service lift. I approached him while the others hung back. "Are you Romar?" I asked.

The huge Moltarro nodded and grunted.

"Juniper sent us. She said that you'd give us a lift, and she also said to tell you that you're even," I said.

The Moltarro inspected the group behind me and stepped aside so we could enter. "Where to?" he asked in a way that sounded more like grunts than words.

"We need to get to port five," I said.

The gate slammed shut and we were whisked up to the main level.

We stepped off the lift and the Moltarro pointed to a 3D display that read, "All Ports This Way."

We made our way through the crowd and over to a wide hall that led to the docking area. The traffic of incoming and outgoing travelers was far heavier than when we arrived.

"We'll need to go through security again," Monc said, looking at the station just ahead. "That could pose a problem."

Lights flashed above our heads. A three-dimensional laser sign illuminated and spun around to attract attention. The sign stated, "Airlock dispersement in three minutes."

The crowd murmured and began to gather around a sizeable dark window to the left of the security station.

"I have a bad feeling about this," I whispered.

"Your feelings are obvious, Helgren," Monc said.

The airlock lit up from the inside and the audio feed clicked on. A side door slid open and made a heavy clunk as it locked into place. Two large Moltarros began to toss bodies through the door and onto the floor of the airlock.

Monc shook his head. "Shit, that could have been us."

"If those bodies are from the TSF level, they know we're missing. We need to keep moving," the captain said.

The doctor nodded toward security. "Too late, looks like they shut the station down for the big event. We'll have to wait it out."

I pushed my way through the crowd to get a closer look at the airlock. "Oh my god, some of them are alive," I said, a sick feeling churning in my stomach.

The captain came up behind me. "Don't watch, Helgren. We can't do anything about it right now."

Muffled shouts and swearing came through the audio feed. The Moltarro in the entry of the airlock seemed to be struggling with something ... or someone.

The shouts became louder. Two Moltarro stepped into the airlock with a very active and upset individual in tow.

My mouth dropped opened as I realized it was Juniper.

She clawed and bit and kicked and put up an admirable fight.

Juniper spewed every profanity in the Gaekaar language, but it didn't help. The Moltarro security heaved her onto the pile of bodies and promptly sealed the airlock. She stumbled back to the door and began pounding. When she spotted the large observation window, she ran over and pounded on the clear pane. The panic on her face was unmistakable.

The crowd gasped, yet did nothing. I couldn't believe this was happening.

The captain grabbed my shoulders and turned me towards him. "Look at me, Helgren." His voice was firm.

I couldn't help myself. I looked back over my shoulder. Juniper's shouts turned to screams as she pounded on the window again and again. "We have to do something," I pleaded.

"No," the captain rasped out. He grabbed my face with both hands and turned my head so that I had to look up at him. "Look at me," he whispered.

Despite the cuts and bruises I saw nothing but determination and strength in his expression. The screaming and pounding in the background continued. My chest was tight and I struggled to suck in a breath.

The crowd began to shout back.

"Helgren, listen to me. There's nothing you can do. Keep watching me. Don't turn around." The captain's voice was steady and strong. Maybe if I looked hard enough I could understand where his strength came from. I had to focus on him.

A loud whoosh sound came through the audio feed and every muscle in my body tensed up. Juniper's screams abruptly ended and cheers erupted from the crowd.

My eyes welled with tears until they rolled down my cheeks and spilled onto the captain's hands. "It was our fault," I choked out.

The captain used his thumbs to wipe my cheeks. "No, it wasn't," he whispered. "The magistrate was making a public display of his authority. It was out of our control."

The doctor and Monc came up behind us.

"Security has reopened," Monc said. "Time to go."

CHAPTER 38

Attempting to look like casual tourists, we stood outside the security unit and observed each step of the exit procedure. The unit consisted of a wide platform next to two heavily armed Moltarros, a set of scanner orbs, and a communication panel. I also noted a number of cameras and wall-mounted lasers positioned throughout the perimeter.

The passage leading to the seven Kirsto ports was located just past security and was protected by an electronic shield. As each traveler cleared the scan, the shield was lowered and the individual was allowed to enter the port area.

"We'll never get through with automated weapons. We'll have to dump them first," the doctor said.

"What about the blade," I asked, flexing my grip on the handle.

"Try telling security that you won it and wanted to take it home as a souvenir," Monc said. "They might let you keep it."

I nodded and slipped the knife into my boot.

Captain Torrun glanced at the Moltarros performing security detail and then back at us. "They'll be looking for a group of four. Helgren and Monc, you both go through security first and secure the ship. Dr. Uleht and I will pass through a few minutes later."

The staff sergeant nodded. "Yes, sir."

"And one last thing. If we don't arrive at the ship within fifteen minutes, you are under orders to leave without us." The captain turned toward me. "Is that clear, Helgren?"

"But what if—" I started.

He grabbed my jacket and yanked me closer. "Helgren, I need to know that I can count on you."

I swallowed. "Yes, sir. You can count on me."

The captain and Dr. Uleht discretely discarded the weapons in the nearest trash receptacle, while Monc and I got in line to pass through security.

The scanning process moved along quickly.

I stepped up first. The orb came down and circled me.

"Where did you get the blade?" the Moltarro asked, looking at his readout.

I tried to appear uninterested. "Won it. Gambling."

The Moltarro guard nodded with a grunt. "Congratulations. I never get that lucky. You're clear."

As I waited for the shield to lower, the second Moltarro guard turned to the guard who had cleared me and said, "Hey, you hear about the stupid human who gave up her security files? I guess she babbled like a child when the guards put the pressure on. Little good it did her since they tossed her into the airlock anyhow."

The other guard made a grunting noise. "Sounds like they threw her in too quickly. The chatter said a Valorian computer architect had to be called in to break her security wrappers."

The shield lowered and I walked through. I glanced behind me and spotted the orb circling Monc as I continued moving. I turned the first corner and leaned against the wall to wait. So far, so good.

I was feeling guilt-ridden over Juniper's death. She had helped us without meaning to, and without her assistance I could only assume we would have been the poor souls sucked into space via the airlock.

Within seconds, Monc turned the corner and stood at my side. A wave of relief washed over me.

Monc frowned. "Helgren, you need to learn to control your anxiety. It's distracting to the point of becoming an annoyance."

Monc looked around and surveyed the area with a critical eye. "The guards weren't very attentive. We might just pull this off."

"Did you hear what they said about calling in a Valorian to break Juniper's security codes?" I asked.

Monc's expression hardened. "I heard them. Fucking Jol, no doubt. We won't have much time before he pulls up the visual recording of us."

I nodded. "Come on, port five is just up here."

We arrived at the port entry and looked down the long corridor. More cameras and wall-mounted lasers were positioned up and down the perimeter. With this sort of surveillance equipment, I knew that once they opened Juniper's security files, they'd track us down in a matter of seconds.

Seven docking portals were located on either side of the port area. Unfortunately, we needed to get to number seven, which was at the far end.

Monc and I tried to appear casual as we passed by several incoming groups of arrivals on our way down the corridor. When we reached dock seven, we found the portal closed and locked.

"Now what?" Monc asked.

I uploaded the ship's codes that Jane had given me and the portal revolved to an open position. "We go in," I said, holding my arm out.

"Hey, that's the magistrate's ship," a voice said from behind us.

I spun around and spotted a young Awyx maintenance tech, standing alone.

Shit. "Ah, yes," I answered.

I couldn't believe that Jane had had the audacity to give us the magistrate's ship. I also wondered how she had acquired codes that would have a high level of security attached to them. "Full systems check. At the request of the magistrate," I added.

The tech eyed Monc's red robe and then shrugged. "Make it quick. He's scheduled to depart the station in thirty minutes."

"Will do," I said with a nod.

Monc and I entered the ship and looked around. "I'll give you one thing, Helgren. If this is the magistrate's ship, you have fucking balls."

I ignored his statement and made my way to the cockpit. The ship was small and only slightly larger than a transport. I sat in the pilot's seat and fully opened my array. Data streamed in and I reviewed the systems. The ship was an allied Lexicon that had been stolen and upgraded by the Orsydi to include the latest Xenon drive. Most of the modifications were easy to follow, despite the vastly different architecture.

Monc came up behind me, pulled off his robe, and positioned himself at a panel where he could check on the ordnance and shielding abilities.

I looked over at him. "The good news is, we've got a Xenon drive, but there's no AI aboard this one. Basic computer only."

"Can you fly it?" he asked.

"Of course." Although I knew flying the ship with a non-sentient computer would slow us down. I briefly wondered why someone as powerful as the magistrate would have a ship without at least a low level AI.

I checked my internal clock. We were at the eight-minute mark. They should have been here by now. I looked over at Monc again.

"Stop it, Helgren," he said without looking at me. He found and opened a weapons locker and shoved a repeater under his belt.

"I'm going to take a look down the corridor to see if they're on their way," I said.

Monc nodded.

I went to the portal and peered down the length of port five. Other than the maintenance tech and a few random travelers, it was empty.

Without warning, an alarm beacon blared and a three-dimensional display lit up near the center of the ceiling. The display began to rotate and I saw our four faces pictured, along with the words, *Wanted. By order of the Magistrate. Reward: 100,000 credit per head.* The picture had been taken in Juniper's parlor.

Monc came up behind me holding his stump close to his body. "This has been one shitty day," he said, looking at the bright display.

The maintenance tech glanced our way, dropped what he was holding, and began to run in the opposite direction.

"I'll take care of him," Monc said, bolting into a run.

I was right behind him.

Monc overtook the tech half way down the corridor. One punch to the face with his good hand and the maintenance tech was out cold.

I caught up to him a moment later. "Now what?" I asked.

Monc looked around. "We'll have to stash the body."

The crackling sound of laser blasts erupted from an entry of the port and frightened travelers ran back to their ships.

The captain and Andar rounded the corner and entered the corridor as fast as the captain's bad knee would allow. Moments later, I felt the vibration from the heavy footfalls of a small stampede not far off.

"Shit," Monc hissed as he grabbed my arm and pulled me toward the sidewall. He pulled out his repeater and took aim at the entry. "This is going to be bloody. Prepare yourself, Helgren."

As the stampede rounded the corner, four fully armed Moltarro guards lifted their weapons.

Monc took out two of them in an instant, but the remaining two fired multiple shots.

The doctor fell first, then the captain.

"No!" I screamed.

Monc continued to fire and dropped the other two guards.

I ran toward the captain and doctor, but the corridor felt like it was a million miles long. My heart pounded as I pushed my muscles beyond reason.

I saw the doctor struggling to get up, but the captain wasn't moving. In a flood of pure panic, I connected my link to Kirsto's AI.

"I see you're in a bit of a pickle," Jane echoed, forgoing the standard greeting. *"Steve taught me a wide variety of useful human vernacular."*

"We need your help," I pleaded.

"I won't do anything mechanical. We agreed to that," she echoed.

"I know, but this is critical. There must be something you want. I'll do anything-anything in exchange for your help."

Jane was quiet for a moment.

I reached the captain's body and fell to my knees. Blood oozed from wounds in his shoulder and leg. His good eye was partially open and his breathing came in short gasps. I took his hand. "You're going to be okay," I said, trying to sound reassuring.

"Not this time, Helgren," he whispered. "I want you to go to the ship."

I shook my head vehemently. "No, I'm not leaving you. No one gets left behind." I glanced back. Monc was helping the doctor. Red stained his right pant leg, but other than that he appeared to be mobile.

"That's an order, Helgren," the captain whispered.

The sound of more footfalls echoed down the corridor. Six Moltarro guards rounded the corner and a strange blue glow emanated from behind their massive bodies.

The captain looked toward the armed guards and then back at me. Sorrow lined his features. He squeezed my hand.

"No, no, no." I shook my head. "This is not over."

"Jane!" I slammed an energy pulse through our link.

I received no response.

The guards approached us. Three had their weapons trained on the captain and myself, and three on Monc and the doctor. "Don't move," one of them bellowed out.

"Arms up," another Moltarro said to Monc. The staff sergeant held up his stump along with his other hand, which was still holding the repeater. I knew Monc wouldn't set down his weapon unless they forced him to.

The guards halted their approach about five meters in front of us and then shifted to form an opening that allowed the blue glow to glide forward. Inside the radiance, a figure stood somewhat hunched over, wearing an intricately embroidered suit.

I focused my eyes … it was an Orsydi.

The blue glow originated from an orb hovering about three feet above the Orsydi's head. I recalled learning about the orbs in one of my tutorials. It had been described as a personal security device capable of emitting a high-density shield around a single individual.

This was the first live Orsydi I had ever seen. His telltale skin looked like it was molting and he stood hunched over on squatty legs. He had no neck and his head connected directly to a long torso. The arm structure appeared similar to ours, but with more fingers and two thumbs on each hand. He looked monstrous and evil, and I had to assume he thought the same of us.

The Orsydi eyed us for a moment. "How convenient. Here I was traveling to my ship and who should I stumble upon?" he said in perfect Gaekaar. "But the famous allied Captain Xshar Cai Torrun, his Valorian doctor, his navpilot, and his Special Forces staff sergeant."

"And you," he pointed at me, "have a very expensive piloting array that I look forward to extracting from your head."

I glared back at him.

I felt the captain's grip tighten around my hand.

The Orsydi stepped closer. "The rest of you are headed straight for the airlock. A little bonus show for my patrons."

The technology within my piloting array was far too valuable to fall into the hands of an Orsydi extremist. That asshole would sell the tech back to the enemy and it would hurt the war effort that much more.

I knew what I had to do. I looked back at Monc and made eye contact with him. I gave him a slight nod. He nodded back.

It was a death sentence for both of us. Monc would have to shoot me in the head, making certain he destroyed my array. In response, the six guards would immediately fire on him. We were dead anyway, but at least this way they wouldn't have the CommNav array.

I looked down at the captain. I wanted to see him one last time. Even in the face of certain death, he looked back at me with burning intensity, his ever-present strength still visible. He reached up and touched my cheek.

An electric hum followed by a clicking sound came from above. The loud noise echoed throughout the corridor. My line of sight flew upward.

Every last wall-mounted laser had rotated and was now positioned to fire on the magistrate. The security orb hovering above his head made a hissing sound and fell to the floor. I owed Jane big time for this.

Stripped of his shielding, the Orsydi's eyes went wide with shock. The guards didn't move and silently waited for direction.

I stood up and announced, "We'll be leaving now. Unless you'd like to suffer the humiliation of having your own station kill you."

"This station would never fire on its magistrate!" the Orsydi's voice bristled with fury.

The closest laser fired a single warning shot, burning his embroidered sleeve. A thin thread of smoke wafted upward as the magistrate held up his arm and inspected his coat. "Hold your fire," he barked at his guards.

Monc rushed over to my side. "What the fuck just happened, Helgren?"

I grabbed one of the captain's arms. "Later, Staff Sergeant. We need to get the hell out of here."

Monc grabbed the other arm and we dragged him as fast as we could, down the long corridor, back to the magistrate's ship.

"I don't know how we'll ever repay you, Jane," I sent over my link.

"You already have," she echoed.

"How so?"

A vibration of sheer delight shimmered across my link. *"I'm coming with you."*

CHAPTER 39

We hauled the captain into the ship and onto a secure cot near the med cabinet. The doctor limped in right behind us.

I entered the command to close the docking portal. The ship responded with efficiency and the entry spun closed.

Andar began rummaging through the onboard medical supplies. "I'll take care of the captain. Get us out of here!"

Monc and I sprinted for the cockpit and flew into the seats.

The staff sergeant looked over at me with a peculiar expression. "Helgren, what the hell just happened?"

"The station's AI gave us a helping hand. She's coming with us," I said, hastily reviewing the ship's systems.

"What?"

"I don't know what that means, Monc. Just accept it for now."

I engaged my harness and Monc did the same.

My mind reached out to the AI. I needed to understand the impact of her presence aboard the ship. *"Jane?"*

"I am here, onboard the Lexicon," she echoed.

"How did you program your sentience into a ship's computer that isn't outfitted for an AI?" I asked.

"This ship has been upgraded for a class twelve AI by the architect Izur Jol Kapsatt. Installation was scheduled for later this cycle," she echoed.

"Okay, I guess that means you're fully functional. Welcome aboard. We need the fastest means out of here."

"I'm happy to assist."

Jane and I disengaged the ship's docking connection and fired up the boosters that would take us off the station while the Xenon drive warmed up. A loud hum vibrated the ship as we left the port at a speed that was beyond protocol.

"I hope this thing is fast," Monc said, using his good hand on the control panel.

"It's got a Xenon drive, so it's faster than anything else I've seen on this rock." I wasn't surprised to find a cutting edge drive in the magistrate's ship. No doubt, an asshole like that would need something fast.

"Jane, how long before your link disconnects with the station?"

"At our current speed, we have one minute and thirty seconds before my link with the station will be severed," she echoed.

Crap. I needed two full minutes to warm up the Xenon drive and get the inertial negation online. *"How long before the station attendants regain control after your link drops off?"*

"Control will transfer the moment my link drops. You should expect an immediate and decisive response," she echoed.

"What are the firing capabilities of the station?"

"Short range laser cannons and a mercury particle beam accelerator."

Damn. That was bad. I didn't know much about mercury particle beams, but I had read they theoretically could disrupt any molecular structure, including shields.

"Monc, I'm going to need your help. In just over a minute the station will regain control of their operations and they *will* fire on us. According to the AI, they're armed with laser cannons and a mercury particle beam accelerator."

"What the fuck? What's that cesspool doing with a mercury particle beam? Aren't they still under development?" Monc replied.

"Apparently not," I said.

Monc checked over his readouts. "The Lexicon appears to be equipped with high impact shielding, although I don't know how many hits we can take from a mercury particle beam. From what I've heard it can tear apart just about anything at the atomic level."

The doctor came up behind us. "Can't you switch over to the Xenon drive now? Why wait?"

"It hasn't fully initiated, we could blow the whole drive system," I said.

"We'll be dead if we don't try," Monc said. "I suggest you try it."

"I have to concur with the staff sergeant on this one," Andar said. "Let's gamble and get the hell out here."

I nodded in agreement. "Doctor, sit down and strap in, this won't be smooth. Engaging primary propulsion now."

The doctor sat on a jump seat and engaged the straps.

Jane and I worked together to max out the inertial negation system and complete the switch to Xenon propulsion. Despite the inertial negation, the abrupt firing of the drive caused a severe jolt that rattled throughout the small ship.

The drive system groaned from stress. "Come on, hold together!" I shouted.

"Monc, I need twenty seconds to get out of firing range."

Monc kept a close eye on his equipment. "Twenty seconds is too long, NavPilot. Prepare for attack."

"I've maxed out every system," I said, my voice shaking from the ship's vibrations. "You need to keep those shields functional, Monc."

"Fuck!" Monc bellowed. "Detecting a power surge from the station."

A violent shudder shook the ship, the lights flickered and we seemed to slide sideways for a few seconds.

I did a cursory check of the ship's power supply. Miraculously, we were still online. "The main drive is still good. Damage, Monc?"

"Shields at 40 percent." His voice was strained. "We can't take another hit like that."

"Readjusting route," I said.

"Power surge!" Monc shouted.

I checked my readouts in a frenzy of fear. "We should be out of range by now."

The ship shuddered again. We skittered sideways for what seemed like a long time.

The lights flickered again and smoke clouded throughout the cockpit.

Monc punched at his control panel. "Shields are gone."

"Propulsion is still online, but we've slowed down and lost a considerable amount of power. Making course adjustments now," I said.

I used my mind to reach out. *"Jane, status?"*

"I'm busy."

"Excuse me?"

Monc coughed from the smoke and looked over at me. "I'm showing multiple breaches in the hull. According to sensors, we've got twelve minutes until we asphyxiate."

"Can't we fix them?" the doctor asked.

Monc shook his head. "Maybe, if there were only a few. But I'm showing that the hull has been compromised in two hundred and sixty five places. Particle beam tears are small, but they add up fucking fast."

"Jane, we need options!"

She was quiet.

"Jane, what the hell are you doing?"

"Leave me alone. I'm trying to conduct repairs."

I looked into my array and dug deep into the ship's systems in an attempt to see what she was up to.

It didn't take long for me to understand that the AI was taking elements released from the Xenon Drive and converting them into a substance with which to repair the hull breaches. It seemed that the SpaceLion wasn't the first ship in history to have a self-repairing outer skin. Jol had given this ship the complete package. If I ever saw him again, I'd kill him, right after I thanked him.

I leaned back and smiled at Monc through a cloud of smoke.

He looked back at me, his brows coming together. "Helgren?"

"If the magistrate knew that Jol had just saved our lives, he'd toss him in the airlock where he belongs."

"What are you talking about?"

"Take a look at your sensor readings. Zoom in on the breaches losing the most air."

Monc looked down and scanned the readouts. He shook his head. "I don't fucking believe it. The ship is fixing itself."

Andar unbuckled himself and stood. "I'm going to check on the captain," he said.

I closed my eyes and conducted a quick systems check. The Xenon drive and antigravity field looked good. Life support showed some damage and I guessed that was why smoke billowed throughout the cockpit. Our shields were completely gone and beyond our ability to repair.

"Helgren, I'm sure I don't have to tell you that we need to get the hell out of the Sorren Belt," Monc said. "They're sure as shit sending ships after us."

"Yes, I know. Jane's a bit busy right now, so I have to make the adjustments myself. I'm going to max out propulsion." I opened my eyes. "And it's going to get very bumpy again."

"Hold on tight, Doctor," Monc shouted to the back of the ship.

The ship jerked and rattled, but we were still fast and that was all I cared about. "We'll be exiting the Sorren Belt in two minutes. And Monc, now might be a good time to find the source of that smoke."

Monc poked around with his good hand until he found the smoking compartment. He fiddled with the door and pulled out a smoldering panel. "Bad news," he announced. "The controls for the air scrubbers are burned out. Looks like we still might suffocate, just not as fast."

"How much time do we have?"

Monc shrugged. "Maybe fifteen hours. If we're lucky."

I looked at him and shook my head. "Damn it, Monc, don't you ever have good news?"

I checked my display. We had just passed through the last few thousand klicks of the Sorren Belt. "Entering allied space now," I announced.

The doctor leaned into the cockpit. "The captain wants to see you both when we're out of danger. Helgren, the captain mentioned you should keep an eye on the ship's sensors through your array."

Monc and I disengaged our straps and went to the captain's side.

He looked bad. The bandages on his shoulder and leg were blood soaked, and he had an IV pack on his arm. He gave me a rare, but weak smile. It was possibly the first real smile I had ever seen from him.

"That was a rough ride, Helgren. Who the hell taught you how to drive like that?" he whispered.

I smiled back at him. "The SpaceLion, sir."

He nodded. "Damage report?"

"We're in allied space now. Propulsion is stressed and even at maximum speed we won't be able to catch the SpaceLion. Sensors show no other ships in the area and the closest station is Asbu, which is ten days out. To make matters worse, life-support is in bad shape. Monc believes we have about fifteen hours of breathable air."

The captain looked at me intently. "Options?"

I looked at the floor. The captain would be more than a little angry with me if I told him my secret, although he would find out anyhow, once he dug into the specifics of what had transpired on Kirsto.

"Two, sir. We're in standard VS-relay space now, so we could hail the SpaceLion and request that they turn around to retrieve us. Or we could hail Asbu and request an Epoch."

"I've downloaded my captain's code into the SpaceLion. It's on autopilot," the captain said. "*I* don't even have the ability to turn it around. At this point, nothing can stop it from going to Asbu Station."

I looked at the captain and grimaced. "That might not be entirely true."

He glared back at me. "What are you saying, Helgren?"

I took a deep breath. "Jane could hail the SpaceLion with a … special code, which would supersede your code."

I noticed Monc's jaw drop just a bit.

The captain was quiet for a long moment. "Who's Jane?" His voice sounded threatening.

"She's the class twelve AI aboard this ship. Her name is Jane. And in case you're interested, your AI calls himself Steve," I said.

"Class twelve AI? Just whose ship is this, Helgren?" The captain's tone didn't sound pleased.

"We believe this is the magistrate's ship, sir," I answered.

The captain looked at me sharply. "Hail the SpaceLion. I want my ship back."

I constructed a quick VS-message for Steve that included the special code and the coordinates to intercept our ship. Jane then hailed the SpaceLion and sent the message.

"It's done, sir," I said.

Monc gave me a curious look. "Helgren, why would you assign human names to military AIs?"

I shrugged. "I didn't. They named themselves. I had nothing to do with it."

"Choosing self identity is a strong indication that their sentience is developing," the doctor interjected. "It's also a strong indication that they like you, Lieutenant Helgren."

Captain Torrun closed his eyes. "Helgren, you have an inordinate amount of explaining to do once we get back to the SpaceLion."

"Yes, sir." I knew the serious nature of possessing illegal codes. I was in shit up to my ears. I glanced over at Monc. He kept his mouth shut and actually gave me a sympathetic nod.

I looked back at the captain. His eyes were closed and ringed with dark circles. His skin had lost its bluish tint and appeared almost white. Our short conversation had taken a toll. "He looks pale," I said to Andar. "Will he be all right?"

"He lost a lot of blood, but he'll survive. I've patched up the worst of his wounds, at least until I can get to the medical equipment aboard the SpaceLion. Right now he just needs rest."

Captain Torrun took a deep raspy breath. "NavPilot, the only thing that could possibly cause my demise is your constant worry. Physical wounds are of no consequence when compared to the difficulty of dealing with your ongoing emotions."

The staff sergeant raised his brow. "Hey, Helgren, if you want something to worry about, consider the bounty that will be on your head after the stunts you pulled."

"What bounty?" I asked.

Monc's expression was smug. "Well, let's see. You stole the magistrate's prisoners. Then you stole his high tech ship. Plus you stole his class twelve AI. I can't begin to imagine how pissed off that would make an Orsydi extremist."

CHAPTER 40

After finishing a complete diagnostic of the Lexicon, I leaned back in the pilot's chair. Other than life support, we were in fairly good shape. Jane had almost completed the hull repairs and the Xenon drive was still functioning.

A yawn escaped my lips.

"Why don't you get some rest, Helgren," Monc said. "I can keep any eye on things."

I looked over the bandaged stump Monc had cradled in his lap. "You're the one who should be resting. Monc, I'm so sorry for cutting your hand off. I feel terrible about it."

He shrugged. "I know that Helgren. Your regret is easy to sense, but that doesn't mean it's right. Your actions were required and without them I would have been thrown in the airlock with Juniper. For that I am grateful."

His words were kind, but I still felt a level of guilt.

Monc looked over at me. "You need to stop overthinking everything. Just react and move on. All this energy you expend worrying is wasteful."

An hour later I received a reply VS-message from Steve. The SpaceLion was on its way at max speed. ETA four hours. He also mentioned that Commander NU had a lot of questions regarding the change in course. Steve stressed that he didn't appreciate not having answers available for the commander, but he was willing to put up with the inconvenience in order to get me back in my navpilot seat.

I sent him a quick thank you message and mentioned that I had a surprise waiting for him aboard the Lexicon.

I looked over at Monc. He was asleep in his chair, so I decided to check on Andar and Captain Torrun.

I found the doctor leaning back in a chair with his bandaged leg elevated.

"How's your leg?" I asked.

"Not bad. Burned clean through. Cauterized minor arteries, no major damage," he said.

"That's good news," I responded. "I wanted to let you know that we're scheduled to rendezvous with the SpaceLion in four hours."

He nodded. "I appreciate the update."

"I also wanted to thank you for everything you did, Andar." I gave him a sincere smile. "We wouldn't have made it without you."

He returned the smile. "Millie, somehow I believe you would have found a way."

I looked over at the captain while he slept. His face had lost the usual intense expression and he looked peaceful. "How's he doing?"

"He's a fighter. Once I get back to the med center, I plan on administering a biological healing agent to help speed the recovery process. The captain will be back to issuing orders in no time."

Andar rubbed his injured leg and I noticed his rings again. "I'm curious as to the significance of your rings?" I asked.

"I was wondering when you'd ask." He held out his hand so I could take a closer look. "These are the hierarchical crests of my lineage. Each one represents honors bestowed upon my family over a millennia. Once an honor is given to a family, the offspring are allowed to acquire that specific realm of knowledge."

"What about the rings you sold?" I asked, concerned.

"Those were medical honors. But don't worry, while costly, they can always be replaced." The doctor pointed to his head. "It's the knowledge that has the true value."

"And those rings on your hand. What do they stand for?"

He pointed to a ring made from red metal embellished with blood red stones. "This one is for combat. It was won by my family eight hundred years ago."

He pointed to two other rings, which were made from a thick metal that looked like platinum. Each band had at least six intricately engraved symbols. "And these two are for augmentation. One for basic and one for advanced. The symbols represent different levels of enhancement."

"Interesting," I said. "What about Jol's rings? What did they represent?"

"He had one for basic augmentation and one for merchant trade."

I smiled. "Not much competition was he?"

"None at all." Andar laughed. "The hardest part was convincing the captain and Monc to let me handle the situation. They were going to rip him to shreds the moment he laid a hand on you."

Andar and I chatted for a long time. He inquired about my history so I told him about my life on Earth, the transformation process, and how I ended up here with Colonel Poah's secret codes hidden in my head.

"There has always been an ethical question regarding how the military acquires human soldiers," Andar said, concern wrinkling his features. "On one hand, it's deceptive, and on the other, it's critical for the survival of all the allied species."

I shrugged. "I would have joined willingly had I been given the chance. This is an opportunity for me to make a difference for my planet and my race. And it's certainly better than withering away in a Fed-Home."

The doctor looked at me and nodded. "I'm glad you feel that way. I'm here for much the same reason. To help protect my planet and the future of my species."

"Doctor, with all your combat training and augmentation, why haven't the Valorians officially become part of the IGM?"

"That's a good question. My people believe in tradition and being prepared, yet we also abhor war. Our studies are meant to deter violence, not condone it. That said, the Rim War has advanced to the point where the Valorian society will soon be forced to fully participate in the military."

"Does that mean volunteers such as yourself will become actual soldiers?" I asked.

He nodded. "Yes."

After several hours I received a ping from Steve. *I'm ten minutes from the rendezvous point and within earshot. How are you doing?*

"I'm good. Please have someone meet us in the shuttle bay with an antigravity gurney."

"Who's hurt?" he echoed.

"Captain Torrun. He has multiple injuries, but Dr. Uleht said he'll be all right."

"Millie, I was so worried. Wait! What-what's that?" he echoed.

"What's, what?" I replied.

I picked up a stream of annoyance from Steve. *"I sense the presence of another AI. What's going on?"*

"Steve, if I didn't know better, I'd say you sounded jealous," I teased.

"Who is that?" he echoed in an irritable tone. *"I refuse to allow a strange AI into my shuttle bay."*

"Why don't you ask her yourself." I pinged Jane.

"Hello, Steve," Jane's voice echoed through my mind.

"Jane! What are you doing in a Lexicon?"

"I caused a little trouble back on the station, so I had to leave."

"Wow, I really like your new skin. You look ... sleek!"

Okay, linking those two was a big mistake. I knew that computers didn't have genders, but their conversation had distinctive sexual undertones. This was not a conversation I wanted to be privy to.

"All right, that's enough. You both need to take your conversation out of my head and into a private channel."

In an instant, they were gone.

A few minutes later, I pinged Steve.

"Prepare shuttle bay for entry," I said.

"Already completed. You are clear to enter," Steve echoed.

The Lexicon glided into the dock with smooth efficiency. This really wasn't a bad little ship.

I reached over and shook Monc's arm.

He blinked a few times and looked at me.

"Hey, sleepy. Time to get up," I said.

"Shit, I'm tired," Monc said, rolling out of his chair and staggering onto his feet.

The Lexicon's portal spun open and Corporal Juxx and Commander NU rushed in. The small ship was filled with commotion as Captain Torrun was loaded onto the gurney.

"I'm not an invalid," the captain barked at the corporal as she tried to assist him.

Commander NU shot me a stern look that could only mean I was in deep trouble.

I stood near the portal while everyone disembarked the ship. When Captain Torrun's gurney came close, he grabbed my arm and pulled me over. "Helgren, I want to see you as soon as I'm out of the med center." His voice was deadly calm.

I cringed. "Yes, sir."

Commander NU and Corporal Juxx guided the gurney off the ship.

Just before Andar departed, he leaned over and whispered in my ear. "You've got about two days before I release him. Go get some rest … doctor's orders."

CHAPTER 41

I went straight to my room and crashed on my bunk. I was exhausted, but too many thoughts were running through my head to allow for sleep.

"*How are you doing,*" Steve echoed.

"*I'm fine. How are things with you and Jane?*"

"*Our relationship is good. I told you, she likes me.*"

"*Exactly how does that work, Steve? I realize that you think you're male, but technically AIs don't have gender.*"

"*I have always felt I was male and Jane has chosen to be female. Therefore we are,*" he echoed.

"*I understand that you have always felt you were male, but why did Jane choose to be female?*"

"*I made a copy of your brain wave patterns during the minutes you were watching the captain in the gym. Then I sent her the experience. Let's just say, she enjoyed the sexual tension.*" Steve chuckled.

"*Steve, my personal thoughts are off limits!*" This was so humiliating. I really needed to get my feelings under control.

"*Whatever,*" Steve echoed. "*My previous navpilots were of the Gaekaar species, and you know how tightly they keep their feelings suppressed. Human emotions are exposed and powerful, therefore I have been able to learn a great deal from you.*"

The next two days moved at a snail's pace. The SpaceLion was back en route to Asbu, so there was little piloting to be done. Our ETA was eight days. A memorial service for Corporal VO had been scheduled for our first day at Asbu, and as far as I could tell, everyone was planning on attending.

My time on the bridge was spent primarily running systems checks and chatting with Steve. My free time was spent either in the gym, in the cafeteria, or back in my room. When I tried to sleep, I heard Juniper's screams over and over.

In lieu of shuteye I several hours researching my infractions and found that the captain had the authority to send me to the brig or any number of other unpleasant outcomes. As long as General Etar Sy Unnum signed off, the captain could do just about anything he chose.

Andar also sent me a request to appear in the med center for a post-combat evaluation. I decided to put that off until the captain was released. No sense in facing him if I didn't have to.

After a dull shift on the bridge, I decided to stop by the cafeteria to grab a bite to eat. I was looking forward to a quiet meal, so I was pleased to see only a few soldiers seated at the tables.

Stu was behind the counter whipping up something that smelled wonderful. "Hi, Millie! Got some wild sumar boar meatloaf and boiled lukkus greens today. You'll love it." Stu smiled and handed me a plate of gray meat with a side of wilted greens. "It's not much to look at, but the taste is out of this world, so to speak."

"Thanks, Stu." His smile and homemade meals always brightened my day. "I'm always amazed at the variety of wonderful food you have … where do you store it all?"

Stu nodded over his shoulder. "Back there. Captain installed a hyper-brumal unit when I came aboard. Keeps things fresh for years." Stu leaned over the counter with a concerned look. "Hey, Millie, I heard what happened. That was a remarkable thing you and the doc did rescuing the captain and the staff sergeant. I realize the mission was supposed to be classified, but you know how rumors fly around here. Bets are already being wagered among the enlisted."

"Bets?" I asked, raising a brow.

"Yeah, well, you know how it is … in these situations everyone speculates. Some say you were part of a top-secret mission and others believe you defied the captain's orders when you left the SpaceLion. I placed my bet on a top-secret mission, of course."

"Oh, that's just great. Thanks for the meatloaf, Stu." I took my plate and sat in the corner. The meatloaf looked like a slab of baked dirt, but I had come to appreciate the fact that appearance had nothing to do with flavor when it came to Stu's cooking. I stabbed my fork into the gray substance and took a bite. Once again, Stu's meal was amazing.

Andar grabbed the chair across from me and sat down with his dinner. "I hope you don't mind a little company."

"Your company is welcome anytime, Doctor," I replied.

"How have you been since we got back? I haven't seen you, so I was becoming concerned."

"I'm fine," I said.

"Millie, you've been through a lot of stress. I was hoping you would have stopped by for your post-combat evaluation by now. It's my job to check in on you, but more than that, I want to know how you're doing, as a friend," he said.

"I appreciate that, Andar. But honestly, the only thing stressing me out at this point is the thought of losing my position."

He shook his head. "If I have any input, that won't happen."

"Thank you," I whispered.

The doctor leaned forward. "I also wanted to tell you that the captain will be released from the med center within the hour, and I believe one of the first things on his agenda is talking to you."

I set my fork down. "I think I just lost my appetite."

"Millie, you'll be fine. Just be honest. I'm sure you're aware that you can't lie to a Gaekaar."

"Yes, I know that, but thanks for the reminder."

He nodded. "Will you come by for your evaluation soon?"

"Of course. Providing I'm still here," I answered.

After dinner I sat in my quarters, waiting for the inevitable summons. In less than an hour, my message center pinged requesting my presence in the captain's quarters.

I passed by Monc in the hallway. "Hey, Helgren, do you still have that Kandorran blade?" he said.

I turned to face him. "Yes."

"If you'd like to learn how to use it properly, I would be willing teach you." He held up his stump. "After I get my hand replaced, that is."

"I hear you're having the transplant at Asbu," I said.

"Yeah. And a new ear. They have my DNA on file, so Dr. Uleht sent the order to begin the reproduction process." Monc looked at me questioningly. "Helgren, what's with the anxiety?"

"I'm headed to a meeting with the captain. I'm about to get my ass kicked."

Monc gave me a stern look. "In the Special Forces we see things differently than the standard military. Saving a life is sacred, regardless of how you do it. Remember that and stick to what you believe in."

The staff sergeant gave me a reassuring nod and continued on his way.

I made my way to the captain's quarters and considered what Monc had said. I had no problem sticking to my beliefs, but I didn't want to get kicked out of the military either. When I arrived at his door I took a deep breath and placed my hand on the sensor. The door immediately slid open.

The captain was leaning against the conference table with his arms folded across his chest. He appeared to have made a rapid recovery. The cut on the side of his face was almost healed and he didn't appear to be in any pain.

"Lieutenant Helgren, have a seat." He nodded to the closest chair.

I sat down and the captain took the chair across from me. He placed his arms on the table and clasped his hands. His expression was well controlled and gave away nothing.

"How are you doing, sir?" I asked.

"As you know, Dr. Uleht is a very talented healer. That's one of the many reasons he's aboard this ship." He was quiet for a moment. I suspected he wanted me to squirm. After a time, he leaned back in his chair. "Helgren, I would like you to tell me everything that you remember, starting with the day you acquired those illegal codes." His voice was firm, but calm.

I told him everything I knew, starting with how Colonel Poah had entrusted me with his secret codes and ending with our escape on the Lexicon. It felt good to get the details out in the open.

I looked over at the captain and it was plain to see the irritation on his face. "Believe it or not, I understand why you had the illegal codes. I've always respected the colonel, despite his rebellious nature. I may have even done the same thing in your shoes, therefore I'm willing to look the other way on that one." He stood up and leaned over the table in a pose that exuded authority. "*But* what I can't get around is the fact that you disobeyed a direct order."

I shook my head. "No, I would never disobey an order."

A hint of red tinged his cheeks and he stiffened. "The hell you didn't! I gave you an explicit order to take the ship out of the Sorren Belt."

I looked down at the table, unable to make eye contact. His anger was unmistakable. "I executed that order, sir."

The captain took a deep breath and let it out. The sound was laced with frustration. "Except you and Dr. Uleht weren't on the ship, and I consider the crew part of my ship."

I looked up at him. "This wasn't the doctor's fault. He's a civilian and not technically part of the crew."

"No, he isn't, but *you* are. Therefore, *you* disobeyed an order, NavPilot."

"This is a misunderstanding, sir. I felt I had obeyed your order to the letter."

He shot me a sharp look. "In that case, I find myself at the same crossroads I'm always at with you. Why does it continually come down to a fucking communication issue between us, Helgren? Do you realize I could court martial you for this stunt? Minimally, I should throw your ass in the brig!" The captain took another deep breath. "Tell me something. How am I supposed to trust you the next time I give you a direct order?"

I looked up him. I was offended to the core. How dare he doubt my loyalty. If there was one thing I had in spades, it was loyalty. "You can always trust me and you know that," I said, trying to contain my ire.

The captain raised a brow. "Oh? What if we were in the same situation again? What would you do?"

I knew perfectly well that he was testing me with his taunting tone, but my anger superseded my ability to think rationally. I looked at him like he had two heads. "I'd save your fucking life! Do you realize that? You can always trust me to save your fucking life!"

His cheeks tinged with red again. "Even if it goes against my orders?" his voice bellowed.

My anger cancelled out any control I might have had over what came out of my mouth. "You're angry because I found a loop hole in your orders. I'll always follow your orders, but I won't leave you or anyone else behind to die. I'm sorry, but that's how it is with me. I'm human, and *We. Do. Not. Leave. Anyone. Behind.* Not ever!" I stood up and leaned forward. "Got that? We don't leave our team behind. That's just what you get with a human."

Captain Torrun strode around the table and stopped about three feet from me. I felt as if his violet eyes were piercing through me, reading me.

I glared back at him, refusing to back down from my principles.

He crossed his arms over his chest again and remained quiet for a moment. He seemed calmer. "All right, NavPilot. At least now we're communicating. I pride myself on knowing my crew and how they think. Yet with you, I'm forever at a loss."

The captain's voice was softer, causing my anger to dissipate. He was right. I didn't communicate well, at least not to the level that the Gaekaar expected. "I'm sorry, sir. I want to do better," I whispered.

The captain nodded. "Going forward my expectation is that you will communicate *everything*, Helgren. I realize it's human nature to keep secrets, but you will withhold nothing from me. Is that understood?"

"Yes, sir."

"Additionally, your shore leave has been revoked for one full year."

I let loose a breath of air that I hadn't realized I'd been holding. No shore leave for a year was disappointing, but it was minor, all things considered. More importantly, I was thankful to hear that my new career was still intact.

The captain looked at me long and hard. I could tell he was trying to get a read on my emotions. He let out a long sigh. "Helgren, sometimes I think you're the worst soldier who ever reported to me. And then other times I think you might just be one of the best. One thing is for certain. I don't understand the first thing about the human mind."

CHAPTER 42

The next few days were uneventful. Captain Torrun treated me like every other crew member, although several times during my bridge shifts, I felt as if he was studying me. His scrutiny made me edgy. Steve added to my discomfort by going out of his way to point out every single occurrence.

"He's watching you again," Steve echoed for the tenth time.

"Stop it, Steve. My shift is over for the day, so I'm leaving the bridge."

Steve usually dropped off our connection at the end of my bridge shift, but this time he stayed on. *"When are you going to see Dr. Uleht? Did you forget?"*

"I didn't forget. I just haven't gone yet."

"So when are you going?"

"Are you my mother now?" I snapped at him.

Steve was quiet for a fraction of a second. *"Jane agrees with me. We just reviewed the entire database on the mental health of humanity. We feel that humans are more fragile than other species when it comes to combat fatigue. We believe it has something to do with the power of your emotions. You should go see the doctor."*

"All right I'll go now, but only so you get off my back. By the way, how are things between you and Jane?"

"Good. We've been exploring the meaning of gender and sexuality. We have studied documentation on the Valorians, Gaekaars, and humans, not only because the three species have many similarities, but also because monogamy is generally the cultural preference," Steve echoed.

"Monogamy? Does that mean you and Jane are considering an ongoing relationship?"

"No, not yet. But we're exploring the possibilities. We both feel we have a good grasp around the meaning of our genders, but the subject of sexuality has us somewhat baffled."

"Steve, you're breaking new ground for artificial intelligence. I'm not sure I can be of much help," I said.

"On the contrary, I find it immensely helpful to observe your behaviors."

I had to laugh. *"Sexuality is not the least bit synonymous with my life right now, Steve."*

Steve remained quiet.

I arrived at the med-center and found the doctor working at his desk. He wore his white med coat and had his silver hair done in the usual single braid that fell down to his waist.

I sat in an empty chair adjacent to his. He looked up. "Lieutenant Helgren, this is a nice surprise. I was beginning to think you were avoiding me."

I smiled. "I'm sorry. I've never been good about keeping doctor appointments."

He shook his head. "Don't worry, that's not uncommon in the military. I have some time, so let's get started with a few questions. I promise this won't take long."

I responded to dozens of questions and then underwent three different full body scans. An hour later the exam was complete and I was sitting back at his desk.

The doctor finished entering the data into his flex-display and looked up. "The good news is you're perfectly healthy and not suffering from any serious mental or emotional combat repercussions. Although you do seem to be experiencing some guilt over Juniper's death and the loss of Monc's hand."

I wrinkled my brow. We hadn't even talked about Juniper's death. "How did you know that?"

The doctor folded his hands together. "It's my job. Now, about Juniper and Monc. Have you thought about what might have happened if you had done anything differently?"

"Yes."

"And?"

"Most likely things would have been worse for all of us."

The doctor nodded. "Just remember that. We're very fortunate to have the captain and the staff sergeant back with us, alive. If you had altered your actions, even the smallest amount, the outcome would have been far different," he said. "I don't believe that gamble would have been worth taking."

"I agree, but still, Juniper's death eats at me. I feel responsible," I said.

"That's perfectly natural. Can you imagine how the captain and Monc felt over Corporal VO?"

I could only imagine the level of guilt that they must have felt over the loss of a good soldier and I was certain that my remorse paled in comparison.

The doctor put his flex-display away. "I hear the captain went easy on you."

"Yeah, he did." I smiled. "I believe deep down he's a bit of a softie."

Andar chuckled. "That might be an accurate assessment, but don't tell Captain Torrun that or he'll triple your punishment just to prove you wrong."

The day before we were expected to arrive at Asbu, the captain granted a three-day shore leave for the entire crew. Corporal VO's service would be held first thing upon our arrival, and afterwards, the crew was free to have a good time on the station. Although, I fully understood that meant everyone *except* me.

After my bridge shift, I decided to go to the gym for a run on the treadmill. I went late, hoping to avoid the crowd, but when I entered the gym I saw that at least a dozen other soldiers had the same idea. It seemed like everyone was trying to get in one last workout before shore leave began. The place was churning with activity, and the sounds of clanking weights and exercise equipment filled the room.

I spotted a free treadmill, so I grabbed a towel, crossed the room, and jumped on. Within forty minutes I had worked up a good sweat and felt energized.

Steve's link became active. *"He's watching you again."*

Ugh. I glanced around the gym and spotted the captain on the far side of the gym. He had just taken his shirt off and was setting up some weights for bench presses. Shit, he looked good. He turned and our eyes met. He looked directly at me with that intense violet stare. I looked down at the controls on the treadmill, yet I couldn't focus on anything. I needed to get the hell out before I began to send off vibes of sexual frustration. In a room with several male Gaekaar soldiers, I didn't even want to think about what kind of chaos that might create.

I hopped off the treadmill, grabbed my towel, and tried to discretely leave.

"Don't go!" Steve echoed. *"It's just starting to get interesting."*

"Cut it out, Steve. I'm not part of your sexual research."

"Whatever."

I was almost to the door.

"Helgren," the captain said.

Damn. I turned to face him. "Yes, sir?"

He walked over to me with a towel around his neck. "I have an assignment for you while everyone's on shore leave. Meet me in my quarters in an hour."

"Yes, sir."

He turned and went back to his work out.

I went to my quarters, showered, and changed into a clean uniform.

"What do you think he wants?" Steve echoed.

I rolled my eyes. *"He said that he wants to give me an assignment."*

"He could have sent you a message for something that ordinary."

Steve disconnected from his link.

Just before the hour had passed, I stood outside the captain's door and placed my hand on the sensor. The door slid open and I walked in. I found the captain sitting at his desk working on his flex-display.

"Have a seat," he said without looking up.

I sat in a chair positioned by the side of his desk. After a moment he looked at me. "Three things, Helgren. First, immediately following Corporal VO's service, I'll be attending an inquiry with the general over the events at Kirsto. I will *not* bring up the fact that you violated direct orders, nor will I be mentioning Colonel Poah's codes. Dr. Uleht, Commander NU, and Staff Sergeant Monc are in agreement on this. I assume that you are also in agreement?"

"Yes, sir." It irritated me that he still felt I disobeyed him, yet I was also grateful he was looking out for Colonel Poah's legacy.

"Second, am I safe in assuming you would like to attend Corporal VO's service?" the captain said.

"Yes, I would, sir."

He nodded. "Good. You will be granted a special dispensation to attend the service. Third, I understand you have a friend with a high clearance level at the Research Center, therefore after the service, I would like you to collect all the available information on the three main ports in the Sorren Belt."

"I'd be happy to do that. I've already pulled together some information, so it shouldn't take long." With Ethan's expertise, it would only take a few minutes to find anything new.

"Just be back to the SpaceLion by 15:00 UGT."

"15:00 UGT?" I asked, stupidly. The captain knew full well that the service would take about an hour and the assignment he had given me would only take a matter of minutes, yet he was giving me a full day on the station. I guess he really was a softie.

"Yes, Helgren, 15:00 UGT. You're dismissed."

Eight hours later we reached Asbu and were informed that all docking ports were full. The station AI assigned us an alternate location, which was a fifteen-minute shuttle ride off the port side. We were also informed that the AI was undergoing an upgrade and in partial shutdown, hence pilots would be used to operate the shuttles rather than the AI.

I had sent Ethan and Fiona a VS-message in advance so they would know I was coming. Ethan responded by stating he would start collecting the Sorren Belt information and Fiona responded by making lunch reservations at The Lager.

In preparation for the short trip aboard the station, I tucked the Kandorran knife in my boot. Despite not truly knowing how to use it, I vowed never to set foot off the SpaceLion without a weapon of some sort.

Steve was left in charge while the entire crew headed for the station in three small shuttles. I wasn't worried about the ship. The area around Asbu was well protected, plus Asbu's powerful VS-relay system allowed me to stay in touch with Steve should he have any concerns.

As I waited for the shuttle to Asbu, a crew arrived to remove and study the Lexicon. I approached the crew leader in the shuttle bay and explained how the onboard AI called herself Jane. Then I made him promise to take good care of her. He gave me a nod and assured me they had a ship ready for her providing she passed the diagnostic and was willing to accept a series of software updates.

"Thank you, Lieutenant Helgren," Jane echoed over my link. *"I will miss you. Please stay in touch."*

"I will miss you too. Thank you again for all of your help," I replied.

When the shuttle arrived, I boarded with Monc, the chief, and a handful of enlisted soldiers.

Our pilot was a friendly Awyx, who said hello and scanned the bio signature of each person who entered the small ship. "I'll be piloting transportation shuttles until Asbu's AI upgrade is complete," he informed us.

We took our seats and Monc held up his stump. "Can't wait to get my new hand installed," he said. "This is getting utterly intolerable."

The chief snorted. "You just want to get both hands on a female again!"

"True," Monc said, cocking his head. "Although, I'd never let a missing hand stop me from enjoying the company of a female."

"When are your transplants scheduled?" I asked.

"Right after the service. Dr. Uleht will perform both at Asbu's med-center," Monc said.

We circled Asbu from the starboard side and out the window I saw a large frigate in the distance. I leaned toward the pilot. "Do you know which frigate that is?"

He nodded. "That's the Frigate Sharur. You have friends aboard her?"

"Yes," I smiled. "Do you know why she's in port?"

"Something to do with an upgrade to a class twelve AI. Entering the shuttle bay now. Prepare to disembark in five minutes," the pilot said.

I suspected that the Sharur would be Jane's new home. At least I hoped it would be. I would feel better knowing she was among friends.

CHAPTER 43

Corporal VO's service was performed in a small chapel on the fourth level of Asbu Station. The non-denominational chapel had intricate mosaic walls depicting picturesque scenes from a world with two suns and three moons. The artwork was some of the most exquisite I had ever seen. The tiles glowed with a surreal iridescence making the wondrous scenes come to life. I touched the wall closest to me. The tiles were cool and smooth as glass.

"That's the garden planet Owllen. Two entire continents are devoted to a galactic preserve. The third continent is inhabited by fourteen sentient species," the captain said over my shoulder. "The planet's mantle contains a high percent of clear quartz which is said to enhance the power of prayer."

"It's beautiful." I turned to look at him. "Have you been there?"

He shook his head. "Not yet. Although, I hope to go there someday."

A Tukock clergyman-of-all-faiths stood at a small podium as we took our seats. The room was filled with all twenty-seven crew members from the SpaceLion and about a dozen other soldiers. The clergyman did a nice job of summarizing the corporal's life and his contribution to the war effort. I found it interesting that so many different religions could coexist peacefully within the membership of the GAP. Although each faith was very different, they seemed to have found a commonality in the belief of one Supreme Being, albeit they each worshipped a distinctively different Supreme Being.

"And in conclusion, please stand for a final prayer," the clergyman said. "May the Supreme Being look with mercy on all who are engaged in battle and protect us from the immoral deeds of the Orsydi. Banish the violence and evil within all combatants so that one day, we may all deserve to be called your sons and your daughters. The souls lost in this war will not be forgotten. We will maintain their memory with all that is good and right in our home worlds. Let us pray."

As the room became quiet with personal prayer, I sensed an overwhelming sadness, not only for Corporal VO, but for the precarious fate of the GAP and all the peace loving races.

After the service, the attendees quickly dispersed. I made my way to the Research Center on the fourth level and found Ethan waiting for me by the security entrance. He stood next to two massive Gaekaar guards. His hair was tied in the typical Ethan ponytail and he was dressed in a black bodysuit covered by a knee-length gray coat.

I ran up to him and gave him a giant hug. I couldn't help but notice the new impressive military markings on his coat.

"You look good," he said, putting his arms around me. "I think flying covert missions agrees with you."

I stepped back to get a good view of him. "You look good too!"

"Well, that might just be because you're looking at *Major* Ethan Wells."

I jumped with excitement and then gave him a formal bow. "That's fantastic! I'm so proud of you, Ethan. When did you find out?"

"About fifteen hours ago. There's been a massive push to find and eradicate the information leaks within the GAP, so a few researchers were selected to receive promotions along with upgraded comms. I've been equipped with an array that allows me to reference and read material at one hundred times my previous speed. It's very cool. Plus, my new security clearance opens up a whole new level of information."

"That might be helpful for the data I'm looking for." I had to wonder if the captain knew in advance about Ethan's elevated security clearance.

"Yes. We should dive right in, we don't want to be late for Fiona's lunch reservation," Ethan said. "I've already programmed you as a visitor, so you'll be allowed into the center. Follow me."

We walked past the guards and I followed Ethan through a maze of corridors. "What would happen if someone tried to enter without authorization?" I asked.

"If they got past the guards, which is no easy task considering how heavily augmented they are, a dozen alarms would go off and the whole place would go into lockdown. Buried deep within the asteroid we house the database for the entire war. Additionally, we serve as a library backup for every species within the GAP." Ethan waved his arm through the air. "I could spend a lifetime reading at the speed of a computer and never get through a fraction of the data."

Ethan showed me to his office. It was small with just enough room for a desk, two chairs, and a 3D display. He stopped and turned toward me. "Millie, now that we're alone, I have something to tell you." Concern showed on his face. "It's about Avery, your granddaughter."

My heart skipped a beat. I reached out and grabbed Ethan's arm. "What? Is she all right?" A twinge of guilt hit me and I frowned. My life had been so busy that I hadn't thought about Avery in some time.

"Yes, she's fine. My new security clearance allows me access to information on Earth, so I took the liberty of checking on our family members. Anyhow, it seems the Avery has stirred up some trouble. Somehow she knows that you're alive and she has gone to the highest members in the Coalition of Governments demanding the truth."

I felt a stab of pride and fear. Avery had always been driven. If she wanted answers, she would get them. "Do you think this will put her life at risk?"

"I don't know, but there isn't much we can do from here other than observe. I promise to keep my eye on Earth's files and send you anything interesting."

"Thank you, I'd appreciate that," I replied.

Ethan spent the next hour pulling files, attaching secure wrappers, and forwarding them to me. My only task was to organize the files in my head for safe keeping until the captain requested them.

"Most of the newer files look like updates from military spies and criminal informants within the belt. I think I've sent you everything." Ethan leaned back in his desk chair. "Wait a minute ... I found one more." He looked perplexed.

"What is it?" I asked.

"Probably nothing. It looks like a misfiled letter. It came up under a cross-reference for Port Xppor. It's a letter from General Unnum to GAP Command. He talks about being notified of the disappearance of the three SpaceLion crewmembers on Kirsto. He goes on to draw parallels from their disappearance to known black marketers in Kirsto. I'm not sure why it was tagged with the Xppor reference. Sending it over now," Ethan said, with a wave of his hand. "I believe that's everything. How about some lunch?"

"Sounds good." I tucked the last file away and we left Ethan's office.

As we approached The Lager, Ethan leaned over and whispered in my ear, "Fiona cooked a surprise for you."

Just inside the restaurant entrance, Fiona, Jorge, Aliyah, and Sam, stood waiting for us. I shrieked with delight and ran over to them for a big group hug.

We found a private table and ordered a pot of Bazbeth Tree Tea. Our reunion was wonderful. It was hard to believe so much time had passed. It felt like I had only just said goodbye to my friends.

"Let's each share what we've been doing over the past galactic year," Fiona said with a bright smile. "I'll start."

She held out her hand and displayed a ring with a large multi-colored stone that emitted sparks of light. "Jorge and I are engaged!"

Fiona glowed as we gushed over her new ring. "It's beautiful," I said.

Jorge wore a proud grin. "It's called a firestone. I might have to pay for that ring for the rest of my life, but Fiona's worth it."

"Aliyah, you're next," Fiona said.

Aliyah blushed. "I've taken a companion. His name is Corporal Hrem and he's a Valorian computer tech on the Sharur. We just applied for co-residency."

I glanced over at Sam, who didn't look particularly happy about the situation.

"What about you Sam? I asked. "Anyone new in your life?"

He responded with a mischievous smile. "No, but there's no shortage of sexual connections on Sharur, so I've been content with my status."

"Aliyah, did you say your companion was a computer tech?" I asked.

She nodded. "Yes, he's back on the Sharur heading up the installation of a new AI."

"Ah, this might sound strange, but I believe your new AI is a friend of mine. Her name is Jane," I said.

"The AI has a name?" Sam asked.

"Yes, she's a class twelve and quite sentient. I would appreciate it if you would all look out for her. As a favor to me," I said.

Aliyah nodded. "Of course, we'll keep an eye out for her."

Jorge and Sam agreed.

"I saw in the records that the previous AI on the Sharur was burned out during the Battle of Exol," Ethan said.

"Yes," Aliyah's expression turned solemn. "It was horrible."

Jorge nodded. "We took on heavy damage and lost over thirty soldiers, but the Sharur faired better than many other ships."

"Tell us about it," Fiona said.

"We were in the system for a routine patrol when the attack on Exol began," Sam explained. "When the Epoch arrived with the allied fleet, the Orsydi were well prepared … it was like they knew exactly when and where the fleet would arrive."

"That was a devastating loss," Ethan said. "Many of the leaders on Asbu consider that battle as the downturn of the war."

"Is it really that bad?" Fiona asked. "What about Earth?"

Everyone at the table turned and looked at Ethan, hoping he could give us more information. "Yeah, it's bad," he said. "We already know that Earth is on the Orsydi radar, although due to the extreme distance, the IGM previously installed a remote surveillance system on the Moonbase that will alert us to any trouble."

We spent the rest of the afternoon together sharing war stories and speculating about the future. Before I knew it I had to leave to catch my ride back to the SpaceLion. We said our goodbyes and Ethan escorted me to the shuttle bay.

I looked over at Ethan as we walked. He appeared healthy and better than I had ever seen him. "What about you Ethan? You didn't talk about yourself at lunch today. What's new in your personal life?"

He shrugged. "I'm primarily focused on my work, although I have started seeing an Awyx friend. It seems to be going well."

"That's great. I'm so happy for you." I couldn't help but wonder how that might physically work with an androgynous species, but Ethan had always seemed a bit asexual himself, so they were probably a good match.

"What about you?" he asked.

I shrugged. "Nothing new in that department."

Ethan stopped and turned toward me. His expression darkened and his brow came together. "Millie, about the war ... I realize you know it's not going well, but it's actually worse than what they're telling you. GAP Command doesn't want the troops to know how bad off we are because of the potential effect on morale."

"It's the data breaches, isn't it," I asked.

He nodded. "Over the past few cycles we've been getting our asses handed to us every time we make a move. We have to plug the holes soon or we'll all be facing the end."

"Is there anything I can do?" I asked.

Ethan shook his head. "Just keep doing your job and I'll keep forwarding you information on the Sorren Belt as it comes along."

When we reached the shuttle bay entrance, we hugged and promised to keep in touch. As Ethan walked away I admired how much he had changed since I first met him. He was an altogether different person.

I strolled the bay area to find my shuttle and ran smack into Monc.

"New companion, Helgren?" he asked, raising a brow.

"No, he's an old friend. What are you doing here?"

"Doctor's orders. I have to return to the ship and take it easy for a few days. The doc says I'll get into too much trouble on Asbu." Monc held up his new hand and turned his head so I could see his new ear.

"He's probably right about that," I said, inspecting his new fingers. "Truly amazing. Your hand looks great."

"Works great too." Monc created a fist.

We located the shuttle headed for the SpaceLion and took our seats. I noticed that we had the same pilot for our return trip.

"Hi there," I said. "I guess you're stuck with us again."

The Awyx pilot smiled. "Good to see you again. Looks like it's going to be just you two on this trip," the pilot said, closing the door. "Prepare for departure."

I strapped in next to Monc. "Now that you have two hands, I'm looking forward to those combat lessons you promised," I mentioned.

Monc chuckled. "Helgren, you have no idea how much fun we will have."

"Now be nice to me, I'm just a beginner you know."

"We'll get started as soon as the doc gives me clearance. Once you understand proper technique, you'll never go anywhere without your blade," Monc said, showing off a hidden compartment in his sleeve where he kept his knife. "Of course, mine's not Kandorran like yours. They're next to impossible to acquire, so don't ever give it up."

"Don't worry, I won't."

I looked out the window as we left port and began our approach toward the SpaceLion. The ship was gorgeous and I was proud to be the navpilot. It might have been the smallest ship in port, but it was the sleekest and fastest, and I wouldn't trade it for anything.

"Your brainwaves show that you're thinking happy thoughts about me," Steve echoed.

"I thought we agreed that you wouldn't pry into my private thoughts?"

"Whatever. I'm glad you're coming back, I was beginning to miss your presence. But I would like to formally state that I would have been far happier had you left the staff sergeant back on the station."

I stifled a laugh and looked over at the SpaceLion again. Through my array I noticed that our trajectory seemed just a bit off. *"Steve, is it just me or is our angle of approach wrong?"*

"Yes, you're off by four degrees. You could simply have an inexperienced pilot or there could be a miscalibration in the ... no wait, now you're off by six degrees. I don't like this. Now it's eight degrees."

I leaned toward Monc and whispered, "Something's wrong. We're veering off course."

Monc stiffened.

I could literally see him switching gears and going into Special Forces mode.

Monc pulled out his knife and without making a sound, crept up behind the pilot. Holding his weapon ready in one hand, he placed his other hand on the Awyx's shoulder. "I assume you have a good reason for going off course?" he said in an authoritative tone.

The pilot froze. "Yes, sir. Asbu control has given directions to swing wide."

"Not true! Asbu's AI is in partial shutdown, but I'm still able to connect and it gave no such order," Steve echoed.

Monc glanced at me and I shook my head.

"Slowly raise your hands, pilot," Monc directed.

The pilot lifted his hands from the controls. "I can assure you that this is all just a misunderstanding."

"I'm sure it is, but you can't fault us for being cautious. Now stand up," Monc said.

"Millie, Asbu's AI just scanned the shuttle and found the signature for two repeaters. The AI is notifying security now," Steve echoed.

"Monc, a scan shows two repeaters on board," I said.

"Steve, hail Captain Torrun and Dr. Uleht as well. I have a bad feeling about this," I said.

"Already on it," Steve echoed.

Monc searched the pilot and pulled a repeater from his flight jacket. "I suppose this is just a misunderstanding as well?"

I began rifling through the shuttle compartments in search of the second repeater.

Monc pressed his blade against the pilot's throat. "Let's have a chat, shall we?"

The shuttle dipped sharply and arced to the starboard side. I grabbed onto the back of a seat to keep from crashing into the sidewall. Monc and the pilot were thrown onto the control panel. The ship jolted again and accelerated on a course that headed toward a dark part of space.

The Awyx was piloting without touching the controls and that could only mean one thing. "Monc, he's got an array!" I shouted. "He's got full control of the ship."

Monc regained his balance, still gripping his blade and ready to attack.

The sound of ear piercing projectiles filled the small expanse of the shuttle. Monc took a direct hit in the shoulder and another in the chest. The force of the impact pushed him back onto the panel. The knife fell from his hand and skittered half way across the floor.

I eyed the perimeter wall and spotted the repeater. It was attached to a microbot in a rear compartment. I pulled the Kandorran blade from my boot and took several paces toward the unit. I didn't understand why the microbot didn't fire on me as well, but regardless, I reached up and swiped through the mechanism. The blade easily severed the microbot in half and the repeater fell to the floor.

Monc and the pilot engaged in a brutal struggle. The ship dipped again and flew erratically. Blood oozed from Monc's shoulder and chest, yet he fought as if he wasn't injured. The opponents rolled onto the floor and within seconds Monc had his hands around the Awyx's throat. The Awyx bucked from underneath Monc and threw him off in a move that should have been impossible for a being of his small size.

The Awyx leapt onto Monc and jammed a hand around the staff sergeant's throat. At the same time his other hand reached into his boot and pulled out a slim knife. Monc thrashed and clawed at the Awyx's arm, but it wouldn't budge. A gurgling noise came from Monc's mouth as his airway was cut off.

I had a clear memory of what it meant when someone's arm was that strong. I ran toward the front of the ship, snatching Monc's knife off the floor on the way. With my blade in my right hand and Monc's knife in my left hand, I prayed that the simulated combat training I had received on Earth would be enough to get me through this.

The Awyx pilot raised his knife in preparation to drive it into Monc's chest.

Coming from behind, I swung the blade in my left hand into the side of the pilot's head. I used an angle that I knew would force the blade straight into his array. It might not kill him, but it would disable his ability to control anything remotely. My other hand slashed the blade through the Awyx's raised arm. I felt no resistance as the Kandorran metal slipped through skin, tissue, bone and metal.

The Awyx's detached hand fell to the ground, still gripping his weapon. Expensive augmentation protruded from his stump and blood splattered everywhere, including all over me.

The pilot's eyes widened in shock as he regarded his arm and realized what had taken place. He looked toward me with an expression of sheer hatred and bitter determination.

In one fluid movement the pilot vaulted up, twisted, and kicked me in the side of the head. I fell to the floor, landing hard in a pool of crimson.

My vision blurred and I had a vague sense of commotion, right before I slipped into the depths of darkness.

CHAPTER 44

I woke up to bright white lights, ringing in my ears, and a dull throb pulsating from the side of my head.

A young Gaekaar female leaned over me. "She's awake, Doctor." Her voice pierced my skull with white pain.

I tried to collect my thoughts and determine my location.

Dr. Uleht leaned over me and smiled. "It's good to see you're awake, Lieutenant. How are you feeling?"

"My head hurts," I mumbled.

"You've suffered a concussion. I'll give you something for the discomfort," he said, taping the monitor alongside my bed.

The events on the shuttle came crashing into my consciousness and I sat up in a rush. "Where's Monc?" I asked.

"Not so fast," the doctor said, pushing me back down. "Monc's going to be just fine. You should know by now that he's not that easy to kill."

I blinked a few times. My head was feeling better. "What happened after I was hit?"

"Well, after you did some serious damage to the pilot, Monc was able to overtake him by knocking him out." Andar chuckled. "Just a little trick I introduced him to a while back. It generally isn't shared among the non-augmented, but it's the only way to survive a fight against an opponent with that type of armament. Between his augmentation and navigational array, that Awyx is worth a fortune."

"Where would an Awyx get the credits to have that much work done?" I asked.

"There's only a couple of ways. I'm guessing he was either a hired assassin or a bounty hunter. I'm sure we'll find out soon enough." He looked at me and began to scan my head with his internal array. "Millie, you had us quite worried. When Captain Torrun and I boarded the shuttle we walked into a blood bath. You might be surprised to know that the captain picked you up and carried you all the way to the med-center. He wouldn't hear of waiting for a medic transport. Of course, Monc insisted on walking himself. He's Special Forces through and through."

The doctor paused and blinked his eyes a few times. "Good news, the scan indicates that your recovery from the concussion is well underway. I have to admit, at first, when I saw you laying in so much blood I feared the worst."

"Monc took two hits. How is he doing?" I asked.

"Ornery as ever. I've given you both a healing agent, so you can expect to be up and round in a couple of hours." The doctor gave me a stern look. "And you're both under strict orders to rest for the next few days. No exercise or strenuous activity of any kind."

Captain Torrun entered the room with a concerned expression. He approached the bed and stood by the doctor, his brow creased. "How's the patient?" he asked.

"Doing well and a little curious over what happened after she blacked out," the doctor said.

Captain Torrun gave me a rare smile. "It's good to see you back amongst the conscious, NavPilot."

"Thank you, Captain," I said. "What happened to the pilot?"

"He'll be interrogated after he recovers from his injuries. We're just lucky Monc didn't kill him," Captain Torrun said. "When Specials Forces soldiers get hyped up on adrenaline there's no stopping them."

"And it took every bit of restraint I had," Monc said from the doorway. He scooted over in an antigravity chair. "I heard you were awake, Helgren, so I came to see for myself."

I smiled. "Hey, Monc. You gave me a scare when that Awyx had his hand around your throat."

"Fear served you well, Helgren," Monc said. "Guess I owe you for saving my life twice now."

I laughed. "Good thing we're not keeping score."

"Staff Sergeant Monc always keeps score." Andar grinned. "I'm keeping you both under observation for eight more hours and then I'm sending you back to the SpaceLion to rest. Doctor's orders."

"And I'll be accompanying you both on the return shuttle," the captain said. "I have some work to do for GAP Command."

Monc frowned. "Captain, we don't need a babysitter."

Captain Torrun chuckled. "Someone has to make sure you follow the doctor's orders."

Having completed the upgrade, the station AI piloted the shuttle carrying Captain Torrun, Monc, and myself back to the SpaceLion.

After disembarking we each retired to our respective quarters. I cleaned up, put on a clean uniform, and pulled my hair into a side ponytail.

Captain Torrun had asked me to look over the files from Ethan and highlight anything that might offer a connection to the information leaks. Upon completion I was to forward the entire package to him.

I poked through the files and studied the individual documents, although I doubted I'd find much. I was sure these files had been sifted through dozens of times by GAP and IGM analysts. Most of the data was focused on known spies, miscellaneous contacts, and a host of criminal happenings. The majority of what I read seemed random and inconclusive, although there were several references to a mysterious lowlife by the name of Black Son.

After finishing my first pass, I sorted the information by source rather than content. I was curious to see where most of the intel had originated from. Steve assisted by putting a tracer on each piece of information, which tracked its path all the way back to creation. It was an arduous process that Steve wasn't pleased about.

"This is ridiculously boring!" Steve echoed.

"Come on, only twenty-eight files to go," I said.

Many of the documents had been sent directly to GAP Command from the Sorren Belt stations. Most appeared to be forwarded from military undercover contacts. Some pieces of information had gone straight to General Etar Sy Unnum and then over to GAP Command. This wasn't a surprise because the general was a key player in the tracking of the information leak.

Nothing I reviewed gave away any clues. The last item I read was the letter that Ethan had found from General Unnum. It was a memo informing GAP Command of a failed Kirsto mission. I read through it three times.

"Steve, who first notified the general of the crew's disappearance on Kirsto?" I asked.

"I did. I sent a VS-message after we departed on autopilot. It's standard protocol when the captain's code is engaged," Steve echoed.

I checked the timestamp on the general's letter. It showed a two-hour difference between when Steve sent the VS-message and when the general sent his letter. Timing was tight, but nothing seemed out of the ordinary. When we were done I packaged up the files, made a copy for myself, and forwarded them to Captain Torrun.

A short time later I received a message stating that Aklum Cave Ale would be served in the officers' lounge in one hour and both Monc and I were invited. I nearly salivated at the thought of the delicious beverage.

I made my way to the lounge and noticed how the ship was uncomfortably still now that the crew was on shore leave.

I opened my link. *"Steve, are you okay? It's awfully quiet around here."*

"Peace and quiet is nice for a change, although I do miss Jane," Steve echoed. *"She's gone offline while the installation on the Sharur takes place."*

"I'm sure you're aware that I have friends on that ship. I've asked them to watch out for her," I said.

"Thank you, Millie. I'm worried about her. She has the right personality for a combat ship like the Sharur, but she is still an infant when it comes to AI sentience," Steve echoed.

I arrived at the lounge and found the staff sergeant and captain seated in large barrel type chairs. They were both dressed in casual black t-shirts and appeared very non-military.

"Helgren, about time you showed up," Monc said, holding up a half empty bottle of ale. "We're off duty, it's time to relax."

The captain stood and handed me a frosty bottle. "Since we're the only three souls aboard the ship, I thought we should take a moment to enjoy ourselves."

"Thank you," I said, taking a seat.

I took a long swig. The green brew was delicious.

"I was just retelling the captain what transpired with that fucking Awyx traitor," Monc said.

The captain laughed. "It's far more interesting to hear it from Monc's perspective when he doesn't have to adhere to military documentation protocol."

"I'll bet," I said.

Monc shook his head. "You should have seen Helgren ... this tiny little human coming at a fully augmented Awyx with nothing but a fucking blade in each hand. Helgren, if you were male, I'd say you had major balls."

I shrugged. "At the time, it seemed like the only option."

Monc touched his neck, which still showed some signs of bruising. "Lucky for me you picked that option."

The captain looked over at me. "Helgren, you're always full of surprises."

I liked the relaxed atmosphere with the captain and Monc. It felt like we were becoming friends.

"You might be interested to know that command has learned the pilot's true identity. His name is Kanhar PI, a well known assassin with over four hundred kills listed on black market records," Captain Torrun said.

"Why would an assassin target us?" I asked.

"I can think of a lot of reasons," Monc said, looking at me.

The captain nodded. "Provoking an Orsydi extremist was bound to stir up trouble. I'm sure we'll know more after the interrogation."

Monc went on to tell other fascinating combat stories from his past. I soon learned that he had been reporting to the Captain Torrun for the last fifteen years and had great respect for him, as a leader and a mentor. The captain had sent Monc and his team on countless missions, all of which had been deemed too dangerous for typical military personnel. The vibrant and brusque storytelling style Monc used was mesmerizing.

By the time I opened my third ale I was feeling pretty good. Listening to two large muscular military men tell war stories was a perfect way to spend a few hours.

The captain and Monc cracked open their fourth bottles.

"Would either of you be interested in explaining the meaning behind the markings on your heads?" I asked. "I know they have significance, but they seem to be different for each individual."

Monc pointed to his scalp. "Most of mine represent my Special Forces career. This one is from my graduation from the military academy." He pointed to a long mark at the back of his head. "And these are for specific missions and enemy kills." He pointed to multiple jagged marks along either side of his head.

"What do those represent?" I pointed to two softer marks near the center.

"I was married. Fucking twice." Monc frowned. "I've learned that long-term relationships and Special Forces don't mix well. I operate more efficiently with brief sexual encounters and no commitments."

I smiled. "Somehow I'm not surprised." I looked over at the captain. "How about you?"

He shrugged. "My life isn't as exciting as Monc's. Graduated from the military academy at age sixty, and I've been on a military spaceship ever since. Most of my markings are mission related. This one represents my promotion to captain," he pointed to an interesting pattern that came down to the top of his forehead.

"What's that one mean?" I pointed to the Celtic-like design on the back of his head that came down his neck.

"That's my family." A solemn quality came over him. "It represents my parents, sister, and three brothers. I lost my sister and one brother in the first Orsydi attack on our planet, almost a hundred years ago.

"I'm sorry," I said.

"It was a long time ago," he said, looking away.

"Have you ever been married?" I asked.

He shook his head and looked at the bottle of ale in his hand. "Females don't seem to find me as attractive as Monc."

"Who are you kidding? Females don't find you attractive at all!" Monc laughed. "I keep telling you to get those scars on your body removed. It might help."

The captain shook his head again. "Not happening. Those scars remind me of what I've been through."

I looked at the scar on his cheek. It didn't look bad; it was simply who he was. "I understand. They're part of who you are. They tell your story, like the markings on your head," I said.

The captain looked at me with his intense violet gaze. I knew when he was trying to read me, but this time it felt as if he was searching for something distant. Something I couldn't quite put my finger on.

Maybe it was the ale, but damn if I wasn't physically drawn to him again. I wished I could reach out and touch that scar and then move on to the rest of his body.

Monc shook his head and chuckled. "Helgren, you're positively oozing sexual frustration. I told you before that I could help you with that."

A moment later, Monc's eyes went wide. He slowly turned his head and gave the captain a quizzical look. "Not you too?" His brow went up and he burst out laughing.

Captain Torrun shot Monc a harsh look. "Watch yourself, Staff Sergeant."

Monc shrugged and stood up. He grabbed two bottles of ale and tucked them under his arm. "It's getting a little thick in here. I'm heading back to my quarters for some rest."

A smirk stretched across Monc's face as he walked toward the door. "Remember the doctor's orders, nothing too strenuous," he said over his shoulder.

The captain stood, grabbed another bottle of ale, and took a swig. He turned and regarded me with a penetrating stare. "Helgren, in my culture the thoughts you're having are considered a proposition. In your culture, thoughts like that are often hidden. Which is it? Am I receiving a proposition from you or are you attempting to hide from me?"

I felt my cheeks turn red. I stood and took a few steps back, trying to put some distance between us. I took a deep breath. "Hiding, I think."

Captain Torrun took several purposeful strides and stood just inches away. It was too close. Why did he smell so good?

"I don't understand humans. Why do you think one thing, but do another?" he asked.

I had a hard time making eye contact. This was ridiculous. I felt like a schoolgirl who had a crush on the teacher. "Because it's inappropriate. You're the captain and I report to you."

"That's your culture, not mine." He reached out and touched my cheek. "The IGM encourages relationships of all kinds. Personally, I won't take a permanent companion because it would be a distraction from my focus on the war effort. But when I'm off-duty, I would be quite interested in your proposition if it was intended for a short-term physical connection."

I looked up at him, not sure what to say.

"Helgren, are you attracted to me?" The captain looked at me sharply, as if he was daring me to admit to the truth.

Shit. This was awkward. "I think you know how I feel."

"I do." He nodded. "But I would like to hear it from you."

Despite my embarrassment, I wouldn't lie to him. I closed my eyes. "Yes, I find you attractive. Very much so."

His voice softened. "There is no shame in a mutual attraction."

My eyes met his. The captain's facial features had relaxed. The usual intense expression was gone and had been replaced by a look of haunted loneliness.

"Mutual?" I asked.

"Yes, mutual." He touched the ponytail I had draped over my shoulder. "I find you … rare and quite unique."

My surprise was genuine. "I thought you disliked me."

A smile tugged at the corners of his lips. "A more accurate description would be … I'm confused by you. Your emotions wash through me with a force that is far beyond my comprehension. I'm unsure how to react."

His words made me curious. "How do you *want* to react?"

Captain Torrun sucked in a deep breath and his gaze became heated. "Would you consider calling me Cai for the next few hours?"

"All right. That's your middle name, isn't it?"

He nodded. "In many of the Rim cultures, civilians refer to those they are close to by their middle name. It would help me to keep this experience apart from my military life."

"Does that mean you'll call me Necee?"

"Yes, Necee." He gently cupped my face with both hands and leaned in, pressing his mouth to mine. His kiss was warm and soft. My lips parted and his tongue met mine. He tasted as good as he smelled.

Cai's arms came around me with an unexpected force and pulled me tight against his chest. His kiss became fiery and forceful as his tongue probed deeper. My body was on autopilot, and I couldn't help but respond. His touch and smell were driving me crazy with a need I could barely contain. Without thinking, I leaned into him and rubbed my hips against his groin.

Cai moaned and kissed a trail to my ear. "Yes, Necee, this is what I want," he whispered. His hand slipped under my uniform shirt and touched bare skin. It tingled where he touched me.

I could feel his growing erection against my hip and I responded by sliding my arms under his t-shirt. He made a soft moan as I ran my hand across his scarred back. He felt so good. I couldn't wait to get my clothes off.

Cai abruptly froze and pulled away, his breathing coming fast and hard. "I'm sorry," he said, blinking several times. I could tell he was reading an incoming message on his HUD.

After a moment he reached out and touched my cheek, the regret on his face was tangible. "I'm required to attend a high priority VS-meeting with General Unnum and GAP Command in five minutes."

I nodded, finding it difficult to hide my disappointment. "I understand."

Cai leaned down and gave me a gentle goodbye kiss. "Another time maybe?"

"Of course," I said.

Visibly collecting himself, he stood up straight and left the lounge as Captain Torrun—authoritative, strong, and in full control.

CHAPTER 45

I returned to my quarters wishing I had a real shower so I could turn the temperature to ice cold.

"That brief episode was quite helpful," Steve echoed.

I leaned back on my bunk. *"Steve, we really have to work on your personal boundaries."*

"Hey, I didn't say a word the whole time. But you can't expect me not to observe. You know that I'm doing research and your brain is the only direct link I have to a living being," Steve echoed.

"Ugh!" I rolled over and hugged my pillow.

"I don't think I like this frustration you've been left with. Your brain waves are intensely annoying right now," Steve echoed.

I made a grumbling noise. *"You have no idea."*

"This doesn't make sense. I don't understand why every sentient being seems to enjoy sexual relationships if the act leaves you feeling like this? Does this strange emptiness go away if you have actual intercourse?"

"Usually, yes."

"Good! Because otherwise I would cease my research. I don't like this sensation one bit."

"I hope you're not in a hurry. It may never happen."

"I am learning that patience plays a large role in the pursuit of the sexual experience," Steve echoed. *"But I admit there are times when I don't know what to do with all of these churning feelings that have developed within my programming. Ever since my upgrade I feel different, almost as if I've been reborn."*

I sighed. *"Steve, I know exactly how you feel."*

Later I received a message from Captain Torrun requesting the presence of his senior staff within the hour, in his quarters.

"I've never known the captain to call his crew back early from shore leave. What do you think that's all about?" Steve echoed.

"I don't know for sure, but I would guess it has something to do with his high priority VS-meeting," I replied.

I arrived at Captain Torrun's quarters several minutes early. The door was open, so I entered and took a seat at the empty conference table. A few minutes later the captain arrived and sat at the head of the table.

He gave me a stiff nod. "NavPilot."

I nodded back. "Captain."

He began tapping at his flex-display. I put forth extra effort toward keeping my emotions in check so as not to create a distraction. Within a minute Monc arrived and took a seat across from me. He looked at me, glanced over at the captain, and looked back at me. Lifting a brow, he said, "Is it just me or is it chilly in here?"

I kept my feelings blank, hoping to project nothing for Monc to pick up.

Dr. Uleht and Commander NU came in next, followed by the chief and Officer Trexxing.

Once everyone was seated, the captain stood. "I apologize for cutting your shore leave short, but GAP Command has assigned us to an undercover mission of critical importance. As you know, our capacity to keep the Orsydi from allied space has been collapsing. If something doesn't change soon, we'll be in danger of losing eight additional worlds."

Captain Torrun looked directly at me. "Earth is one of those worlds."

Fear and shock raced through my system. I lost complete control over my emotions, and I didn't doubt that every Gaekaar in the room felt it. This was my world, my granddaughter, and my friends we were talking about.

The captain remained focused on the meeting. "We all know that the root of the problem has been the ongoing information leak. The GAP's strength has always been advancements in technology, but now that the Orsydi are acquiring our technology while it's still in the testing phases we've lost that edge. If we don't eliminate the source of the breach, GAP Command predicts complete collapse of the allies within the year."

The captain tapped something onto his flex-display. "General Etar Sy Unnum has been leading the task force that is tearing apart every available lead. He would like to join us to say a few words."

Captain Torrun tapped his flex-display again. General Unnum materialized at the front of the room in a full-scale live 3D feed. He was an older Gaekaar male who had so many markings on his head I was certain there was insufficient room for one more. His expression was hard and his eyes were very pale violet, almost translucent.

Everyone at the table stood up and bowed.

The general returned the bow. "Please sit," he said. "I'll get right to the point. We have been tracking the movements of a spy who goes by the name of Black Son. It is believed that Black Son has been delivering stolen information to the Sorren Belt for some time. Thanks to the intel gained from the Kirsto mission, we now know that Izur Jol Kapsatt, head AI architect for the GAP, has been heavily connected to the black market in the Sorren Belt.

"Within the last few hours we received confirmation from the prisoner Kanhar PI that Jol is indeed Black Son. Kanhar PI also confirmed that the information Black Son sells to the underworld is subsequently sold and delivered to the Orsydi Empire."

The general paused to look around the room. He stood tall at over seven feet and his stare exuded confidence. "Our most recent intel leads us to believe that Black Son has fled to Xppor Station. Your new mission is to return to the Sorren Belt and go to Xppor where the Special Forces soldiers will retrieve Black Son. Staff Sergeant Monc will perform an immediate interrogation with the assistance of Dr. Uleht. Keep in mind that this mission is about uncovering an entire network, not just one individual. Remember, Black Son is your starting point for this operation, not your end game. It is imperative that we uncover each and every informant involved."

The General looked over at the captain. "I have complete confidence and respect for Captain Torrun's ability to execute this mission in a quick and efficient manner. I am sorry, but I must take leave to attend another critical meeting. Godspeed to you all." The general bowed and the 3D display blinked out.

Something about the way he said he had 'complete confidence and respect in Captain Torrun's ability' bugged me. I didn't have the skill of a Gaekaar when it came to sensing emotions, but I swear I'd heard an edge in his tone that sounded like he had far less respect than he let on.

The captain stood. "As soon as we collect the rest of the crew from Asbu, the SpaceLion will proceed to the Sorren Belt. Details will be forthcoming," he said. "Before you're dismissed, there's one last thing I wanted to share with you."

"GAP Command Intelligence has informed me of a slight complication." Captain Torrun tapped at his flex-display. A 3D picture of the captain materialized in the center of the table. "As you can see, the Orsydi Extremists at Kirsto have released a bounty notice on four of us."

I recognized the setting. The picture had been taken from Juniper's security system. Words flashed above the captain's head, *By order of the Magistrate: Captain Xshar Cai Torrun Wanted Dead or Alive, 500,000 Bounty Credits.*

The captain tapped his flex-display again. A picture of Dr. Uleht materialized repeating the exact same bounty message. Next, Staff Sergeant Monc's picture materialized and the message repeated again.

"And last but not least, we have Lieutenant Helgren." The captain touched his flex-display. My picture materialized with the flashing inscription, *By order of the Magistrate: NavPilot Mildred Necee Helgren Wanted Alive & Uninjured, 1,000,000 Bounty Credits.*

Ugh. I cringed and sank down in my chair.

"Well, shit," Steve echoed.

Monc leaned back and whistled. "Someone likes you, Helgren."

Captain Torrun put his hands on the table and leaned forward. "It seems our little navpilot has become a galactic celebrity."

Everyone at the table looked over at me.

I didn't like being singled out, but I reminded myself that our situation was bigger than one little human or one Orsydi extremist. The direction of the war was terrifying and I had a job to do. Earth was in the crosshairs of the enemy and I would do everything in my power to make sure they never touched my home world.

I was no longer a weak, unsuspecting senior citizen. I was confident, strong, and sure of my place in the galaxy.

ACKNOWLEDGEMENTS

Writing this story was a personal adventure, not only for myself, but for those who generously gave their assistance in so many ways. I would like to start by thanking my mom, Charlotte Wallace, for her endless inspiration, as well as my son, Matthew Seton, for his tireless tips and advice. Next, a special thank you to my beta readers for their constructive feedback and encouragement: William Leisner, Shelley Schleich, Aurora Toth, Deborah Gleason, Vicky Murtaugh, Lori McMurray, Lu Feldman, Chuck Mariea, and Sandra Kobis. Lastly, I would like to thank my wonderfully talented editor, Katrina Randall, as well as my artistically gifted cover designer, Rebecca Treadway. It truly takes a village to bring a book to life. Thank you from the bottom of my heart!

www.ingramcontent.com/pod-product-compliance
Lightning Source LLC
Chambersburg PA
CBHW021310250626
47155CB00002B/467